The Dreaming Jewels

This is the strange tale of Horty, a little boy who ran away from home and took refuge in the bizarre world of the carnival. With him went his favourite toy – an old jack-in-the-box whose jewelled eyes sparkled and shone, hypnotic in their brilliance. And among the freaks and oddities of the side-shows he found friends – 'jewel' people like him, who tried to protect him from the terrible secret of his existence.

To Marry Medusa

The Medusa was the intergalactic conqueror, a hive-like being with a consuming appetite to absorb all life in the universe. Now the Medusa had reached Earth. It had taken control of its first human being. Through him it would possess all his fellows. But there was one thing the Medusa had not reckoned on. One tiny factor in the complex human equation. A desperate last chance for the stubborn and independent creature known as Man to save himself …

Venus Plus X

The Ledom had made a world without war, without fear – a world in which each individual was free to love, create and explore. A gentle and kindly new race, they made their twentieth-century guest, Charlie Johns, welcome to their paradise. Charlie thought he was in heaven. But when he found out just where – and when – he was, an Eden turned into a nightmare!

Also by Theodore Sturgeon

Novels

The Dreaming Jewels (1950) (aka The Synthetic Man)
More Than Human (1952)
To Marry Medusa (1958)
Venus Plus X (1960)
Some of Your Blood (1961)
Godbody (1986)

The Complete Short Stories of Theodore Sturgeon

The Ultimate Egoist (1994)
Microcosmic God (1995)
Killdozer! (1996)
Thunder and Roses (1997)
The Perfect Host (1998)
Baby is Three (1999)
A Saucer of Loneliness (2000)
Bright Segment (2002)
And Now the News … (2003)
The Man Who Lost the Sea (2005)
The Nail and the Oracle (2007)
Slow Sculpture (2009)
Case and the Dreamer (2010)

Theodore Sturgeon
SF GATEWAY OMNIBUS

THE DREAMING JEWELS
TO MARRY MEDUSA
VENUS PLUS X

GOLLANCZ
LONDON

This omnibus copyright © The Estate of Theodore Sturgeon 2014
The Dreaming Jewels copyright © The Estate of Theodore Sturgeon 1950
To Marry Medusa copyright © The Estate of Theodore Sturgeon 1958
Venus Plus X copyright © The Estate of Theodore Sturgeon 1960
Introduction copyright © SFE Ltd 2014

All rights reserved

The right of Theodore Sturgeon to be identified as the author
of this work has been asserted by him in accordance with the
Copyright, Designs and Patents Act 1988.

First published in Great Britain in 2014 by
Gollancz
An imprint of the Orion Publishing Group
Orion House, 5 Upper St Martin's Lane,
London WC2H 9EA

An Hachette UK Company

A CIP catalogue record for this book
is available from the British Library

ISBN 978 0 575 11715 0

1 3 5 7 9 10 8 6 4 2

Typeset by Jouve (UK), Milton Keynes

Printed and bound by CPI Group (UK) Ltd, Croydon CR0 4YY

The Orion Publishing Group's policy is to use papers
that are natural, renewable and recyclable products and
made from wood grown in sustainable forests. The logging
and manufacturing processes are expected to conform to
the environmental regulations of the country of origin.

www.orionbooks.co.uk
www.gollancz.co.uk

CONTENTS

Introduction from The
Encyclopedia of Science Fiction   ix

The Dreaming Jewels   1

To Marry Medusa   123

Venus Plus X   219

ENTER THE SF GATEWAY . . .

Towards the end of 2011, in conjunction with the celebration of fifty years of coherent, continuous science fiction and fantasy publishing, Gollancz launched the SF Gateway.

Over a decade after launching the landmark SF Masterworks series, we realised that the realities of commercial publishing are such that even the Masterworks could only ever scratch the surface of an author's career. Vast troves of classic SF and fantasy were almost certainly destined never again to see print. Until very recently, this meant that anyone interested in reading any of those books would have been confined to scouring second-hand bookshops. The advent of digital publishing changed that paradigm for ever.

Embracing the future even as we honour the past, Gollancz launched the SF Gateway with a view to utilising the technology that now exists to make available, for the first time, the entire backlists of an incredibly wide range of classic and modern SF and fantasy authors. Our plan, at its simplest, was – and still is! – to use this technology to build on the success of the SF and Fantasy Masterworks series and to go even further.

The SF Gateway was designed to be the new home of classic science fiction and fantasy – the most comprehensive electronic library of classic SFF titles ever assembled. The programme has been extremely well received and we've been very happy with the results. So happy, in fact, that we've decided to complete the circle and return a selection of our titles to print, in these omnibus editions.

We hope you enjoy this selection. And we hope that you'll want to explore more of the classic SF and fantasy we have available. These are wonderful books you're holding in your hand, but you'll find much, much more … through the SF Gateway.

www.sfgateway.com

INTRODUCTION
from The Encyclopedia of Science Fiction

Theodore Sturgeon (1918–1985) was the working name of the US author born Edward Hamilton Waldo in New York City, later adopting his stepfather's surname and taking on a new first name; *Argyll* (1993) prints a long anguished letter Sturgeon wrote to his stepfather, plus an autobiographical essay from 1965, both of which more than confirm the hints of emotional turmoil underlying these name changes. Certainly Sturgeon early suffered or entered into several exiles and life crises. Illness cut him off from any chance he might become a gymnast, which had been his first ambition. When still a teenager he went to sea, where he spent three years in spiritual isolation, during which period he made his first fiction sales – beginning in 1937 – to McClure's syndicate, for newspaper publication. After beginning to publish SF with 'Ether Breather' (1939) he remained active as a member of the small band of pre-War Genre SF writers for only a year or so before he abruptly stopped writing, the first of several droughts. He then spent half a decade abroad, variously employed, before returning to his primary career in 1946. The next fifteen years saw him produce, in an almost constant flood, virtually all the stories and novels for which he is remembered and loved. Then, for the last twenty-five years of his life, except for two or three short periods of renewed flow, he was relatively silent. Given that all of Sturgeon's best work somehow or other moves from alienation to some form of Transcendent community, it might – crassly – be suggested that, in his own life, it was story-writing itself which represented that blissful movement towards acceptance and resolution which makes so many of his tales so emotionally fulfilling, and that silence for him was a reliving of exile. Certainly there can be no denying the green force that shoots through even the silliest Pulp-magazine conceits to which he put his mind, or the sense of achieved and joyful *tour de force* generated by his best work.

He had, one might say, a binary career: either he was writing nothing or he was writing at a high pitch. Of his approximately 200 stories, a very high proportion are as successful as he was allowed to be in a field not well designed, during his active years, to accommodate SF tales told with raw passion. Sturgeon was, in fact, initially less comfortable with *Astounding Science Fiction* than with *Unknown*, whose remit was moderately less restrictive, and that magazine's demise may have had something to do with his first departure from the field. In those first three years, however, he produced more than twenty-five stories, all in *Astounding* and *Unknown*, using the pseudonyms E. Waldo Hunter or E. Hunter Waldo on occasions when he had two stories in an issue; several of the twenty-five remain among his best known, including *It* (1948) and 'Microcosmic God' (1941). Along with A. E. van Vogt, Robert A. Heinlein and Isaac Asimov, Sturgeon was a central contributor to and shaper of John W. Campbell Jr's so-called Golden Age of SF, though less comfortably than his colleagues, as even in those early years, while obeying the generic commands governing the creation of Campbellian technological or Hard SF, he was also writing sexually threatening, explorative tales, which he found difficult to publish domestically; 'Bianca's Hands' (1947), for instance, never appeared in an American magazine.

In the late 1940s and the 1950s Sturgeon came into his full stride, and almost all his collections sort and resort this material, though not comprehensively; the most important individual titles are *Without Sorcery* (1948; republished as *Not Without Sorcery* 1961), *E Pluribus Unicorn* (1953), *A Way Home* (1955), *Caviar* (coll 1955), *A Touch of Strange* (1958) and *Aliens 4* (1959). Although he continued to contribute to *Astounding* for several years, most of the work assembled in these collections first appeared in newer and more flexible markets like *Galaxy*, where he published much of his best work after 1950. In order to gain a full sense of the emotional range and technical skill of these productive years, the Complete Stories of Theodore Sturgeon (published in thirteen volumes, 1994–2010) is both necessary and definitive; the first eleven volumes were edited by Paul Williams. Though shibboleths still haunted editors of Genre SF, he clearly felt increasingly free to write stories expressive of his sense that Sex in all its innumerable manifestations – including the then dangerous subject of homosexuality – was the most intense and central form of Communication the human race was capable of, and constituted a set of codes or maps capable of leading maimed adolescents out of alienation and into the light. Most of his explorations of this material may seem unexceptionable in the present century, an advance in human honesty and relevance he helped make possible; but stories like 'The World Well Lost' (1953), about Aliens exiled from their own culture because of their homosexuality, created considerable stir in the 1950s. And although the road to liberation (or transcendent community) was sometimes solely internal, the dictates of SF and fantasy, and Sturgeon's own romantic impulses, generated a large number of tales in which Children, gifted with paranormal powers, must fight against a repressive world until they meet others of their kind. Sturgeon's short stories read like instruction manuals for finding the new world.

The most famous examples of the sense of enablement he generated, however, were his three first SF novels, beginning with *The Dreaming Jewels*

(1950) (see below). *More Than Human* (1953), winner of the 1954 International Fantasy Award and Sturgeon's most famous single title – though not necessarily his finest novel – consists of three connected parts, 'Baby is Three' (1952), preceded and followed in terms of internal chronology by two novella-length narratives. With very considerable intensity it depicts the coming together of six 'deficient' human beings into a Psi-Powered gestalt, where their various powers – including Telepathy, Telekinesis, Teleportation – are sorted by Baby, a human Computer who invents Antigravity en passant, and harnessed by a co-ordinating personality. The complicated but episodic storyline involves two cases of Amnesia, extended flashbacks, a mechanical trust in laws of Psychology, and what might seem a distracting disinclination to focus on any one character; but transcends these genuine problems, closing with a powerful paean to human Evolution. Others of their kind, who are Secret Masters, have been Uplifting the human race for centuries; the protagonists of the novel, who understand that together they are a new species, *Homo gestalt*, join their fellows in the long task. The third novel in this sequence of exploratory tales is *The Cosmic Rape* (1958), which was later retitled *To Marry Medusa* (see below).

Less noticed at the time, but increasingly admired in recent years, was his last genuinely successful novel, *Venus Plus X* (1960) (see below). None of Sturgeon's later novels were told with the same emotional intensity and control, though *Some of Your Blood* (1961), a non-SF study of a blood-drinking psychotic Vampire, is moderately effective. *Godbody* (1986), a short novel on which he had been working for several years before his death, less sustainedly reiterates earlier paeans to Transcendence.

Sturgeon won both Hugo and Nebula awards for one of his infrequent later stories, 'Slow Sculpture' (1970), but his later career was not happy, mainly because of an incurably complex recurring writer's block, though the continued publication of stories from the years of his prime helped maintain an appropriate sense of very considerable stature. His influence upon writers like Harlan Ellison and Samuel R. Delany was seminal, and in his life and work he was a powerful and generally liberating influence in post-World War Two American SF. Though his mannerisms were sometimes self-indulgent, though his excesses of sympathy for tortured adolescents sometimes gave off a sense of self-pity, and though his technical experiments were perhaps less substantial than their exuberance made them seem, his very faults illuminated the stresses of being an American author writing for pay in restrictive markets, in an alienating era, and in the solitude of his craft. Out of that solitude, he remained, all the same, capable of writing a story as strong, immeasurably complex, word-perfect and deeply fixative in the reader's memory as 'The Man Who Lost the Sea' (1959), a tale which – along with everything else – is a tone-perfect eulogy to the world and ambitions of the traditional American SF he knew so well. Like much of his early work, most of his later stories were variously assembled in individual volumes; but the Complete Stories of Theodore Sturgeon again remains the central source for understanding his achievement in short forms. In late 1985 Sturgeon was posthumously accorded the World Fantasy Award for lifetime achievement; and he was inducted into the Science Fiction Hall of Fame in 2000.

The Dreaming Jewels (1950), which was later retitled *The Synthetic Man*, is the first novel here presented. Its early critical reception demonstrates how difficult it was for Sturgeon to persuade his readers that a suspenseful genre plot could be married to an intensive examination of human (and para-human) emotions. Later readers know better. Young Horty is both human and – by virtue of the eponymous jewels – a hybrid experiment, undertaken by aliens, in the creation of a species unspoiled by humanity's deadly avarice and lack of self-knowledge. Forced by his wicked step-parents to run away to a circus, Horty gradually becomes aware of his nature, and through melodramas and epiphanies defeats the evil forces about him, and gives us hope.

The Cosmic Rape (1958), which was later retitled *To Marry Medusa*, is the second tale of the three given here, and recasts, in compact, highly professional form, elements of the first. A Hive Mind from the stars has infiltrated mankind but finds itself – to its ultimate betterment – catalysing *Homo sapiens* as a racial entity into one Transcendent gestalt, but with the incomparable benefit that each element in the gestalt, each human mind, remains conscious. The sense of homecoming and empowerment generated by the final pages of this short book is deeply touching.

Less emotionally charged, but more strongly argued, *Venus Plus X* (1960) closes this trio of radical tales. Along with Ursula K. LeGuin's *The Left Hand of Darkness* (1969), which it may have inspired, *Venus Plus X* is one of the very few successful American SF efforts in the creation of the liveable Utopia. Charlie Johns awakens in Ledom (that is, Model), a melodious unisex society, longingly and effectively depicted by Sturgeon as having transcended that sexual divisiveness of mankind against which he always argued. After Charlie discovers that Ledom occupies a Pocket Universe, and that he has been transported here in order to judge its success, he then realizes that the androgynous bliss of Ledom depends not on a mutation but on surgery immediately after birth. This understanding is consistent with Sturgeon's clear belief that *Homo sapiens* is probably doomed if left to its own devices; the final message of *Venus Plus X* is that help may be possible. Charlie himself, and a woman native to Ledom, discover together the joys of sex, and the chance to make a new world, in which passionate loving kindness may prevail. This was Sturgeon's dream from the beginning. May it be ours.

*

For a more detailed version of the above, see Theodore Sturgeon's author entry in *The Encyclopedia of Science Fiction*: http://sf-encyclopedia.com/entry/sturgeon_theodore

Some terms above are capitalised when they would not normally be so rendered; this indicates that the terms represent discrete entries in *The Encyclopedia of Science Fiction*.

THE DREAMING JEWELS

CHAPTER I

They caught the kid doing something disgusting out under the bleachers at the high-school stadium, and he was sent home from the grammar school across the street. He was eight years old then. He'd been doing it for years.

In a way it was a pity. He was a nice kid, a nice-looking kid too, though not particularly outstanding. There were other kids, and teachers, who liked him a little bit, and some who disliked him a little bit; but everyone jumped on him when it got around. His name was Horty – Horton, that is – Bluett. Naturally he caught blazes when he got home.

He opened the door as quietly as he could, but they heard him, and hauled him front and centre into the living-room, where he stood flushing, with his head down, one sock around his ankle, and his arms full of books and a catcher's mitt. He was a good catcher, for an eight-year-old. He said, 'I was—'

'We know,' said Armand Bluett. Armand was a bony individual with a small moustache and cold wet eyes. He clapped his hands to his forehead and then threw up his arms. 'My God, boy, what in Heaven's name made you do a filthy thing like that?' Armand Bluett was not a religious man, but he always talked like that when he clapped his hands to his head, which he did quite often.

Horty did not answer. Mrs Bluett, whose name was Tonta, sighed and asked for a highball. She did not smoke, and needed a substitute for the smoker's thoughtful match-lit pause when she was at a loss for words. She was so seldom at a loss for words that a fifth of rye lasted her six weeks. She and Armand were not Horton's parents. Horton's parents were upstairs, but the Bluetts did not know it. Horton was allowed to call Armand and Tonta by their first names.

'Might I ask,' said Armand icily, 'how long you have had this nauseating habit? Or was it an experiment?'

Horty knew they weren't going to make it easy on him. There was the same puckered expression on Armand's face as when he tasted wine and found it unexpectedly good.

'I don't do it much,' Horty said, and waited.

'May the Lord have mercy on us for our generosity in taking in this little swine,' said Armand, clapping his hands to his head again. Horty let his breath out. Now that was over with. Armand said it every time he was angry. He marched out to mix Tonta a highball.

'Why did you do it, Horty?' Tonta's voice was more gentle only because her vocal chords were more gently shaped than her husband's. Her face showed the same implacable cold.

'Well, I – just felt like it, I guess.' Horty put his books and catcher's mitt down on the footstool.

Tonta turned her face away from him and made an unspellable, retching syllable. Armand strode back in, bearing a tinkling glass.

'Never heard anything like it in my life,' he said scornfully. 'I suppose it's all over the school?'

'I guess so.'

'The children? The teachers too, no doubt. But of course. Anyone say anything to you?'

'Just Dr Pell.' He was the principal. 'He said – said they could …'

'Speak up!'

Horty had been through it once. Why, why go through it all again? 'He said the school could get along without f-filthy savages.'

'I can understand how he felt,' Tonta put in, smugly.

'And what about the other kids? They say anything?'

'Hecky brought me some worms. And Jimmy called me Sticky-tongue.' And Kay Hallowell had laughed, but he didn't mention that.

'Sticky-tongue. Not bad, that, for a kid. Ant-eater.' Again the hand clapped against the brow. 'My God, what am I going to do if Mr Anderson greets me with "Hi Sticky-tongue!" Monday morning? This will be all over town, sure as God made little apples.' He fixed Horty with the sharp wet points of his gaze. 'And do you plan to take up bug-eating as a profession?'

'They weren't bugs,' Horty said diffidently and with accuracy. 'They were ants. The little brown kind.'

Tonta choked on her highball. 'Spare us the details.'

'My God,' Armand said again, 'what'll he grow up as?' He mentioned two possibilities. Horty understood one of them. The other made even the knowledgeable Tonta jump. 'Get out of here.'

Horty went to the stairs while Armand thumped down exasperatedly beside Tonta. 'I've had mine,' he said. 'I'm full up to here. That brat's been the symbol of failure to me ever since I laid eyes on his dirty face. This place isn't big enough – *Horton!*'

'Huh.'

'Come back here and take your garbage with you. I don't want to be reminded that you're in the house.'

Horty came back slowly, staying out of Armand Bluett's reach, picked up his books and the catcher's mitt, dropped a pencil-box – at which Armand my-Godded again – picked it up, almost dropped the mitt, and finally fled up the stairs.

'The sins of the stepfathers,' said Armand, 'are visited on the stepfathers, even unto the thirty-fourth irritation. What have I done to deserve this?'

Tonta swirled her drink, keeping her eyes on it and her lips pursed appreciatively as she did so. There had been a time when she disagreed with Armand. Later, there was a time when she disagreed and said nothing. All that had been too wearing. Now she kept an appreciative exterior and let it soak in as deeply as it would. Life was so much less trouble that way.

Once in his room, Horty sank down on the edge of the bed with his arms still full of his books. He did not close the door because there was none, due to Armand's conviction that privacy was harmful for youngsters. He did not turn on the light because he knew everything in the room, knew it with his eyes closed. There was little enough. Bed, dresser, closet with a cracked cheval glass. A child's desk, practically a toy, that he had long outgrown. In the closet were three oiled-silk dress-covers stuffed full of Tonta's unused clothes, which left almost no space for his.

His …

None of this was really his. If there had been a smaller room, he would have been shoved into it. There were two guest bedrooms on this floor, and another above, and they almost never had guests. The clothes he wore weren't his; they were concessions to something Armand called 'my position in this town'; rags would have done if it weren't for that.

He rose, the act making him conscious of the clutter he still clutched in his arms. He put it down on the bed. The mitt was his, though. He'd bought it for seventy-five cents from the Salvation Army store. He got the money by hanging around Dempledorff's market and carrying packages for people, a dime a trip. He had thought Armand would be pleased; he was always talking about resourcefulness and earning ability. But he had forbidden Horty ever to do that again. 'My God! People will think we are paupers!' So the mitt was all he had to show for the episode.

All he had in the world – except, of course, Junky.

He looked, through the half-open closet door, at the top shelf and its clutter of Christmas-tree lights (the Christmas tree was outside the house, where the neighbours could see – never inside), old ribbons, a lampshade, and – Junky.

He pulled the oversized chair away from the undersized desk and carried it – if he had dragged it, Armand would have been up the stairs two at a time to see what he was up to, and if it was fun, would have forbidden it – and set it down carefully in the closet doorway. Standing on it, he felt behind the leftovers on the shelf until he found the hard square bulk of Junky. He drew it out, a cube of wood, gaudily painted and badly chipped, and carried it to the desk.

Junky was the kind of toy so well-known, so well-worn, that it was not necessary to see it frequently, or touch it often, to know that it was there.

Horty was a foundling – found in a park one late fall evening, with only a receiving blanket tucked about him. He had acquired Junky while he was at the Home, and when he had been chosen by Armand as an adoptee (during Armand's campaign for City Counsellor, which he lost, but which he thought would be helped along if it were known he had adopted a 'poor little homeless waif'). Junky was part of the bargain.

Horty put Junky softly on the desk and touched a worn stud at the side. Violently at first, then with rusted-spring hesitancy, and at last defiantly, Junky emerged, a jack-in-the-box, a refugee from a more gentle generation. He was a Punch, with a chipped hooked nose which all but met his upturned, pointed chin. In the gulch between these stretched a knowing smile.

But all Junky's personality – and all his value to Horty – was in his eyes. They seemed to have been cut, or moulded, blunt-faceted, from some leaded glass with gave them a strange, complex glitter, even in the dimmest room. Time and again Horty had been certain that those eyes had a radiance of their own, though he could never quite be sure.

He murmured, 'Hi, Junky.'

The jack-in-the-box nodded with dignity, and Horty reached and caught its smooth chin. 'Junky, let's get away from here. Nobody wants us. Maybe we wouldn't get anything to eat, and maybe we'd be cold, but gee … Think of it, Junky. Not being scared when we hear *his* key in the lock, and never sitting at dinner while he asks questions until we have to lie, and – and all like that.' He did not have to explain himself to Junky.

He let the chin go, and the grinning head bobbed up and down, and then nodded slowly, thoughtfully.

'They shouldn't 'a been like that about the ants,' Horty confided. 'I didn't *drag* nobuddy to see. Went off by myself. But that stinky Hecky, he's been watching me. An' then he sneaked off and got Mr Carter. That was no way to do, now was it, Junky?' He tapped the head on the side of its hooked nose, and it shook its head agreeably. 'I hate a sneak.'

'You mean me, no doubt,' said Armand Bluett from the doorway.

Horty didn't move, and for a long instant his heart didn't either. He half crouched, half cowered behind the desk, not turning towards the doorway.

'What are you doing?'

'Nothin'.'

Armand belted him across the cheek and ear. Horty whimpered, once, and bit his lip. Armand said, 'Don't lie. You are obviously doing something. You were talking to yourself, a sure sign of a degenerating mind. What's this – oh. Oh yes, the baby toy that came with you. Your estate. It's as repulsive as you are.' He took it from the desk, dropped it on the floor, wiped his hand on the side of his trousers, and carefully stepped on Junky's head.

Horty shrieked as if it were his own head which was being crushed, and leapt at Armand. So unexpected was the attack that the man was bowled right off his feet. He fell heavily and painfully against the bedpost, grabbed at it and missed, and went to the floor. He sat there for a moment grunting and blinking, and then his little eyes narrowed and fixed themselves on the trembling Horty. 'Mmm – *hm!*' said Armand in a tone of great satisfaction, and rose. 'You should be exterminated.' He grasped the slack of Horty's shirt and struck him. As he spoke, he hit the boy's face, back and forth, back and forth, by way of punctuation. 'Homicidal, that's what you are. I was going to. Send you away. To a school. But it isn't safe. The police will. Take care of you. They have a place. For juvenile delinquents. Filthy little pervert.'

He rushed the sodden child across the room and jammed him into the closet. 'This will keep you safe until the police get here,' he panted, and slammed the door. The hinge side of it caught three fingers of Horty's left hand.

At the boy's shriek of very real agony Armand snapped the door open again. 'No use in your yelling. You – My God! What a mess. Now I suppose I'll have to get a doctor. There's no end – absolutely no end to the trouble you cause. Tonta!' He ran out and down the stairs. 'Tonta!'

'Yes, Peaches.'

'That young devil stuck his hand in the door. Did it on purpose, to excite sympathy. Bleeding like a stuck pig. You know what he did? He struck me. He attacked me, Tonta! It's not safe to have him in the house!'

'You poor darling! Did he hurt you?'

'A wonder he didn't kill me. I'm going to call the police.'

'I'd better go up while you're phoning,' said Tonta. She wet her lips.

But when she reached the room, Horty was gone. There was a lot of excitement for a while after that. At first Armand wanted to get his hands on Horty for his own purposes, and then he began to be afraid of what people might say if the boy gave his own garbled version of the incident. Then a day went by, and a week and a month and it was safe to look to heaven and say mysteriously, 'He's in safe hands now, the poor little tyke,' and people could answer, 'I understand …' Everyone knew he was not Armand's child, anyway.

But Armand Bluett tucked one idea snugly away in the corner of his mind. That was to look out, in the future, for any young man with three fingers missing from his left hand.

CHAPTER II

The Hallowell's lived at the edge of town, in a house that had only one thing wrong with it; it was at the intersection where the State Highway angled into the end of Main Street, so that the traffic roared night and day past both the front and back gates.

The Hallowell's taffy-headed daughter, Kay, was as full of social consciousness as only a seven-year-old can be. She had been asked to empty the trash, and as usual she opened the back gate a crack and peeped out at the highway, to see if anyone she knew would catch her at the menial task.

'Horty!'

He shrank into the fog-swirled shadows of the traffic-light standard.

'Horton Bluett, I see you.'

'Kay …' He came to her, staying close to the fence. 'Listen, don't tell nobody you saw me, huh?'

'But wh – oh. You're running away!' she blurted, noticing the parcel tucked under his arm. 'Horty – are you sick?' He was white, strained. 'Did you hurt your hand?'

'Some.' He held his left wrist with his right hand, tightly. His left hand was wrapped in two or three handkerchiefs. 'They was going to get the police. I got out of the window on to the shed roof and hid there all afternoon. They was lookin' all over the street and everywhere. You won't tell?'

'I won't tell. What's in the package?'

'Nothin'.'

If she had demanded it, grabbed at it, he would probably never have seen her again. Instead she said, 'Please, Horty.'

'You can look.' Without releasing his wrist, he turned so she could pull the package out from under his arm. She opened it – it was a paper bag – and took out the hideous broken face of Junky. Junky's eyes glittered at her, and she squeaked, 'What is it?'

'It's Junky. I had him since before I was born. Armand, he stepped on it.'

'Is that why you're running away?'

'*Kay! What are you doing out there?*'

'Coming, Mother! Horty, I got to go. Horty, are you coming back?'

'Not ever.'

'Gee … that Mister Bluett, he's so *mean* …'

'*Kay Hallowell! Come in this instant. It's raining!*'

'Yes, Mother! Horty, I wannit to tell you. I shouldn'ta laughed at you today. Hecky brought you the worms, and I thought it was a joke, thass all. I didn't know you really did eat ants. Gee … I et some shoe-polish once. That's nothin'.'

Horty held out his elbow and she carefully put the package under it. He said, as if he had just thought of it – and indeed he had – 'I *will* come back, Kay. Someday.'

'Kay!'

''Bye, Horty.' And she was gone, a flash of taffy hair, yellow dress, a bit of lace, changed before his eyes to a closed gate in a board fence and the sound of dwindling quick footsteps.

Horton Bluett stood in the dark drizzle, cold, but with heat in his ruined hand and another heat in his throat. This he swallowed, with difficulty, and, looking up, saw the broad inviting tailgate of a truck which was stopped for the traffic light. He ran to it, tossed his small bundle on it, and squirmed up, clawing with his right hand, trying to keep his left out of trouble. The truck lurched forward; Horty scrabbled wildly to stay on. The package with Junky in it began to slide back towards him, past him; he caught at it, losing his own grip, and began to slip.

Suddenly there was a blur of movement from inside the truck, and a flare of terrible pain as his smashed hand was caught in a powerful grip. He came very close to fainting; when he could see again he was lying on his back on the jolting floor of the truck, holding his wrist again, expressing his anguish in squeezed-out tears and little, difficult grunts.

'Gee, kid, you don't care how long you live, do you?' It was a fat boy, apparently his own age, bending over him, his bowed head resting on three chins. 'What's the matter with your hand?'

Horty said nothing. He was quite beyond speech for the moment. The fat boy, with surprising gentleness, pressed Horty's good hand away from the handkerchiefs and began laying back the cloth. When he got to the inner layer, he saw the blood by the wash of light from a street-light they passed, and he said, 'Man.'

When they stopped for another traffic signal at a lighted intersection, he looked carefully and said, 'Oh, man' with all the emphasis inside him somewhere, and his eyes contracted into two pitying little knots of wrinkles. Horty knew the fat boy was sorry for him, and only then did he begin to cry openly. He wished he could stop, but he couldn't, and didn't while the boy bound up his hand again and for quite a while afterwards.

The fat boy sat back on a roll of new canvas to wait for Horty to calm down. Once Horty subsided a little and the boy winked at him, and Horty, profoundly susceptible to the least kindness, began to wail again. The boy picked up the paper bag, looked into it, grunted, closed it carefully and put it out of the way on the canvas. Then to Horty's astonishment, he removed from his inside coat pocket a large silver cigar case, the kind with five metal cylinders built together, took out a cigar, put it all in his mouth and turned it to wet it down, and lit up, surrounding himself with sweet-acrid blue smoke. He did not try to talk, and after a while Horty must have dozed off, because he opened his eyes to find the fat boy's jacket folded as a pillow under his head, and he could not remember its being put there. It was dark then; he sat up, and immediately the fat boy's voice came from the blackness.

'Take it easy, kid.' A small pudgy hand steadied Horty's back. 'How do you feel?'

Horty tried to talk, choked, swallowed and tried again. 'All right, I guess. Hungry … gee! We're out in the country!'

He became conscious of the fat boy squatting beside him. The hand left his back; in a moment the flame of a match startled him, and for an etched moment the boy's face floated before him in the wavering light, moonlike, with delicate pink lips acrawl on the black cigar. Then with a practised flick of his fingers, he sent the match and its brilliance flying out into the night. 'Smoke?'

'I never did smoke,' said Horty. 'Some corn-silk, once.' He looked admiringly at the red jewel at the end of the cigar. 'You smoke a lot, huh.'

'Stunts m'growth,' said the other, and burst into a peal of shrill laughter. 'How's the hand?'

'It hurts some. Not so bad.'

'You got a lot of grit, kid. I'd be screamin' for morphine if I was you. What happened to it?'

Horty told him. The story came out in snatches, out of sequence, but the fat boy got it all. He questioned briefly, and to the point, and did not comment at all. The conversation died after he had asked as many questions as he apparently wanted to, and for a while Horty thought the other had dozed off. The cigar dimmed and dimmed, occasionally sputtering around the edges, once in a while brightening in a wavery fashion as vagrant air touched it from the back of the truck.

Abruptly, and in a perfectly wide-awake voice, the fat boy asked him, 'You lookin' fer work?'

'Work? Well – I guess maybe.'

'What made you eat them ants?' came next.

'Well, I – I don't know. I guess I just – well, I wanted to.'

'Do you do that a lot?'

'Not too much.' This was a different kind of question than he had had from Armand. The boy asked him about it without revulsion, without any more curiosity, really, than he had asked him how old he was, what grade he was in.

'Can you sing?'

'Well – I guess so. Some.'

'Sing something. I mean, if you feel like it. Don't strain y'self. Uh – know *Stardust?*'

Horty looked out at the starlit highway racing away beneath the rumbling wheels, the blaze of yellow-white which turned to dwindling red tail-light eyes as a car whisked by on the other side of the road. The fog was gone, and a lot of the pain was gone from his hand, and most of all he was gone from Armand and Tonta. Kay had given him a feather-touch of kindness, and this odd boy, who talked in a way he had never heard a boy talk before, had given him another sort of kindness. There were the beginnings of a wonderful warm glow inside him, a feeling he had had only twice before in his whole life – the time he had won the sack-race and they gave him a khaki handkerchief, and the time four kids had whistled to a mongrel dog, and the dog had come straight to him, ignoring the others. He began to sing, and because the truck rumbled so, he had to sing out to be heard; and because he had to sing out, he leaned on the song, giving something of himself to it as a high-steel worker gives part of his weight to the wind.

He finished. The fat boy said, 'Hey.' The unaccented syllable was warm praise. Without any further comment he went to the front of the truck body and thumped on the square pane of glass there. The truck immediately slowed, pulled over and stopped by the roadside. The fat boy went to the tail-gate, sat down, and slid off to the road.

'You stay right there,' he told Horty. 'I'm gonna ride up front for a while. You hear me now – don't go 'way.'

'I won't,' said Horty.

'How the hell can you sing like that with your hand mashed?'

'I don't know. It doesn't hurt so much now.'

'Do you eat grasshoppers too? Worms?'

'No!' cried Horty, horrified.

'Okay,' said the boy. He went to the cab of the truck; the door slammed, and the truck ground off again.

Horty worked his way carefully forward until, squatted by the front wall of the truck-body, he could see through the square pane.

The driver was a tall man with a curious skin, lumpy and grey-green. He had a nose like Junky's, but almost no chin, so that he looked like an aged parrot. He was so tall that he had to curve over the wheel like a fern-frond.

Next to him were two little girls. One had a round bush of white hair – no, it was platinum – and the other had two thick ropes of pigtails, bangs, and beautiful teeth. The fat boy was next to her, talking animatedly. The driver seemed not to pay any attention to the conversation at all.

Horty's head was not clear, but he did not feel sick either. Everything had an exciting, dreamlike quality. He moved back in the truck body and lay down with his head on the fat boy's jacket. Immediately he sat up, and crawled among the goods stacked in the truck until his hand found the long roll of canvas and moved along it until he found his paper bag. Then he lay down again, his left hand resting easily on his stomach, his right inside the bag, with his index and little fingers resting between Junky's nose and chin. He went to sleep.

CHAPTER III

When he woke again the truck had stopped, and he opened unfocused eyes to a writhing glare of light – red and orange, green and blue, with an underlying sheet of dazzling gold.

He raised his head, blinking, and resolved the lights into a massive post bearing neon signs: ICE TWENTY FLAVOURS CREAM and CABINS and BAR – EAT. The wash of gold came from floodlights over the service area of a gas station. Three tractor-trailer trucks were drawn up behind the fat boy's truck; one of them had its trailer built of heavily-ribbed stainless steel and was very lovely under the lights.

'You awake, kid?'

'Uh – Hi! Yes.'

'We're going to grab a bite. Come on.'

Horty rose stiffly to his knees. He said, 'I haven't got any money.'

'Hell with that,' said the fat boy. 'Come on.'

He put a firm hand under Horty's armpits as he climbed down. A jukebox throbbed behind the grinding sound of a gasoline pump and their feet crunching pleasantly on cinders. 'What's your name?' Horty asked.

'They call me Havana,' said the fat boy. 'I never been there. It's the cigars.'

'My name's Horty Bluett.'

'We'll change that.'

The driver and the two girls were waiting for them by the door of a diner. Horty hardly had a chance to look at them before they all crowded through and lined up at the counter. Horty sat between the driver and the silver-haired girl. The other one, the one with dark ropes of braided hair took the next stool, and Havana, the fat boy, sat at the end.

Horty looked first at the driver – looked, stared, and dragged his eyes away in the same tense moment. The driver's sagging skin was indeed a grey-green, dry, loose, leather-rough. He had pouches under his eyes, which were red and inflamed-looking, and his underlip drooped to show long white lower incisors. The backs of his hands showed the same loose sage-green skin, though his fingers were normal. They were long and the nails were exquisitely manicured.

'That's Solum,' said Havana, leaning forward over the counter and talking across the two girls. 'He's the Alligator-Skinned Man, an' the ugliest human in captivity.' He must have sensed Horty's thought that Solum might resent this designation, for he added, 'He's deaf. He don't know what goes on.'

'I'm Bunny,' said the girl next to him. She was plump – not fat like Havana, but round – butter-ball round, skintight round. Her flesh was flesh coloured and blood coloured – all pink with no yellow about it. Her hair was as white as cotton, but glossy, and her eyes were the extraordinary ruby of a white rabbit's. She had a little midge of a voice and an all but ultrasonic giggle, which she used now. She stood barely as high as his shoulder, though they sat at the same height. She was out of proportion only in this one fact of the long torso and the short legs. 'An' this is Zena.'

Horty turned his gaze full on her and gulped. She was the most beautiful little work of art he had ever seen in his life. Her dark hair shone, and her eyes shone too, and her head planed from temple to cheek, curved from cheek to chin, softly and smoothly. Her skin was tanned over a deep, fresh glow like the pink shadows between the petals of a rose. The lipstick she chose was dark, nearly a brown red; that and the dark skin made the whites of her eyes like beacons. She wore a dress with a wide collar that lay back on her shoulders, and a neckline that dropped almost to her waist. That neckline told Horty for the very first time that these kids, Havana and Bunny and Zena, weren't kids at all. Bunny was girl-curved, puppy-fat curved, the way even a four-year-old girl – or boy – might be. But Zena had breasts, real, taut, firm, separate breasts. He looked at them and then at the three small faces, as if the faces he had seen before had disappeared and were replaced by new ones. Havana's studied, self-assured speech and his cigars were his badges of maturity, and albino Bunny would certainly show some such emblem in a minute.

'I won't tell you his name,' said Havana. 'He's fixin' to get a new one, as of now. Right, kid?'

'Well,' said Horty, still struggling with the strange shifting of estimated place these people had made within him, 'Well, I guess so.'

'He's cute,' said Bunny. 'You know that kid?' She uttered her almost inaudible giggle. 'You're cute.'

Horty found himself looking at Zena's breasts again and his cheeks flamed. 'Don't rib him,' said Zena.

It was the first time she had spoken … One of the earliest things Horty could remember was a cat-tail stalk he had seen lying on the bank of a tidal creek. He was only a toddler then, and the dark-brown sausage of the cat-tail fastened to its dry yellow stem had seemed a hard and brittle thing. He had, without picking it up, run his fingers down its length, and the fact that it was not dried wood but velvet, was a thrilling shock. He had such a shock now, hearing Zena's voice for the first time.

The short-order man, a pasty-faced youth with a tired mouth and laugh-wrinkles around his eyes and nostrils lounged up to them. He apparently felt no surprise at seeing the midgets or the hideous green-skinned Solum. 'Hi, Havana. You folks setting up around here?'

'Not fer six weeks or so. We're down Eltonville way. We'll milk the State Fair and work back. Comin' in with a load o' props. Cheeseburger fer the glamour-puss there. What's yer pleasure, ladies?'

'Scrambled on rye toast,' said Bunny.

Zena said, 'Fry some bacon until it's almost burned—'

'– an' crumble it over some peanut-butter on whole wheat, I remember, princess,' grinned the cook. 'What say, Havana?'

'Steak. You too, huh?' he asked Horty. 'Nup – he can't cut it. Ground sirloin, an' I'll shoot you if you bread it. Peas an' mashed.'

The cook made a circle of his thumb and forefinger and went to get the order.

Horty asked, timidly, 'Are you with a circus?'

'Carny,' said Havana.

Zena smiled at his expression. It made his head swim. 'That's a carnival. You know. Does your hand hurt?'

'Not much.'

'That kills me,' Havana exploded. 'Y'oughta see it.' He drew his right hand across his left fingers and made a motion like crumbling crackers. 'Man.'

'We'll get that fixed up. What are we going to call you?' asked Bunny.

'Let's figure out what he's going to do first,' said Havana. 'We got to make the Maneater happy.'

'About those ants,' said Bunny, 'would you eat slugs and grasshoppers, and that?' She asked him straight out, and this time she did not giggle.

'No!' said Horty, simultaneously with Havana's, 'I already asked him that. That's out, Bunny. The Maneater don't like to use a geek, anyway.'

Regretfully, Bunny said, 'No carny ever had a midge that would geek. It would be a card.'

'What's a geek?' asked Horty.

'He wants to know what's a geek.'

'Nothing very nice,' said Zena. 'It's a man who eats all sorts of nasty things, and bites the heads off live chickens and rabbits.'

Horty said, 'I don't think I'd like doing that,' so soberly that the three midgets burst into a shrill explosion of laughter. Horty looked at them all, one by one, and sensed that they laughed with, not at him, and so he laughed too. Again he felt that inward surge of warmth. These folk made everything so easy. They seemed to understand that he could be a little different from other folks, and it was all right. Havana had apparently told them all about him, and they were eager to help.

'I told you,' said Havana, 'he sings like an angel. Never heard anything like it. Wait'll you hear.'

'You play anything?' asked Bunny. 'Zena, could you teach him guitar?'

'Not with that left hand,' said Havana.

'*Stop* it!' Zena cried. 'Just when did you people decide he was going to work with us?'

Havana opened his mouth helplessly. Bunny said, 'Oh – I thought …' and Horty stared at Zena. Were they trying to give and take away all at the same time?

'Oh, kiddo, don't look at me like that,' said Zena. 'You'll tear me apart …' Again, in spite of his distress, he could all but feel her voice with fingertips. She said, 'I'd do anything in the world for you, child. But – it would have to be something good. I don't know that this would be good.'

'Sure it'd be good,' scoffed Havana. 'Where's he gonna eat? Who's gonna take him in? Listen, after what he's been through he deserves a break. What's the matter with it, Zee? The Maneater?'

'I can handle the Maneater,' she said. Somehow, Horty sensed that in that casual remark was the thing about Zena that made the others await her decision. 'Look, Havana,' she said, 'what happens to a kid his age makes him what he will be when he grows up. Carny's all right for us. It's home to us. It's the one place where we can be what we are and like it. What would it be for him, growing up in it? That's no life for a kid.'

'You talk as if there was nothing in a carnival but midges and freaks.'

'In a way that's so,' she murmured. 'I'm sorry,' she added. 'I shouldn't have said that. I can't think straight tonight. There's something …' She shook herself. 'I don't know. But I don't think it's a good idea.'

Bunny and Havana looked at each other. Havana shrugged helplessly. And Horty couldn't help himself. His eyes felt hot, and he said, 'Gee.'

'Oh, Kid, don't.'

'Hey!' barked Havana. 'Grab him! He's fainting!'

Horty's face was suddenly pale and twisted with pain. Zena slid off her stool and put her arm around him. 'Sick, honey? Your hand?'

Gasping, Horty shook his head. 'Junky,' he whispered, and grunted as if his windpipe were being squeezed. He pointed with his bandaged hand towards the door. 'Truck,' he rasped. 'In – Junky – oh, truck!'

The Midgets looked at one another, and then Havana leaped from his stool and, running to Solum, punched his arm. He made quick motions, pointing outside, turning an imaginary steering wheel, beckoning towards the door.

Moving with astonishing speed, the big man slipped to the door and was gone, the others following. Solum was at the truck almost before the midgets and Horty were outside. He bounded catlike past the cab, throwing a quick glance into it, and in two more jumps was at the tailgate and inside. There were a couple of thumps and Solum emerged, the tattered figure of a man dangling from his parti-coloured hands. The tramp was struggling, but when the brilliant golden light fell on Solum's face, he uttered a scratchy ululation which must have been clearly audible a quarter of a mile away. Solum dropped him on to the cinders; he landed heavily on his back and lay there writhing and terrified, fighting to get wind back into his shocked lungs.

Havana threw away his cigar stub and pounced on the prone figure, roughly going through the pockets. He said something unprintable and then, 'Look here – our new soupspoons and four compacts and a lipstick and – why, you little sneak,' he snarled at the man, who was not large but was nearly three times his size. The man twitched as if he would throw Havana off him; Solum immediately leaned down and raked a large hand across his face. The man screamed again, and this time did surge up and send Havana flying; not, however, to attack, but to run sobbing and slobbering with fear from the gaunt Solum. He disappeared into the darkness across the highway with Solum at his heels.

Horty went to the tailgate. He said, timidly, to Havana, 'Would you look for my package?'

'That ol' paper bag? Sure.' Havana swung up on the tailgate, reappeared a moment later with the bag, and handed it to Horty.

Armand had broken Junky very thoroughly, breaking the jack-in-the-box's head away from the rest of the toy, flattening it until all that Horty could salvage was the face. But now the ruin was complete.

'Gee,' said Horty. 'Junky. He's all busted.' He drew out the two pieces of the hideous face. The nose was crushed to a coarse powder of papier-mâché, and the face was cracked in two, a large piece and a small piece. There was an eye in each, glittering. 'Gee,' Horty said again, trying to fit them together with one hand.

Havana, busy gathering up the loot, said over his shoulder, "Sa damn shame, kid. The guy must've put his knee on it while he was goin' through our stuff.' He tossed the odd collection of purchases into the cab of the truck while Horty wrapped Junky up again. 'Let's go back inside. Our order'll be up.'

'What about Solum?' asked Horty.

'He'll be along.'

Horty was conscious, abruptly, that Zena's deep eyes were fixed on him. He almost spoke to her, didn't know what to say, flushed in embarrassment, and led the way into the restaurant. Zena sat beside him this time. She leaned across him for the salt, and whispered, 'How did you know someone was in the truck?'

Horty settled his paper bag in his lap, and saw her eyes on it as he did so, 'Oh,' she said; and then in quite a different tone, slowly, 'Oh-h.' He had no answer to her question, but he knew, suddenly, that he would not need one. Not now.

'How'd you know there was someone out there?' demanded Havana, busy with a catsup bottle.

Horty began to speak, but Zena interrupted. 'I've changed my mind,' she said suddenly. 'I think carny can do the kid more good than harm. It's better than making his way on the outside.'

'Well now.' Havana put down the bottle and beamed. Bunny clapped her hands. '*Good*, Zee! I knew you'd see it.'

Havana added, 'So did I. I … see somp'n else, too.' He pointed.

'Coffee urn?' said Bunny stupidly, 'Toaster?'

'The mirror, stoopid. Will you look?' He leaned close to Horty and put an arm around his head, drawing his and Zena's faces together. The reflections looked back at them – small faces, both brown, both deep-eyed, oval, dark-haired. If Horty were wearing lipstick and braids, his face would have been different from hers – but very little.

'Your long-lost brother!' breathed Bunny.

'My cousin – and I mean a *girl* cousin,' said Zena. 'Look – there are two bunks in my end of the wagon … stop that cackling, Bunny; I'm old enough to be his mother and besides – oh, shut up. No; this is the perfect way to do it. The Maneater never has to know who he is. It's up to you two.'

'We won't say anything,' said Havana.

Solum kept on eating.

Horty asked, 'Who's the Maneater?'

'The boss,' said Bunny. 'He used to be a doctor. He'll fix up your hand.'

Zena's eyes looked at something that was not in the room. 'He hates people,' she said. 'All people.'

Horty was startled. This was the first indication among these odd folk that there might be something to be afraid of. Zena, understanding, touched his arm. 'Don't be afraid. His hating won't hurt you.'

CHAPTER IV

They reached the carnival in the dark part of the morning, when the distant hills had just begun to separate themselves from the paling sky.

To Horty it was all thrilling and mysterious. Not only had he met these people, but there was also the excitement and mystery ahead, and the way of starting it, the game he must play, the lines he must never forget. And now, at dawn, the carnival itself. The wide dim street, paved with wood shavings, seemed faintly luminous between the rows of stands and bally-platforms. Here a dark neon tube made ghosts of random light rays from the growing dawn; there one of the rides stretched hungry arms upwards in bony silhouette. There were sounds, sleepy, restless, alien sounds; and the place smelled of damp earth, popcorn, perspiration, and sweet exotic manures.

The truck threaded its way behind the western row of midway stands and came to a stop by a long house-trailer with doors at each end.

'Home,' yawned Bunny. Horty was riding in front with the girls now, and Havana had curled up in the back. 'Out you get. Scoot, now; right into that doorway. The Maneater'll be asleep, and no one will see you. When you come out you'll be somebody different, and then we'll go fix your hand up.'

Horty stood on the truck step, glanced around, and then arrowed to the door of the trailer and skinned inside. It was dark there. He stood clear of the door and waited for Zena to come in, close it, and draw the curtains on the small windows before turning on the lights.

The light seemed very bright. Horty found himself in a small square room. There was a tiny bunk on each side, a compact kitchenette in one corner, and what appeared to be a closet in the other.

'All right,' said Zena, 'take off your clothes.'

'*All* of 'em?'

'Of course all of them.' She saw his startled face, and laughed. 'Listen, Kiddo. I'll tell you something about us little people. Uh – how old did you say you were?'

'I'm almost nine.'

'Well, I'll try. Ordinary grown-up people are very careful about seeing each other without clothes. Whether or not it makes any sense, they are that way because there's a big difference between men and women when they're grown up. More than between boys and girls. Well, a midget stays like a child, in most ways, all his life except for maybe a couple of years. So a lot of us don't let such things bother us. As for us, you and me, we might as well make up our minds right now that it's not going to make any difference. In the first place, no one but Bunny and Havana and me know you're a boy. In the second place, this little room is just too small for two people to live in if they're going to be stooping and cringing and hiding from each other because of something that doesn't matter. See?'

'I – I guess so.'

She helped him out of his clothes, and he began his careful education on how to be a woman from the skin outwards.

'Tell me something, Horty,' she said, as she turned out a neat drawer, looking for clothes for him. 'What's in the paper bag.'

'That's Junky. It's a jack-in-the-box. It was, I mean. Armand busted it – I told you. Then the man in the truck busted it more.'

'Could I see?'

Worrying into a pair of her socks, he nodded towards one of the bunks. 'Go ahead.'

She lifted out the tattered bits of papier-mâché. '*Two* of them!' she exploded. She turned and looked at Horty as if he had turned bright purple, or sprouted rabbit's ears.

'Two!' she said again. 'I thought I saw only one, there at the diner. Are they really yours? Both of them?'

'They're Junky's eyes,' he explained.

'Where did Junky come from?'

'I had him before I was adopted. A policeman found me when I was a baby. I was put in a Home. I got Junky there. I guess I never had any folks.'

'And Junky stayed with you – here, let me help you into that – Junky stayed with you from then on?'

'Yes. He had to.'

'Why had to?'

'How do you hook this?'

Zena checked what seemed to be an impulse to push him into a corner and hold him still until she extracted the information from him. 'About Junky,' she said patiently.

'Oh. Well, I just had to have him near me. No, not near me. I could go a long way away as long as Junky was all right. As long as he was mine, I mean. I mean, if I didn't even see him for a year it was all right, but if somebody moved him, I knew it, and if somebody hurt him, I hurt too. See?'

'Indeed I do,' said Zena surprisingly. Again Horty felt that sweet shock of delight; these people seemed to understand everything so well.

Horty said, 'I used to think everybody had something like that. Something they'd be sick if they lost it, like. I never thought to ask anyone about it, even. And then Armand, he picked on me about Junky. He used to hide Junky to get me excited. Once he put him on a garbage truck. I got so sick I had to have a doctor. I kept yelling for Junky, until the doctor told Armand to get this Junky back to me or I would die. Said it was a fix something. Ation.'

'A fixation. I know the routine,' Zena smiled.

'Armand, he was mad, but he had to do it. So anyway he got tired of fooling with Junky, and put him in the top of the closet and forgot about him pretty much.'

'You look like a regular dream-girl,' said Zena admiringly. She put her hands on his shoulders and looked gravely into his eyes. 'Listen to me, Horty. This is *very* important. It's about the Maneater. You're going to see him in a few minutes, and I'm going to have to tell a story – a whopper of a story. And you've got to help me. He just *has* to believe it, or you won't be able to stay with us.'

'I can remember real good,' said Horty anxiously. 'I can remember anything I want to. Just tell me.'

'All right.' She closed her eyes for a moment, thinking hard. 'I was an orphan,' she said presently. 'I went to live with my Auntie Jo. After I found out I was going to be a midget I ran away with a carnival. I was with it for a few years before the Maneater met me and I came to work for him. Now …' She wet her lips. 'Auntie Jo married again and had two children. The first one died and you were the second. When she found out you were a midget too, she began to be very mean to you. So you ran away. You worked a while in summer stock. One of the stagehands – the carpenter – took a shine to you. He caught you last night and took you into the wood shop and did a terrible thing to you – so terrible that you can't even talk about it. Understand? If he asks you about it, just cry. Have you got all that?'

'Sure,' said Horty casually. 'Which one is going to be my bed?'

Zena frowned. 'Honey? – this is *terribly* important. You've got to remember every single word I say.'

'Oh, I do,' said Horty. And to her obvious astonishment he reeled off everything she had said, word for word.

'My!' she said, and kissed him. He blushed. 'You *are* a quick study! That's wonderful. All right then. You're nineteen years old and your name's – uh – Hortense. (That's in case you hear someone say 'Horty' some day and the Maneater sees you look around.) But everybody calls you Kiddo. All right?'

'Nineteen and Hortense and Kiddo. Uh-huh.'

'Good. Gosh, honey, I'm sorry to give you so many things to think of at once! Now, this is something just between us. First of all, you must never, *never* let the Maneater know about Junky. We'll find a place for him here, and I don't want you to ever talk about him again, except to me. Promise?'

Wide-eyed, Horty nodded. 'Uh-huh.'

'Good. And one more thing, just as important. The Maneater's going to fix your hand. Don't worry; he's a good doctor. But I want you to push every bit of old bandage, every little scrap of cotton he uses, over towards me if you can, without letting him notice it. I don't want you to leave a drop of your blood in his trailer, understand? Not a drop. I'm going to offer to clean up for him – he'll be glad; he hates to do it – and you help me as much as you can. All right?'

Horty promised. Bunny and Havana pounded just then. Horty went out first, holding his bad hand behind him, and they called him Zena, and Zena pirouetted out, laughing, while they goggled at Horty. Havana dropped his cigar and said, 'Hey.'

'Zee, he's *beautiful!*' cried Bunny.

Zena held up a tiny forefinger. '*She's* beautiful, and don't you forget it.'

'I feel awful funny,' said Horty, twitching his skirt.

'Where on earth did you get that hair?'

'A couple of false braids. Like 'em?'

'And the dress?'

'Bought it and never wore it,' said Zena. 'It won't fit my chest expansion ... Come on, kids. Let's go wake the Maneater.'

They made their way among the wagons. 'Take smaller steps,' said Zena. 'That's better. You remember everything?'

'Oh, sure.'

'That's a good – a good girl, Kiddo. And if he should ask you a question and you don't know, just smile. Or cry. I'll be right beside you.'

A long silver trailer was parked next to a tent bearing a brilliantly coloured poster of a man in a top-hat. He had long pointed moustachios and zig-zags of lightning came from his eyes. Below it, in flaming letters, was the legend.

WHAT DO YOU THINK?
Mephisto Knows.

'His name isn't Mephisto,' said Bunny. 'It's Monetre. He used to be a doctor before he was a carny. Everyone calls him Maneater. He don't mind.'

Havana pounded on the door. 'Hey, Maneater! Y'going to sleep all afternoon?'

'You're fired,' growled the silver trailer.

'Okay,' said Havana casually. 'Come on out and see what we got.'

'Not if you want to put it on the payroll,' said the sleepy voice. There were movements inside. Bunny pushed Horty over near the door and waved to Zena to hide. Zena flattened against the trailer wall.

The door opened. The man who stood there was tall, cadaverous, with hollows in his cheeks and a long bluish jaw. His eyes seemed, in the early morning light, to be just inch-deep black sockets in his head. 'What is it?'

Bunny pointed at Horty. 'Maneater, who's that?'

'Who's that?' He peered. 'Zena, of course. Good morning, Zena,' he said, his tone suddenly courtly.

'Good morning,' laughed Zena, dancing out from behind the door.

The Maneater stared from Zena to Horty and back. 'Oh, my aching bankroll,' he said. 'A sister act. And if I don't hire her you'll quit. And Bunny and Havana will quit.'

'A mind-reader,' said Havana, nudging Horty.

'What's your name, kid sister?'

'My pa named me Hortense,' recited Horty, 'but everyone calls me Kiddo.'

'I don't blame them,' said the Maneater in a kindly voice. 'I'll tell you what I'm going to do, Kiddo. I'm going to call your bluff. Get off the lot, and if the rest of you don't like it, you can go along with her. If I don't see any of you on the midway at eleven o'clock this morning, I'll know what you decided.' He closed the door softly and with great firmness.

'Oh – *gee*!' said Horty.

'It's all right,' grinned Havana. 'He don't mean it. He fires everybody 'most every day. When he means it he pays 'em. Go get 'im, Zee.'

Zena rippled her knuckles on the aluminium door. 'Mister Maneater!' she sang.

'I'm counting your pay,' said the voice from inside.

'Oh-oh,' said Havana.

'Please. Just a minute,' cried Zena.

The door opened up again. The Maneater had one hand full of money. 'Well?'

Horty heard Bunny mutter, 'Do good, Zee. Do good!'

Zena beckoned to Horty. He stepped forward hesitantly. 'Kiddo, show him your hand.'

Horty extended his ruined hand. Zena peeled off the soiled, bloody handkerchiefs one by one. The inner one was stuck fast; Horty whimpered as she disturbed it. Enough could be seen, however, to show the Maneater's trained eye that three fingers were gone completely and the rest of the hand in a bad way.

'How in creation did you do a thing like this, girl?' he barked. Horty fell back, frightened.

'Kiddo, go over there with Havana, hm?'

Horty retreated, gratefully. Zena began talking rapidly in a low voice. He could only hear part of it. 'Terrible shock, Maneater. Don't remind her of it, ever … carpenter … and took her to his shop … when she … and her hand in the vice.'

'No wonder I hate people,' the Maneater snarled. He asked her a question.

'No,' said Zena. 'She got away, but her hand …'

'Come here, Kiddo,' said the Maneater. His face was something to see. His whip of a voice seemed to issue from his nostrils which, suddenly, were not carven slits but distended, circular holes. Horty turned pale.

Havana pushed him gently. 'Go on, Kiddo. He's not mad. He's sorry for you. Go *on*!'

Horty inched forward and timidly climbed the step.

'Come in here.'

'We'll see you,' called Havana. He and Bunny turned away. As the door closed behind him and Zena, Horty looked back and saw Bunny and Havana gravely shaking hands.

'Sit down there,' said the Maneater.

The inside of his trailer was surprisingly spacious. There was a bed across the front end, partially curtained. There was a neat galley, a shower, and a safe; a large table, cabinets, and more books than one would ever expect to fit into such space.

'Does it hurt?' murmured Zena.

'Not much.'

'Don't worry about that,' growled the Maneater. He put alcohol, cotton, and a hypodermic case on the table. 'Tell you what I'm going to do. (Just to be different from other doctors.) I'm going to block the nerve on your whole arm. When I poke the needle into you it'll hurt, like a bee-sting. Then your arm will feel very funny, as if it were a balloon being blown up. Then I'll clean up that hand. It won't hurt.'

Horty smiled up at him. There was something in this man, with his frightening changes of voice and his treacherous humour, his kindness and his cruel aura, which the boy found deeply appealing. There was a kindness like Kay's, little Kay who hadn't cared if he ate ants. And there was a cruelty like Armand Bluett's. If nothing else, the Maneater would serve as a link with the past for Horty – for a while at least. 'Go ahead,' said Horty.

'That's a good girl.'

The Maneater bent to his work, with Zena, fascinated, looking on, deftly moving things out of his way, making things more convenient for him. So absorbed he became that if he had any further questions to ask about 'Kiddo' he forgot them.

Zena cleared up afterwards.

CHAPTER V

Pierre Monetre had graduated from college three days before he was sixteen, and from medical school when he was twenty-one. A man died under his hands during a simple appendectomy, which was not Pierre Monetre's fault.

But someone – a hospital trustee – made a slighting reference to it. Monetre went to him to protest and stayed to break the man's jaw. He was immediately banned from the surgical theatre, and rumour blamed it on the appendectomy alone. Instead of proving to the world matters which he felt needed no proof, he resigned from the hospital. He then began to drink. He took this drunkenness before the world as he had taken his brilliance and his skill – front and centre, and damn the comments. The comments on his brilliance and his skill had helped him. The comments on his drunkenness shut him out.

He got over the drunkenness; alcoholism is not a disease, but a symptom. There are two ways of disposing of alcoholism. One is to cure the disorder which causes it. The other is to substitute some other symptom for it. That was Pierre Monetre's way.

He chose to despise the men who had shut him out, and let himself despise the rest of humanity because it was kin to those men.

He enjoyed his disgust. He built himself a pinnacle of hatred and stood on it to sneer at the world. This gave him all the altitude he needed at the time. He starved while he did it; but since riches were of value to the world at which he sneered, he enjoyed his poverty too. For a while.

But a man with such an attitude is like a child with a whip – or a nation with battleships. For a while it is sufficient to stand in the sun, with one's power in plain sight for all to see. Soon, however, the whip must whistle and crack, the rifles must thunder, the man must take more than a stand; he must take action.

Pierre Monetre worked for a while with subversive groups. It was of no importance to him which group, or what it stood for, as long as its aim was to tear down the current structure of the majority. He did not confine this to politics, but also did what he could to introduce modern non-objective art into traditional galleries, agitated for atonal music in string quartets, poured beef extract on the serving table of a vegetarian restaurant, and made a score of other stupid, petty rebellions – rebellions for their own sake always, having nothing to do with the worth of any art or music or food-taboos.

His disgust, meanwhile, fed on itself, until it was neither stupid nor petty. Again he found himself at a loss for a means of expressing it. He grew increasingly bitter as his clothes wore out, as he was forced out of one sordid garret after another. He never blamed himself, but felt victimised by humanity – a humanity that was, part and parcel, inferior to him. And suddenly he was given what he wanted.

He had to eat. All his corrosive hatreds focused there. There was no escaping it, and for a while there was no means of eating except doing work which would be of some value to some part of humanity. This galled him, but there was no other way of inducing humanity to pay for his work. So he turned to a phase of his medical training and got a job in a biological laboratory doing cellular analyses. His hatred of mankind could not change the characteristics of his interested, inquiring, brilliant mind; he loved the work, hating only the fact that it benefited people – employers and their clients, who were mostly doctors and their patients.

He lived in a house – an ex-stable – near the edge of a small town, where he could take long walks by himself in the woods and think his strange thoughts. Only a man who had consciously turned away, for years, from everything human would have noticed what he had noticed one fall afternoon, or would have had the curiosity to examine it. Only a man with his unusual combination of training and ability would have had the equipment to explain it. And certainly, only such a social monster could have used it as he did.

He saw two trees.

Each was a tree like any other tree – an oak sapling, twisted from some early accident, young and alive. Never in a thousand years would he have noticed either of them, particularly had he seen it alone. But he saw them together; his eye swept over them, he raised his eyebrows in slight surprise and walked on. Then he stopped and went back and stood staring at them. And suddenly he grunted as if he had been kicked, and went between the trees – they were twenty feet apart – and gaped from one to the other.

The trees were the same size. Each had a knotted primary limb snaking off to the north. Each had a curling scar on the first shoot from it. The first cluster on the primary on each tree had five leaves on it.

Monetre went and stood closer, running his gaze from tree to tree, up and down, one, then the other.

What he saw was impossible. The law of averages permits of such a thing as two absolutely identical trees, but at astronomical odds. Impossible was the working word for such a statistic.

Monetre reached and pulled down a leaf from one tree, and from the other took down its opposite number.

They were identical – veining, shape, size, texture.

That was enough for Monetre. He grunted again, looked searchingly around to fix the location in his mind, and headed back to his shack at a dead run.

Far into the night he laboured over the oak leaves. He stared through a magnifying glass until his eyes ached. He made solutions of what he had in the house – vinegar, sugar, salt, a little phenol – and marinated parts of the leaves. He dyed corresponding parts of them with diluted ink.

What he found out about them checked and double-checked when he took them to the laboratory in the morning. Qualitative and quantitative analysis, volumetric and kindling temperature and specific gravity tests, spectrographics and pH ratings – all said the same thing; these two leaves were incredibly and absolutely identical.

Feverishly, in the months that followed, Monetre worked on parts of the trees. His working microscopes told the same story; he talked his employer into letting him use the 300-power mike which the lab kept in a bell-jar, and it said the same thing. The trees were identical, not leaf for leaf, but cell for cell. Bark and cambrium and heartwood, they were the same.

It was his own incessant sampling which gave him his next lead. He took his specimens from the trees after the most meticulous measurements. A core-drill 'take' from Tree A was duplicated on Tree B, to the fractional millimetre. And one day Monetre positioned his drill on both trees, got his sample from Tree A, and, in removing it, broke the drill before he could obtain his specimen from the second tree.

He blamed it, of course, on the drill, and therefore on the men who made it, and therefore on all men; and he fumed home, happily in his own ground.

But when he came back the next day he found a hole in Tree B, exactly on the corresponding spot to his tap on Tree A.

He stood with his fingers on the inexplicable hole, and for a long moment his active mind was at a complete stop. Then, carefully, he took out his knife and cut a cross in Tree A, and, in the same place on Tree B, a triangle. He cut them deep and clear, and went home again to read more esoteric books on cell structure.

When he returned to the forest, he found both trees bearing a cross.

He made many more tests. He cut odd shapes in each tree. He painted swatches of colour on them.

He found that overlays, like paint and nailed-on pieces of board, remained as he applied them. But anything affecting the structure of the tree – a cut or scrape or laceration or puncture – was repeated, from Tree A to Tree B.

Tree A was the original, Tree B was some sort of a ... copy.

Pierre Monetre worked on Tree B for two years before he found out, with the aid of an electron microscope, that aside from the function of exact duplication,

Tree B was different. In the nucleus of each cell of Tree B was a single giant molecule, akin to the hydrocarbon enzymes, which could transmute elements. Three cells removed from a piece of bark or leaf-tissue meant three cells replaced within an hour. The freak enzyme, depleted, would then rest for an hour or two, and slowly begin to restore itself, atom by captured atom, from the surrounding tissue.

The control of restoration in damaged tissue is a subtle business at its simplest. Any biologist can give a lucid description of what happens when cells begin to rebuild – what metabolistic factors are present, what oxygen exchange occurs, how fast and how large and for what purpose new cells are developed. But they cannot tell you *why*. They cannot say what gives the signal 'Start!' to a half-ruined cell, and what says 'stop'. They know that cancer is a malfunction of this control mechanism, but what the mechanism is they do not say. This is true of normal tissue.

But what of Pierre Monetre's Tree B? It never restored itself normally. It restored itself only to duplicate Tree A. Notch a twig of Tree A. Break off the corresponding twig of Tree B and take it home. For twelve to fourteen hours, that twig would work on the laborious process of reforming itself to be notched. After that it would stop, and be an ordinary piece of wood. Return then to Tree B, and you would find another restored twig, and this one with its notch perfectly duplicated.

Here even Pierre Monetre's skill bogged down. Cell regeneration is a mystery. Cell duplication is a step beyond an unfathomable enigma. But somewhere, somehow, this fantastic duplication was controlled, and Monetre doggedly set about finding what did it. He was a savage, hearing a radio and searching for the signal source. He was a dog, hearing his master cry out in pain because a girl wrote that she did not love him. He saw the result, and he tried, without adequate tools, without the capacity to understand it if it were thrust under his nose, to determine the cause.

A fire did it for him.

The few people who knew him by sight – none knew him any other way – were astonished that he joined the volunteer fire-fighters that autumn, when the smoke blasted through the hills driven by a flame-whipped wind. And for years there was a legend about the skinny feller who fought the fire like a soul promised release from hell. They told about cutting the new fire-trail, and how the skinny feller threatened to kill the forest ranger if he did not move his fire line a hundred yards north of where it had been planned. The skinny feller made history with his battle of the back-blaze, watering it with his very sweat to keep it out of a certain patch of wood. And when the fire advanced to the edge of the back-blaze, and the men broke and fled before it, the skinny feller was not with them, but stayed, crouched in the smoking moss between two oak saplings, with a spade and an axe in his bleeding hands and a fire in his eyes hotter than any that ever touched a tree. They saw all of that—

They did not see Tree B begin to tremble. Their eyes were not with Monetre's, to peer through heat and smoke and the agonised cloud of exhaustion which hovered around him, and see the scientist's mind reaching out to seize on the fact that the shuddering of Tree B was timed exactly with the rolling flames over a clearing fifty feet away.

He watched it, red-eyed. Flame touched the rocky clearing, and the tree shivered. Flame tugged the earth like hair in a hurricane pulling a scalp, and when the fire wavered and streamed upwards, Tree B stood firm. But when a tortured gust of cold air rushed in to fill the heat-born vacuum, and was pursued along the ground by fingers of fire, the tree shook and tensed, wavered and trembled.

Monetre dragged his half-flayed body to the clearing and watched the flames. A spear of red-orange there; the tree stood firm. A lick of a fiery tongue here, and the tree moved.

So he found it, in the middle of a basalt outcropping. He turned over a rock with fingers which sizzled when they touched it, and under it he found a muddy crystal. He thrust it under his armpit and staggered, tottered, back to his trees, which were now in a small island built of earth and sweat and fire by his own demoniac energy, and he collapsed between the oak saplings while the fire roared past him.

Just before dawn he staggered through a nightmare, a spitting, dying inferno, to his house, and hid the crystal. He dragged himself a quarter of a mile further towards the town before he collapsed. He regained consciousness in the hospital and immediately began demanding to be released. First they refused, next they tied him to his bed, and finally he left, at night, through the window, to be with his jewel.

Perhaps it was because he was at the ragged edge of insanity, or because the fusion between his conscious and unconscious minds was almost complete. More likely it was because he was peculiarly equipped, with that driving, searching mind of his. Certainly few, if any, men had ever done it before, but he did it. He established a contact with the jewel.

He did it with the bludgeon of his hatred. The jewel winked passively at him through all his tests – all that he dared give it. He had to be careful, once he found out that it was alive. His microscope told him that; it was not a crystal, but a super-cooled liquid. It was a single cell, with a faceted wall. The solidified fluid inside was a colloid, with an index of refraction like that of polystyrene, and there was a complex nucleus which he did not understand.

His eagerness quarrelled with his caution; he dared not run excessive heat, corrosion, and bombardment tests on it. Wildly frustrated, he sent to it a blast of the refined hatred which he had developed over the years, and the thing – screamed.

There was no sound. It was a pressure in his mind. There was no word, but the pressure was an agonised negation, a 'no'-flavoured impulse.

Pierre Monetre sat stunned at his battered table, staring out of the dark of his room at the jewel, which he had placed in the pool of light under a gooseneck lamp. He leaned forward and narrowed his eyes, and with complete honesty – for he had a ravening dislike of anything which bid to defy his understanding – he sent out the impulse again.

'No!'

The thing reacted, by that soundless cry, as if he had prodded it with a hot pin.

He was, of course, quite familiar with the phenomena of piezoelectricity, wherein a crystal of quartz or Rochelle salts would yield a small potential when squeezed, or would slightly change its dimensions when voltage was applied across it. Here was something analogous, for all the jewel was not a true crystal. His thought-impulse apparently brought a reaction from the jewel in thought 'frequencies'.

He pondered.

There was an unnatural tree, and it had been connected, in some way, with this buried jewel, fifty feet away; for when flame came near the jewel, the tree trembled. When he flicked the jewel with the flame of his hatred, it reacted.

Could the jewel have *built* that tree, with the other as a model? But how? How?

'Never mind how,' he muttered. He'd find that out in good time. He could hurt the thing. Laws and punishment hurt; oppression hurts; power is the ability to inflict pain. This fantastic object would do what he wanted it to do for he would flog it to death.

He caught up a knife and ran outside. By the light of a waning moon he dug up a sprig of basil which grew near the old stable and planted it in a coffee can. In a similar can he put earth. Bringing them inside, he planted the jewel in the second can.

He composed himself at the table, gathering a particular strength. He had known that he had extraordinary power over his own mind; in a way he was like a contortionist, who can make a shoulder muscle, or a thigh or part of an arm, jump and twitch individually. He did a thing like tuning an electronic instrument, with his brain. He channelled his mental energy into a specific 'wave-length' which hurt the jewel, and suddenly, shockingly, spewed it out.

Again and again he struck out at the jewel. Then he let it rest while he tried to bring into the cruel psychic blows some directive command. He visualised the drooping basil shrub, picturing it in the second can.

> *Grow one.*
> *Copy that.*
> *Make another.*
> *Grow one.*

Repeatedly he slashed and slugged the jewel with the order. He could all but hear it whimper. Once he detected, deep in his mind, a kaleidoscopic flicker of impressions – the oak tree, the fire, a black, star-studded emptiness, a triangle cut into bark. It was brief, and nothing like it was repeated for a long time, but Monetre was sure that the impressions had come from the jewel; that it was protesting something.

It gave in; he could feel it surrender. He bludgeoned it twice more for good measure, and went to bed.

In the morning he had two basil plants. But one was a freak.

CHAPTER VI

Carnival life plodded steadily along, season holding the tail of the season before. The years held three things for Horty. They were – belonging; Zena; and a light with a shadow.

After the Maneater fixed up his – 'her' – hand, and the pink scar-tissue came in, the new midget was accepted. Perhaps it was the radiation of willingness, the delighted, earnest desire to fit in and to be of real value that did it, and perhaps it was a quirk or a carelessness on the Maneater's part, but Horty stayed.

In the carnival the pinheads and the roustabouts, the barkers and their shills, the dancers and fire-eaters and snake-men and ride mechanics, the layout and advance men, had something in common which transcended colour and sex and racial and age differences. They were carny, all of them, interested in gathering their tips and turning them – which is carnivalese for collecting a crowd and persuading it to file past the ticket-taker – for this, and for this alone, they worked. And Horty was a part of it.

Horty's voice was a part of Zena's in their act, which followed Bets and Bertha, another sister team with a total poundage in the seven hundreds. Billed as The Little Sisters, Zena and Kiddo came on with a hilarious burlesque of the preceding act, and then faded to one of their own, a clever song-and-dance routine which ended in a bewilderment vocal – a harmonising yodel. Kiddo's voice was clear and true, and blended like keys on an organ with Zena's full contralto. They also worked in the Kiddies' Village, a miniature town with its own fire station, city hall, and restaurants, all child-sized; adults not admitted. Kiddo served weak tea and cookies to the round-eyed, freckle-faced moppets at the country fairs, and felt part of their wonder and part of their belief in this magic town. Part of … part of … it was a deep-down, thrilling theme to everything that Kiddo did; Kiddo was part of Horty, and Horty was part of the world, for the first time in his life.

Their forty trucks wound among the Rockies and filed out along the Pennsylvania Turnpike, snorted into the Ottawa Fairgrounds and blended themselves into the Fort Worth Exposition. Once, when he was ten, Horty helped the giant Bets bring her child into the world, and thought nothing of it, since it was so much a part of the expected–unexpected of being a carny. Once a pinhead, a happy, brainless dwarf who sat gurgling and chuckling with joy in a corner of the freak show, died in Horty's arms after drinking lye, and the scar in Horty's memory of that frighteningly scarlet mouth and the pained and puzzled eyes – that scar was a part of Kiddo, who was Horty, who was part of the world.

And the second thing was Zena, who was hands for him, eyes for him, a brain for him until he got into the swing of things, until he learned to be, with utter naturalness, a girl midget. It was Zena who made him belong, and his starved ego soaked it up. She read to him, dozens of books, dozens of kinds of books, in that deep, expressive voice which quite automatically took the parts of all the characters in a story. She led him, with her guitar and her phonograph records, into music. Nothing he learned changed him; but nothing he learned was forgotten. For Horty-Kiddo had eidetic memory.

Havana used to say it was a pity about that hand. Zena and Kiddo wore black gloves in their act, which seemed a little odd; and besides, it would have been nice if they both played guitar. But of course that was out of the question. Sometimes Havana used to remark to Bunny, at night, that Zena was going to wear her fingers plump off if she played all day on the bally-platform and all night to amuse Horty; for the guitar would cry and ring for hours after they bedded down. Bunny would say sleepily that Zena knew that she was doing – which was, of course, perfectly true.

She knew what she was doing when she had Huddie thrown out of the carnival. That was bad, for a while. She violated the carny's code to do it, and she was carny through and through. It wasn't easy, especially because there was no harm in Huddie. He was a roustabout, with a broad back and wide tender mouth. He idolised Zena, and was happy to include Kiddo in his inarticulate devotion. He brought them cookies and cheap little scatter-pins from the towns, and squatted out of sight against the base of their bally-platform to listen raptly while they rehearsed.

He came to the trailer to say goodbye when he was fired. He had shaved, and his store suit didn't fit very well. He stood on the step holding a battered straw 'keyster' and chewed hard on some half-formed words that he couldn't quite force out. 'I got fired,' he said finally.

Zena touched his face. 'Did – did the Maneater tell you why?'

Huddie shook his head. 'He jus' called me in and handed me my time. I ain't done nothin', Zee. I – I didn't say nothin' t'him, though. Way he looked, he like to kill me. I – I jus' wish …' He blinked, set down his suitcase, and wiped his eyes on his sleeve. 'Here,' he said. He reached into his breast pocket, thrust a small package at Zena, turned and ran.

Horty, sitting on his bunk and listening wide-eyed, said, 'Aw … Zee, what's he done? He's such a *nice* feller!'

Zena closed the door. She looked at the package. It was wrapped in gilt gift paper and had a red ribbon with a multiple, stringy bow. Huddie's big hands must have spent an hour over it, Zena slipped the ribbon off. Inside was a chiffon kerchief, gaudy and cheap and just the bright present that Huddie would choose after hours of careful searching.

Horty suddenly realised that Zena was crying. 'What's the matter?'

She sat beside him and took his hands. 'I went and told the Maneater that Huddie was – was bothering me. That's why he was fired.'

'But – Huddie never did anything to you! Nothing bad.'

'I know,' Zena whispered. 'Oh, I know. I lied. Huddie had to go – right away.'

Horty stared at her. 'I don't understand about that, Zee.'

'I'm going to explain it to you,' she said carefully. 'It's going to hurt, Horty, but maybe that'll prevent something else happening that will hurt much more. Listen. You always remember everything. You were talking to Huddie yesterday, remember?'

'Oh yes. I was watching him and Jenny and Ole and Stinker drive stakes. I love to watch 'em. They stand around in a circle with their big heavy sledge-hammers and each one taps easy – plip, plip, plip, plip – and then each one swings the hammer right over their head and hits with all their might – blap, blap, blap, blap! – *so fast!* An' that ol' stake, it jus' *melts* into the ground!' He stopped, his eyes shining, hearing and seeing the machine-gun rhythm of the sledge crew with all the detail of his sound-camera mind.

'Yes, dear,' said Zena patiently. 'And what did you say to Huddie?'

'I went to feel the top of the stake inside the iron band, where it was all splintery. I said, "My, it's all mashed!" And Huddie, he said, "Jus' think how mashed your hand'd be iff'n you lef' it there while we'uns drove it." And I laughed at him an' said, "It wouldn't bother me for long, Huddie. It would grow back again." That's all, Zee.'

'None of the others heard?'

'No. They were starting the next stake.'

'All right, Horty. Huddie had to go because you said that to him.'

'But – but he thought it was a joke! He just laughed … what did I do, Zee?'

'Horty, sweetheart, I told you that you must never say the slightest, tiniest word to anyone about your hand, or about anything growing back after it gets cut off, or anything at all like that. You've got to wear a glove on your left hand day and night, and never do a thing with—'

'– with my three new fingers?'

She clapped a hand over his mouth. 'Never talk about it,' she hissed, 'to anyone but me. *No one* must know. Here.' She rose and tossed the dazzling kerchief on his lap. 'Keep this. Look at it and think about it and – and leave me alone for a while. Huddie was – I … I can't like you very much for a little while, Horty. I'm sorry.'

She turned away from him and went out, leaving him shocked and hurt and deeply ashamed. And when, very late that night, she came to his bed and slid her warm, small arms around him and told him it was all right now, he needn't cry any more, he was so happy he could not speak. He burrowed his face into her shoulder and trembled, and he made a promise – a deep promise, to himself, not to her, that he would always, always do as she said. They never spoke of Huddie again.

Sights and smells were treasures; he treasured the books they read together – fantasies like *The Worm Ouroborus* and *The Sword in the Stone* and *The Wind in the Willows*; strange, quizzical, deeply human books, each the only one of its kind, like *Green Mansions*. Bradbury's *Martian Chronicles*, Capek's *War with the Newts*, and *The Innocent Voyage*.

Music was a treasure – laughing music like the Polka from the 'Isle of Gold' and the cacaphonous ingenuities of Spike Jones and Red Ingalls; the rich romanticism of Crosby, singing 'Adeste Fideles' or 'Skylark' as if each were his only favourite, and Tchaikovsky's azure sonorities; and the architects, Franck building with feathers, flowers, and faith, Bach with agate and chrome.

But the things Horty treasured most were the drowsy conversations in the dark, sometimes on a silent fairground after hours, sometimes bumping along a moon-washed road.

'Horty—' (She was the only one who called him Horty. No one else heard her do it. It was like a private pet-name.)

'Mmm?'

'Can't you sleep?'

'Thinkin'.'

'Thinking about your childhood sweetheart?'

'How'd you know? Uh – don't kid me, Zee.'

'Oh, I'm sorry, honey.'

Horty said into the darkness, 'Kay was the only one who ever said anything nice to me, Zee. The only one. It wasn't only that night I ran away. Sometimes in school she'd just smile, that's all. I – I used to wait for it. You're laughing at me.'

'No, Kiddo, I'm not. You're so sweet.'

'Well,' he said defensively, 'I like to think about her sometimes.'

He did think about Kay Hallowell, and often; for this was the third thing, the light with a shadow. The shadow was Armand Bluett. He could not think of Kay without thinking of Armand, though he tried not to. But sometimes the cold wet eyes of a tattered mongrel in some farmyard, or the precise, heralding sound of a key in a Yale lock, would bring Armand and Armand's flat sarcasm and Armand's hard and ready hands right into the room with him. Zena knew of this, which is why she always laughed at him when he mentioned Kay …

He learned so much in those somnolent talks. About the Maneater, for example. 'How'd he ever get to be carny, Zee?'

'I can't say exactly. Sometimes I think he hates carny. He seems to despise the people who come in, and I guess he's in the business mostly because it's the only way he can keep his—' She fell silent.

'What, Zee?'

She was quiet until he spoke again. 'He has some people he – thinks a lot of,' she explained at length. 'Solum. Gogol, the Fish Boy. Little Pennie was one of them.' Little Pennie was the pinhead who had drunk lye. 'A few others. And some of the animals. The two-legged cat, and the Cyclops. He – likes to be near them. He kept some of them before he got into show business. But it must have cost a lot. This way, he can make money out of them.'

'Why does he like them, 'specially?'

She turned restlessly. 'He's the same kind they are,' she breathed. Then, 'Horty, don't ever show him your hand!'

One night in Wisconsin something woke Horty.

Come here.

It wasn't a sound. It wasn't in words. It was a call. There was a cruel quality to it. Horty lay still.

Come here, come here. Come! Come!

Horty sat up. He heard the prairie wind, and the crickets.

Come! This time it was different. There was a coruscating blaze of anger in it. It was controlled and directive, and had in it a twinge of the pleasure of an Armand Bluett in catching a boy in an inarguable wrong. Horty swung out of bed and stood up, gasping.

'Horty? Horty – what is it?' Zena, naked, came sliding out of the dim whiteness of her sheets like the dream of a seal in surf.

'I'm supposed to – go,' he said with difficulty.

'What is it?' she whispered tensely. 'Like a voice inside you?'

He nodded. The furious command struck him again, and he twisted his face.

'Don't go,' Zena whispered. 'You hear me, Horty? Don't you move.' She spun into a robe. 'You get back into bed. Hold on tight; whatever you do, don't leave this trailer. The – it will stop. I promise you it will stop quickly.' She pressed him back to his bunk. 'Don't you go, now, no matter what happens.'

Blinded, stunned by this urgent, painful pressure, he sank back on the bunk. The call flared again within him; he started up. 'Zee—' But she was gone. He stood up, his head in his hands, and then remembered the furious urgency of her orders, and sat down again.

It came again and was – incomplete. Interrupted.

He sat quite still and felt for it with his mind, timidly, as if he were tonguing a sensitive tooth. It was gone. Exhausted, he fell back and went to sleep.

In the morning Zena was back. He had not heard her come in. When he asked her where she had been, she gave him a curious look and said, 'Out.' So he did not ask her anything more. But at breakfast with Bunny and Havana, she suddenly gripped his arm, taking advantage of a moment when the others had left the table to stove and toaster. 'Horty! If you ever get a call like that again, wake me. Wake me right away, you hear?' She was so fierce he was frightened; he had only time to nod before the others came back. He never forgot it. And after that, there were not many times when he woke her and she slipped out, wordlessly, to come back hours later; for when he realised the calls were not for him, he no longer felt them.

The seasons passed and the carnival grew. The Maneater was still everywhere in it, flogging the roustabouts and the animal men, the daredevils, and the drivers with his weapon – his contempt, which he carried about openly like a naked sword.

The carnival grew – larger. Bunny and Havana grew – older, and so did Zena, in subtle ways. But Horty did not grow at all.

He – she – was a fixture now, with a clear soprano voice and black gloves. He passed with the Maneater, who withheld his contempt in saying 'Good Morning' – a high favour – and who had little else to say. But Horty-Kiddo was loved by the rest, in the earnest, slap-dash way peculiar to carnies.

The show was a flat-car rig now, with press-agents and sky-sweeping searchlights, a dance pavilion and complicated epicyclic rides. A national magazine had run a long picture story on the outfit, with emphasis on its 'Strange People' ('Freak Show' being an unpopular phrase). There was a press office now, and there were managers, and annual re-bookings from big organisations. There were public-address systems for the bally-platforms, and newer – not new, but newer, trailers for the personnel.

The Maneater, had long since abandoned his mind-reading act, and, increasingly, was a presence only to those working on the lot. In the magazine stories, he was a 'partner', if mentioned at all. He was seldom interviewed and never photographed. He spent his working hours with his staff, and stalking about the grounds, and his free time with his books and his rolling laboratory and his 'Strange People'. There were stories of his being found in the dark hours of the morning, standing in the breathing blackness with his hands behind him and his gaunt shoulders stooped, staring at Gogol in his tank, or peering over the two-headed snake or the hairless rabbit. Watchmen and animal men had learned to keep away from him at such times; they withdrew silently, shaking their heads, and left him alone.

*

'Thank you, Zena.' The Maneater's tone was courtly, mellow.

Zena smiled tiredly, closed the door of the trailer against the blackness outside. She crossed to the chrome and plastic-web chair by his desk and curled up with her robe tucked over her toes. 'I've had enough sleep,' she said.

He poured wine – shimmering Moselle. 'An odd hour for it,' he offered, 'but I know you like it.'

She took the glass and set it on the corner of the desk. She waited. She had learned to wait.

'I found some new ones today,' said the Maneater. He opened a heavy mahogany box and lifted a velvet tray out of it. 'Mostly young ones.'

'That's good,' said Zena.

'It is and it isn't,' said Monetre irascibly. 'They're easier to handle – but they can't do as much. Sometimes I wonder why I bother.'

'So do I,' said Zena.

She thought his eyes moved to her and away in their deep sockets, but she couldn't be sure. He said, 'Look at these.'

She took the tray on her lap. There were eight crystals lying on the velvet, gleaming dully. They had been freshly cleaned of the layer of dust, like dried mud, that always covered them when they were found – the layer that made them look like clods, like stones. They were not quite translucent, yet the nucleus could be seen by one who knew just what internal hovering shadow to look for.

Zena picked one up and held it to the light. Monetre grunted, and she met his gaze.

'I was wondering which one you would pick up first,' he said. 'That one's very alive.' He took it from her and stared at it, narrowing his eyes. The bolt of hatred he aimed at it made Zena whimper. 'Please don't …'

'Sorry … but it screams so,' he said softly, and put it back with the others. 'If I could only understand how they think,' he said. 'I can hurt them. I can direct them. But I can't talk to them. But some day I'll find out …'

'Of course,' said Zena, watching his face. Was he going to have another of his furies? He was due for one …

He slumped into his chair, his clasped hands between his knees and stretched. She could hear his shoulders crackle. 'They dream,' he said, his organ voice dwindling to an intense whisper. 'That's as close to describing them as I've come yet. They dream.'

Zena waited.

'But their dreams live in our world – in our kind of reality. Their dreams are not thoughts and shadows, pictures and sounds like ours. They dream in flesh and sap, and wood and bone and blood. And sometimes their dreams aren't finished, and so I have a cat with two legs, and a hairless squirrel, and Gogol, who should be a man, but who has no arms, no sweat glands, no brain. They're not finished … they all lack formic acid and niacin, among other things. But – they're alive.'

'And you don't know – yet – how the crystals do it.'

He looked up at her without moving his head, so that she saw his eyes glint through his heavy brows. 'I hate you,' he said, and grinned. 'I hate you because I have to depend on you – because I have to talk to you. But sometimes I like what you do. I like what you said – *yet*. I don't know how the crystals do their dreaming *yet*.'

He leaped to his feet, the chair crashing against the wall as he moved. 'Who understands a dream fulfilled?' he yelled. Then, quietly, as if there were no excitement in him, he continued evenly. 'Talk to a bird and ask it to understand that a thousand-foot tower is a man's finished dream, or that an artist's sketch is part of one. Explain to a caterpillar the structure of a symphony – and the dream that based it. Damn structure! Damn ways and means!' His fist crashed down on the desk. Zena quietly picked up her wine glass. 'How this thing happens isn't important. Why it happens isn't important. But it *does* happen, and I can control it.' He sat down and said to Zena, courteously, 'More wine?'

'Thank you, no. I still—'

'The crystals are alive,' Monetre said conversationally. 'They think. They think in ways which are utterly alien to ours. They've been on this earth for hundreds, thousands of years … clods, pebbles, shards of stone … thinking their thoughts in their own way … striving for nothing mankind wants, taking nothing mankind needs … intruding nowhere, communing only with their own kind. But they have a power that no man has ever dreamed of before. And I want it. I want it. I want it, and I mean to have it.'

He sipped his wine and stared into it. 'They breed,' he said. 'They die. And they do a thing I don't understand. They die in pairs, and I throw them away. But some day I'll force them to give me what I want. I'll make a perfect thing – a man, or a woman … one who can communicate with the crystals … one who will do what I want done.'

'How do – how can you be sure?' Zena asked carefully.

'Little things I get from them when I hurt them. Flashes, splinters of thought. For years I've been prodding them, and for every thousand blows I give them, I get a fragment. I can't put it into words; it's a thing I *know*. Not in detail, not quite clearly … but there's something special about the dream that gets *finished*. It doesn't turn out like Gogol, or like Solum – incomplete or wrongly made. It's more like that tree I found. And that finished thing will probably be human, or near it … and if it is, I can control it.'

'I wrote an article about the crystals once,' he said after a time. He began to unlock the deep lower desk drawer. 'I sold it to a magazine – one of those veddy lit'ry quarterly reviews. The article was pure conjecture, to all intents and purposes. I described these crystals in every way except to say what they look like. I demonstrated the possibility of other, alien life-forms on earth, and how they could live and grow all around us without our knowledge – *provided they didn't compete.* Ants compete with humans, and weeds do, and amoebae. These crystals do not – they simply live out their own lives. They may have a group consciousness like humans – but if they do, they don't use it for survival. And the only evidence mankind has of them is their dreams – their meaningless, unfinished attempts to copy living things around them. And what do you suppose was the learned refutation stimulated by my article?'

Zena waited.

'One,' said Monetre with a frightening softness, 'countered with a flat statement that in the asteroid belt between Mars and Jupiter there is a body the size of a basketball which is made of chocolate cake. That, he said, is a statement which must stand as a truth because it cannot be scientifically disproved. *Damn* him!' he roared, and then went on, as softly as before, 'Another explained away every evidence of malformed creatures by talking eclectic twaddle about fruit-flies, X-rays, and mutation. It's that blind, stubborn, damnable attitude that brought such masses of evidence to prove that planes wouldn't fly (for if ships needed power to keep them afloat as well as to drive them, we'd have no ships) or that trains were impractical (because the weight of the cars on the tracks would overcome the friction of the locomotive's wheels, and the train would never start). Volumes of logical observer's proof showed the world was flat. Mutations? Of course there are natural mutations. But why must one answer be the only answer? Hard radiation mutations – demonstrable. Purely biochemical mutations – very probable. And the crystals' dreams …'

From the deep drawer he drew a labelled crystal. He took his silver cigarette lighter from the desk, thumbed it alight, and stroked the yellow flame across the crystal.

Out of the blackness came a faint, agonised scream.

'Please don't,' said Zena.

He looked sharply at her drawn face. 'That's Moppet,' he said. 'Have you now bestowed your affections on a two-legged cat, Zena?'

'You didn't have to hurt her.'

'Have to?' he brushed the crystal with the flame again, and again the scream drifted to them from the animal tent. 'I had to develop my point.' He snapped the lighter out, and Zena visibly relaxed. Monetre dropped lighter and crystal on the desk and went on calmly. 'Evidence. I could bring that fool with his celestial chocolate cake here to this trailer, and show him what I just showed you, and he'd tell me the cat was having a stomach ache. I could show him electron photomicrographs of a giant molecule inside that cat's red corpuscles actually transmuting elements – and he'd accuse me of doctoring the films. Humanity has been accursed for all its history by its insistence that what it already knows must be right, and all that differs from that must be wrong. I add my curse to the curse of history, with all my heart. Zena …'

'Yes, Maneater.' His abrupt change in tone startled her; she had never got used to it.

'The complex things – mammals, birds, plants – the crystals only duplicate them if they want to – or if I flog them half to death. But some things are easy.'

He rose, and drew drapes aside from the shelves behind and above him. He lifted down a rack on which was a row of chemist's watch-glasses. Setting it under the light, he touched the glass covers fondly. 'Cultures,' he said, in a lover's voice. 'Simple, harmless ones, now. Rod bacilli in this one, and spirella here. The *cocci* are coming along slowly, but coming for all that. I'll plant glanders, Zena, if I like, or the plague. I'll carry nuisance-value epidemics up and down this country – or wipe out whole cities. All I need to be sure of it is that middle-man – that fulfilled dream of the crystals that can teach me how they think. I'll find that middle-man, Zee, or make one. And when I do, I'll do what I like with mankind, in my own time, in my own way.'

She looked up at his dark face and said nothing.

'Why do you come here and listen to me, Zena?'

'Because you call. Because you'll hurt me if I don't,' she said candidly. Then, 'Why do you talk to me?'

Suddenly, he laughed. 'You never asked me that before, in all these years, Zena, thoughts are formless, coded … impulses without shape or substance or direction – until you convey them to someone else. Then they precipitate, and become ideas that you can put out on the table and examine. You don't know what you think until you tell someone else about it. That's why I talk to you. That's what you're *for*. You didn't drink your wine.'

'I'm sorry.' Dutifully, she drank it, looking at him wide-eyed over the rim of the glass that was too big to be her glass.

After that he let her go.

The seasons passed and there were other changes. Zena very seldom read aloud any more. She heard music or played her guitar, or busied herself with costumes and continuities, quietly, while Horty sprawled on his bunk, one hand cupping his chin, the other flipping pages. His eyes moved perhaps four times to scan each page, and their turning was a rhythmic susurrus. The books were Zena's choice, and now they were almost all quiet beyond her. Horty swept the books of knowledge, breathed it in, stored it, filed it. She used to look at him, sometimes, in deep astonishment, amazed that he was Horty … he was Kiddo, a girl-child, who, in a few minutes would be on the bally-platform singing the 'Yodelin' Jive' with her. He was Kiddo, who giggled at Cajun Jack's horseplay in the cook-tent and helped Lorelei with her brief equestrienne costumes. Yet, still giggling, or still chattering about bras and sequins, Kiddo was Horty, who would pick up a romantic novel with a bosomy dust-jacket, and immerse himself in the esoteric matter concealed – texts disguised under the false covers – books on microbiology, genetics, cancer, dietetics, morphology, endocrinology. He never discussed what he read, never, apparently, evaluated it. He simply stored it – every page, every diagram, every word of every book she brought him. He helped her put the false covers on them, and he helped her secretly dispose of the books when he had read them – he never needed them for reference – and he never questioned her once about why he was doing it.

Human affairs refuse to be simple … human goals refuse to be clear. Zena's task was a dedication, yet her aims were speckled and splotched and surmise and ignorance, and the burden was heavy …

The rain drove viciously against the trailer in one morning's dark hours, and there was an October chill in the August air. The rain spattered and hissed like the churning turmoil she sensed so often in the Maneater's mind. Around her was the carnival. It was around her memories too, for more years than she liked to count. The carnival was a world, a good world, but it exacted a bitter payment for giving her a place to belong. The very fact that she belonged meant a stream of goggling eyes and pointing fingers: *You're different. You're different.*

Freak!

She turned restlessly. Movies and love-songs, novels and plays … here was a woman – they called her dainty, too – who could cross a room in five strides instead of fifteen, who could envelope a doorknob in one *small* hand. She stepped up into trains instead of clambering like a little animal, and used restaurant forks without having to distort her mouth.

And they were loved, these women. They were loved, and they had choice. Their problems of choice were subtle ones, easy ones – differences between men which were so insignificant they really couldn't matter. They didn't have to look at a man and think first, first of all before anything else, *What will it mean to him that I'm a freak?*

She was little, little in so many ways. Little and stupid. The one thing she had been able to love, she had put into deadly jeopardy. She had done what she could, but there was no way of knowing if it was right.

She began to cry, silently.

Horty couldn't have heard her, but he was there. He slid into bed beside her. She gasped, and for a moment could not release her breath from her pounding throat. Then she took his shoulders, turned him away from her. She pressed her breasts against his warm back, crossed her arms over his chest. She drew him close, close, until she heard breath hissing from his nostrils. They lay still, curled, nested together like two spoons.

'Don't move, Horty. Don't say anything.'

They were quiet for a long time.

She wanted to talk. She wanted to tell him of her loneliness, her hunger. Four times she pursed her lips to speak, and could not, and tears wet his shoulder instead. He lay quiet, warm and with her – just a child, but so much *with* her.

She dried his shoulder with the sheet, and put her arms around him again. And gradually, the violence of her feeling left her, and the all but cruel pressure of her arms relaxed.

At last she said two things that seemed to mean the pressure she felt. For her swollen breasts, her aching loins, she said, 'I love you, Horty. I love you.'

And later, for her hunger, she said, 'I wish I was big, Horty. I want to be big …'

Then, she was free to release him, to turn over, to sleep. When she awoke in the dripping half-light, she was alone.

He had not spoken, he had not moved. But he had given her more than any human being had ever given her in her whole life.

CHAPTER VII

'Zee …'

'Mmm?'

'Had a talk with the Maneater today while they were setting up our tent.'

'What'd he say?'

'Just small-talk. He said the rubes like our act. Guess that's as near as he can get to saying he likes it himself.'

'He doesn't,' said Zena with certainty. 'Anything else?'

'Well – no, Zee. Nothing.'

'Horty, darling. You just don't know how to lie.'

He laughed. 'Well, it'll be all right, Zee.'

There was a silence. Then, 'I think you'd better tell me, Horty.'

'Don't you think I can handle it?'

She turned over to face him across the trailer. 'No.'

She waited. Although it was pitch black, she knew Horty was biting his lower lip, tossing his head.

'He asked to see my hand.'

She sat bolt upright in her bunk. 'He didn't!'

'I told him it didn't give me any trouble. Gosh – when was it that he fixed it? Nine years ago? Ten?'

'Did you show it to him?'

'Cool down, Zee! No, I didn't. I said I had to fix some costumes, and got away. But he called after me and said to come to his lab before ten tomorrow. I'm just trying to think of some way to duck it.'

'I was afraid of this,' she said, her voice shaking. She put her arms around her knees, resting her chin on them.

'It'll be all right, Zee,' said Horty sleepily. 'I'll think of something. Maybe he'll forget.'

'He won't forget. He has a mind like an adding machine. He won't attach any importance to it until you don't show up then, look out!'

'Well, s'pose I do show it to him.'

'I've told you and told you, Horty, you must *never* do that!'

'All right, all right. Why?'

'Don't you trust me?'

'You know I do.'

She did not answer, but sat rigidly, in thought. Horty dozed off.

Later – probably two hours later – he was awakened by Zena's hand on his shoulder. She was crouched on the floor by his bunk. 'Wake up, Horty. Wake up!'

'Wuh?'

'Listen to me, Horty. You remember all you've told me – *please* wake up! – remember, about Kay, and all?'

'Oh, sure.'

'What was it you were going to do, some day?'

'You mean about going back there and seeing Kay again, and getting even with that old Armand?'

'That's right. Well, that's exactly what you're going to do.'

'Well, sure.' He yawned and closed his eyes. She shook him again. 'I mean now, Horty. Tonight. Right now.'

'Tonight? Right now?'

'Get up, Horty. Get dressed. I mean it.'

He sat up blearily. 'Zee … it's night-time!'

'Get dressed,' she said between her teeth. 'Hop to it, Kiddo. You can't be a baby all your life.'

He sat on the edge of the bed and shivered away the last smoky edges of sleep. 'Zee!' he cried. 'Go away? You mean, leave here? Leave the carnival and Havana and – and you?'

'That's right. Get dressed, Horty.'

'But – where will I go?' He reached for his clothes. 'What will I do? I don't know anybody out there?'

'You know where we are? It's only fifty miles to the town you came from. That's as near as we'll get this year. Anyway, you've been here too long,' she added, her voice suddenly gentle. 'You should have left before – a year ago, two years, maybe.' She handed him a clean blouse.

'But why do I have to?' he asked pitiably.

'Call it a hunch, though it isn't really. You wouldn't get through that appointment with the Maneater tomorrow. You've got to get out of here and stay out.'

'I can't go!' he said, childishly protesting even as he obeyed her. 'What are you going to tell the Maneater?'

'You had a telegram from your cousin, or some such thing. Leave it to me. You won't ever have to worry about it.'

'Not ever – can't I ever come back?'

'If you ever see the Maneater again, you turn and run. Hide. Do anything, but never let him near you as long as you live.'

'What about you, Zee? I'll never see you again!' He zipped up the side of a grey pleated skirt and held still for Zee's deft application of eyebrow pencil.

'Yes you will,' she said softly. 'Some day. Some way. Write to me and tell me where you are.'

'Write to you? Suppose the Maneater should get my letter? Would that be all right?'

'It would not.' She sat down, casting a woman's absent, accurate appraisal over Horty. 'Write to Havana. A penny postcard. Don't sign it. Pick it out on a typewriter. Advertise something – hats or haircuts, or some such. Put your return address on it but transpose each pair of numbers. Will you remember that?'

'I'll remember,' said Horty vaguely.

'I know you will. You never forget anything. You know what you're going to learn now, Horty?'

'What?'

'You're going to learn to *use* what you know. You're just a child now. If you were anyone else, I'd say you were a case of arrested development. But all the books we've read and studied … you remember your anatomy, Horty? And the physiology?'

'Sure, and the science and history and music and all that. Zee, what am I going to do out there? I got nobody to tell me anything!'

'You'll have to tell yourself now.'

'I don't know what to do *first*!' he wailed.

'Honey, honey …' She came to him and kissed his forehead and the tip of his nose. 'You walk out to the highway, see? And stay out of sight. Go down the road about a quarter of a mile and flag a bus. Don't ride in anything else but a bus. When you get to town wait at the station until about nine o'clock in the morning and then find yourself a room in a rooming house. A quiet one on a small street. Don't spend too much money. Get yourself a job as soon as you can. You better be a boy, so the Maneater won't know where to look.'

'Am I going to grow?' he asked, voicing the professional fear of all midgets.

'Maybe. That depends. Don't go looking for Kay and that Armand creature until you're ready for it.'

'How will I know when I'm ready?'

'You'll know. Got your bankbook? Keep on banking by mail, the way you always have. Got enough money? Good. You'll be all right, Horty. Don't ask anyone for anything. Don't tell anyone anything. Do things for yourself, or do without.'

'I don't – belong out there,' he muttered.

'I know. You will, though; just the way you came to belong here. You'll see.'

Moving gracefully and easily on high heels, Horty went to the door. 'Well, goodbye, Zee. I – I wish I – Couldn't you come with me?'

She shook her glossy dark head. 'I wouldn't dare, Kiddo. I'm the only human being the Maneater talks to – really talks to. And I've – got to watch what he's doing.'

'Oh.' He never asked what he should not ask. Childish, helpless, implicitly obedient, the exact, functional product of his environment, he gave her a frightened smile and turned to the door. 'Goodbye, honey,' she whispered, smiling.

When he had gone she sank down on his bunk and cried. She cried all night. It was not until the next morning that she remembered Junky's jewelled eyes.

CHAPTER VIII

A dozen years had passed since Kay Hallowell had seen, from the back window, Horty Bluett climb into a brilliantly painted truck, one misty night. Those years had not treated the Hallowells kindly. They had moved into a smaller house, and then into an apartment, where her mother died. Her father had hung on for a while longer, and then had joined his wife, and Kay, at nineteen, left college in her junior year and went to work to help her brother through pre-medical school.

She was a cool blonde, careful and steady, with eyes like twilight. She carried a great deal on her shoulders, and she kept them squared. Inwardly she was afraid to be frightened, afraid to be impressionable, to be swayed, to be moved, so that outwardly she wore carefully constructed poise. She had a job to do; she had to get ahead herself so that she could help Bobby through the arduous process of becoming a doctor. She had to keep her self-respect, which meant decent housing and decent clothes. Maybe some day she could relax and have fun, but not now. Not tomorrow or next week. Just some day. Now, when she went out to dance, or to a show, she could only enjoy herself cautiously, up to the point where late hours, or a strong new interest, or even enjoyment itself, might interfere with her job. And this was a great pity, for she had a deep and brimming reservoir of laughter.

'Good morning, Judge.' How she hated that man, with his twitching nostrils and his limp white hands. Her boss, T. Spinney Hartford, of Benson, Hartford, and Hartford, was a nice enough man but he certainly hobnobbed with some specimens. Oh well; that's the law business. 'Mr Hartford will be with you in a moment. Please sit down, Judge.'

Not there, Wet-Eyes! Oh dear, right next to her desk. Well, he always did.

She flashed him a meaningless smile and went to the filing cabinets across the room before he could start that part weak, part bewildering line of his. She hated the waste of time; there was nothing she needed from the files. But she couldn't sit there and ignore him, and she knew he wouldn't shout across the office at her; he preferred the technique described by Thorne Smith as 'a voice as low as his intentions'.

She felt his moist gaze on her back, on her lips, rolling up and down the seams of her stockings, and she had an attack of gooseflesh that all but itched. This wouldn't do. Maybe short range would be better; perhaps she could parry what she couldn't screen. She returned to her desk, gave him the same lipped smile, and pulled out her typewriter, swinging it up on its smooth counterspring swivels. She ran in some letterhead and began to type busily.

'Miss Hallowell.'

She typed.

'Miss Hallowell.' He reached and took her wrist. 'Please don't be so very busy. We have such a brief moment together.'

She let her hands fall into her lap – one of them, at least. She let the other hang unresisting in the Judge's limp white clasp until he let it go. She folded her hands and looked at them. That voice! If she looked up she was sure she would see a trickle of drool on his chin. 'Yes, Judge?'

'Do you enjoy it here?'

'Yes. Mr Hartford is very kind.'

'A most agreeable man. Most agreeable.' He waited until Kay felt so stupid, sitting there staring at her hands, that she had to raise her face. Then he said, 'You plan to stay here for quite a while, then.'

'I don't see why – that is, I'd like to.'

'The best-laid plans …' He murmured. Now, what was that? A threat to her job? What did this slavering stuffed-shirt have to do with her job? *'Mr Hartford is a most agreeable man.'* Oh. Oh dear. Mr Hartford was a lawyer, and frequently had cases in Surrogate. Some of those were hairline decisions on which a lot depended. *'Most agreeable.'* Of course Mr Hartford was an agreeable man. He had a living to make.

Kay waited for the next gambit. It came.

'You really won't have to work here more than two more years, as I understand it.'

'Wh-why? Oh. How did you know about that?'

'My dear girl,' he said, with an insipid modesty. 'I naturally know the contents of my own files. Your father was most provident, and very wise. When you are twenty-one, you'll be in for a comfortable bit of money, eh?'

It's none of your business, you old lynx. 'Why, I'll hardly notice that, Judge. That's earmarked for Bobby, my brother. It will put him through his last two years and a year of specialisation too, if he wants it. And we won't have to lose a wink of sleep over anything from then on. We're just keeping above water until then. But I'll go on working.'

'Admirable.' He twitched his nostrils at her, and she bit her lip and looked down at her hands again. 'Very lovely,' he added appreciatively. Again she waited. Move Three took place. He sighed. 'Did you know there was lien on your father's estate, for an old partnership matter?'

'I – had heard that. The old agreements were torn up when the partnership was dissolved in Daddy's trucking business.'

'One set of papers were not torn up. I still have them. Your father was a trusting man.'

'That account was squared twice over, Judge!' Kay's eyes could, sometimes, take on the slate colour of thunderclouds. They did now.

The Judge leaned back and put his fingertips together. 'It is a matter which could get to court. To Surrogate, by the way.'

He could get her job. Maybe he could get the money and with it, Bobby's career. The alternative ... well, she could expect that now.

She was so right.

'Since my dear wife departed—' (She remembered his dear wife. A cruel, empty-headed creature with wit enough to cater to his ego in the days before he became a judge, and nothing else.) '– I am a very lonely man, Miss Hallowell. I have never met anyone quite like you. You have beauty, and you could be clever. You can go far. I would like to know you better,' he simpered.

Over my dead body. 'You would?' she said inanely, stiff with disgust and fear.

He underlined it. 'A lovely girl like you, with such a nice job, and with that little nest-egg coming to you – if nothing happens.' He leaned forward. 'I'm going to call you Kay from now on. I'm sure we understand each other.'

'No!' She said it because she did understand, not because she didn't.

He took it his way. 'Then I'd be happy to explain further,' he chuckled. 'Say tonight. Quite late tonight. A man in my position can't – haw! – trip the light fantastic where the lights are bright.'

Kay said nothing.

'There's a little place,' sniggered the Judge, 'called Club Nemo, on Oak Street. Know it?'

'I think I have – noticed it,' she said with difficulty.

'One o'clock,' he said cheerfully. He stood up and leaned over her. He smelled like soured after-shave. 'I do not like to stay up late for nothing. I'm sure you'll be there.'

Her thoughts raced. She was furious, and she was frightened, two emotions which she had avoided for years. She wanted to do several things. She wanted primarily to scream, and to get rid of her breakfast then and there. She wanted to tell him some things about himself. She wanted to storm into Mr Hartford's office and demand to know if this, this, and that were included in her duties as a stenographer.

But then, there was Bobby, so close to a career. She knew what it was to have to quit on the homestretch. And poor, fretting, worried Mr Hartford; he meant no harm, but he wouldn't know how to handle a thing like this. And one more thing, a thing the Judge apparently did not suspect – her proven ability to land on her feet.

So instead of doing any of the things she wanted to do, she smiled timidly and said, 'We'll see ...'

'We'll see each other,' he amended. 'We'll see a great deal of each other.' She felt that moist gaze again on the nape of her neck as he moved off, felt it on her armpits.

A light on her switchboard glowed. 'Mr Hartford will see you now, Judge Bluett,' she said.

He pinched her cheek. 'You can call me Armand,' he whispered. 'When we're alone, of course.'

CHAPTER IX

He was there when she arrived. She was late – only a few minutes, but they cost a great deal. They were minutes added to the hours of fuming hatred, of disgust, and of fear which she had gone through after the Judge's simpering departure from the Hartford offices that morning.

She stood for a moment just inside the club. It was quiet – quiet lights, quiet colours, quiet music from a three-piece orchestra. There were very few customers, and one she knew. She caught a glimpse of silver hair in the corner back of the jutting corner of the bandstand at a shadowed table. She went to it more because she knew he would choose such a spot than because she recognised him.

He stood up and pulled out a chair for her. 'I knew you'd come.'

How could I get out of it, you toad? 'Of course I came,' she said. 'I'm sorry you had to wait.'

'I'm glad you're sorry. I'd have to make you sorry if you weren't.' He laughed when he said it, and only served to stress the pleasure he felt at the thought. He ran the back of his hand over her forearm, leaving a new spoor of gooseflesh. 'Kay. Pretty little Kay,' he moaned. 'I've got to tell you something. I really put some pressure on you this morning.'

You don't say! 'You did?' she asked.

'You must have realised it. Well, I want you to know right away, right now, that I didn't mean any of that – except about how lonely I am. People don't realise that as well as being a judge, I'm a man.'

That makes me one of the people. She smiled at him. This was a rather complicated process. It involved the fact that in this persuasive, self-pitying speech his voice had acquired a whine, and his features the down-drawn character of a spaniel's face. She half-closed her eyes to blur this image, and got such a startling facsimile of a mournful hound's head over his wing collar that she was reminded of an overheard remark: 'He's that way through having been annoyed, at an early age, by the constant barking of his mother.' Hence the smile. He misunderstood it and the look that went with it and stroked her arm again. Her smile vanished, though she still showed her teeth.

'What I mean is,' he crooned, 'I just want you to like me for myself. I'm sorry I had to use any pressure. It's just that I didn't want to fail. Anyway, all's fair ... you know.'

'– in love and war,' she said dutifully. And this means war. Love me for myself alone, or else.

'I won't ask much of you,' he said out of wet lips. 'It's only that a man wants to feel cherished.'

She closed her eyes so he could not see them roll heavenward. He wouldn't ask much. Just sneaking and skulking to protect his 'position' in the town. Just that face, that voice, those hands ... the swine, the blackmailer, the doddering, slimy-fingered old *wolf! Bobby, Bobby,* she thought in anguish, *be a good doctor ...*

There was more of it, much more. A drink arrived. His choice for a sweet young girl. A sherry flip. It was too sweet and the foam on it grabbed unpleasantly at her lipstick. She sipped and let the Judge's sentimental slop wash over her, nodded and smiled, and, as often as she could, tuned out the sound of his voice and listened to the music. It was competent and clean – Hammond Solovox, string bass, and guitar – and for a while it was the only thing in the whole foul world she could hold on to.

Judge Bluett had, it seemed, a little place tucked away over a store in the slums. 'The Judge works in the court and his chambers,' he intoned, 'and has a fine residence on The Hill. But Bluett the Man has a place too, a comfortable spot, a diamond in a rough setting, a place where he can cast aside the black robes, his dignities and his honours, and learn again that he has red blood in his veins.'

'It must be very nice,' she said.

'One can hide there,' he said expansively. 'I should say, *two* can hide there. All the conveniences. A cellar at your elbow, a larder at your beck and call. A civilised wilderness for a loaf of bread, a jug of wine, and – th-h-owoo.' He ended with a hoarse whisper, and Kay had the insane feeling that if his eyes protruded another inch, a man could sit on one and saw the other off.

She closed her eyes again and explored her resources. She felt that she had possibly twenty seconds of endurance left. Eighteen. Sixteen. Oh, this is fine. Here goes Bobby's career up in smoke – in a mushroom-shaped cloud at a table for two.

He gathered his feet under him and rose. 'You'll excuse me for a moment,' he said, not quite clicking his heels. He made a little joke about powder rooms, and obviously being human. He turned away and turned back and pointed out that this was only the first of the little intimacies they would come to learn of each other. He turned away and turned back and said 'Think it over. Perhaps we can slip away to our little dreamland this very night!' He turned away and if he had turned back again he would have got a French heel in the area of his watchpocket.

Kay sat alone at the table and visibly wilted. Anger and scorn had sustained her; now, for a moment, fear and weariness took their places. Her shoulders sagged and turned foward and her chin went down, and a tear slid out on to her cheek. This was three degrees worse than awful. This was too much to pay for a Mayo Clinic full of doctors. She wanted out. Something had to happen, right now.

Something did. A pair of hands appeared on the tablecloth in front of her.

She looked up and met the eyes of the young man who stood there. He had a broad, unremarkable face. He was nearly as blond as she, though his eyes were dark. He had a good mouth. He said, 'A lot of people don't know the difference between a musician and a potted palm when they go to pour their hearts out. You're in a spot, Ma'am.'

Some of her anger returned, but it subsided, engulfed in a flood of embarrassment. She could say only, 'Please leave me alone.'

'I can't. I heard that routine.' He tossed his head towards the rest rooms. 'There's a way out, if you'll trust me.'

'I'll keep the devil I know,' she said coldly.

'You listen to me. I mean listen, until I'm finished. Then you can do as you like. When he comes back, stall him off for tonight. Promise to meet him here tomorrow night. Make it a real good act. Then tell him you shouldn't leave here together; you might be seen. He'll think of that anyway.'

'And he leaves, and I'm at your tender mercies?'

'Don't be a goon! Sorry. No, you leave first. Go straight to the station and catch the first train out. There's a northbound at three o'clock and a southbound at three twelve. Take either one. Go somewhere else, hole up, find yourself another job, and stay out of sight.'

'On what? Three dollars mad-money?'

He flipped a long wallet out of his inside jacket pocket. 'Here's three hundred. You're smart enough to make out all right on that.'

'You're crazy! You don't know me, and I don't know you. Besides, I haven't anything up for sale.'

He made an exasperated gesture. 'Who said anything about that? I said take a train – any train. No one's going to follow you.'

'You *are crazy*. How could I get it back to you?'

'You worry about that. I work here. Drop by some time – during the day when I'm not here, if you like, and leave it for me.'

'What on earth makes you want to do a thing like that?'

His voice was very gentle. 'Say it's the same thing makes me bring raw fish to alley-cats. Oh, stop arguing. You need an out and this is it.'

'I can't do a thing like that!'

'You got a good imagination? The kind that makes pictures?'

'I – suppose so.'

'Then, forgive me, but you need a kick in the teeth. If you don't do what I just told you, that crumb is going to—' and in a half-dozen simple, terse words, he told her exactly what that crumb was going to do. Then, with a single deft motion, he slipped the bills into her handbag and got back on the bandstand.

She sat, sick and shaken, until Bluett returned from the men's room. She had an unusually vivid pictorial imagination.

'While I was gone,' he said, settling into his chair and beckoning to the waiter for the cheque, 'know what I was doing?'

That, she thought, is just the kind of question I need right now. Limpidly, she asked, 'What?'

'I was thinking about that little place, and how wonderful it would be if I could slip away after a hard day at court, and find you there waiting for me.' He smiled fatuously. 'And no one would ever know.'

Kay sent up a 'Lord-forgive-me, I-know-not-what-I-do,' and said distinctly, 'I think that's a charming idea. Just charming.'

'And it wouldn't – *what?*'

For a moment she almost pitied him. Here he had his lines flaked out, his hooks sharpened and greased, and his casting arm worked up to a fine snap, and she'd robbed him of his sport. She'd driven up behind him with a wagon-load of fish. She'd surrendered.

'Well,' he said. 'Well, I, hm. Hm-m-m! Waiter!'

'But,' she said archly, 'Not tonight, Ar-mand.'

'Now, Kay. Just come up and look at it. It's not far.'

She figuratively spit on her hands, took a deep breath and plunged – wondering vaguely at just what instant she had decided to take this fantastic course. She batted her eyelashes only a delicate twice, and said softly, 'Armand, I'm not an experienced person like you, and I' – she hesitated and dropped her eyes – 'I want it to be perfect. And tonight, it's all so sudden, and I haven't been able to look forward to anything, and it's terribly late and we're both tired, and I have to work tomorrow but I won't the day after, and besides—' and here she capped it. Here she generated, on the spot, the most diffuse and colourful statement of her entire life – 'Besides,' she said, fluttering her hands prettily, 'I'm not *ready.*'

She peeped at him from the sides of her eyes and saw his bony face undergo four distinct expressions, one after the other. Again there was that within her which was capable of astonishment; she had been able to think of only three possible reactions to a statement like that. At the same moment the guitarist behind her, in the middle of a fluid *glissando,* got his little finger trapped underneath his A string.

Before Armand Bluett could get his breath back, she said, 'Tomorrow, Armand. But—' She blushed. When she was a child, reading *Ivanhoe* and *The Deerslayer,* she used to practise blushing before the mirror. She never could do it. Yet she did it now. 'But earlier,' she finished.

Her astonishment factor clicked again, this time with the thought, why haven't I ever tried this before?

'Tomorrow night? You'll come?' he said. 'You really will?'

'What time, Ar-mand?' she asked submissively.

'Well now. Hmp. Ah – say eleven?'

'Oh, it would be crowded here then. Ten, before the shows are over.'

'I knew you were clever,' he said admiringly.

She grasped the point firmly and pressed it. 'There are always too many people,' she said, looking around. 'You know, we shouldn't leave together. Just in case.'

He shook his head in wonder, and beamed.

'I'll just—' She paused, looking at his eyes, his mouth. 'I'll just go, like that.' She snapped her fingers. 'No goodbyes …'

She skipped to her feet and ran out, clutching her purse. And as she passed the end of the bandstand, the guitarist, speaking in a voice just loud enough to reach her, and barely moving his lips, said:

'Lady, you ought to have your mouth washed out with bourbon.'

CHAPTER X

His honour, the Surrogate Armand Bluett, left his chambers early the next afternoon. Dressed in a dark brown business suit and seeing alternately from the corners of his eyes, he taxied across town, paid off the driver, and skulked down a narrow street. He strolled past a certain doorway twice to be sure he was not followed, and then dodged inside, key in hand.

Upstairs, he went through the compact two-and-kitchenette with a fine-toothed comb. He opened all the windows and aired the place out. Stuffed between the cushions on the couch he found a rainbow-hued silk scarf redolent with cheap, dying scent. He dropped it in the incinerator with a snort. 'Won't need *that* any more.'

He checked the refrigerator, the kitchen shelves, the bathroom cabinet. He ran the water and tested the gas and the lights. He tried the end-table lamps, the torchere, the radio. He ran a small vacuum cleaner over the rugs and the heavy drapes. Finally, grunting with satisfaction, he went into the bathroom and shaved and showered. There followed clouds of talc and a haze of cologne. He pared his toenails, after which he stood before the cheval glass in various abnormal chest-out poses, admiring his reflection through a rose-coloured ego.

He dressed carefully in a subdued hound's-tooth check and a tie designed for the contracting pupil, returned to the mirror for a heady fifteen minutes, sat down and painted his nails with colourless polish, and wandered dreamily around fluttering his flabby hands and thinking detailed thoughts, reciting, half-aloud, little lines of witty, sophisticated dialogue. 'Who polished your eyes?' he muttered, and 'My dear, dear child, that was nothing, really nothing. A study in harmony, before the complex instrumentation of the flesh … no, she's not old enough for that one. Mm. You're the cream in my coffee. No! *I'm* not old enough for that.'

So he passed the evening, very pleasantly indeed. At 8.30 he left, to dine sumptuously at a seafood restaurant. At 9.50 he was ensconced at the corner table at Club Nemo, buffing his glittering nails on his lapel and alternately wetting his lips and dabbing at them with a napkin.

At ten o'clock she arrived.

Last night he had risen to his feet as she crossed the dance floor. Tonight he was up out of his chair and at her side before she reached it.

This was Kay transformed. This was the conception of his wildest dreams of her.

Her hair was turned back from her face in soft small billows which framed her face. Her eyes were skilfully shadowed, and seemed to have taken on a violet tinge with their blue. She wore a long cloak of some heavy material, and under it, a demure but skin-tight jacket of black ciré satin and a black hem-slashed skirt.

'Armand …' she whispered, holding out both hands.

He took them. His lips opened and closed twice before he could say anything at all, and then she was past him, walking with a long, easy stride to the table. Walking behind her, he saw her pause as the orchestra started up, and throw a glance of disdain at the guitarist. At the table she unclasped the cloak at her throat and let it fall away confidently. Armand Bluett was there to receive it as she slid into her chair. He stood there goggling at her for so long that she laughed at him. 'Aren't you going to say anything at all?'

'I'm speechless,' he said, and thought, my word, that came out effectively.

A waiter came, and he ordered for her. Daiquiri, this time. No woman he had ever seen reminded him less of a sherry flip.

'I am a very lucky man,' he said. That was twice in a row he had said something unrehearsed.

'Not as lucky as I am,' she said, and she seemed quite sincere as she said it. She put out just the tip of a pink tongue; her eyes sparkled, and she laughed. For Bluett, the room began to gyrate. He looked down at her hands, toying with the clasp of a tiny cosmetic case.

'I don't think I ever noticed your hands before,' he said.

'Please do,' she twinkled. 'I love the things you say, Armand,' and she put her hands in his. They were long, strong hands with square palms and tapered fingers and what certainly must be the smoothest skin in the world.

The drinks came. He let go reluctantly and they both leaned back, looking at each other. She said, 'Glad we waited?'

'Oh yes. Hm. Yes indeed.' Suddenly, waiting was intolerable. Almost inadvertently he snatched up his drink and drained it.

The guitarist fluffed a note. She looked pained. Armand said, 'It's not too nice here tonight, is it?'

Her eyes glistened. 'You know a better place?' she asked softly.

His heart rose up and thumped the lower side of his Adam's apple. 'I certainly do,' he said when he could.

She inclined her head with an extraordinary, controlled acquiescence that was almost like a deep pain to him. He threw a bill on the table, put her cloak over her shoulders, and led her out.

In the cab he lunged for her almost before the machine was away from the kerb. She hardly seemed to move at all, but her body twisted away from him inside the cloak; he found himself with a double handful of cloth while Kay's profile smiled slightly, shaking its head. It was unspoken, but it was a flat 'no'. It was also a credit to the low frictional index of ciré satin.

'I never knew you were like this,' he said.

'Like what?'

'You weren't this way last night,' he floundered.

'What way, Ar-mand?' she teased.

'You weren't so – I mean, you didn't seem to be sure of yourself at all.'

She looked at him. 'I wasn't – ready.'

'Oh, I see,' he lied.

Conversation lapsed after that, until he paid off the cab at the street intersection near his hideout. He was beginning to feel that the situation was out of his control. If she controlled it, however, as she had so far, he was more than willing to go along.

Walking down the dirty, narrow street, he said, 'Don't look at any of this, Kay. It's quite different upstairs.'

'It's all the same, when I'm with you,' she said, stepping over some garbage. He was very pleased.

They climbed the stairs, and he flung open the door with a wide gesture. 'Enter, fair lady, the land of the lotus-eaters.'

She pirouetted in and cooed over the drapes, the lamps, the pictures. He closed the door and shot the bolt, dropped his hat on the couch and stalked towards her. He was about to put his arms around her from behind when she darted away. 'What a way to begin!' she sang. 'Putting your hat there. Don't you know it's bad luck to put a hat on a bed?'

'This is my lucky day,' he pronounced.

'Mine too,' she said. 'So let's not spoil it. Let's pretend we've been here forever, and we'll be here forever.'

He smiled. 'I like that.'

'I'm glad. That way,' she said, stepping away from a corner as he approached, 'there's no hurry. Could we have a drink?'

'You may have the moon,' he chanted. He opened the kitchenette. 'What would you like?'

'Oh, how wonderful. Let me, let me. You go into the other room and sit down, Mister Man. This is woman's work.' She shunted him out, and began to mix, busily.

Armand lounged back on the couch with his feet on the rock-maple coffee table, and listened to the pleasant clinking and swizzling noises from the other room. He wondered idly if he could get her to bring his slippers every evening.

She glided in, balancing two tall highballs on a small tray. She kept one hand behind her back as she knelt and put the tray down on the coffee table and slipped into an easy-chair.

'What are you hiding?' he asked.

'It's a secret.'

'Come over here.'

'Let's talk a little while first. Please.'

'A little while.' He sniggered. 'It's your fault, Kay. You're so beautiful. Hm. You make me feel mad – impetuous.' He began rubbing his hands together. She closed her eyes. 'Armand ...'

'Yes, my little one,' he answered, patronisingly.

'Did you ever hurt anyone?'

He sat up. 'I? Kay, are you afraid?' He puffed his chest out a bit. 'Afraid of me? Why, I won't hurt you, baby.'

'I'm not talking about me,' she said, a little impatiently. 'I just asked you – did you ever hurt anyone?'

'Why, of course not. Not intentionally, that is. You must remember – my business is justice.'

'Justice.' She said it as if it tasted good. 'There are two ways of hurting people, Armand – outside, where it shows, and inside, in the mind, where it scars and festers.'

'I don't follow you,' he said, his pomposity returning as his confesion grew. 'Whom have I ever hurt?'

'Kay Hallowell, for one,' she said detachedly, 'with the kind of pressure you've been putting on. Not because she's a minor; you are only a criminal on paper for that, and even that wouldn't apply in some states.'

'Now, look here, young lady—'

'– but because,' she went on calmly, 'you have been systematically wrecking what faith she has in humanity. If there is a basic justice, then for that you are a criminal by its standards.'

'Kay – what's come over you? What are you talking about? I won't have any more of this!' He leaned back and folded his arms. She sat quietly.

'I know,' he said, half to himself, 'you're joking. Is that it, baby?'

In the same level, detached tone, she went on speaking. 'You are guilty of hurting others in both the ways I mentioned. Physically, where it shows, and psychically. You will be punished in both those ways, *Justice* Bluett.'

He blew air from his nostrils. 'That is quite enough. I did not bring you here for anything like this. Perhaps I shall have to remind you, after all, that I am not a man to be trifled with. Hm. The matter of your estate—'

'I am not trifling, Armand.' She leaned across the low table to him. He put up his hands. 'What do you want?' he breathed, before he could stop himself.

'Your handkerchief.'

'My h – *what*?'

She plucked it out of his breast pocket. 'Thank you.' As she spoke she shook it out, brought up two corners and knotted them together. She slipped her left hand through the loop and settled the handkerchief high on her forearm. 'I am going to punish you first in the way it doesn't show,' she said informatively, 'by reminding you, in a way you can't forget, of how you once hurt someone else.'

'What kind of nonsense—'

She reached behind her with her right hand and brought out what she had been hiding – a new, sharp, heavy cleaver.

Armand Bluett cowered away, back into the couch cushions. 'Kay – no! No!' he panted. His face turned green. 'I haven't touched you, Kay! I only wanted to talk. I wanted to help you and – and your brother. Put that thing down, Kay!' He was drooling with terror. 'Can't we be friends, Kay?' he whimpered.

'Stop it!' she hissed. She lifted the cleaver high, resting her left hand on the table and leaning towards him. Her face made, line upon plane upon carven curve, a mask of utter contempt. 'I told you that your physical punishment comes later. Think about this while you wait for it.'

The cleaver arced over and came down, with every ounce of a lithe body behind it. Armand Bluett screamed – a ridiculous, hoarse, thin sound. He closed his eyes. The cleaver crashed into the heavy top of the coffee-table. Armand twisted and scrabbled back into the cushions, crabbed sidewise and backwards along the wall until he could go no farther. He stopped ludicrously, on all fours, on the couch, backed into the corner, sweat and spittle running off his chin. He opened his eyes.

It had apparently taken him only a split second to make the hysterical move, for she still stood over the table; she still held the handle of the cleaver. Its edge had buried itself in the thick wood, after passing through the flesh and bone of her hand.

She snatched up the bronze letter-opener and thrust it under the handkerchief on her forearm. As she straightened, bright arterial blood spouted from the stumps of three severed fingers. Her face was pale under the cosmetics, but not one whit changed otherwise; it still wore its proud, unadulterated contempt. She stood straight and tall, twisting the handkerchief with the handle of the letter-opener, making a tourniquet, and she stared him down. As his eyes fell, she spat, 'Isn't this better than what you planned? Now you've got a part of me to keep for your very own. That's much better than using something and giving it back.'

The spurting blood had slowed to a dribble as she twisted. Now she went to the chair on which she had left her cosmetics case. Out of it she worried a rubber glove. Holding the tourniquet against her side, she pulled the glove over her hand and snugged it around the wrist.

Armand Bluett began to vomit.

She shouldered into her cloak and went to the door.

When she had drawn back the bolt and opened it, she called back in a seductive voice, 'It's been so wonderful, Armand darling. Let's do it again soon …'

It took Armand's mind nearly an hour to claw its way up out of the pit of panic into which it had fallen. During the hour he hunkered there on the couch in his own filth, staring at the cleaver and the three still white fingers.

Three fingers.

Three *left* fingers.

Somewhere, deep in his mind, that meant something to him. At the moment he refused to let it surface. He feared it would. He knew it would. He knew that when it did, he would know consuming terror.

CHAPTER XI

Bobby dear, she wrote, I can't bear to think of you getting letters back with 'address unknown' on them. I'm all right. That's first and foremost. I'm all right, monkey-face, and you're not to worry. Your big sister is *all right*.

I'm also all mixed up. Maybe in that nice orderly hospital this will make more sense to you. I'll try to make it short and simple.

I was working one morning at the office when that awful Judge Bluett came in. He had to wait for a few minutes before he could see old Wattles Hartford, and he used it to make his usual wet soggy string of verbal passes. My brush worked fine until the seamy old weasel got on the subject of Daddy's money. You know that we'll get it when I'm twenty-one – unless that old partnership deal comes up again. It would have to go to court. Bluett not only was the partner – he's the Surrogate. Even if we could get him disqualified from hearing the case, you know how he could fix anyone else who might take the bench. Well, the idea was that if I would be nice and sweet to Hizzoner, in any nasty way he wanted, the will wouldn't be contested. I was terribly frightened, Bobby; you know the rest of your training has to come out of that money. I didn't know what to do. I needed time to think. I promised to meet him that night, real late, in a night club.

Bobby, it was awful. I was just at the point of blowing up, there at the table, when the old drooler left the room for a minute. I didn't know whether to fight or run away. I was scared, believe me. All of a sudden there was somebody standing there talking to me. I think he must be my guardian angel. Seems he had overheard the Judge talking to me. He wanted me to cut and run. I was afraid of him, too, at first, and then I saw his face. Oh, Bobby, it was such a *nice* face! He wanted to give me some money, and before I could say no he told me I could return it whenever I wanted to. He told me to get out of town right now – take a train, any train; he didn't even want to know which one. And before I could stop him he shoved $300 into my bag and walked off. The last thing he said was to accept a date for the next evening with the Judge. I couldn't do a thing – he'd only been there two minutes and he was talking practically every second of it. And then the Judge came back. I flapped my eyelids at the old fool like a lost woman, and cut out. I got a train to Eltonville twenty minutes later and didn't even register in a hotel when I got here. I waited around until the stores opened and bought an overnight case and a tooth brush and got myself a room. I slept a few hours and the very same afternoon I had a job in the only record shop in the place. It's $26 a week but I can make it fine.

Meanwhile I don't know what's happening back home. I'm sort of holding my breath until I hear something. I'm going to wait, though. We have time, and in the meantime, I'm all right. I'm not going to give you my address, honey, though I'll write often. Judge Bluett just might be able to get his hands on mail, some way. I think it pays to be careful. He's dangerous.

So, honey, that's the situation as far as it's gone. What next? I'll watch the home town papers for any item about His Dishonour the Surrogate, and hope for the best. As for you, don't worry your little square head about me, darling. I'm doing fine. I'm only making a few dollars a week less than I was at home and I'm a lot safer here. And the work isn't hard; some of the nicest people like music. I'm sorry I can't give you my exact address, but I do think it's better not to just now. We can let this thing ride for a year if we have to, and small loss. Work hard, baby; I'm behind you a thousand per cent. I'll write often.

Your loving
Big Sis Kay.

X X X

(This is the letter that Armand Bluett's hired second-storey man found in Undergraduate Robert Hallowell's room at the State Medical School.)

CHAPTER XII

'Yes – I am Pierre Monetre. Come in.' He stood aside and the girl entered.

'This is good of you, Mr Monetre. I know you must be terribly busy. And probably you won't be able to help me at all.'

'I might not if I were able,' he said. 'Sit down.'

She took a moulded plywood chair which stood at the end of the half desk, half lab bench which took up almost an end wall of the trailer. He looked at her coldly. Soft yellow hair, eyes sometimes slate-blue, sometimes a shade darker than sky-blue; a studied coolness through which he, with his schooled perceptions, could readily see. She is disturbed, he thought; frightened and ashamed of it. He waited.

She said, 'There's something I've got to find out. It happened years ago. I'd almost forgotten about it, and then saw your posters, and I remembered ... I could be wrong, but if only—' She kneaded her hands together. Monetre watched them, and then returned his cold stare to her face.

'I'm sorry, Mr Monetre. I can't seem to get to the point. It's all so vague and so – terribly important. The thing is, when I was a little girl, seven or eight years old, there was a boy in my class in school who ran away. He was about my age, and had some sort of horrible run-in with his stepfather. I think he was hurt. His hand. I don't know how badly. I was probably the last one in town to see him. No one ever saw him again.'

Monetre picked up some papers, shifted them, put them down again. 'I really don't know what I can do about that, Miss—'

'Hallowell. Kay Hallowell. Please hear me out, Mr Monetre. I've come thirty miles just to see you, because I can't afford to pass up the slightest chance—'

'If you cry, you'll have to get out,' he rasped. His voice was so rough that she started. Then he said, with gentleness, 'Please go on.'

'Th-thank you. I'll be quick ... it was just after dark, a rainy, misty night. We lived by the highway, and I went out back for something ... I forget ... anyway, he was there, by the traffic light. I spoke to him. He asked me not to tell anyone that I had seen him, and I never have, till now. Then' – she closed her eyes, obviously trying to bring back every detail of the memory – 'I think someone called me. I turned to the gate and left him. But I peeped out again, and saw him climbing on the back of a truck that was stopped for the night. It was one of your trucks. I'm sure it was. The way it was painted ... and yesterday, when I saw your posters, I thought of it.'

Monetre waited, his deep-set eyes expressionless. He seemed to realise, suddenly, that she had finished. 'That happened twelve years ago? And, I suppose, you want to know if that boy reached the carnival.'

'Yes.'

'He did not. If he had, I should certainly have known of it.'

'Oh ...' It was a faint sound, stricken, yet resigned; apparently she had not expected anything else. She pulled herself together visibly, and said, 'He was small for his age. He had very dark hair and eyes and a pointed face. His name was Horty – Horton.'

'Horty ...' Monetre searched his memory. There was a familiar ring to those two syllables, somehow. Now, where ... He shook his head. 'I don't remember any boy called Horty.'

'Please try. *Please!* You see—' She looked at him searchingly, her eyes asking a question. He answered it, saying, 'You can trust me.'

She smiled, 'Thank you. Well, there's a man, a horrible person. He was once responsible for that boy. He's doing a terrible thing to me; it's something to do with an old law case, and he might be able to keep me from getting some money that is due me when I come of age. I need it. Not for myself; it's for my brother. He's going to be a doctor, and—'

'I don't like doctors,' said Monetre. If there is a great bell for hatred as there is one for freedom, it rang in his voice as he said that. He stood up. 'I know nothing about any boy named Horty, who disappeared twelve years ago. I am not interested in finding him in any case, particularly if doing so would help a man make a parasite of himself and fools of his patients. I am not a kidnapper, and will have nothing to do with a search which reeks of that and blackmail to boot. Goodbye.'

She had risen with him. Her eyes were round. 'I – I'm sorry. Really, I—'

'Goodbye.' It was the velvet this time, used with care, used to show her that his gentleness was a virtuosity, an overlay. She turned to the door, opened it. She stopped and looked back over her shoulder. 'May I leave you my address, just in case, some day, you—'

'You may not,' he said. He turned his back on her and sat down. He heard the door close.

He closed his eyes, and his arched, slit nostrils expanded until they were round holes. Humans, humans, and their complex, useless, unimportant machinations. There was no mystery about humans; no puzzle. Everything human could be brought to light by asking simply. 'What does it gain you?' ... What could humans know of a life-form to which the idea of gain was alien? What could a human say of his crystal-kin, the living jewels which could communicate with each other and did not dare to, which could cooperate with each other and scorned to?

And what – he let himself smile – what would humans do when they had to fight the alien? When they were up against an enemy which would make an advance and then scorn to consolidate it – and then make a different *kind* of advance, in a different way, in another place?

He sank into an esoteric reverie, marshalling his crystallines against teeming, stupid mankind; losing, in his thoughts, the pointless perturbations of a girl in a search for a child long missing, for some petty gainful reason of her own.

'Hey, Maneater.'

'*Damn* it! What now?'

The door opened diffidently. 'Maneater, there's—'

'Come in, Havana, and speak up. I don't like mumblers.'

Havana edged in, after setting his cigar down on the step. 'There's a man outside wants to see you.'

Monetre glowered over his shoulder. 'Your hair's getting grey. What's left of it. Dye it.'

'Okay, okay. Right away, this afternoon. I'm sorry.' He shifted his feet miserably. 'About this man—'

'I've had my quota for today,' said Monetre. 'Useless people wanting impossible things of no importance. Did you see that girl go out of here?'

'Yes. That's what I'm trying to tell you. So did this guy. See, he was waiting to see you. He asked Johnward where he could find you, and—'

'I think I'll fire Johnward. He's an advance man, not an usher. What business has he, bringing people to annoy me?'

'I guess he thought you ought to see this one. A big-shot,' said Havana timidly. 'So when he got your trailer, he asked me were you busy. I told him yes, you were talking to someone. He said he'd wait. About then the door opens, and that girl comes out. She puts a hand on the side and turns back to say something to you, and this guy, this big-shot, he blows a fuse. No kidding, Maneater, I never seen anything like it. He grabs my shoulder. I'll have a bruise there for a week. He says, "It's her! It's her!" and I says "Who?" and he says, "She mustn't see me! She's a devil! She cut those fingers off, and they've grown back again!"'

Monetre sat bolt upright and turned in his swivel chair to face the midget. 'Go on, Havana,' he said in his gentle voice.

'Well, that's all. 'Cept he ducked back behind Gogol's bally-platform and hunkered down out of sight, and peeped out at that girl as she walked past him. She never saw him.'

'Where is he now?'

Havana glanced through the door. 'Still right there. Looks pretty bad. I think he's having some kind of a fit.'

Monetre left his chair and shot through the door, leaving it completely up to Havana whether he got out of the way or not. The midget leaped to the side, out of Monetre's direct path, but not far enough to avoid the bony edge of Monetre's pelvis, which glanced stunningly off Havana's pudgy cheekbone.

Monetre bounded to the side of the man who cowered down behind the bally-platform. He knelt and placed a sure hand on the man's forehead, which was clammy and cold.

'It's all right now, sir,' he said in a deep, soothing voice. 'You'll be perfectly safe with me.' He urged the idea 'safe', because, whatever the cause might be, the man was sodden, trembling, all but ecstatic with fear. Monetre asked no questions, but kept crooning. 'You're in good hands now, sir. Quite safe. Nothing can happen now. Come along; we'll have a drink. You'll be all right.'

The man's watery eyes fixed themselves on him, slowly. Awareness crept into them, and a certain embarrassment. He said, 'Hm. Uh – slight attack of – hm … vertigo, you know. Sorry to be … hm.'

Monetre courteously helped him up, picked up a brown homburg and dusted it off. 'My office is just there. Do come in and sit down.'

Monetre kept a firm hand on the man's elbow, led him to the trailer, handed him up the two steps, reached past him and opened the door. 'Would you like to lie down for a few minutes?'

'No, no. Thank you; you're very kind.'

'Sit here, then. I think you'll find it comfortable. I'll get you something that will make you feel better.' He fingered a simple combination latch, chose a bottle of tawny port. From a desk drawer he took a small phial and put two drops of liquid into a glass, filling it with wine. 'Drink this. It will make you feel better. A little sodium amytal – just enough to quiet your nerves.'

'Thank you, thank' – he drank it greedily – 'you. Are you Mr Monetre?'

'At your service.'

'I am Judge Bluett. Surrogate, you know. Hm.'

'I am honoured.'

'Not at all, not at all. I am the one who … I drove fifty miles to see you, sir, and would gladly have done twice that. You have a wide reputation.'

'I hadn't realised it,' said Monetre, and thought, this deflated creature is as insincere as I am. 'What can I do for you?'

'Hm. Well, now. Matter of – ah – scientific interest. I read about you in a magazine, you know. Said you know more about fr – ah, strange people, and things like that, than anyone alive.'

'I wouldn't say that,' said Monetre. 'I have worked with them for a great many years, of course. What was it you wanted to know?'

'Oh … the kind of thing you can't get out of reference books. Or ask any so-called scientist, for that matter; they just laugh at things that aren't in some book, somewhere.'

'I have experienced that, Judge. I do not laugh readily.'

'Splendid. Then I shall ask you. Namely, do you know anything about – ah – regeneration?'

Monetre cloaked his eyes. Would the fool ever get to the point – 'What kind of regeneration? The girdle of the nematodes? Cellular healing? Or are you talking about old-time radio receivers?'

'Please,' said the judge, and made a flabby gesture. 'I'm quite the layman, Mr Monetre. You'll have to use simple language. What I want to know is – how much of a restoration is possible after a serious cut?'

'How serious a cut?'

'Hm. Call it an amputation.'

'Well, now. That depends, Judge. A fingertip, possibly. A chipped bone can grow surprisingly. You – you know of a case where a regeneration has been, shall we say, a bit more than normal?'

There was a long pause. Monetre noticed that the Judge was paling. He poured him more port, and filled a glass for himself. Excitement mounted within him.

'I do know of such a case. At least, I mean … hm. Well, it seemed so to me. That is, I saw the amputation.'

'An arm? A leg, perhaps, or a foot?'

'Three fingers. Three whole fingers,' said the Judge. 'It would seem that they grew back. And in forty-eight hours. A well-known osteologist treated the whole thing as a great joke when I asked him about it. Refused to believe I was serious.' Suddenly he leaned forward so abruptly that the loose skin of his jaw quivered. 'Who was the girl who just left here?'

'An autograph hound,' said Monetre in a bored tone. 'A person of no importance. Do proceed.'

The Judge swallowed with difficulty. 'Her name is – Kay Hallowell.'

'Perhaps so, perhaps so. Have you changed the subject?' asked Monetre impatiently.

'I have not, sir,' the Judge answered hotly. 'That girl, that monster – in good light, and right before my eyes, *chopped off three fingers of her left hand*!' He nodded, pushing his lower lip out, and sat back.

If he expected a sharp reaction, he was not disappointed. Monetre leaped to his feet and bellowed, 'Havana!' He strode to the door and yelled again. 'Where is that little fat – oh; there you are, Havana. Go and find that girl who just left here. Understand? Find her and bring her back. I don't care what you tell her; find her and bring her back here.' He clapped his hands explosively. '*Run!*'

He returned to his chair, his face working. He looked at his hands, then at the judge. 'You're quite sure of this.'

'I am.'

'Which hand?'

'The left.' The Judge ran a finger around his collar. 'Ah – Mr Monetre. If that boy should bring her back here, why, ah – I, that is—'

'I gather you are afraid of her.'

'Now, ah – I wouldn't say that,' said the Judge. 'Startled, yes. Hm. Wouldn't you be?'

'No,' said Monetre. 'You are lying, sir.'

'I? Lying?' Bluett puffed up his chest and glowered at the carny boss.

Monetre half-closed his eyes and began ticking off items on his fingers. 'It would seem that what frightened you a few minutes ago was the sight of that girl's left hand. You told the midget that the fingers had grown back. It was obviously the first time you had seen the hand regenerated. And yet you tell me that you have already consulted an osteologist about it.'

'There are no lies involved,' said Bluett stiffly. 'True, I did see the restored hand when she stood in this doorway, and it was the first time. But I also saw her cut those fingers off!'

'Then why,' asked Monetre, 'come to me to ask questions about regeneration?' Watching the Judge flounder about for an answer, he added, 'Come now, Judge Bluett, either you have not stated your original purpose in coming here, or – you have seen a case of this regeneration before. Ah, I see that's it.' His eyes began to burn. 'I think you'd better tell me the whole story.'

'That *isn't* it!' the Judge protested. 'Really, sir, I am not enjoying this cross-questioning. I fail to see—'

Shrewdly, Monetre reached out to touch the fear which hovered so close to this wet-eyed man. 'You are in greater danger than you suspect,' he interrupted. 'I know what that danger is, and I am probably the only man in the world who can help you. You will co-operate with me, sir, or you will leave this instant – and take the consequences.' He said this with his flexible voice toned down to a soft, resonating diapason, which apparently frightened the Judge half out of his wits. The chain of imaginary horrors which mirrored themselves on Bluett's paling face must have been colourful, to say the least. Smiling slightly, Monetre leaned back in his chair and waited.

'M-may I ...' The Judge poured himself more wine. 'Ah. Now, sir. I must tell you at the outset that this whole matter has been one of – ah – conjecture on my part. That is, up until I saw the girl just now. By the way – I do not want to have her see me. Could you—'

'When Havana brings her back, I'll get you out of sight. Go on.'

'Good. Thank you, sir. Well, some years ago I brought a child into my house. Ugly little monster. When he was seven or eight years old, he ran away from home. I have not heard of him since. I imagine he would be nineteen or so by this time – if he's alive. And – and there seems to be some connection between him and this girl.'

'What connection?' Monetre prompted.

'Well, sh-she seemed to know something about him.' As Monetre shifted his feet impatiently, he blurted, 'Fact is, there was a little trouble. The boy was downright rebellious. I thrashed him and shoved him into a closet. His hand, quite accidentally, you realise – his hand was crushed in the hinge of the door. Hm. Yes – very unpleasant.'

'Go on.'

'I've been – ah – looking, you know – that is, if that boy has grown up, he might be resentful, you understand … besides, he was a most unbalanced child, and one never knows how these things might affect a weak mind—'

'You mean you feel guilty as hell and scared to boot, and you've been watching for a young man with some fingers missing. Fingers – get to the point! What has this to do with the girl?' Monetre's voice was a whip.

'I can't – say exactly,' mumbled the Judge. 'She seemed to know something about the boy. I mean, she hinted something about him – said that she was going to remind me of a way I had – hurt someone once. And then she took a cleaver and cut off her fingers. She disappeared. I had a man locate her. He found out she was due here – my man sent for me. That's all.'

Monetre closed his eyes and thought hard. 'There was nothing wrong with her fingers when she was in here.'

'Damn it, I know that! But I tell you, I saw, with my own eyes—'

'All right, all right. She cut them off. Now, exactly why did you come here?'

'I – that's all. When something like that happens it makes you forget everything you know and start right from scratch. What I saw was impossible, and I began thinking in a way that let anything be possible … anyth—'

'Come to the point!' roared the Maneater.

'There is none!' Bluett roared back. They glared at each other for a crackling moment. 'That's what I'm trying to tell you; I don't know. I remembered that child and his crushed fingers, and there was this girl and what she did. I began wondering if she and the boy were the same … I told you "impossible" didn't matter any more. Well, the girl had a perfectly good hand before she chopped into it. If, somehow, she was that boy, he must have grown the fingers back. If he could do it once, he could do it again. If he knew he could do it again, he wouldn't be afraid to cut them off.' The judge threw up his hands and shrugged, and let his arms fall limply. 'So I began to wonder what manner of creature could grow fingers at will. That's all.'

Monetre made wide eaves of his lids, his burning dark eyes studying the Judge. 'This – boy who might be a girl,' he murmured. 'What was his name?'

'Horton. Horty, we called him. Vicious little scut.'

'Think, now. Was there anything strange about him as a child?'

'I should say so! I don't think he was sane. Clinging to baby-toys – that sort of thing. And he had filthy habits.'

'What filthy habits?'

'He was expelled from school for eating insects.'

'Ah! Ants?'

'How did you know?'

Monetre rose, pased to the door and back. Excitement began to thump in his chest. 'What baby-toys did he cling to?'

'Oh, I don't remember. It isn't important.'

'I'll decide that,' snapped Monetre. 'Think, man! If you value your life—'

'I can't think! I can't!' Bluett looked up at the Maneater, and quailed before those blazing eyes. 'It was some sort of a jack-in-the-box. A hideous thing.'

'What did it look like? Speak up, damn it!'

'What does it – oh, all right. It was this big, and it had a head on it like a Punch – you know, Punch and Judy. Big nose and chin. The boy hardly ever looked at it. But he had to have it near him. I threw it away one time and the doctor made me find it and bring it back. Horton almost died.'

'He did, eh?' grunted Monetre tautly, triumphantly. 'Now tell me – that toy had been with him since he was born, hadn't it? And there was something about it – some sort of jewelled button, or something glittery?'

'How did you know—' Bluett began again, and again quailed under the radiation of furious, excited impatience from the carny boss. 'Yes. The eyes.'

Monetre flung himself on the Judge. He grasped his shoulders, shook him. 'You said "eye", did you? There was only one jewel?' he panted.

'Don't – don't—' wheezed Bluett, pushing weakly at Monetre's taloned hands. 'I said "eyes". Two eyes. They were both the same. Nasty looking things. Seemed to have a light of their own.'

Monetre straightened slowly, backed off. 'Two of them,' he breathed. 'Two …'

He closed his eyes, his brain humming. Disappearing boy, fingers … fingers crushed. Girl … the right age, too … Horton. Horton … Horty. His mind looped and wheeled back over the years. A small brown face, peaked with pain, saying, 'My folks called me Hortense, but everyone calls me Kiddo.' Kiddo, who had arrived with a crushed hand, and had left the carnival two years ago. What had happened when she left? He had wanted something, wanted to examine her hand, and she left during the night.

That hand. When she first arrived, he had cleaned it up, trimmed away the ruined flesh, sewed it up. He had treated it every day for weeks, until the scar-tissue was fused over, and there was no further danger of infection; and then, somehow or other he had never looked at it again. Why not? Oh – Zena, Zena had always told him how Kiddo's hand was getting along.

He opened his eyes – slits, now. 'I'll find him,' he snarled.

There was a knock at the door, and a voice. 'Maneater—'

'It's the midget,' babbled Bluett, leaping up. 'With the girl. What shall I – where shall—'

Monetre sent him a look which wilted him, tumbled him back in his chair. The carny boss rose and stilted to the door, opening it a crack. 'Get her?'

'Gosh, Maneater, I—'

'I don't want to hear it,' said Monetre in a terrible whisper. 'You didn't bring her back. I sent you to get her and you didn't do it.' He closed the door with great care and turned to the Judge. 'Go away.'

'Eh? Hm. But what about the—'

'Go away!' It was a scream. As his glare had made Bluett limp, his voice stiffened him. The Judge was on his feet and moving doorwards before the scream had ceased to be a sound. He tried to speak, and succeeded only in moving his wet mouth.

'I'm the only one in the world who can help you,' said Monetre; and the Judge's face showed that this easy, quiet, conversational tone was the most shocking thing of all. He went to the door and paused. Monetre said, 'I will do what I can, Judge. You'll hear from me very soon, you may be sure of that.'

'Ah,' said the Judge. 'Mm. Anything I can do, Mr Monetre. Call on me. Anything at all.'

'Thank you. I shall certainly need your help.' Monetre's bony features froze the instant he stopped speaking, Bluett fled.

Pierre Monetre stood staring at the space where the Judge's bloated face had just been. Suddenly he balled his fist and smashed it into his palm. 'Zena!' said only his lips. He went pale with fury, weak with it, and went to his desk. He sat down, put his elbows on the blotter and his chin in his hand, and began to send out waves of feral hatred and demand.

Zena!
Zena!
Here! Come Here!

CHAPTER XIII

Horty laughed. He looked at his left hand, at the three stubs of fingers which rose, like unspread mushrooms, from his knuckles, touched the scar-tissue around them with his other hand, and he laughed.

He rose from the studio couch and crossed the wide room to the cheval glass, to stare at his face, to stand back and look critically at his shoulders, his profile. He grunted in satisfaction and went to the telephone in the bedroom.

'Three four four,' he said. His voice was resonant, well suited to the cast of his solid chin and his wide mouth. 'Nick? This is Sam Horton. Oh, fine. Sure, I'll be able to play again. The doc says I was lucky. A broken wrist usually heals pretty stiff, but this one won't. No – don't worry. Hm? About six weeks. Positively … Gold? Thanks Nick, but I'll get along. No, don't worry – I'll yell if I need any. Thanks, though. Yeah, I'll drop by every once in a while. I was in there a couple of days ago. Where did you find that three-chord bubble-head you have on guitar? He does by accident what Spike Jones does on purpose. No, I didn't want to hit him. I wanted to husk him.' He laughed. 'I'm kidding. He's okay. Well, thanks Nick. 'Bye.'

Going to the studio couch, he flung himself down with the confident relaxation of a well-fed feline. He pressed his shoulders luxuriously into the foam mattress, rolled and reached for one of the four books on the end table.

They were the only books in the apartment. Long ago he had learned of the physical encroachment of books, and the difficulties of overflowing bookcases. His solution was to get rid of them all, and make an arrangement with his dealer to send him four books a day – new books, on a rental basis. He read them all, and always returned them on the next day. It was a satisfactory solution, for him. He had total recall. What use, then, were bookcases?

He owned two pictures – a Markell, meticulously unmatched irregular shapes, varying in their apparent transparency, superimposed one on the other so that the tone of each affected the others, and so that the colour of the background affected everything. The other was a Mondrian, precise and balanced, and conveying an almost-impression of something which could never quite be anything.

He owned, however, miles of magnetic tape on which was recorded a magnificent collection of music. Horty's fabulous mind could retain the whole mood of a book, and recall any part of it. It could do the same with music; but to recall music is to generate it to a certain degree, and there is a decided difference in the colouration of the mind which hears music and one which makes it. Horty could do both, and his music library made it possible for him to do either.

He had the classics and the romantics which had been Zena's favourites, the symphonies, concerti, ballads, and virtuosic showpieces which had been his introduction to music. But his tastes had widened and deepened, and now included Honnegger and Copland, Shostakovitch and Walton. In the popular field he had discovered Tatum's sombre choridings and the incredible Thelonius Monk. He had the occasionally inspired trumpet of Dizzy Gillespie, the bewildering cadenzas of Ella Fitzgerald, the faultless production of Pearl Bailey's voice. His criterion in all of it was humanity and the extensions of humanity. He lived with books that led to books, art that led him to conjecture, music that led him to worlds beyond worlds of experience.

Yet for all these riches, Horty's rooms were simply furnished. The only unconventional article of furniture was the tape recorder and reproducer – a massive incorporation of high-fidelity components which Horty had been led to assemble because of an ear that demanded every nuance, every overtone, of every instrumental voice. Otherwise his rooms were like anyone's comfortably appointed, tastefully decorated apartment. It occurred to him, fleetingly and at long intervals, that with his resources he could surround himself with automatic luxury-machines like back-kneading chairs and air-conditioned drying chambers for after his shower. But he was never moved in such directions. His mind was simply and steadily acquisitve. His analytical abilities were phenomenal, but he was seldom moved to use them extensively. Therefore to acquire knowledge was sufficient; its use could wait for demand, and there was little demand coexistent with his utter and demonstrable confidence in his own powers.

Halfway through his book he stopped, a puzzled expression in his eyes. It was as if a special sound had reached him – yet none had.

He closed the book and racked it, rose to stand listening, turning his head slightly as if he were trying to fix the source of the sensation.

The doorbell rang.

Horty stopped moving. It was not a freeze, the startled immobilisation of a frightened animal. It was more a controlled, relaxed split second for thought. Then he moved again, balanced and easy.

At the door he paused, staring at the lower panel. His face tightened, and a swift frown rippled on his brow. He flung the door open.

She stood crookedly in the hallway, looking up at him with her eyes. Her head was turned sidewise and a little downward. She had to strain her eyes painfully to meet his; she was only four feet tall.

She said, faintly, 'Horty?'

He made a hoarse sound and knelt, pulling her into his arms, holding her with power and gentleness. 'Zee … Zee, what happened? Your face, your—' He picked her up and kicked the door shut and carried her over to the studio couch, to sit with her across his knees, cradled in his arms, her head resting in the warm hollow of his right hand. She smiled at him. Only one side of her mouth moved. Then she began to cry, and Horty's own tears curtained from him the sight of her ravaged face.

Her sobs stopped soon, as if she were simply too tired to continue. She looked at his face, all of it, part by part. She brought her hand up and touched his hair. 'Horty …' she whispered. 'I loved you so much the way you were …'

'I haven't changed,' he said. 'I'm a big grown-up man now. I have an apartment and a job. I have this voice and these shoulders and I weigh a hundred pounds more than I did three years ago.' He bent and kissed her quickly. 'But I haven't changed, Zee. I haven't changed.' He touched her face, a careful, feathery contact. 'Do you hurt?'

'Some.' She closed her eyes and wet her lips. Her tongue seemed unable to reach one corner of her mouth. 'I've changed.'

'You've *been* changed,' he said, his voice shaking. 'The Maneater?'

'Of course. You knew, didn't you?'

'Not really. I thought once you were calling me. Or he was … it was far away. But anyway, no one else would have – would … what happened? Do you want to tell me?'

'Oh yes. He – found out about you. I don't understand how. Your – that Armand Bluett – he's a judge or something now. He came to see the Maneater. He thought you were a girl. A big girl, I mean.'

'I was, for a while.' He smiled tensely.

'Oh. Oh, I see. Were you really at the carnival that day?'

'At the carnival? No. What day, Zee? You mean when he found out?'

'Yes. Four – no; five days ago. You weren't there. I don't under—' She shrugged. 'Anyway, a girl came to see the Maneater and the Judge followed her and thought she was you. The Maneater thought so too. He sent Havana looking for her. Havana couldn't find her.'

'And then the Maneater got hold of you.'

'Mm. I didn't mean to tell him, Horty. I didn't. Not for a long time, anyway. I – forget.' She closed her eyes again. Horty trembled suddenly, and then could breathe.

'I don't … remember' she said with difficulty.

'Don't try. Don't talk any more,' he murmured.

'I want to. I've got to. He mustn't find you!' she said. 'He's hunting for you right this minute!'

Horty's eyes narrowed and he said, 'Good.'

Her eyes were still closed. She said, 'It was a long time. He talked very quietly. He gave me cushions and some wine that tasted like autumn. He talked about the carnival and Solum and Gogol. He mentioned 'Kiddo' and then talked about the new flat cars and the commissary tent and the trouble with the roustabouts' union. He said something about the musicians' union and something about music and something about the guitar and then about the act we used to have. Then he was off again about the menageries and the shills and the advance men, and back again. You see? Just barely mentioning you and going away and coming back and back. All night, Horty, all, all *night!*'

'Sh-h-h.'

'He wouldn't ask me! He talked with his head turned away watching me out of the corners of his eyes. I sat and tried to sip the wine, and tried to eat when Cooky brought dinner and midnight lunch and breakfast, and tried to smile when he stopped for a minute. He didn't touch me, he didn't hit me, he didn't *ask* me!'

'He did later,' breathed Horty.

'Much later. I don't remember … his face over me like a moon, once. I hurt all over. He shouted. Who is Horty, where is Horty, who is Kiddo, why did I hide Kiddo … I woke up and woke up. I don't remember the times I slept, or fainted, or whatever it was. I woke up with my blood in my eyes, drying, and he was talking about the ride mechanics and the power for the floodlights. I woke up in his arms, he was whispering in my ear about Bunny and Havana, they must have known what Horty was. I woke up on the floor. My knee hurt. There was a terrible light. I jumped up with the pain of it. I ran out of the door and fell down, my knee wouldn't work, it was in the afternoon and he caught me and dragged me back again and threw me on the floor and made the light again. He had a burning glass and he gave me vinegar to drink. My tongue swelled, I—'

'Sh-h-h. Zena, honey, hush. Don't say any more.'

The flat, uninflected voice went on. 'I lay still when Bunny looked in and the Maneater didn't know she saw what he was doing and Bunny ran away and Havana came and hit the Maneater with a piece of pipe and the Maneater broke his neck he's going to die and I—'

Horty's eyelids felt dry. He raised a careful hand and slapped her smartly across her undamaged cheek. 'Zena. *Stop it!*'

At the impact she uttered a great shriek, and screamed. 'I don't *know* any more, *truly* I don't!' and burst into painful, writhing sobs. Horty tried to speak to her but could not be heard through her weeping. He stood, turned, put her down gently on the couch, ran and wrung out a cloth in cold water and bathed her face and wrists. She stopped crying abruptly and fell asleep.

Horty watched her until her breathing assured him that she was at peace. He put his head slowly down beside hers as he knelt on the floor beside the couch. Her hair was on his forehead. Half-crossing his arms, he grasped his elbows and began to pull them. He kept the tension until his shoulders and chest throbbed with pain. He needed to be near her, would not move, yet must relieve the black tension of fury which built in him, and the work his muscles did against each other saved his sanity without the slightest movement to disturb the sleeping girl. He knelt there for a long time.

At breakfast the next morning she could laugh again. Horty had not moved her or touched her except to remove her shoes and cover her with a down quilt. In the small hours of the morning he had taken a pillow from the bedroom and put it on the floor between the studio couch and the door, and had stretched out to listen to her breathing and, with feline attention, to each sound from the stairway and hall outside.

He was standing, bent over her, when she opened her eyes. He said immediately, 'I'm Horty and you're safe, Zee.' The spiralling panic in her eyes died unborn, and she smiled.

While she bathed, he took her clothes to a neighbourhood machine laundry and in half an hour was back with them washed and dried. The food he had picked up on the way was not needed; she had breakfast well on the way when he returned – 'gas-house' eggs (fried in the centre of slices of bread punched out with a water glass) and crisp bacon. She took the groceries from him and scolded him. 'Kippers – papaya juice – Danish ring. Horty, that's *company* eatments!'

He smiled, more at her courage and her resilience than at her protests. He leaned against the wall with his arms folded, watching her hobbling about the kitchen, draped from neck to heels in what was, for him, a snug-fitting bathrobe, and tried not to think of the fact that she had used it at all. He understood, though, seeing the limp, seeing what had happened to her face …

It was a gay breakfast, during which they happily played 'Remember when—' which is, in the final analysis, the most entrancing game in the world. Then there was a silent time, when to each, the sight of the other was enough communication. At last Horty asked, 'How did you get away?'

Her face darkened. The effort for control was evident – and successful. Horty said, 'You'll have to tell me everything, Zee. You'll have to tell me about – me, too.'

'You've found out a lot about yourself?' It was not a question.

Horty waved this aside. 'How did you get away?'

The mobile side of her face twitched. She looked down at her hands, slowly lifted one, put it on and around the other, and as she talked, squeezed. 'I was in a coma for days, I guess. Yesterday I woke up on my bunk, in the trailer. I knew I had told him everything – except that I knew where you were. He still thinks you are that girl.

'I heard his voice. He was at the other end of the trailer, in Bunny's room.

Bunny was there. She was crying. I heard the Maneater taking her away. I waited and then dragged myself outside and over to Bunny's door. I got in. Havana was there on the bed with a stiff thing around his neck. It hurt him to talk. He said the Maneater was taking care of him, fixing his neck. He said the Maneater is going to make Bunny do a job for him.' She looked up swiftly at Horty. 'He can, you know. He's a hypnotist. He can make Bunny do anything.'

'I know.' He considered her. 'Why the hell didn't he use it on you?' he flared.

She fingered her face. 'He can't. He – it doesn't work like that on me. He can reach me, but he can't make me do anything. I'm too—'

'Too what?'

'Human,' she said.

He stroked her arm and smiled at her. 'That you are … Go on.'

'I went back to my part of the trailer and got some money and a few other things and left. I don't know what the Maneater will do when he learns I'm gone. I was very careful, Horty. I hitch-hiked fifty miles and then took a bus to Eltonville – that's three hundred miles from here – and a train from there. But I know he'll find me somehow, sooner or later. He doesn't give up.'

'You're safe here,' he said, and there was blued steel in his soft voice.

'It isn't me! Oh, Horty – don't you understand? It's you he's after!'

'What does he want with me? I left the carnival three years ago and it didn't seem to bother him much.' He caught her eye; she was looking at him in amazement. 'What is it?'

'Aren't you curious about yourself at all, Horty?'

'About myself? Well, sure. Everybody is, I guess. But about what, especially?'

She was silent a moment, thinking. Abruptly she asked, 'What have you done since you left the carnival?'

'I've told you in my letters.'

'The bare outlines, yes. You got a furnished room and lived there for a while, reading a lot and feeling your way. Then you decided to grow. How long did that take?'

'About eight months. I got this by mail and moved in at night so no one saw me, and changed. Well, I had to. I'd be able to get a job as a grown man. I buskined awhile – you know, playing the clubs for whatever the customers would throw to me – and bought a really good guitar and went to work at the Happy Hours. When that closed I went to Club Nemo. Been there ever since, biding my time. You told me I'd know when it was time … that's always been true.'

'It would be,' she nodded. 'Time to stop being a midget, time to go to work, time to start on Armand Bluett – you'd know.'

'Well, sure,' he said, as if the fact deserved no further comment. 'And when I needed money, I wrote things … some songs and arrangements, articles, and even a story or two. The stories weren't so good. It's easy to put things together, but awful hard to make them up. Hey – you don't know what I did to Armand, do you?'

'No.' She looked at his hand. 'It has something to do with that, hasn't it?'

'It has.' He inspected it and smiled. 'Last time you saw my hand like this was about a year after I came to the carnival. Want to know something? I lost these fingers just three weeks ago.'

'And they've grown that much?'

'It doesn't take as long as it did,' he said.

'It did start slowly,' she said.

He looked at her, seemed about to ask a question, and then went on. 'One night at Club Nemo he walked in with her. I'd never dreamed that I'd see them together – I know what you're thinking! I always thought of them at the same time! Ah, but that was check and balance. Good and evil. Well …' He drank coffee. 'They sat right where I could hear them talk. He was the oily wolf and she was the distressed maiden. It was pretty disgusting. So, he got up to powder his nose, and I made like Lochinvar. I mixed right in. I gave her some succinct language and some carfare, and she got away, after promising him a date for the next night.'

'You mean she got away from him for the moment.'

'Oh no. She got clear away, by train. I don't know where she went. Well, I sat there chording that guitar and thinking hard. You said that I'd always know when it was time. I knew that night that it was time to get Armand Bluett. Time to start, that is. He gave me a treatment once that lasted for six years. The least I could do was to give him a long stretch too. So I made my plans. I put in a tough night and day.' He stopped, smiling without humour.

'Horty—'

'I'll tell it, Zee. It's simple enough. He got his date. Took the gal to a sybaritic little pest-hole he had hidden away in the slums. He was very easy to lead along the primrose paving. At the critical point his "conquest" said a few well-chosen words about cruelty to children and left him to mull them over while staring at the three fingers she had chopped off as souvenirs.'

Zena glanced at his left hand again. 'Uh! What a treatment! But Horty – you got ready in one night and day?'

'You don't know the things I can do,' he said. He rolled back his sleeve. 'Look.'

She stared at the brown, slightly hairy right forearm. Horty's face showed deep concentration. There was no tension; his *eyes* were quiet and his brow unfurrowed.

For a moment the arm remained unchanged. Suddenly the hair on it moved – *writhed*. One hair fell off; another; a little shower of them, finding their way down among the small checks of the tablecloth. The arm remained steady and, like his brow, showed no tension beyond its complete immobility.

It was naked now, and the creamy brown colour that was typical of both him and Zena. But – was it? Was it the effect of staring with such concentration? No; it was actually paler, paler and more slender as well. The flesh on the back of the hand and between the fingers contracted until the hand was slim and tapered rather than square and thick as it had been.

'That's enough,' said Horty conversationally, and smiled. 'I can restore it in the same length of time. Except for the hair, of course. That will take two or three days.'

'I knew about this,' she breathed. 'I did know, but I don't think I ever really believed … your control is quite complete?'

'Quite. Oh, there are things I can't do. You can't create or destroy matter. I could shrink to your size, I suppose. But I'd weigh the same as I do now, pretty much. And I couldn't become a twelve-foot giant overnight; there's no way to assimilate enough mass quickly enough. But that job with Armand Bluett was simple. Hard work, but simple. I compacted my shoulders and arms and the lower part of my face. Do you know I had twenty-eight tooth-aches the whole time? I whitened my skin. The hair was a wig, of course, and as for the female form deevine, that was taken care of by what Elliot Springs calls the "bust-bucket and torso-twister trade".'

'How can you joke about it?'

His voice went flat as he said, 'What should I do; grind my teeth *every* minute? This kind of wine needs a shot of bubbles every now and then, honey, or you can't swallow much. No; what I did to Armand Bluett was just a starter. I'm making him do it himself. I didn't tell him who I am. Kay's out of the picture; he doesn't know who she is or who I am or, for that matter, who he is himself.' He laughed; an unpleasant sound. 'All I gave him was a powerful association with three ruined fingers from 'way back. They'll work in his sleep. The next thing I do to him will be as good – and nothing like that at all.'

'You'll have to change your plans some.'

'Why?'

'Kay isn't out of the picture. I'm beginning to understand now. She came out to the carnival to see the Maneater.'

'Kay did? But why?'

'I don't know. Anyway, the Judge followed her there. She left, but Bluett and the Maneater got together. I know one thing, though. Havana told me – the Judge is terrified of Kay Hallowell.'

Horty slapped the table. 'With her hand intact! Oh, how wonderful! Can you imagine what that must have been?'

'Horty, darling – it isn't all fun. Don't you see that that's what started all this – that's what made the Maneater suspect that "Kiddo" was something else besides a girl midget? Don't you realise that the Maneater thinks you and Kay are the same one, no matter what the Judge thinks?'

'Oh, my God.'

'You remember everything you hear,' said Zena. 'But you just don't figure things out very fast, sweetheart.'

'But – but – getting smashed up like this … Zena, it's my fault! It's as if I'd done it to you!'

She came around the table and put her arms around him, pulling his head to her breast. 'No, darling. That was coming to me, from years back. If you want to blame someone – besides the Maneater, blame me. It was my fault for taking you in twelve years ago.'

'What did you do it for? I never really knew.'

'To keep you away from the Maneater.'

'Away fr – but you kept me right next to him!'

'The last place in the world he'd think of looking.'

'You're saying he was looking for me then.'

'He's been looking for you ever since you were one year old. And he'll find you. He'll find you, Horty.'

'I hope he does,' grated Horty. The doorbell rang.

There was a frozen silence. It rang again.

'I'll go,' said Zena, rising.

'You will like hell,' said Horty roughly. 'Sit down.'

'It's the Maneater,' she whimpered. She sat down.

Horty stood where he could look through the living-room at the front door. Studying it, he said, 'It isn't. It's, it's – well, what do you know! Old Home Week!'

He strode out and flung the door open. 'Bunny!'

'Wh – Excuse m – is this where …' Bunny hadn't changed much. She was a shade more roly-poly, and perhaps a little more timid.

'Oh, Bunny …' Zena came running unevenly out, tripped on the hem of the bathrobe. Horty caught her before she could fall. The girls hugged each other frantically, shouting tearful endearments over the rich sound of Horty's relieved laughter. 'But darling, how did you find—' 'It's so good to—' 'I thought you were—' 'You doll! I never thought I'd—'

'*Cut!*' roared Horty. 'Bunny, come in and have some breakfast.'

Startled, she looked at him, her albino eyes round. Gently he asked, 'How's Havana?'

Without taking her eyes off his face, Bunny fumbled for Zena and held on. 'Does he know Havana?'

'Honey,' said Zena. 'That's *Horty*!'

Bunny shot Zena a rabbit-like glance, craned to peer behind Horty, and suddenly seemed to realise just what Zena had said. 'That?' she demanded, pointing. 'Him?' She stared. 'He's – Kiddo, too?'

Horty grinned. 'That's right.'

'He grew,' said Bunny inanely. Zena and Horty bellowed with laughter, and, as Horty had done once so long ago, so Bunny gaped from one to the other, sensed that they were laughing with and not at her, and joined her tinkling giggle to the noise. Still laughing, Horty went into the kitchen and called out, 'You still take canned milk and half a teaspoon of sugar, Bunny?' and Bunny began to cry. Into Zena's shoulder she sobbed happily. 'It is Kiddo, it is, it is …'

Horty put the steaming cup on the end table and settled down beside the girls. 'Bunny, how in time did you find me?'

'I didn't find you. I found Zee. Zee, maybe Havana's goin' to die.'

'I – remember,' Zee whispered. 'Are you sure?'

'The Maneater did what he could. He even called in another doctor.'

'He *did*? Since when has he taken to doctors?'

Bunny sipped her coffee. 'You just can't know how he's changed, Zee. I couldn't believe it myself until he did that, called a doctor in, I mean. You know about m-me and Havana. You know how I feel about what the Maneater did to him. But – it's as if he had come up from under a cloud that he's lived with for years He's really changed. Zee, he wants you to come back. He's *so* sorry about what happened. He's really broken up.'

'Not enough,' muttered Horty.

'Does he want Horty to come back too?'

'Horty – oh, Kiddo.' Bunny looked at him. 'He couldn't do an act now. I don't know, Zee. He didn't say.'

Horty noticed the swift, puzzled frown on Zena's brow. She took Bunny's upper arm and seemed to squeeze it impatiently. 'Honey – start from the beginning. Did the Maneater send you?'

'Oh no. Well, not exactly. He's changed so, Zee. You don't believe me … Well, you'll see for yourself. He needs you and I came to get you back, all by myself.'

'Why?'

'Because of Havana!' Bunny cried. 'The Maneater might be able to save him, don't you see? But not when he's all torn apart by what he did to you.'

Zena turned a troubled face to Horty. He rose. 'I'll fix you a bite to eat, Bunny,' he said. A slight sidewise movement of his head beckoned to Zena; she acknowledged it with an eyelid and turned back to Bunny. 'But how did you know where I was, honey?'

The albino leaned forward and touched Zena's cheek. 'You poor darling. Does it hurt much?'

Horty, in the kitchen, called, 'Zee! What did you do with the tabasco?'

'Be right back,' said Zee. She hobbled across to the kitchen. 'It should be right there on the … yes. Oh – you haven't started the toast! I'll do it, Horty.'

They stood side by side at the stove, busily. Under his breath Horty said, 'I don't like it, Zee.'

She nodded. 'There's something ... we've asked her twice, three times, how she found this place, and she hasn't said.' She added clearly, 'See? *That's* the way to make toast. Only you have to watch it.'

A moment later, 'Horty. How did you know who it was at the door?'

'I didn't. Not really. I knew who it *wasn't*. I know hundreds of people, and I knew it wasn't any of them.' He shrugged. 'That left Bunny. You see?'

'I can't do that. Nobody I know can do that. 'Cept maybe the Maneater.' She went to the sink and clattered briskly. 'Can't you tell what people are thinking?' she whispered when she came close to him again.

'Sometimes, a little. I never tried, much.'

'Try now,' she said, nodding towards the living-room.

His face took on that unruffled, deeply occupied expression. At the same moment there was a flash of movement past the open kitchen door. Horty, who had his back to it, turned and sprang through into the living-room. 'Bunny?'

Bunny's pink lips curled back from her teeth like an animal's and she scuttled to the front door, whipped it open and was gone. Zena screamed. 'My purse! She's got my purse!'

In two huge bounds Horty was in the hall. He pounced on Bunny at the head of the stairs. She squealed and sank her teeth into his hand. Horty clamped her head under his arm, jamming her chin against his chest. Having taken a bite, she was forced to keep it – and meanwhile was efficiently gagged.

Inside, he kicked the door closed and pitched Bunny to the couch like a sack of sawdust. Her jaws did not relax; he had to lean over her and pry them apart. She lay with her eyes red and glittering, and blood on her mouth.

'Now, what do you suppose made her go off like that?' he asked, almost casually.

Zena knelt by Bunny and touched her forehead. 'Bunny. Bunny, are you all right?'

No answer. She seemed conscious. She kept her mad ruby eyes fixed on Horty. Her breath came in regular, powerful pulses like those of a slow freight. Her mouth was rigidly agape. 'I didn't do anything to her,' said Horty. 'Just picked her up.'

Zena rescued her handbag from the floor and fumbled through it. Seemingly satisfied, she set it down on the coffee-table. 'Horty, what did you do in the kitchen just now?'

'I – sort of ...' He frowned. 'I thought of her face, and I made it kind of open like a door, or – well, blow away like fog, so I could see inside. I didn't see anything.'

'Nothing at all?'

'She moved,' he said simply.

Zena began to knead her hands together. 'Try again.'

Horty went to the couch. Bunny's eyes followed him. Horty folded his arms. His face relaxed. Bunny's eyes closed immediately. Her jaw slackened. Zena barked, 'Horty – be careful!'

Without moving otherwise, Horty nodded briefly.

For a moment nothing happened. Then Bunny trembled. She threw out an arm, clenched her small hand. Tears appeared between her lids, and she relaxed. In a few seconds she began to move vaguely, purposelessly, as if unfamiliar hands tested her motor centres. Twice she opened her eyes; once she half sat up, and then lay back. At last she released a long, shuddering sigh, pitched almost as low as Zena's voice, and lay still, breathing deeply.

'She's asleep,' said Horty. 'She fought me, but now she's asleep.' He fell into a chair and covered his face for a moment. Zena watched him restore himself as he had restored his whitened arm earlier. He sat up briskly and said, his voice strong again, 'It was more than her strength, Zee. She was full to the brim with something that wasn't hers.'

'Is it all gone now?'

'Sure. Wake her and see.'

'You've never done anything like this before, Horty? You seem as sure of yourself as old Iwazian.' Iwazian was the carnival's photo-gallery operator. He had only to take a picture to know how good it was; he never looked at a proof.

'You keep saying things like that,' said Horty with a trace of impatience. 'There are things a man can do and things he can't. When he does something, what's the point of wondering whether or not he's actually done it? Don't you think he knows?'

'I'm sorry, Horty. I keep underestimating you.' She sat beside the albino midget. 'Bunny,' she cooed. 'Bunny …'

Bunny turned her head, turned it back, opened her eyes. They seemed vague, unfocused. She turned them on Zena, and recognition crept into them. She looked around the room, cried out in fear. Zena held her close. 'It's all right, darling,' she said. 'That's Kiddo, and I'm here, and you're all right now.'

'But how – where—'

'Sh-h. Tell us what's happened. You remember the carnival? Havana?'

'Havana's goin' to die.'

'We'll try to help, Bunny. Do you remember coming here?'

'Here?' She looked around, as if one part of her mind were trying to catch up with the rest. 'The Maneater told me to. He was nothing but eyes. After a while I couldn't even see his eyes. His voice was inside my head. I don't remember,' she said piteously. 'Havana's going to die.' She said this as if it were the first time.

'We'd better not ask her questions now,' said Zena.

'Wrong,' said Horty. 'We'd better, and fast.' He bent over Bunny. 'How did you find this place?'

'I don't remember.'

'After the Maneater talked inside your head, what did you do?'

'I was on a train.' Her answers were almost vague; she did not seem to be withholding information – rather, she seemed unable to extend it. It had to be lifted out.

'Where did you go when you got off the train?'

'A bar. Uh – Club … Nemo. I asked the man where I could find the fellow who hurt his hand.'

Zena and Horty exchanged a look. 'The Maneater said Zena would be with this fellow.'

'Did he say the man was Kiddo? Or Horty?'

'No. He didn't say. I'm hungry.'

'All right, Bunny. We'll get you a big breakfast in a minute. What were you supposed to do when you found Zena? Bring her back?'

'No. The jewels. She had the jewels. There had to be two of them. He'd give me twice what he gave Zena if I came back without them. But he'd kill me if I came with only one.'

'How he's changed,' Zena said, scornful horror in her voice.

'How did he know where I was?' Horty demanded.

'I don't know. Oh; that girl.'

'What girl?'

'She's a blonde girl. She wrote a letter to someone. Her brother. A man got the letter.'

'What man?'

'Blue. Judge Blue.'

'Bluett?'

'Yes, Judge Bluett. He got the letter and it said the girl was working in a record shop in town. There was only one record shop. They found her easily.'

'*They found her?* Who?'

'The Maneater. And that Blue. Bluett.'

Horty brought his fists together. 'Where is she?'

'The Maneater's got her at the carnival. Can I have my breakfast now?'

CHAPTER XIV

Horty left.
He slipped into a light coat and found his wallet and keys, and he left. Zena screamed at him. Intensity injected raucousness into her velvet voice. She caught his arm; he did not shake her off, but simply kept moving, dragging her as if she were smoke in the suction of his movement. She turned to the table, snatched up her bag, found two glittering jewels. 'Horty, wait, wait!' She held out the jewels. 'Don't you remember, Horty? Junky's eyes, the jewels – they're *you*, Horty!'
He said, 'If you need anything at all, no matter what, call Nick at Club Nemo. He's all right,' and opened the door.
She hobbled after him, caught at his coat, missed her hold, staggered against the wall. 'Wait, wait. I have to tell you, you're not ready, you just don't *know!*' she sobbed. 'Horty, the Maneater—'
Halfway down the stairs he turned. 'Take care of Bunny, Zee. Don't go out, not for anything. I'll be back soon.'
And he left.
Holding the wall, Zena crept down the hall and into the apartment. Bunny sat on the couch, sobbing with fright. But she stopped when she saw Zena's twisted face, and ran to her. She helped her to the easy-chair and crouched on the floor at her feet, hugging her legs, her round chin against Zena's knees. The vibrant colour was gone from Zena; she stared drily down, black eyes in a grey face.
The jewels fell from her hand and glittered on the rug. Bunny picked them up. They were warm, probably from Zena's hand. But the little hand was so cold ... They were hard, but Bunny felt that if she squeezed them they would be soft. She put them on Zena's lap. She said nothing. She knew, somehow, that this was not the time to say anything.
Zena said something. It was unintelligible; her voice was a hoarseness, nothing more. Bunny made a small interrogative sound, and Zena cleared her throat and said, 'Fifteen years.'
Bunny waited quietly after that, for minutes, wondering why Zena did not blink her eyes. Surely that must hurt her ... she reached up presently and touched the lids. Zena blinked and stirred uneasily. 'Fifteen years I've been trying to stop this from happening. I knew what he was the instant I saw those jewels. Maybe even before ... but I was sure when I saw the jewels.' She

closed her eyes; it seemed to give more vitality to her voice, as if her intense gaze had been draining her. 'I was the only one who knew. The Maneater only hoped. Even Horty didn't know. Only me. Only me. Fifteen years—'

Bunny stroked her knee. A long time passed. She became certain that Zena was asleep, and had begun to think thoughts of her own when the deep, tired voice came again.

'They're alive.' Bunny looked up; Zena's hand was over the jewels. 'They think and they speak. They mate. They're alive. These two are Horty.'

She sat up and brushed her hair back. 'That's how I knew. We were in that diner, the night we found Horty. A man was robbing our truck, remember? The man put his knee on these crystals, and Horty got sick. He was indoors and a long way from the truck but he knew. Bunny, do you remember?'

'Mm-hm. Havana, he used to talk about it. Not to you, though. We always knew when you didn't want to talk, Zena.'

'I do now,' said Zena wearily. She wet her lips. 'How long have you been with the show, Bun?'

'I guess eighteen years.'

'Twenty for me. Almost that, anyway. I was with Kwell Brothers when the Maneater bought into it. He had a menagerie. He had Gogol and a pinhead and a two-headed snake and a bald squirrel. He used to do a mind-reading act. Kwell sold out for nothing. Two late springs and a tornado taught Kwell all the carny he ever wanted to know. Lean years. I stuck with the show because I was there, mostly. Just as tough there as anywhere else.' She sighed, scanning over twenty years. 'The Maneater was obsessed by what he called a hobby. Strange people aren't his hobby. Carny isn't his hobby. Those things are because of his hobby.' She lifted the jewels and clicked them together like dice. 'These are his hobby. These things sometimes make strange people. When he got a new freak' – the word jolted both of them as she said it – 'he kept it by him. He got into show business so he could keep them and make money too. That's all. He kept them and studied them and made more of them.'

'Is that really what makes strange people?'

'No! Not all of them. You know about glands and mutations, and all that. These crystals make them too, that's all. They do it – I *think* they do it – on purpose.'

'I don't understand, Zee.'

'Bless your heart! Neither do I. Neither does the Maneater, although he knows an awful lot about them. He can talk to them, sort of.'

'How?'

'It's like his mind-reading. He puts his mind on them. He – hurts them with his mind until they do what he wants.'

'What does he want them to do?'

'Lots of things. They all amount to one thing, though. He wants a – a middle-man. He wants them to make something that he can maybe talk to, give orders to. Then the middleman would turn around and make the crystals do what he wanted.'

'I guess I'm sort of stupid, Zee.'

'No you're not, honey … oh, Bunny, Bunny, I'm so *glad* you're here!' She pulled the albino up into the chair and hugged her fervently. 'Let me talk, Bun. I've got to talk! Years and years, and I haven't said a word …'

'I won't understand one word in ten, I bet.'

'Yes you will, lamb. Comfy? Well … you see, these crystals are a sort of animal, kind of. They're not like any other animal that ever lived on earth. I don't think they came from anywhere on earth. The Maneater told me he sees a picture sometimes of white and yellow stars in a black sky, the way space would look away outside the earth. He thinks they drifted here.'

'He told you? You mean he talked to you about them?'

'By the hour. I guess everybody has to talk to someone. He talked to me. He threatened to kill me, time and time again, if I ever said a word. But that's not why I kept it a secret. See, he was good to me, Bunny. He's mean and crazy, but he was always good to me.'

'I know. We used to wonder.'

'I didn't think it made any difference to anyone. Not at first, not for years. When I did learn what he was really trying to do I *couldn't* tell anyone; no one would've believed me. All I could do was to learn as much as I could and hope I could stop him when the time came.'

'Stop him from what, Zee?'

'Well – look; let me tell you a little more about the crystals. Then you'll see. These crystals used to *copy* things. I mean, one would be near a flower, and it would make another flower almost like it. Or a dog, or a bird. But mostly they didn't come out right. Like Gogol. Like the two-headed snake.'

'Gogol is one of those?'

Zena nodded. 'The Fish-Boy. I think he was supposed to be a human being. No arms, no legs, no teeth, and he can't sweat so he has to be kept in a tank or he'll die.'

'But what do the crystals do that for?'

She shook her head. 'That's one of the things the Maneater was trying to find out. There isn't anything regular about the things the crystals make, Bunny. I mean, one will look like the real thing and another will come up all strange, and another won't live at all, it's such a botch. That's why he wanted a middle-man – someone who could communicate with the crystals. He couldn't except in flashes. He could no more understand them than you or I could understand advanced chemistry or radar or something. But one thing did not come clear. There are different kinds of crystals; some are more complicated than others, and can do more. Maybe they're all the same kind, but some are older. They never helped each other; didn't seem to have anything to do with each other.

'But they bred. The Maneater didn't know that. He knew that sometimes a pair of crystals would sometimes stop responding when he hurt them. At first he thought they were dead. He dissected one pair. And once he gave a couple to old Worble.'

'I remember him! He used to be a strong man, but he was too old. He used to help the cook, and all. He died.'

'Died – that's one way to say it. Remember the things he used to whittle?'

'Oh yes – dolls and toys and all like that.'

'That's right. He made a jack-in-the-box and used these for eyes.' She tossed the crystals and caught them. 'He was always giving things away to kids. He was a good old man. I know what happened to that jack-in-the-box. The Maneater never found out, but Horty told me. Somehow or other it passed from hand to hand and got into an orphanage. That's where Horty was, when he was a tiny baby. Inside of six months they were a part of Horty – or he was a part of them.'

'But what about Worble?'

'Oh, maybe a year later the Maneater began wondering if the crystals bred, and what happened when they did. He was afraid that he had given away two big, well-developed crystals that weren't dead after all. When Worble told him he had put them in toys he made and some kid had them, he didn't know where, why, the Maneater hit him. Knocked him down. Old Worble never woke up again though it was two weeks before he died. No one knew about it but me. It was out behind the cook-tent. I saw.'

'I never knew,' breathed Bunny, her ruby eyes wide.

'No one did,' Zena repeated. 'Let's have some coffee – why, *honey*! You never did get your breakfast, you poor baby!'

'Oh gosh,' said Bunny. 'That's all right. Go on talking.'

'Come into the kitchen,' she said, as she rose stiffly. 'No. don't be surprised when the Maneater seems to be inhuman. He – *isn't* human.'

'What is he, then?'

'I'll get to it. About the crystals; the Maneater says that the closest you can come to the way they make things – plants and animals, and so on, is to say they *dream* them. You dream sometimes. You know how the things in your dreams are sometimes sharp and clear, and sometimes fuzzy or crooked or out of proportion?'

'Yup. Where's the eggs?'

'Here, dear. Well, the crystals dream sometimes. When they dream sharp and clear they make pretty good plants, and real rats and spiders and birds. They usually don't, though. The Maneater says they're erotic dreams.'

'What d'ye mean?'

'They dream when they're ready to mate. But some are too – young, or undeveloped, and maybe some just don't find the right mate at that time. But when they dream that way, they change molecules in a plant and make it like another plant, or change a pile of mould into a bird … no one can say what they'll choose to make, or why?'

'But – why should they make things so they can mate?'

'The Maneater doesn't think they do it so they *can* mate, exactly,' said Zena, her voice patient. She skilfully flipped an egg in the pan. 'He calls it a by-product. It's as if you were in love and you were thinking of nothing but the one you love, and you made a song. Maybe the song wouldn't be about your lover at all. Maybe it'd be about a brook, or a flower, or something. The wind. Maybe it wouldn't be a whole song, even. That song would be a by-product. See?'

'Oh. And the crystals make things – even complete things – like Tin Pan Alley makes songs.'

'Something like it.' Zena smiled. It was the first smile in a long while. 'Sit down, honey; I'll bring the toast. Now – this is my guess – when two crystals mate, something different happens. They make a whole thing. But they don't make it from just anything the way the single crystals do. First they seem to die together. For weeks they lie like that. After that they begin a together-dream. They find something near them that's alive, and they make it over. They replace it, cell by cell. You can't see the change going on in the thing they're replacing. It might be a dog; the dog will keep on eating and running around; it will howl at the moon and chase cats. But one day – I don't know how long it takes – it will be completely replaced, every bit of it.'

'Then what?'

'Then it can change itself – if it ever thinks of changing itself. It can be almost anything if it wants to be.'

Bunny stopped chewing, thought, swallowed, and asked, 'Change how?'

'Oh, it could get bigger or smaller. Grow more limbs. Go into a funny shape – thin and flat, or round like a ball. If it's hurt it can grow new limbs. And it could do things with thought that we can't even imagine. Bunny, did you ever read about werewolves?'

'Those nasty things that change from wolves to men and back again?'

Zena sipped coffee. 'Mmm. Well, those are mostly legends, but they could have started when someone saw a change like that.'

'You mean these crystal-things aren't new on earth?'

'Oh, heavens no! The Maneater says they're arriving and living and breeding and dying here all the time.'

'Just to make strange people and werewolves,' breathed Bunny in wonder.

'No, darling! Making those things is nothing to them! They live a life of their own. Even the Maneater doesn't know what they do, what they think about. The things they make are absent-minded things, like doodles on a piece of paper that you throw away. But the Maneater thinks he could understand them if he could get that middle-man.'

'What's he want to understand a crazy thing like that for?'

Zena's small face darkened. 'When I found that out, I began listening carefully – and hoping that some day I could stop him. Bunny, the Maneater hates people. He hates and despises all people.'

'Oh yes,' said Bunny.

'Even now, with the poor control he has over the crystals, he's managed to make some of them do what he wants. Bunny, he's planted crystals in swampland with malaria mosquito eggs all around them. He's picked up poisonous coral snakes in Florida and planted them in Southern California. Things like that. It's one of the reasons he keeps the carnival. It covers the country, the same route year after year. He goes back and back, finding the crystals he's planted, seeing how much harm they've done to people. He keeps finding more. He finds them all over. He walks in the woods and out on the prairies, and every once in a while he sends out a – a kind of thought he knows how to do. It hurts the crystals. When they feel pain, he knows it. He hunts around, hurting the crystals until their pain leads him right to them. But anyway, there are plenty around. They look like pebbles or clods until they're cleaned.'

'Oh, how – how awful!' Tears brightened Bunny's eyes. 'He ought to be – killed!'

'I don't know if he can *be* killed.'

'You mean he really is one of those things from the crystals?'

'Do you think a human being could do what he does?'

'But – what would he do if he got that middle-man?'

'He'd train him up. Those creatures that are made by two crystals, they're whatever they think they are. The Maneater would tell the middle-man that he was a servant; he was under orders. The middle-man would believe him, and think that of himself. Through him the Maneater would have real power over the crystals. He could probably even make them mate, and dream-together any horrible thing he wanted. He could spread disease and plant-blight and poison until there wouldn't be a human being left on earth! And the worst thing about it is that the crystals don't even seem to want that! They're satisfied to go on as they are, making a flower or a cat once in a while, and thinking their own thoughts, and living whatever strange sort of life they live. They aren't after people! They just don't *care*.'

'Oh, Zee! And you've been carrying all this around with you for years!' Bunny ran around the table and kissed her. 'Oh, baby, why didn't you tell someone?'

'I didn't dare, sweetheart. They would think I was out of my mind. And besides – there's Horty.'

'What about Horty?'

'Horty was a baby in an orphanage when, somehow, that toy with the crystal eyes was brought in. The crystals picked on him. It all fits. He told me that when the jack-in-the-box – he called it Junky – was taken away from him; he almost died. The doctors there thought it was some kind of psychosis. It wasn't, of course; the child was in some strange bondage to the married crystals and could not exist away from them. It seems that it was far simpler to leave the toy with the child – it was an ugly toy, Horty tells me – than to try to cure the psychosis. In any case, Junky went along with Horty when he was adopted – by that Armand Bluett, incidentally; that judge.'

'He's awful! He looks all soft and – wet.'

'The Maneater has been looking for one of those twin-crystal creatures for twenty years or more, only he didn't know it. Why, the very first crystal he found was probably one of a pair, and he didn't realise it. Not ever – not until he found out about Horty. He guessed it, but he never knew until now. I knew that night we picked up Horty. The Maneater would give everything he owns in the world for Horty – a human. Not a human; Horty isn't human and hasn't been since he was a year old. But you know what I mean.'

'And that would be his middle-man?'

'That's right. So when I saw what Horty was, I jumped at the chance to hide him the last place in the world Pierre Monetre would think of looking – right under his nose.'

'Oh, Zee! What a terrible chance to take! He was bound to find out!'

'It wasn't too much of a chance. The Maneater can't read my mind. He can prod it; he can call me in a strange way; but he can't find out what's in it. Not in the way Horty did on you before. The Maneater hypnotised you to make you steal the jewels and bring them back. Horty went right into your mind and cleared all that away.'

'I – I remember. It was crazy.'

'I kept Horty by me and worked on him constantly. I read everything I could get my hands on and fed it to him. Everything, Bunny, comparative anatomy and history and music and mathematics and chemistry – everything I could think of that would help him to a knowledge of human beings. There's an old Latin saying, Bunny: *Cogito ergo sum* – "I think, therefore I am." Horty is the essence of that saying. When he was a midget he believed he was a midget. He didn't grow. He never thought of his voice changing. He never thought of applying what he learned to himself; he let me make all his decisions for him. He digested everything he learned in a reservoir with no outlet, and it never touched him until he decided himself that it was time to use it. He has eidetic memory, you know.'

'What's that?'

'Camera memory. He remembers perfectly everything he has seen or read or heard. When his fingers began to grow back – they were smashed hopelessly, you know – I kept it a secret. That was the one thing that would have told the Maneater what Horty was. Humans can't regenerate fingers. Single-crystal creatures can't either. The Maneater used to spend hours in the dark, in the menagerie tent, trying to force the bald squirrel to grow hair, or trying to put gills on Gogol the Fish Boy, by prodding at them with his mind. If any of them had been twin-crystal creatures, they would have repaired themselves.'

'I think I see. And what you were doing was to convince Horty that he was human?'

'That's right. He had to identify himself first and foremost with humanity. I taught him guitar for that reason, after his fingers grew back, so that he could learn music quickly and thoroughly. You can learn more music theory in a year on guitar than you can in three on a piano, and music is one of the most human of human things … He trusted me completely because I never let him think for himself.'

'I – never heard you talk like this before, Zee. Like out of books.'

'I've been playing a part too, sweet,' said Zena gently. 'First, I had to keep Horty hidden until he had learned everything I could teach him. Then I had to plan some way to make him stop the Maneater, without danger of the Maneater's making a servant of him.'

'How could he do that?'

'I think the Maneater is a single-crystal thing. I think if Horty could only learn to use that mental whip that the Maneater has, he could destroy him with it. If I should kill the Maneater with a bullet, it won't kill his crystal. Maybe that crystal will mate, later, and produce him all over again – with all the power that a twin-crystal creature has.'

'Zee, how do you know the Maneater isn't a twin-crystal thing?'

'I don't,' Zee said bleakly. 'If that's the case, then I can only pray that Horty's estimate of himself as a human being is strong enough to fight what the Maneater wants to make of him. Hating Armand Bluett is a human thing. Loving Kay Hallowell is another. Those are two things that I needled him with, drilled into him, teased him about, until they became part of his blood and bone.'

Bunny was silent before this bitter flood of words. She knew that Zena loved Horty; that she was enough of a woman to feel Kay Hallowell's advent as a deep menace to her; that she had fought and won against the temptation to steer Horty away from Kay; and that, more than anything else, she was face to face with terror and remorse now that her long campaign had come to a head.

She watched Zena's proud, battered face, the lips which drooped slightly on one side, the painfully canted head, the shoulders squared under the voluminous robe, and she knew that here was a picture she would never forget. Humanity is a concept close to the abnormals, who are wistfully near it, who state their membership with aberrated breath, who never cease to stretch their stunted arms towards it. Bunny's mind struck a medallion of this torn and courageous figure – a token and a tribute.

Their eyes met and slowly Zena smiled. 'Hi, Bunny ...'

Bunny opened her mouth and coughed, or sobbed. She put her arms around Zena and snuggled her chin into the cool hollow of the dark-skinned neck. She closed her eyes tight to squeeze away tears. When she opened them she could see again. And then she couldn't speak.

She saw, over Zena's shoulder through the kitchen door, out in the living-room, a huge, gaunt figure. Its lower lip swung loosely as it bent over the coffee-table. Its exquisite hands plucked up one, two jewels. It straightened, sent her a look of dull pity from its sage-green face, and went silently out.

'Bunny, darling, you're hurting me.'

Those jewels are Horty, Bunny thought. *Now I'll tell her Solum has taken them back to the Maneater.* Her face and her voice were as dry and as white as chalk as she said, 'You haven't been hurt yet ...'

CHAPTER XV

Horty pounded up the stairs and burst into his apartment. 'I'm walking under water,' he gasped. 'Every damn thing I reach for is snatched away from me. Everything I do, everywhere I go, it's too early or too late or—' Then he saw Zena on the easy-chair, her eyes open and staring, and Bunny crouched at her feet. 'What's the matter here?'

Bunny said, 'Solum came in when we were in the kitchen and took the jewels and we couldn't do anything and Zena hasn't said a word since and I'm scared and I don't know what to do – hoo …' and she began to cry.

'Oh Lord.' He was across the room in two strides. He lifted Bunny up and hugged her briefly and set her down. He knelt beside Zena. 'Zee—'

She did not move. Her eyes were all pupil, windows to a too-dark night. He tilted her chin up and fixed his gaze on her. She trembled and then cried out as if he had burned her, twisted into his arms. 'Don't don't …'

'Oh, I'm sorry, Zee. I didn't know it would hurt you.'

She leaned back and looked up at him, seeing him at last. 'Horty, you're all right …'

'Well, sure. What's this about Solum?'

'He got the crystals. Junky's eyes.'

Bunny whispered, 'For twelve years she's been keeping them away from the Maneater, Horty; and now?'

'You think the Maneater sent him for them?'

'Must have. I guess he must have followed me, and waited until he saw you leave. He was in here and out again before we could do so much as turn and look.'

'Junky's eyes …' There was the time he had almost died, as a child, when Armand threw the toy away. And the time when the tramp had crushed them under his knee, and Horty, in the lunch room two hundred feet away, had felt it. Now the Maneater might … oh, no. This was too much.

Bunny suddenly clasped her hand to her mouth. 'Horty – I just thought – the Maneater wouldn't've sent Solum by himself. He wanted those jewels … you know how he gets when he wants something. He can't bear to wait. He must be in town right now.'

'No.' Zena rose stiffly. 'No, Bun. Unless I'm quite wrong, he was here and is on his way back to the carnival. If he thinks Kay Hallowell is Horty he'll want to have the jewels where he can work on them and watch her at the same time. I'll bet he's burning up the road back to the carnival this minute.'

Horty nodded. 'If only I hadn't gone out! I might've been able to stop Solum, maybe even get to the Maneater and – Damn it! Nick's car was in the garage; first I had to find Nick and borrow it, and then I had to get a parked truck out from in front of the garage, and then there was no water in the radiator, and – oh, you know. Anyway, I have the car now. It's downstairs. I'm going to take off right now. In three hundred miles I ought to be able to catch up with … how long ago was Solum here?'

'An hour or so. You just can't, Horty. And what will happen to you when he goes to work on those jewels, I hate to think.'

Horty took out keys, tossed and caught them. 'Maybe,' he said suddenly, 'Just maybe we can—' He dived for the phone.

Listening to him talk rapidly into the instrument, Zena turned to Bunny. 'A plane. But of course!'

Horty put the phone down, looking at his watch. 'If I can get out to the airport in twelve minutes I can get a feeder flight.'

'You mean "we".'

'You're not coming. This is my party, from here on out. You kids have been through enough.'

Bunny was pulling on her light coat. 'I'm going back to Havana,' she said grimly, and for all her baby features, her face showed case-hardened purpose.

'You're not going to leave me here,' said Zena flatly. She went for her coat. 'Don't argue with me, Horty. I have a lot to tell you, and maybe a lot to do.'

'But—'

'I think she's right,' said Bunny. 'She has a lot to tell you.'

The plane was wobbling out to the runway when they arrived. Horty drove right out on to the tarmac, horn blasting, and it waited. And after they were settled in their seats, Zena talked steadily. They were ten minutes away from their destination when she was finished.

After a long, thoughtful pause, Horty said, 'So that's what I am.'

'It's a big thing to be,' said Zena.

'Why didn't you tell me all this years ago?'

'Because there were too many things I didn't know. There still are … I didn't know how much the Maneater might be able to dig out of your mind if he tried; I didn't know how deep your convictions on yourself had to go before they settled. All I tried to do was to have you accept, without question, that you were a human being, a part of humanity, and grow up according to that idea.'

He turned on her suddenly. 'Why did I eat ants?'

She shrugged. 'I don't know. Perhaps even two crystals can't do a perfect job. Anyway your formic acid balance was out of adjustment. (Did you know the French word for "ant" is *fourmi?* They're full of the stuff.) Some kids eat plaster because they need calcium. Some like burned cake for the carbon. If you had an imbalance, you can bet it would be an important one.'

The flaps went down; they felt the braking effect. 'We're coming in. How far is the carnival from here?'

'About four miles. We can get a cab.'

'Zee, I'm going to leave you outside the grounds somewhere. You've been through too much.'

'I'm going in with you,' said Bunny firmly. 'But, Zee – I think he's right. Please stay outside until – until it's over.'

'What are you going to do?'

He spread his hands. 'Whatever I can. Get Kay out of there. Stop Armand Bluett from whatever filthy thing he plans to do with her and her inheritance. And the Maneater … I don't know, Zee. I'll just have to play it as it comes. But I have to do it. You've done all you can. Let's face it; you're not fast on your feet just now. I'd have to keep looking out for you.'

'He's right, Zee. Please—' said Bunny.

'Oh, be careful, Horty – *please* be careful!'

No bad dream can top this, Kay thought. Locked in a trailer with a frightened wolf and a dying midget, with a madman and a freak due back any minute. Wild talk about missing fingers, about living jewels, and about – wildest of all – Kay not being Kay, but someone or something else.

Havana moaned. She wrung out a cloth and sponged his head again. Again she saw his lips tremble and move, but words stuck in his throat, gurgled and fainted there. 'He wants something,' she said. 'Oh, I wish I knew what he wanted! I wish I knew, and could get it quickly …'

Armand Bluett leaned against the wall by the window, one sack-suited elbow thrust through it. Kay knew he was uncomfortable there and that, probably, his feet hurt. But he wouldn't sit down. He wouldn't get away from the window. Oh no. He might want to yell for help. Old Crawly-Fingers was suddenly afraid of her. He still looked at her wet-eyed and drooling, but he was terrified. Well, let it go. No one likes having his identity denied, but in this case it was all right with her. Anything to keep a room's-breadth between her and Armand Bluett.

'I wish you'd leave that little monster alone,' he snapped. 'He's going to die anyway.'

She turned a baleful glance on him and said nothing. The silence stretched, punctuated only by the Judge's painful foot-shifting. Finally he said, 'When

Mr Monetre gets back with those crystals, we'll soon find out who you are. And don't tell me again that you don't know what all this is about,' he snapped.

She sighed. 'I don't know. I wish you'd stop shouting like that. You can't jolt information out of me that I haven't got. And besides, this little fellow's sick.'

The Judge snorted, and moved even closer to the window. She had an impulse to go over there and growl at him. He'd probably go right through the wall. But Havana moaned again. 'What is it, fellow? What is it?'

Then she stiffened. Deep within her mind she sensed a presence, a concept connected somehow with delicate, sliding music, with a broad pleasant face and a good smile. It was as if a question had been asked of her, to which she answered silently, *I'm here. I'm all right – so far.*

She turned to look at the Judge, to see if he shared the strange experience. He seemed tense. He stood with his elbow on the sill, nervously buffing his nails on his lapel.

And a hand came through the window.

It was a mutilated hand. It rose into the trailer like the seeking head and neck of a waterfowl, passed in over Armand's shoulder and spread itself in front of his face. The thumb and index fingers were intact. The middle finger was clubbed; the other two were mere buttons of scar tissue.

Armand Bluett's eyebrows were two stretched semicircles, bristling over bulging eyes. The eyes were as round as the open mouth. His upper lip turned back and upward, almost covering his nostrils. He made a faint sound, a retch, a screech, and dropped.

The hand disappeared through the window. There were quick footsteps outside, around to the door. A knock. A voice. 'Kay. Kay Hallowell. Open up.'

Inanely, she quavered. 'Wh-who is it?'

'Horty.' The doorknob rattled. 'Hurry. The Maneater's due back, but quick.'

'Horty. I – the door's locked.'

'The key must be in the Judge's pocket. Hurry.'

She went with reluctant speed to the prone figure. It lay on its back, the head propped against the wall, the eyes screwed shut in a violent psychic effort to shut out the world. In the left jacket pocket were keys on a ring and one single. This she took. It worked.

Kay stood blinking at sunlight. 'Horty.'

'That's right.' He came in, touched her arm, grinned. 'You shouldn't write letters. Come on, Bunny.'

Kay said, 'They thought I knew where you were.'

'You do.' He turned away from her and studied the supine form of Armand Bluett. 'What a sight. Something the matter with his stomach?'

Bunny had arrowed to the bunk, knelt beside it. 'Havana ... Oh, Havana ...'

Havana lay stiffly on his back. His eyes were glazed and his lips pouted and dry. Kay said, 'Is – is he … I've done what I could. He wants something. I'm afraid he—' She went to the bedside.

Horty followed. Havana's pale chubby lips slowly relaxed, then pursed themselves. A faint sound escaped. Kay said, 'I *wish* I knew what he wants!' Bunny said nothing. She put her hands on the hot cheeks, gently, but as if she would wrest something up out of him by brute force.

Horty frowned. 'Maybe I can find out,' he said.

Kay saw his face relax, smoothed over by a deep placidity. He bent close to Havana. The silence was so profound, suddenly, that the carnival noises outside seemed to wash in on them, roaring.

The face Horty turned to Kay a moment later was twisted with grief. 'I know what he wants. There may not be time before the Maneater gets here … but—There's got to be time,' he said decisively. He turned to Kay. 'I've got to go to the other end of the trailer. If he moves' – indicating the Judge – 'hit him with your shoe. Preferably with a foot in it.' He went out, his hand, oddly, on his throat, kneading.

'What's he going to do?'

Bunny, her eyes fixed on Havana's comatose face, answered, 'I don't know. Something for Havana. Did you see his face when he went out? I don't think Havana's going to – to—'

From the partition came the sound of a guitar, the six open strings brushed lightly. The A was dropped, raised a fraction. The E was flatted a bit. Then a chord …

Somewhere a girl began to sing to the guitar. *Stardust.* The voice was full and clear, a lyric soprano, pure as a boy's voice. Perhaps it was a boy's voice. There was a trace of vibrato at the ends of the phrases. The voice sang to the lyric, just barely trailing the beat, not quite ad lib, not quite stylised, and as free as breathing. The guitar was not played in complicated chords, but mostly in swift and delicate runs in and about the melody.

Havana's eyes were still open, and still he did not move. But his eyes were wet now, and not glazed, and gradually he smiled. Kay knelt beside Bunny. Perhaps she knelt only to be nearer … Havana whispered, through his smile. 'Kiddo.'

When the song was done, his face relaxed. Quite clearly he said 'Hey.' There was a world of compliment in the single syllable. After that, and before Horty came back, he died.

Entering, Horty did not even glance at the cot. He seemed to be having trouble with his throat. 'Come on,' he said hoarsely. 'We've got to get out of here.'

They called Bunny and went to the door. But Bunny stayed by the bunk, her hands on Havana's cheeks, her soft round face set.

'Bunny, come on. If the Maneater comes back—'

There was a step outside, a thump against the wall of the trailer. Kay wheeled and looked at the suddenly darkened window. Solum's great sad face filled it. Just then Horty screamed shrilly and dropped writhing to the floor. Kay turned to face the opening door.

'Good of you to wait,' said Pierre Monetre, looking about.

CHAPTER XVI

Zena huddled on the edge of the lumpy motel bed and whimpered. Horty and Bunny had been gone for nearly two hours; for the past hour, depression had grown over her until it was like bitter incense in the air, like clothes of lead sheeting on her battered limbs. Twice she had leapt up and paced impatiently, but her knee hurt her and drove her back to the bed, to punch the pillow impotently, to lie passive and watch the doubts circling endlessly about her. Should she have told Horty about himself? Should she not have given him more cruelty, more ruthlessness, about more things than revenging himself on Armand Bluett? How deep had her training gone in the malleable entity which was Horty? Could not Monetre, with his fierce, directive power undo her twelve years' work in an instant? She knew so little: she was, she felt, so small a thing to have undertaken the manufacture of a – a human being.

She wished, fiercely, that she could burrow her mind into the strange living crystals, as the Maneater tried to do, but completely, so that she could find the rules of the game, the facts about a form of life so alien that logic seemed not to work on it at all. The crystals had a rich vitality; they created, they bred, they felt pain; but to what end did they live? Crush one; and the others seemed not to mind. And why, why did they make these 'dream-things' of theirs, laboriously, cell by cell – sometimes to create only a horror, a freak, an unfinished unfunctional monstrosity, sometimes to copy a natural object so perfectly that there was no real distinction between the copy and its original; and sometimes, as in Horty's case, to create something new, something that was not a copy of anything but, perhaps, a mean, a living norm on the surface, and a completely fluid, polymorphic being at its core? What was their connection with these creations? How long did a crystal retain control of its product – and how, having built it, could it abruptly leave it to go its own way? And when the rare syzygy occurred by which two crystals made something like Horty – when would they release him to be his own creature … and what would become of him then?

Perhaps the Maneater had been right when he had described the creatures of the crystals as their dreams – solid figments of their alien imaginations, built any way they might occur, patterned on partial suggestions pictured by faulty memories of real objects. She knew – the Maneater had happily demonstrated – that there were thousands, perhaps millions of the crystals on earth, living their strange lives, as oblivious to humanity as humanity was to them, for the life-cycles, the purpose and aims of the two species were completely separate. Yet – how many men walked the earth who were not men at all; how many trees, how many rabbits, flowers, amoebae, sea-worms, redwoods, eels, and eagles grew and flowered, swam and hunted and stood among their prototypes with none knowing that they were an alien dream, having, apart from the dream, no history?

'Books,' Zena snorted. The books she had read! She had snatched everything she could get her hands on that would give her the slightest lead on the nature of the dreaming crystals. And for every drop of information she had gained (and passed on to Horty) about physiology, biology, comparative anatomy, philosophy, history, theosophy, and psychology, she had taken in a gallon of smug certitude, of bland assumptions that humanity was the peak of creation. The answers … the books had answers for everything. A new variety of manglewort appears, and some learned pundit places his fingers alongside his nose and pronounces, 'Mutation!' Sometimes, certainly. But – always? What of the hidden crystal-creature dreaming in a ditch, absently performing, by some strange telekinesis, a miracle of creation?

She loved, she worshipped Charles Fort, who refused to believe that any answer was the only answer.

She looked at her watch yet again, and whimpered. If she only knew; if she could only guide him … if she could get guidance herself, somewhere, somewhere …

The doorknob turned. Zena froze, staring at it. Something heavy pressed against the door. There was no knock. The crack between door and frame, high up, widened. Then the bolt let go, and Solum burst into the room.

His loose-skinned, grey-green face and dangling lower lip seemed to pull more than usual at the small, inflamed eyes. He took a half-step back to swing the door closed behind him, and crossed the room to her, his great arms away from his body as if to check any move she might make.

His presence told her some terrible news. No one knew where she was but Horty and Bunny, who had left her in this tourist cabin before they crossed the highway to the carnival. And when last heard of, Solum had been on the road with the Maneater.

So – the Maneater was back, and he had contacted Bunny or Horty, or both, and, worst of all, he had been able to extract information that neither would give willingly.

She looked up at him out of a tearing flurry of deadening resignation and mounting terror. 'Solum—'

His lips moved. His tongue passed over his brilliant pointed teeth. He reached for her, and she shrank back.

And then he dropped to his knees. Moving slowly, he took her tiny foot in one of his hands, bent over it with an air that was, unmistakably, reverence.

He kissed her instep, ever so gently, and he wept. He released her foot and crouched there, immersed in great noiseless shuddering sobs.

'But, *Solum*—' she said, stupidly. She put out a hand and touched his wet cheek. He pressed it closer. She watched him in utter astonishment. Long ago she used to wonder at what went on in the mind behind this hideous face, a mind locked in a silent, speechless universe, with all the world pouring in through the observant eyes and never an expression, never a conclusion or an emotion coming out.

'What is it, Solum?' she whispered, 'Horty—'

He looked up and nodded rapidly. She stared at him. 'Solum – can you hear?'

He seemed to hesitate; then he pointed to his ear, and shook his head. Immediately he pointed to his brow, and nodded.

'Oh-h-h …' Zena breathed. For years there had been idle arguments in the carnival as to whether the Alligator-skinned man was really deaf. There was instance after instance to prove both that he was and that he was not. The Maneater knew, but had never told her. He was – telepathic! She flushed as she thought of it, the times that carnies, half-kidding, had hurled insults at him; worse, the horrified reactions of the customers.

'But— What's happened? Have you seen Horty? Bunny?'

His head bobbed twice.

'Where are they? Are they safe?'

He thumbed towards the carnival, and shook his head gravely.

'The-the Maneater's got them?'

Yes.

She hopped off the bed, strode away and back, ignoring the pain. 'He sent you here to get me?'

Yes.

'But why don't you scoop me up and take me back, then?'

No answer. He motioned feebly. She said, 'Let's see. You took the jewels when he asked you to …'

Solum tapped his forehead, spread his hands. Suddenly she understood. 'He hypnotised you then.'

Solum shook his head slowly.

She understood that it had been a matter of indifference to him. But this time it was different. Something had happened to change his mind, and drastically.

'Oh, I wish you could talk!'

He made anxious, lateral circular motions with his right hand. 'Oh, of *course*!' she exploded. She limped to the splintery bureau and her purse. She found her pen; she had no paper but her cheque book. 'Here, Solum. Hurry. Tell me!'

His huge hands enveloped the pen, completely hid the narrow paper. He wrote rapidly while Zena wrung her hands in impatience. At last he handed it to her. His script was delicate, almost microscopic, and as neat as engraving.

He had written, tersely, 'M. hates people. Me too. Not so much. M. wants help, I helped him. M. wanted Horty so he could hurt more people. I didn't care. Still helped. People never liked me.

'I am human, a little. Horty is not human at all. But when Havana was dying, he wanted Kiddo to sing. Horty read his mind. He knew. There was no time. There was danger. Horty knew. Horty didn't say himself. He made Kiddo's voice. He sang for Havana. Too late then. M. came. Caught him. Horty did this so Havana could die happy. It didn't help Horty. Horty knew; did it anyway. Horty is love. M. is hate. Horty more human than I am. I am ashamed. You made Horty. Now I help you.'

Zena read it, her eyes growing very bright. 'Havana's dead, then.'

Solum made a significant gesture, twisting his head in his hands, pointing to his neck, snapping his fingers loudly. He shook his fist at the carnival.

'Yes. The Maneater killed him ... How did you know about the song?'

Solum tapped his forehead.

'Oh. You got it from Bunny, and the girl Kay; from their minds.'

Zena sat on the bed, pressing her knuckles hard against her cheekbones. Think, think ... oh, for guidance; for a word of advice about these alien things! The Maneater, crazed, inhuman; surely a warped crystalline product; there must be some way of stopping him. If only she could contact one of the jewels and ask it what to do ... surely it would know. If only she had the 'middle-man', the interpreter, that the Maneater had been seeking all these years ...

The middle-man! 'I'm blind, I'm stone blind and stupid!' she gasped. All these years her single purpose had been to keep Horty away from the crystals; he must have nothing to do with them, lest the Maneater use him against humanity. But Horty was what he was; he was the very thing the Maneater wanted; he was the one who could contact the crystals. There must be a way in which the crystals could destroy what they created!

But would the crystals tell him of such a thing?

They wouldn't have to, she decided instantly. All Horty would have to do would be to understand the strange mental mechanism of the crystals, and the method would be clear to him.

If only she could tell him! Horty learned quickly, thought slowly; for eidetic memory is the enemy of methodical thought. Ultimately he would think of this himself – but by then he might be the Maneater's crippled slave. What could she do? Write him a note? He might not even be conscious to read it! If only she were a telepath ... Telepath!

'Solum,' she said urgently, 'Can you – *speak*, up here' (she touched her forehead) 'as well as hear?'

He shook his head. But at the same time he picked up the cheque on which he had written and pointed to a word.

'Horty. You can speak to Horty?'

He shook his head, and then made outgoing motions from his brow. 'Oh,' she said. 'You can't project it, but he can read it if he tries.' He nodded eagerly.

'Good!' she said. She drew a deep breath; she knew, at last, exactly what she must do. But the cost … it didn't matter. It couldn't matter.

'Take me back there, Solum. You've caught me. I'm frightened, I'm angry. Get to Horty. You can think of a way. Get to him and think *hard*. Think: *Ask the crystals how to kill one of their dream-things. Find out from the crystals.* Got that, Solum?'

The wall had gone up years ago, when Horty came to the very simple conclusion that the peremptory summonses which awakened him at night in his bunk were for Zena, and not for him. *Cogito, ergo sum;* the wall, once erected, stood untended for years, until Zena suggested that he try reaching into the hypnotised Bunny's mind. The wall had come down for that; it was still down when he used his new sense to locate the trailer in which Kay was a prisoner, and when he sought the nature of Havana's dying wish. His sensitive mind was therefore open and unguarded when the Maneater arrived and hurled at him his schooled and vicious lance of hatred. Horty went down in flames of agony.

In ordinary terms, he was completely unconscious. He did not see Solum catch the fainting Kay Hallowell and tuck her under his long arm while his other hand darted out to snatch up soft-faced, tender-hearted Bunny, who fought and spat as she dangled there. He had no memory of being carried to Monetre's big trailer, of the tottering advent, a few minutes later, of a shaken and murderous Armand Bluett. He was not aware of Monetre's quick hypnotic control of hysterical Bunny, nor of her calm flat voice revealing Zena's whereabouts, nor of Monetre's crackling command to Solum to go to the motor court and bring Zena back. He did not hear Monetre's blunt order to Armand Bluett: 'I don't think I need you and the girl for anything any more. Stand back there out of the way.' He did not see Kay's sudden dash for the door, nor the cruel blow of Armand Bluett's fist which sent her sliding back into the corner as he snarled, 'I need *you* for something, sweetheart, and you're not getting out of my sight again.'

But the blacking out of the ordinary world revealed another. It was not strange; it had co-existed with the other. Horty saw it now only because the other was taken away.

There was nothing about it to relieve the utter lightlessness of oblivion. In it, Horty was immune to astonishment and quite without curiosity. It was a place of flickering impressions and sensations; of pleasure in an integration of abstract thought, of excitement at the approach of one complexity to another, of engrossing concentration in distant and exoteric constructions. He felt the presence of individuals, very strongly indeed; the liaison between them was non-existent, except for the rare approach of one to another and, somewhere far off, a fused pair which he knew were exceptional. But for these, it was a world of self-developing entities, each evolving richly according to its taste. There was a sense of permanence, of life so long that death was not a factor, save as an aesthetic termination. Here there was no hunger, no hunting, no co-operation, and no fear; these things had nothing to do with the bases of a life like this. Basically trained to accept and to believe in that which surrounded him, Horty delved not at all, made no comparison, and was neither intrigued nor puzzled.

Presently he sensed the tentative approach of the force which had blasted him, used now as a goad rather than as a spear. He rebuffed it easily, but moved to regain consciousness so that he might deal with the annoyance.

He opened his eyes and found them caught and held by those of Pierre Monetre, who sat at his desk facing him. Horty was sprawled back in an easy-chair, his head propped in the angle of the back and a small rounded wing. The Maneater was radiating nothing. He simply watched, and waited.

Horty closed his eyes, sighed, moved his jaws as a man does on awakening.

'Horty.' The Maneater's voice was mellow, friendly. 'My dear boy. I have looked forward so long to his moment. This is the beginning of great things for us two.'

Horty opened his eyes again and looked about. Bluett stood glowering at him, a shuddering mixture of fear and fury. Kay Hallowell huddled in the corner opposite the entrance, on the floor. Bunny squatted next to her, holding limply to Kay's forearm, looking out into the room with vacant eyes.

'Horty,' said the Maneater insistently. Horty met his gaze again. Effortlessly he blocked the hypnotic force which the Maneater was exerting. The mellow voice went on, soothingly, 'You're home at last, Horty – really home. I am here to help you. You belong here. I understand you. I know the things you want. I will make you happy. I will teach you greatness Horty. I will protect you, Horty. And you will help me.' He smiled. 'Won't you, Horty?'

'You can drop dead,' said Horty succinctly.

The reaction was instant – a shaft of brutal hatred whetted to a razor-edge, a needle-point. Horty rebuffed it, and waited.

The Maneater's eyes narrowed and his eyebrows went up. 'Stronger than I thought. Good. I'd rather have you strong. You *are* going to work with me, you know.'

Horty blankly shook his head. Again, and twice more, the Maneater struck at him, timing the psychic blow irregularly. Had Horty's defence been a counter-act, like that of a rapier or a boxing-glove, the Maneater would have got through. But it was a wall.

The Maneater leaned back, consciously relaxing. His weapon apparently took quantities of energy. 'Very well,' he purred. 'We'll dull you down a bit.' He drummed his fingers idly.

Long moments passed. For the first time Horty realised that he was paralysed. He could breathe fairly easily, and, with difficulty, move his head. But his arms and legs were leaden, numb. A vague ache in the nape of his neck – and his profound knowledge of anatomy – informed him of a skilfully administered spinal injection.

Kay stirred and was quiet. Bunny looked at her and away, still with that vacant gaping look on her sweet round face. Bluett shifted uncomfortably on his feet.

The door was elbowed aside. Solum came in with Zena in his arms. She was limp. Horty tried frantically and uselessly to move. The Maneater smiled engagingly and motioned with his head. 'Into the corner with the rest of the trash,' he said. 'We might be able to use her. Think our friend would be more co-operative if we cut her down a bit?'

Solum grinned wolfishly.

'Of course,' said the Maneater thoughtfully. 'She isn't very big to begin with. We'd have to be careful. A little at a time.' Belying his offhand tone, his eyes watched every move of Horty's face. 'Solum, old fellow, our boy Horty is a little too alert. Suppose you jolt him a bit. The edge of your hand at the side of his neck, right at the base of the skull. The way I showed you. You know.'

Solum stalked over to Horty. He put one hand on Horty's shoulder, and took careful aim with the other. The hand which rested on his shoulder squeezed slightly, over and over again. Solum's eyes burned down to Horty's. Horty watched the Maneater. He knew the major blow would come from there.

Solum's other hand came down. A fraction of a second after it hit his neck, Monetre's psychic bolt smashed against Horty's barrier. Horty felt a faint surprise; Solum had pulled the punch. He looked up quickly. Solum, his back turned to the Maneater, touched his forehead, worked his lips anxiously. Horty shrugged this off. He had no time for idle wonderments … he heard Zena whimper.

'You're in my way, Solum!' Solum moved reluctantly. 'You'll have another chance at him,' said the Maneater. He opened the drawer in front of him and took out two objects. 'Horty, d'ye know what these are?'

Horty grunted and nodded. They were Junky's eyes. The Maneater chuckled. 'If I smash these, you die. You know that, don't you?'

'Wouldn't be much help to you then, would I?'

'That's right. But I just wanted to let you know I have them handy.' Ceremoniously he lighted a small alcohol blow-lamp. 'I don't have to destroy them. Single-crystal creatures react beautifully to fire. You should do twice as well.' His voice changed abruptly. 'Oh, Horty, my boy, my dear boy – don't force me to play with you like this.'

'Play away,' gritted Horty.

'Hit him again, Solum.' Now the voice crackled.

Solum swept down on him. Horty caught a glimpse of Armand's avid face, the flick of a tongue across his wet lips. The blow was heavier this time, though still surprisingly less powerful than he expected – less powerful, for that matter, than it looked. Horty rolled his head with the impact, and slumped down with his eyes closed. The Maneater hurled no bolts this time, apparently in an attempt to force Horty to use up counter-ammunition while saving his own.

'Too hard, you idiot!'

Kay's voice moaned out of the corner, 'Oh, stop it, stop it …'

'Ah.' The Maneater's chair scraped as he turned. 'Miss Hallowell! How much would the young man do for you? Drag her out here, Bluett.'

The Judge did. He said, with a leer, 'Save some for me, Pierre.'

'I'll do as I like!' snapped the Maneater.

'All right, all right,' said the Judge, cowed. He went back to his corner.

Kay stood erect but trembling before the desk. 'You'll have the police to answer to,' she flared.

'The Judge will take care of the police. Sit down, my dear.' When she did not move, he roared at her. '*Sit down!*' She gulped and sat in the chair at the end of the long desk. He reached out and trapped her wrist, pulled it towards him. 'The Judge tells me you like having your fingers cut off.'

'I don't know what you m-mean. Let me g—'

Meanwhile Solum was on his knees beside Horty, rolling his head, slapping his cheeks. Horty submitted patiently, quite unconscious. Kay screamed.

'Nice noisy carnival we have here,' smiled the Maneater. 'That's quite useless, Miss Hallowell.' He pulled a heavy pair of shears out of the drawer. She screamed again. He put them down and took up the blow-lamp, passing the flame lightly over the crystals which lay winking before him. By some fantastic stroke of luck – or perhaps some subtler thing than luck, Horty flashed a quick look through his lashes at that precise second. As the pale flame touched the jewels, he threw his head back, twisted his features—

But he did it on purpose. He felt nothing.

He looked at Zena. Her face was strained, her whole soul streaming through it, trying to tell him something …

He opened his mind to it. The Maneater saw his eyes open and hurled another of those frightful psychic impulses. Horty slammed his mind shut barely in time; part of the impulse got in and jolted him to the core.

For the first time he fully recognised his lack, his repeated failure to figure things clearly out for himself. He made a grim effort. Zena trying to tell him something. If he had just a second to receive her ... but he was lost if he submitted to another such blow as the first one. There was something else, something about – *Solum*! The signalling hand on his shoulder, the hot eyes, bursting with something unsaid.

'Hit him again, Solum.' The Maneater picked up the shears. Kay screamed again.

Again Solum bent over him; again the hand pressed his shoulder secretly, urgently. Horty looked the green man full in the eyes and opened up to the message which rolled there.

ASK THE CRYSTALS. *Ask the crystals how to kill one of their dreamthings. Find out from the crystals.*

'What are you waiting for, Solum?'

Kay screamed and screamed. Horty closed his eyes and his mind. Crystals ... not the ones on the table. The – the – *all* the crystals, which lived in – in—

Solum's hard hand landed on his neck. He let it drive him under, down and down into that lightless place full of structural, shimmering sensations. Resting in it, he drove his mind furiously about, questing. He was ignored completely, majestically. But there was no guard against him, either. What he wanted was there; he had only to understand it. He would not be helped or hindered.

He recognised now that the crystal-world was not loftier than the ordinary one. It was just – different. These self-sufficient abstracts of ego were the crystals, following their tastes, living their utterly alien existences, thinking with logic and with scales of values impossible to a human being.

He could understand some of it, untrammelled as he was with fixed ideas, though he was hammered into human mould too solidly to be able to merge himself completely with these unthinkable beings. He understood almost immediately that Monetre's theory of the crystal-dreams was true and not-true, like the convenient theory that an atom-nucleus had planetary particles rotating about it. The theory worked in simple practice. The manufacture of living things was a function with a purpose, but that purpose could never be explained in human terms. The one thing that was borne in on Horty was the almost total unimportance, to the crystals, of this function. They did it, but it served them about as much as a man is served by his appendix. And the fate of the creatures they created mattered as little to them as does the fate of a particular molecule of CO_2 exhaled by a man.

Nevertheless, the machinery by which the creation was done was there before Horty. Its purpose was beyond him, but he could grasp its operation. Studying it with his gulping, eidetic mind, he learned … things. Two things. One had to do with Junky's eyes, and the other—

It was a thing to do. It was a thing like stopping a rolling boulder by blocking it with another rolled in its path. It was a thing like lifting the brush-holder on a DC motor, like cutting the tendons at the back of the hind legs of a running horse. It was a thing done with the mind, with a tremendous effort, which said a particular *stop*! to a particular kind of life.

Understanding, he withdrew, not noticed – or ignored – by the strange egos about him. He let in the light. He emerged, and felt his first real astonishment. His neck stung from the blow of Solum's hand, which was still rebounding. The same scream which had begun when he went under came to its gasping conclusion as he came up. Bunny still stared between the slow blink of her drugged-looking lids: Zena still crouched with the same tortured expression of concentration in her pointed face.

The Maneater hurled his bolt. Horty turned it aside, and now he laughed.

Pierre Monetre rose, his face blackening with rage. Kay's wrist slipped out of his hand. Kay bounded for the door; Armand Bluett blocked her. She cowered away, across to Zena's corner, and slumped down, sobbing.

Horty knew what to do, now; he had learned a thing. He tested it with his mind, and knew immediately that it was not a thing which could be done casually. It meant a gathering of mental powers, a shaping of the mass of them, an aiming, a triggering. He turned his mind in on itself and began to work.

'You shouldn't have laughed at me,' said the Maneater hoarsely. He raked in the two jewels and dropped them into a metal ash tray. He picked up the blow-lamp, meticulously adjusting the flame.

Horty worked. And still, a part of his mind was not occupied with the task. You can kill crystal-creatures, it said. The Maneater, yes, but – this is a big thing you are going to do. It may kill others … what others? Moppet? The two-headed snake? Gogol? *Solum?*

Solum, ugly, mute, imprisoned Solum, who had, at the last moment, turned against the Maneater and had helped him. He had carried Zena's message, and it was his own death warrant.

He looked up at the green man, who was backing away, his flaring eyes still anxiously filled with the message, not knowing that Horty had read it and acted upon it seconds before. Poor, trapped, injured creature …

But it was Zena's message. Zena had always been his arbiter and guide. The fact that it was hers meant that she had considered the cost and had decided accordingly. Perhaps it was better this way. Perhaps Solum could, in some unfathomable way, enjoy a peace that life had never yielded him.

The strange force mounted within him, his polymorphic metabolism draining itself into the arsenal of his mind. He felt the drugged strength drain out of his hands, out of the calves of his legs.

'Does this tickle?' snarled the Maneater. He swept the flame over the winking jewels. Horty sat rigidly, waiting, knowing that now this mounting pressure was out of his control, and that it would release itself when it reached its critical pressure. He kept his gaze fixed on the purpling, furious face.

'I wonder,' said the Maneater, 'which crystal builds which part, when two of them go at it.' He lowered the flame like a scalpel, stroking it back and across one of the crystals. 'Does that—'

Then it came. Even Horty was unprepared for it. It burst from him, the thing he had understood from the crystals. There was no sound. There was a monstrous flare of blue light, but it was inside his head; when it had passed he was quite blind. He heard a throttled cry, the fall of a body. Slowly, then, knees, hip, head, another body. Then he gave himself up to pain, for his mind, inside, was like a field after a wind-driven brush fire, raw and burnt and smoking, speckled with hot and dying flames.

Blackness crept over it slowly, with here and there a stubborn luminous pain. His vision began to clear. He lay back drained.

Solum had tumbled to the floor by his side. Kay Hallowell sat against the wall with her hands over her face. Zena leaned against her, her eyes closed. Bunny sat still on the floor, staring, weaving very slightly. Near the door, Armand Bluett was stretched out. Horty thought, *the fool passes out like a corseted Victorian.* He looked at the desk.

Pale and shaken, but erect, the Maneater stood. He said, 'You seem to have made a mistake.'

Horty simply stared at him dully. The Maneater said, 'I would think that, with your talents, you would know the difference between a crystalline and a human being.'

I never thought to look, he cried silently. *Will I ever learn to doubt? Zena always did my doubting for me!*

'You disappoint me. I always have the same trouble. My average is pretty high, though. I can spot 'em about eight times out of ten. I will admit, though, that *that* was a surprise to me.' He tossed a casual thumb at Armand Bluett. 'Oh well. Another heart case on the Fair Grounds. A dead crystalline looks just the same as a dead human. Unless you know what to look for.' With one of those alarming changes of voice, he said, '*You tried to kill me* ...' He wandered over to Horty's chair and looked down at Solum. 'I'll have to learn to get along without old Solum. Nuisance. He was very useful.' He kicked the long body idly, and suddenly swung around and landed a stinging slap on Horty's mouth. 'You'll do twice what he did, and like it!' he shouted. 'You'll jump when I so much as whisper!' He rubbed his hands.

'Oh-h-h-h …'

It was Kay. She had moved slightly. Zena's head had thumped down into her lap. She was chafing the little wrists.

'Don't waste your time,' said the Maneater, casually. 'She's dead.'

Horty's fingertips, especially the growing stubs on his left hand, began to tingle. *She's dead. She's dead.*

At his desk, the Maneater picked up one of the crystals and tossed it, glancing at Zena. 'Lovely little thing. Treacherous snake, of course, but pretty. I'd like to know where the crystal that made her got its model. As nice a job as you'll find anywhere.' He rubbed his hands together. 'Not a patch on what we'll have from now on, hey, Horty?' He sat down, fondling the crystal. 'Relax, boy, relax. That was one hell of a blast. I'd like to learn a trick like that. Think I could? … Maybe I'll leave it to you, at that. Seems to be quite a drain on you.'

Horty tensed muscles without moving. Strength was seeping back into his exhausted frame. Not that it would do him much good. The drug would hold him if he were twice his normal strength.

She's dead. She's dead. When he said that, he meant Zena. Zena had wanted to be a real live normal human being … well, all strange people do, but Zena especially, because she wasn't human, not at all. That was why she'd never let him read her mind. She didn't want anyone to know. She wanted so *much* to be human. But she'd known. She must have known when she sent him the message through Solum. She knew it would kill her too. She was – more of a human being than any woman born.

I'll move now, he thought.

'You'll sit there without food or water until you rot,' the Maneater said pleasantly, 'or at least until you weaken enough to let me into that stubborn head of yours so I can blast out any silly ideas you may have about being your own master. You belong to *me* – three times over.' He handled the two crystals lovingly. 'Stay where you are!' he snarled, whirling on Kay Hallowell, who had begun to rise. Startled and broken, she sank down again. Monetre rose, went and stood over her. 'Now, what to do with you. Hm.'

Horty closed his eyes, and with all his mounting energy, he thought. What was the drug Monetre had used? One of the cocaines, surely – benzocaine, monocaine … He was conscious of approaching vertigo, the first hint of nausea. Which drug would yield just this effect, then demonstrate just this much toxicity? In the back of his mind, he saw the riffling pages of a drug dictionary.

Think!

A dozen drugs could have this effect. But Monetre would certainly choose one that would do all he wanted – and he wanted more than immobility. He wanted psychic stimulation with it.

Got it! The old standby – cocaine hydrochloride. Antidote ... epinephrine. Now I've got to be a pharmacy, he thought grimly, Epinephrine ...

Adrenalin! Close enough – and very easy to supply under the circumstances. He had only to open his eyes and look at the Maneater. His lips curled. The vertigo faded. His heart began to thump. He controlled it. He could feel his body going into a forced-draught condition. His feet began to tingle almost unbearably.

'You could be a heart failure case too,' the Maneater was saying pensively to Kay. 'A little *curare* ... no. The Judge is enough for one day.'

Watching Monetre's back, Horty flexed his hands, pressed his elbows against his sides until his pectoral muscles crackled. He tried to rise, tried again. He all but collapsed, and then freedom and hate combined to accelerate the return of strength to his body. He rose, clenching his hands, trying not to breathe noisily.

'Well, we'll dispose of you in some way,' said the Maneater, returning to his desk, talking over his shoulder at the frightened girl. 'And soon – *uh!*' He found himself face to face with Horty.

The Maneater's hand crept out and closed around the jewels. 'Don't come one small half-inch nearer,' he rasped, 'or I'll smash these. You'll slump together like a bag of rotten potatoes. Don't move, now.'

'Is Zena really dead?'

'As a doornail, son. I'm sorry, I'm sorry that it was so quick, I mean. She deserved a more artistic treatment. *Don't move!*' He held the crystals together in one hand, like walnuts about to be cracked. 'Better go back and sit down where it's comfortable.' Their eyes met, held. Once, twice, the Maneater sent Horty his barbed hate. Horty did not flinch. 'Wonderful defence,' said the Maneater admiringly. 'Now go and *sit* down!' His fingers tightened on the crystals.

Horty said, 'I know a way to kill humans too.' He came forward.

The Maneater scuttled back. Horty rounded the desk and came on. 'You asked for it!' panted the Maneater. He closed his bony hand. There was a faint, tinkling crackle.

'I call it Havana's way,' said Horty thickly, 'after a friend of mine.'

The Maneater's back was against the wall, round-eyed, pasty-faced. He goggled at the single intact crystal in his hand, like walnuts, only one broke when the two were crushed together – uttered a bird-like squeak, dropped the crystal, and ground it under his feet. Then Horty had both hands on his head. He twisted. They fell together. Horty wrapped his legs around the Maneater's chest, got another grip on the head, and twisted again with all his strength. There was a sound like a pound of dry spaghetti being broken in two, and the Maneater slumped.

Blackness showered in descending streamers around Horty. He crawled off the inert figure, pushing his face almost into Bunny's. Bunny's face was looking down and past him, and was no longer vacant and staring. Her lips were curled back from her teeth. Her neck was arched, the cords showing starkly. Gentle Bunny ... she was looking at the dead Maneater, and she was laughing.

Horty lay still. Tired, tired ... it was almost too much effort to breathe. He raised his chin to make it easier for air to pass his throat. This pillow was so soft, so warm ... Feather-touches of hair lay on his upturned face, delicately stroked his closed eyelids. Not a pillow; a round arm curved behind his head. Scented breath at his lips. She was big, now; a regular human girl, the way she always wanted to be. He kissed the lips. 'Zee. Big Zee,' he murmured.

'Kay. It's Kay, darling, you poor brave darling ...'

He opened his eyes and looked up at her, his eyes a child's eyes for the moment, full of weariness and wonder. 'Zee?'

'It's all right. Everything's all right now,' she said soothingly. 'I'm Kay Hallowell. Everything's all right.'

'Kay.' He sat up. There was Armand Bluett, dead. There was the Maneater, dead. There was – was— He uttered a hoarse sound and scrambled uncertainly to his feet. He ran to the wall and picked Zena up and put her gently on the table. She had plenty of room ... Horty kissed her hair. He gathered her hands together and called her quietly, twice, as if she were hiding somewhere near and was teasing him.

'Horty—'

He did not move. With his back to her, he said thickly, 'Kay – where'd Bunny go?'

'She went to sit with Havana. Horty—'

'Go stay with her a little. Go on. Go on ...'

She hesitated, and when she left, she ran.

Horty heard a mourning sound, but he did not hear it with his ears. It was inside his head. He looked up. Solum stood there, silent. The mourning sound appeared again in Horty's head.

'I thought you were dead,' Horty gasped.

I thought you were dead, the silent, startled response came. *The Maneater smashed your jewels.*

'They were through with me. They've been through with me for years. I'm grown ... complete ... finished, and I have been since I was eleven. I just found out, when you sent me to – to speak to the crystals. I didn't know. Zena didn't know. All these years she's been ... oh, Zee, Zee!' Horty raised his eyes after a bit and looked at the green man. 'What about you?'

I'm not a crystalline, Horty. I'm human. I happen to be a receptive telepath. You gave me a nasty jolt right where I felt it most. I don't blame you and the Maneater for thinking I was dead. I did myself for a while. But Zena—

Together they stood over the tiny, twisted body, and their thoughts were their own.

After a time they talked.

'What'll we do with the Judge?'

It's dark now. I'll leave him near the midway. It will be heart failure.

'And the Maneater?'

The swamp. I'll take care of it after midnight.

'You're a big help, Solum. I feel sort of – lost. I would be, too, if it hadn't been for you.'

Don't thank me. I haven't the brains for a thing like that. She did it. Zena. She told me exactly what to do. She knew what was going to happen. She knew I was human, too. She knew everything. She did everything.

'Yeah. Yeah, Solum … What about the girl? Kay?'

Oh. I don't know.

'I think she better go back where she was working. Eltonville. I wish she could forget the whole thing.'

She can.

'She – oh, of course. I can do that. Solum, she—'

I know. She loves you, just as if you were human. She thinks you are. She doesn't understand any of this.

'Yes. I – wish … Never mind. No I don't. She's not my – my kind. Solum – Zena … loved me.'

Yes. Oh yes … and what are you going to do?

'Me? I don't know. Cut out, I guess. Play guitar somewhere.'

What would she want you to do?

'I—'

The Maneater did a lot of harm. She wanted to stop him. Well, he's stopped. But I think perhaps she would like you to right some of the wrongs he's done. All over our carnival route, Horty – anthrax in Kentucky, deadly nightshade in the pasture lands up and down Wisconsin, puff adders in Arizona, polio and Rocky Mountain spotted fever in the Alleghenies; why, he even planted tsetse flies in Florida with his infernal crystals! I know where some of them are, but you could find the rest better even than he could.

'My God … and they mutate, the diseases, the snakes …'

Well?

'Who would I be working for? Who's going to run the – Solum! Why are you staring at the Maneater like that? What's your idea? You – you think I—'

Well?

'He was three inches taller … long hands … narrow face … I don't really see why not, Solum. I could play it that way for a while – at least until "Pierre Monetre" wound up the arrangements to have "Sam Horton" run the carnival so he can retire. Solum, you have a brain.'

No. She told me to suggest it to you if you didn't think of it yourself.

'She—Oh, Zee, Zee ... Solum, if it's all the same to you, I've got to be by myself a while.'

Yes. I'll get this carrion out of here. Bluett first. I'll just tote him to the First Aid tent. No one ever asks old Solum any questions.

Horty stroked Zena's hair, once. His eyes strayed around the trailer and fixed on the Maneater's body. He walked abruptly over to it and turned it over on its face. 'I don't like to be stared at ...' He muttered.

He sat down at the desk on which Zena's body lay. He pulled the chair up close, crossed his forearms and rested his cheek on them. He didn't touch Zena, and his face was turned away from her. But he was *with* her, close, close. Softly, he talked to her, using their old idioms, just as if she were alive.

'Zee ...?

'Does it hurt you, Zee? You look as if you hurt. 'Member about the kitten on the carpet, Zee? We used to tell each other. It's a soft carpet, see, and the kitten digs its claws in and str-r-etches. It goes down in front and up behind, and it yawns, *yeeowarrgh*! And then it tips one shoulder under and jus' *pours* out flat. And if you lift a paw with your finger it's as limp as a tassel and drops back *phup*! on the deep soft rug. And if you think about that until you see it, all if it, the place where the fur's tousled a bit, and the little line of pink that shows on the side because the kitten's just too relaxed to close its mouth all the way – why then, you just *can't* hurt any more.

'There, now ...

'It hurt you to be different from – from folks, didn't it, Zee? I wonder if you know how much there is of that in everybody. The strange people, the little people – they have more than most. And you had more than any of them. Now I know, *now* I know why you wished and wished you were big. You pretended you were human, and had a human sorrow that you weren't big; and that way you hid from yourself that you weren't human at all. And that's why you tried so hard to make me the best kind of human you could think of; because you'd have to be pretty human yourself to do all that for humanity. I think you believed, really believed you were human – until today, when you had to face it.

'So you faced it, and you died.

'You're full of music and laughter and tears and passion like a real woman. You share, and you know about *with*ness.

'Zena, Zena, a jewel dreamed a truly beautiful dream when it made you!

'Why didn't it finish the dream?

'Why don't they finish what they start? Why these sketches and no paintings, these chords with no key signatures, these plays cut off at the second-act climax?

'*Wait!* Shh – Zee. Don't say anything ...

'Must there be a painting for every sketch? Do you have to compose a symphony for every theme? Wait, Zee ... I've got a big think in my head ...

'It comes straight from you. Remember all you taught me – the books, the music, the pictures? When I left the carnival I had Tchaikowsky and Django Rheinhart; I had *Tom Jones, a Foundling* and *1984*. And when I went away I built on these things. I found new beauties. I have Bartok and Gian-Carlo Menotti now, *Science and Sanity* and *The Garden of the Plynck*. Do you see what I mean, honey? New beauties ... things I'd never dreamed of before.

'Zena, I don't know whether it's a large or a small part of the crystals' life, but they have an art. When they're young – as they develop – they try their skills at copying. And when they mate (if it is mating) they make a new something. Instead of copying, they take over a living thing, cell by cell, and build it to a beauty of their own invention.

'I'm going to show them a new beauty. I'm going to point a new direction for them – something they've never dreamed before.'

Horty rose and went to the door. He pulled down the louvres and locked them, and shot the inside bolt. Returning to the desk, he sat down and went through the drawers. From the deep one at the left he lifted a heavy mahogany box, opened it with the Maneater's keys, and took out the trays of crystals. He glanced at them curiously under the desk light. Ignoring the labels, he piled all the crystals in a heap beside Zena's body, and put his head in his hands among them. It was quite dark except for the desk lamp; very little light filtered into the draped oval windows of the trailer.

Horty leaned forward and kissed the smooth, cool elbow. 'Now stay here,' he whispered. 'I'll be right back, honey.'

He bowed his head and closed his eyes, and let his mind go dark. His sense of presence in the trailer slipped away, and he became detached, a wanderer in lightlessness.

Again another sense replaced his sight, and once again he found himself aware of Presences. Profoundly, this time, all 'group' atmosphere was lacking, but for one – no, three quite distant pairs. But all the rest were single, isolated, sharing nothing, each pursuing esoteric, complicated lines of thought ... not thought, but something like it. Horty felt the differences between the creatures sharply. One was concentrated grandeur, dignity and peace. Another's aura was dynamic, haughty, and another closely hid a strange, pulsating, secret idea-series that entranced him, though he knew he'd never understand it.

The strangest thing of all was this: that he, a stranger, was not strange among them. Strangers anywhere on earth, on entering a club, or auditorium, or swimming pool, are, to some extent, made conscious of their lack of membership. But Horty felt no trace of such a thing. And neither did he feel included. Or ignored. He knew they noticed him. They knew he watched them. He could feel it. No one here, however long he stayed, would try communication – he was sure of that. And no one would avoid it.

And in a flash he understood. All earthborn life proceeds and operates from one command: Survive! A human mind cannot conceive of any other base.

The crystals had one – and a very different one.

Horty almost grasped it, but not quite. As simple as 'Survive!', it was a concept so remote from anything he'd ever heard or read that it escaped him. By that token, he was sure that they would find his message complex and intriguing.

So – he spoke to them. There are no words for what he said. He used no words; the thing he had to say came out in one great surge of rich description. Holding every thought that had been sleeping in his mind for twenty years, his books and music; all his fears and joys and puzzlements, and all his motives, this single flash of message coursed among the crystals.

It told of her perfect white teeth and her musical diction. It told of the time she had sent Huddie off, and the turn of her cheek, and the depth of expression which lay in her eyes. It told of her body, and cited a thousand and one human standards by which she was beautiful. It told of the eloquent rustling chords of her half-size guitar, and her generous voice, and the danger she faced in defence of the species denied her by one of the crystals. It pictured her artlessly naked; it brought back the difficult, half-concealed weeping; outbalanced her tears with a peal of arpeggio laughter; and told of her pain, and her death.

Implicit in this was humanity. With it, the base of Survival emerged, a magnificent ethic: *the highest command is in terms of the species, the next is survival of group. The lowest of three is survival of self.* All good and all evil, all morals, all progress, depend on this order of basic commands. To survive for the self at the price of the group is to jeopardise species. For a group to survive at the price of the species is manifest suicide. Here is the essence of good and of greed, and the wellspring of justice for all of mankind.

And back to the girl, the excluded. She has given her life for an alien caste, and has done it in terms of its noblest ethic. It might be that 'justice' and 'mercy' are relative terms; but nothing can alter the fact that her death, upon earning her right to survive, is bad art.

And that, in brief, all weighted down with clumsy, partial words, describes his single phrase of message.

Horty waited.

Nothing. No response, no greeting … nothing.

*

He came back. He felt the desk under his forearms, his forearm on his cheek. He raised his head and blinked at the desk light. He moved his legs. No stiffness. Some day he must investigate the anomaly in time-perception in that atmosphere of alien thought.

It him him then – his failure.

He cried out, hoarsely, and put his arms out to Zena. She lay quite still, quite dead. He touched her. She was rigid. Rigor had accented the crooked smile resulting from the damage the Maneater had done to her motor centres. She looked brave, rueful, and full of regret. Horty's eyes burned. 'You dig a hole, see,' he growled, 'and you drop this in it, and you cover it up. And then what the hell do you do with the rest of your life?'

He sensed someone at the door. He took out his handkerchief and wiped his eyes. They still burned. He turned out the desk lamp and went to the door. Solum.

Horty went out, closed the door behind him, and sat down on the mounting step.

As bad as that?

'I guess it is,' said Horty. 'I – didn't really think she was going to stay dead until just now.' He waited a moment, then said harshly, 'Make conversation, Solum.'

We lost about a third of our strange people. Every one of them within two hundred feet of that blast of yours.

'May they rest in peace.' He looked up at the looming green man. 'I meant that, Solum. It wasn't just a line.'

I know.

A silence. 'I haven't felt like this since I was kicked out of school for eating ants.'

What did you do that for?

'Ask my crystals. While they operate they cause a hell of a formic acid deficiency. I don't know why. I couldn't keep away from 'em.' He sniffed. 'I can smell 'em now.' He bent, sniffed again. 'Got a light?'

Solum handed him a lighter, flaming. 'Thought so,' said Horty. 'Stepped smack on an anthill.' He took up a pinch of the hill and sifted it on his palm. 'Black ants. The little brown ones are much better.' Slowly, almost reluctantly, he turned his hand over and dropped the rubble. He dusted his hands.

Come on over to the mess tent, Horty.

'Yeah.' He rose. On his face was a dawning perplexity. 'No, Solum. You go ahead. I got something to do.'

Solum shook his head sadly and strode off. Horty went back into the trailer, felt his way to the back wall where the Maneater had kept his laboratory racks. 'Ought to have some here,' he muttered, switching on the light. Muriatic, sulphuric, nitric, acetic – ah, here we go.' He took down the bottle of formic acid and opened it. He found a swab, wet it in the acid and touched it to his tongue. 'That goes good,' he muttered. 'Now, what is this? A relapse?' He lifted the swab again.

'That smells *so* good! What is it? Could I have some?'

Horty bit his tongue violently, and whirled.

She came into the light, yawning. 'Of all the crazy places for me to go to sleep ... Horty! What's the matter. You're – are you crying?' Zena asked.

'Me? Never,' he said. He took her into his arms and sobbed. She cradled his head and sniffed at the acid.

After a time, when he had quieted, and when she had a swab of her own, she asked, 'What is it, Horty?'

'I have a lot to tell you,' he said softly. 'Mostly it's about a little girl who was an undesirable alien until she saved a country. Then there was a sort of international citizen's committee that saw to it that she got her first papers, and her husband as well. It's quite a story. Real artistic ...'

CHAPTER XVII

Part of a letter:

… in the hospital just resting up, Bobby Baby. I guess I just cracked under the strain. I don't remember a thing. They tell me I walked out of the store one evening and was found wandering four days later. Nothing had happened to me, really nothing, Bob. It's a weird thing to look back on – a hole in your life. But I'm none the worse for wear.

But here's some good news. Old Crawly-Fingers Bluett died of a heart attack at the carnival.

My job at Hartford's is waiting for me whenever I get back. And listen – remember the wild tale about the young guitarist that lent me $300 that awful night? He sent a note around to Hartford's for me. It said he had just inherited a business worth two million and I was to keep the money. I just don't know what to do. No one knows where he is or anything about him. He's left town permanently. One of the neighbours told me he had two little daughters. Anyway he had two little girls with him when he left. So the money's in the bank and Daddy's legacy in the bag.

So don't worry. Specially about me. As for those four days, they didn't leave a mark on me; well, a little bruise on one cheek, but that's nothing. They were probably good days. Sometimes when I'm waking up, I have a feeling – I can almost put my finger on it – it's sort of a half memory about loving somebody who was very, very good. But maybe I made that up. Now you're laughing at me …

TO MARRY MEDUSA

'To Hal Speer, who was there.'

CHAPTER 1

'I'll bus' your face, Al,' said Gurlick. 'I gon' break your back. I gon' blow up your place, an' you with it, an' all your rotgut licker, who wants it? You hear me, Al?'

Al didn't hear him. Al was back of the bar in his saloon, three blocks away, probably still indignantly red, still twitching his long bald head at the empty doorway through which Gurlick had fled, still repeating what all his customers had just witnessed: Gurlick cringing in from the slick raw night, fawning at Al, stretching his stubble in a ragged brown grin, tilting his head, half-closing his sick-green, muddy-whited eyes. 'Walkin' in here,' Al would be reporting for the fourth time in nine minutes, 'all full of good-ol'-Al this an' hiya-buddy that, an' you-know-me-Al, and how's about a little, *you*-know; an' all I says is I know you all right, Gurlick, shuck on out o' here, I wouldn't give you sand if I met you on the beach; an' him spittin' like that, right on the bar, an' runnin' out, an' stickin' his head back in an' callin' me a—' Sanctimoniously, Al would not sully his lips with the word. And the rye-and-ginger by the door would be nodding wisely and saying, 'Man shouldn't mention a feller's mother, whatever,' while the long-term beer would be clasping his glass, warm as pablum and headless as Anne Boleyn, and intoning, 'You was right, Al, dead right.'

Gurlick, four blocks away now, glanced back over his shoulder and saw no pursuit. He slowed his scamper to a trot and then a soggy shuffle, hunching his shoulders against the blowing mist. He kept on cursing Al, and the beer, and the rye-and-ginger, announcing that he could take 'em one at a time or all together one-handed.

He could do nothing of the kind, of course. It wasn't in him. It would have been success of a sort, and it was too late in life for Gurlick, unassisted, to start anything as new and different as success. His very first breath had been ill-timed and poorly done, and from then on he had done nothing right. He begged badly and stole when it was absolutely safe, which was seldom, and he rolled drunks providing they were totally blacked out, alone, and concealed. He slept in warehouses, box-cars, parked trucks. He worked only in the most extreme circumstances, and had yet to last through the second week. 'I'll cut 'em,' he muttered. 'Smash their face for them, I'll ...'

He sidled into an alley and felt along the wall to a garbage can he knew about. It was a restaurant garbage can and sometimes ... He lifted the lid, and as he did so saw something pale slide away and fall to the ground. It looked like a bun, and he snatched at it and missed. He stooped for it, and part of the misted wall beside him seemed to detach itself and become solid and hairy; it scrabbled past his legs. He gasped in terror and kicked out, a vicious, rat-like motion, a hysterical spasm.

His foot connected solidly and the creature rose in the air and fell heavily at the base of the fence, in the dim wet light from the street. It was a small white dog, three-quarters starved. It yipped twice, faintly, tried to rise and could not.

When Gurlick saw it was helpless he laughed aloud and ran to it and kicked it and stamped on it until it was dead, and with each blow his vengeance became more mighty. There went Al, and there the two barflies and one for the cops, and one for all judges and jailers, and a good one for everyone in the world who owned anything, and to top it, one for the rain. He was a pretty big man by the time he was finished.

Out of breath, he wheezed back to the garbage can and felt around until he found the bun. It was sodden and slippery, but it was half a hamburger which some profligate had tossed into the alley, and that was all that mattered. He wiped it on his sleeve, which made no appreciable difference to sleeve or bun, and crammed the doughy, greasy mass into his mouth.

He stepped out into the light and looked up through the mist at the square shoulders of the buildings that stood around to watch him. He was a man who had fought for, killed for what was rightfully his. 'Don't mess with me,' he growled at the city.

A kind of intoxication flooded him. He felt the way he did at the beginning of that dream he was always having, where he would walk down a dirt path beside a lake, feeling good, feeling strong and expectant, knowing he was about to come to the pile of clothes on the bank. He wasn't having the dream just then, he knew; he was too cold and too wet, but he squared his shoulders anyway. He began to walk, looking up. He told the world to look out. He said he was going to shake it up and dump it and stamp on its fat face. 'You going to know Dan Gurlick passed this way,' he said.

He was perfectly right this time, because it was in him now. It had been in the hamburger and before that in the horse from which most of the hamburger had been made, and before that in two birds, one after the other, which had mistaken it for a berry. Before that … it's hard to say. It had fallen into a field, that's all. It was patient, and quite content to wait. When the first bird ate it, it sensed it was in the wrong place, and did nothing, and the same thing with the second. When the horse's blunt club of a tongue scooped it up with a clutch of meadow-grass, it had hopes for a while. It straightened itself out after the horse's teeth flattened it, and left the digestive tract early, to shoulder its way between cells and fibers until it rested in a ganglion. There it sensed another disappointment, and high time too – once it penetrated into the neurone-chains, its nature would be irreversibly changed, and it would have been with the horse for the rest of its life. As, in fact, it was. But after the butcher's blade missed it, and the meat-grinder wrung it, pinched it, stretched it (but in no way separated any part of it from any other), it could still go on about its job when the time came. Eight months in the deepfreeze affected it not at all, nor did hot fat. It was sold from a pushcart with a bag full of other hamburgers, and wound up in the bottom of the bag. The boy who bit into this particular hamburger was the only human being who ever saw it. It looked like a boiled raisin, or worse. The boy had had enough by then, anyway. He threw it into the alley.

The rain began in earnest. Gurlick's exaltation faded, his shoulders hunched, his head went down. He slogged through the wet, and soon sank to his usual level of feral misery. And there he stayed for a while.

CHAPTER 2

This girl's name was Charlotte Dunsay and she worked in Accounting. She was open and sunny and she was a dish. She had rich brown hair with ruby lights in it, and the kind of topaz eyes that usually belong to a special kind of blonde. She had a figure that Paul Sanders, who was in Pharmaceuticals, considered a waste on an office job, and an outright deprivation when viewed in the light of the information that her husband was a Merchant Marine officer on the Australia run. It was a matter of hours after she caught the attention of the entire plant (which was a matter of minutes after she got there) that news went around of her cheerful but unshakable 'Thanks, but no thanks.'

Paul considered this an outright challenge, but he kept his distance and bided his time. When the water-cooler reported that her husband's ship had come off second best in a bout with the Great Barrier Reef, and had limped to Hobart, Tasmania, for repairs, Paul decided that the day was upon him. He stated as much in the locker room and got good odds – 11 to 2 – and somebody to hold the money. It was, as a matter of fact, one of the suckers who gave him the cue for the single strategic detail which so far escaped him. He had the time (Saturday night), the place (obviously her apartment, since she wouldn't go out) and the girl. All he had to figure out was how to put himself on the scene, and when one of the suckers said, 'Nobody gets into that place but a for-real husband or a sick kitten,' he had the answer. This girl had cried when one of the boss's tropical fish was found belly-up one morning. She had rescued a praying mantis from an accountant who was flailing it against the window with the morning *Times*, and after she let the little green monster out, she had then rescued the accountant's opinion of himself with a comforting word and a smile that put dazzle-spots all over his work for the rest of the afternoon. Let her be sorry for you, and ...

So on Saturday night, late enough so he would meet few people in the halls, but early enough so she wouldn't be in bed yet, Paul Sanders stopped for a moment by a mirror in the hallway of her apartment house, regarded his rather startling appearance approvingly, winked at it, and then went to her door and began rapping softly and excitedly. He heard soft hurrying footsteps behind the door and began to breathe noisily, like someone trying not to sob.

'Who is it? What's the matter?'

'Please,' he moaned against the panel, 'please, please, Mrs Dunsay, help me!'

She immediately opened the door a peering inch. 'Oh, thank God,' he breathed and pushed hard. She sprang back with her hands on her mouth and he slid in and closed the door with his back. She was indeed ready for bed, as he had hardly dared to hope. The robe was a little on the sensible side, but what he could see of the gown was fine, just fine. He said hoarsely, 'Don't let them get me. Don't let them get me!'

'Mr *Sanders!*' Then she came closer, comforting, cheering. 'No one's going to get you. You come on in and sit down until it's safe for you. Oh,' she cried as he let his coat fall open, to reveal the shaggy rip and the bloodstain, 'you're hurt!'

He gazed dully at the scarlet stain. Then he flung up his head and set his features in an approximation of those of the Spartan boy who denied all knowledge of a stolen fox while the fox, hidden under his toga, ate his entrails until he dropped dead. He pulled his coat straight and buttoned it and smiled and said, 'Just a scratch.' Then he sagged, caught the doorknob behind him, straightened up, and again smiled. It was devastating.

'Oh, oh, come and sit down,' she cried. He leaned heavily on her but kept his hands decent, and she got him to the sofa. She helped him off with his coat and the shirt. It was indeed only a scratch, laboriously applied with the tips of his nail scissors, but it was real, and she didn't seem to find the amount of blood too remarkable. A couple of cc's swiped from the plasma lab goes a long way on a white sport shirt.

He lay back limp and breathing shallowly while she flew to get scissors and bandages and warm water in a bowl, and averted his face from the light until she considerately turned it out in favor of a dim end-table lamp, and then he started the routine of not telling her his story because it was too bad … he was not fit to be here … she shouldn't know about such things, he'd been such a fool … and so on until she insisted that he could tell her anything, anything at all if it made him feel better. So he asked her to drink with him before he told her because she surely wouldn't afterward, and she didn't have anything but some sherry, and he said that was fine. He emptied a vial from his pocket into his drink and managed to switch glasses with her, and when she tasted it she frowned slightly and looked down into the glass, but by then he was talking a blue streak, a subdued, dark blue, convoluted streak that she must strain to hear and puzzle to follow. In twenty minutes he let it dwindle away to silence. She said nothing, but sat with slightly glazed eyes on her glass, which she held with both hands like a child afraid of spilling. He took it away from her and set it on the end table and took her pulse. It was slower than normal, and a good deal stronger. He looked at the glass. It wasn't empty, but she'd had enough. He moved over close to her.

'How do you feel?'

She took seconds to answer, and then said slowly, 'I feel …' Her lips opened and closed twice, and she shook her head slightly and was silent, staring out at him from topaz eyes gone all black.

'Charlotte … Lottie … lonely little Lottie. You're lonesome. You've been so alone. You need me, li'l Lottie,' he crooned, watching her carefully. When she did not move or speak, he took the sleeve of her robe in one hand and, moving steadily and slowly, tugged at it until her hand slipped inside. He untied the sash with his free hand and took her arm and drew it out of the robe. 'You don't need this now,' he murmured. 'You are warm, so warm …' He dropped the robe behind her and freed her other hand. She seemed not to understand what he was doing. The gown was nylon tricot, as sheer as they come.

He drew her slowly into his arms. She raised her hands to his chest as if to push him away but there seemed to be no strength in them. Her head came forward until her cheek rested softly against his. She spoke into his ear quietly, without any particular force or expression. 'I mustn't do this with you, Paul. Don't let me. Harry is the … there's never been anyone but him, there never must be. I'm … something's happened to me. Help me, Paul. Help me. If I do it with you I can't live any more; I'm going to have to die if you don't help me now.' She didn't accuse him in any way. Not once.

Paul Sanders sat quite still and silent. It wasn't easy. But sometimes when you rush things they snap out of it, groggy, even sick, but nonetheless out of it, and then that's all, brother … After a silent time he felt what he had been waiting for, the slow, subsiding shiver, and the sigh. He waited for it again and it came.

The blood pounded in his ears. Well, boy, if it isn't now it never will be.

CHAPTER 3

The carcass of the old truck stood forgotten in the never-visited back edge of a junk-yard. Gurlick didn't visit it; he lived in it, more often than not. Sometimes the weather was too bitterly cold for it to serve him, and in the hottest part of the summer he stayed away from it for weeks at a time. But most of the time it served him well. It broke the wind and it kept out most of the rain; it was dirty and dark and cost-free, which three items made it pure Gurlick.

It was in this truck, two days after his encounter with the dog and the hamburger, that he was awakened from a deep sleep by … call it the Medusa.

He had not been having his dream of the pile of clothes by the bank of the pool, and of how he would sit by them and wait, and then of how *she* would appear out there in the water, splashing and humming and not knowing he was there. Yet. This morning there seemed not to be room in his head for the dream nor for anything else, including its usual contents. He made some grunts and a moan, and ground his stubby yellow teeth together, and rolled up to a sitting position and tried to squeeze his pressured head back into shape from the outside. It didn't seem to help. He bent double and used his knees against his temples to squeeze even harder, and that didn't help either.

The head didn't hurt exactly. And it wasn't what Gurlick occasionally called a 'crazy' head. On the contrary, it seemed to contain a spacious, frigid, and meticulous balance, a thing lying like a metrical lesion on the inner surface of his mind. He felt himself capable of looking at the thing, but, for all that it was in his head, it existed in a frightening *direction,* and at first he couldn't bring himself to look that way. But then the thing began to spread and grow, and in a few rocking, groaning moments there wasn't anything in his head *but* the new illumination, this opening casement which looked out upon two galaxies and part of a third, through the eyes and minds of count less billions of individuals, cultures, hives, gaggles, prides, bevies, braces, herds, races, flocks and other kinds and quantities of sets and groupings, complexes, systems and pairings for which the language has as yet no terms; living in states liquid, solid, gaseous and a good many others with combinations and permutations among and between: swimming, flying, crawling, burrowing, pelagic, rooted, awash; and variously belegged, ciliated and bewinged; with consciousness which could be called the skulk-mind, the crash-mind, the paddle-, exaltation-, spring-, or murmuration-mind, and other minds too numerous, too difficult or too outrageous to mention. And over all, the central consciousness of the creature itself (though 'central' is misleading; the hive-mind is permeative) – the Medusa, the galactic man o' war, the superconscious of the illimitable beast, of which the people of a planet were here a nerve and there an organ, where entire cultures were specialized ganglia; the creature of which Gurlick was now a member and a part, for all he was a minor atom in a simple molecule of a primitive cell – this mighty consciousness became aware of Gurlick and he of it. He let himself regard it just long enough to know it was there, and then blanked ten elevenths of his mind away from the very idea. If you set before Gurlick a page of the writings of Immanuel Kant, he would see it; he might even be able to read a number of the words. But he wouldn't spend any time or effort over it. He would see it and discard it from his attention, and if you left it in front of him, or held it there, he would see without looking and wait for it to go away.

Now, in its seedings, the Medusa had dropped its wrinkled milt into many a fantastic fossa. And if one of those scattered spores survived at all, it survived in, and linked with, the person and the species in which it found itself. If the host-integer were a fish, then a fish it would remain, acting as a fish, thinking as a fish; and when it became a 'person' (which is what biologists call the individual polyps which make up the incredible colonies we call hydromedusae), it would *not* put away fishly things. On the contrary, it was to the interest of the Medusa that it keep its manifold parts specialized in the media in which they had evolved; the fish not only remained a fish, but in many cases might become much more so. Therefore in inducting Gurlick into itself, he remained – just Gurlick. What Gurlick saw of the Medusa's environment(s) he would not look at. What the Medusa sensed was only what Gurlick could sense, and (regrettably for our pride of species) Gurlick himself. It could not, as might be supposed, snatch out every particle of Gurlick's information and experience, nor could it observe Gurlick's world in any other way than through the man's own eye and mind. Answers there might be, in that rotted repository, to the questions the Medusa asked, but they were unavailable until Gurlick himself formulated them. This had always been a slow process with him. He thought verbally, and his constructions were put together at approximately oral speed. The end effect was extraordinary; the irresistible demands came arrowing into him from immensity, crossing light-years with considerably less difficulty than it found in traversing Gurlick's thin tough layer of subjective soft-focus, of not-caring, not-understanding-nor-wanting-to-understand. But reach him they did, the mighty unison of voice with which the super-creature conveyed ideas … and were answered in Gurlick's own time, in his own way, and aloud in his own words.

And so it was that this scrubby, greasy, rotten-toothed near-illiterate in the filthy clothes raised his face to the dim light, and responded to the demand-for-audience of the most majestic, complex, resourceful and potent intellect in all the known universe: 'Okay, *okay*. So whaddaya want?'

He was not afraid. Incredible as this might seem, it must be realized that he was now a member, a person of the creature; part of it. It no more occurred to him to fear it than a finger might fear a rib. But at the same time his essential Gurlickness was intact – or, as has been pointed out, possibly more so. So he knew that something he could not comprehend wanted to do something through him of which he was incapable, and would unquestionably berate him because it had not been done …

But this was Gurlick! This kind of thing could hold no fears and no surprises for Gurlick. Bosses, cops, young drunks and barkeeps had done just this to Gurlick all his life! And 'Okay, *okay!* So whaddaya want?' was his invariable response not only to a simple call but also, and infuriatingly, to detailed orders. They had then to repeat their orders, or perhaps they would throw up their hands and walk away, or kick him and walk away. More often than not the demand was disposed of, whatever it was, at this point, and that was worth a kick any time.

The Medusa would not give up. Gurlick would not listen, and would not listen, and … had to listen, and took the easiest way out, and subsided to resentful seething – as always, as ever for him. It is doubtful that anyone else on earth could have found himself so quickly at home with the invader. In this very moment of initial contact, he was aware of the old familiar response of anyone to a first encounter with him – a disgusted astonishment, a surge of unbelief, annoyance, and dawning frustration.

'So whaddaya want?'

The Medusa told him what it wanted, incredulously, as one explaining the utter and absolute obvious, and drew a blank from Gurlick. There was a moment of disbelief, and then a forceful repetition of the demand.

And Gurlick still did not understand.

CHAPTER 4

I am Guido, seventeen, I ... think; nearly seventeen. There is always doubt about us who crawled out of the bones of Anzio and Cassini as infants, as ... maggots out of the bones when the meat is gone. I never look back, never look back. Today the belly is full, tomorrow it must be filled. Yesterday's empty belly is nothing to fear, yesterday's full belly is meaningless today; so never look back, never look back ...

And I am looking back because of Massoni, what he has done. Massoni who will never catch me, has locked me into his house, never knowing I am here. While he goes to all the places I live, all the places I hide, I come straight here to his own house because he is not so clever as I am and will never dream I am here. Perhaps I shall steal from him and perhaps I shall kill him. Massoni's house was part of a fortification in the war, so they say, concrete walls and an iron door and little slits for windows on two sides of the single room. But at the back, where the house is buried in the hill, is plywood, and a panel is loose. Behind is space to climb. Above the room is a flat ceiling; above that a slanted roof, so there is a small space that I, Guido, would think of and he, the clever (but not clever enough) Massoni could live with for years and never suspect. I come here. I find the iron door unlocked. I slip in. I find the loose panel, the climbing space, the dark high hole to hide in, the crack to look through at the room of Massoni. There is time. It is I, Guido, he is looking for and he will look in many places before he comes back tired.

And he comes, and he is tired indeed, falling onto his bed with his overcoat on. It is nearly dark and I can see him staring up and I know he is thinking, *Where is that Guido?* And I know he is also thinking (because he talks this way), *If I could understand that Guido I could be there before he breaks the legs of another beggar, smashes the stained glass of another church, sets another fire in another print shop ...* If Massoni says this aloud I shall laugh aloud, because Massoni does not understand Guido and never will; because what Guido does once, Guido will never do again, so that nobody knows where Guido strikes next.

He sighs, he tightens his lips in the dimness, shakes his head hard. He is thinking, *And though he must make a mistake some day, that is not good enough. If one knew, if one could understand why, one could predict, one could be there at the time – before the time, waiting for him.*

He will never understand, never predict, and never, never be there when

Guido strikes. Because Massoni cannot understand anything as simple as this: that I am Guido, and I hate because I am Guido, and I break and maim and destroy because I am Guido – because that is reason enough. Massoni is afraid because Massoni is a policeman. His life is studying things as they are, and making them into what they should be. But ... he is not like other policemen. He is a detective policeman, without the bright buttons and the stick. The other policemen catch breakers of laws so they may be punished. Some catch them and punish them too. Massoni likes to say he stops the criminal before there is a crime. Massoni is indeed not like the other police. They understand, as I understand, that a crime without witnesses and without clues is not the affair of the police, and that is why they shrug and try to forget the things Guido does. Massoni does not forget. Worse, Massoni knows which are Guido's acts and which are not. When the acid was put in the compressor tank at the bus garage and caused the ruin of sixty-one tires, everyone thought it was Guido's work. Massoni knew it was not; four different people told me what he said. He said it was not the kind of ruin Guido would make. This is why I hide. I never hid before. Eleven times I am arrested and set free, for no clues, no witnesses. I walk in the daytime and I laugh. But now Massoni knows which things I do and which I do not. I do not know how he knows that, so I hide. They are all enemies, every one, but this Massoni, he is my first and greatest enemy. They all want to catch me, *after;* Massoni wants to stop me, *before.* All the rest are making me a plague, a legend, capable of anything; Massoni credits me only with what I do, and says – and says – that I did not do this, I could not do that. Massoni makes me small. Massoni follows everywhere, is behind me; he is beginning to be at my side too often; he will be ahead of me waiting soon, if I do not take care ... by himself he will surround me. I am Guido and I do not underestimate real danger. I am Guido, who looks and talks and behaves like any other seventeen (I think) year old, who fills the belly yesterday and today, and possibly tomorrow, any way he can, like all the others ... but who knows there is more in life than the belly; there is the hating to be done and too short a life to do it all if I live to be a hundred and ten; there is ruin to do, breaking hurting silencing most of all silencing ... silencing their honks and scrapes and everlasting singing.

Massoni, lying on his bed in his overcoat, sighs and rolls over and sits up. From there he can reach the little kerosene stove to light it. When the flame is blue, he sighs, yawns, lifts the kettle to shake it and put it back on the fire. He gets up slowly, walks as if his shoes are too heavy, opens the cabinet, lifts out a –

No! Oh ... *no!*

– lifts out a portable phonograph, sets it on the table, strokes it like a cat, opens it, takes out crank, fits it in, winds it up. Goes to cabinet again, takes a record, looks, another, another, finds one and brings it to the machine –

Not now, not now, Massoni, or you will die in a slow way Guido will plan for you.

– puts it on, puts the needle down, and again it begins, oh why, why, why is everyone in this accursed country forever making music, hearing music, walking from one music to another and humming music while they walk? Why can Massoni not make a pot of coffee without this? It is the one thing I, Guido, cannot bear … and I must bear it now … and I cannot … Ah, look at the fool, swinging his hand, nodding his head, he who was too tired to move not ninety seconds ago; it is as if he drew some substitute for sleep from it, and I do believe all these fools can do it, with their dancing half the night and singing the rest … Why, why must they have music? Why must Massoni make it now, when I am trapped up here hiding and cannot stop it and *cannot stand it* …

Oh look, look at him now, what is he taking from under the bed … surely not a … Oh it is, it is, it's a violin, it's that horror of shingles and catgut and the hair of horses' tails, and he, and he …

I will not listen, I will wrap my arms around my head, I … He goes now, sawing at the thing, and the caterwauling starts and I can't keep him out of my head! …

He plays a lot of notes, this policeman. A lot of notes. He plays with the record, note for note with the swift fall of notes from the machine.

I look at last. His feet are apart, his chin couched on the ebony rest, his eyes half asleep, face quiet, left fingers running like an insect. His whole body … not sways … turns a little, turns back, turned by the music. His right hand with the bow is very … wide, and free. His whole body is … free in a way, like … flying … But this *I cannot stand!* I will—

He has stopped.

The record is finished. He turns it over, sets down the violin on the table, winds the crank, puts on the needle again. I hold my breath, I will roar, I will scream if … But he is looking at the kettle, he is at the cabinet, he is fetching a cookpot, a big can with a cover. Opens. Empty. He is sighing. He goes to phonograph *(stop it, stop it),* he stops it – only to start it over again at the beginning. He takes the big can, he—

He goes out.

Locking the door.

I am alone with this shriek of music, the violin staring up at me from its two long twisted slits.

I can run away now. Can I …?

He has locked the door. Iron door in concrete wall.

And he has left his overcoat. He has left the record playing. He has left the fire in the little stove, the water about to boil on it.

He will be right back then. No time for me to pick that lock and go. I must stay here hidden and hear that gabble of music and look down at that violin, and wait, oh my God, and wait.

This country has music through its blood and bones like a disease, and a man cannot draw in a breath of air that isn't a-thrum with it. You can break the legs of a singing beggar and stop his music, you can burn the printing presses and the stacks of finished paper bearing the fly-specks and chicken-tracks by which men read the music, and still it does not stop; you can throw a brick through the shining window of a shrine and the choir practicing inside will stop, but even as you slip away in the dark you hear a woman singing to a brat, and around the corner some brainless fumbler is tinkling a mandolin …

Ah, God curse that screeching record! What madness could possess what gibbering lunatic to set down such a series of squeaks and stutters? I do not know. (I will not know.) Once he did it it should have killed him, that mishmash of noises, but they are all mad, the Frenchmen, all lunatics to begin with, and can be excused for calling it a good Italian name. Massoni, Massoni, come back and quiet this bellowing box of yours or I shall surely come down in spite of all safety and good sense and smash it along with that grinning fiddle! To be caught, to be caught at last … it might be worth it, for a moment's peace and a breath of air undrenched by the *Rondo Capriccioso*.

I bite my tongue until I grunt from the pain.

I do not know what they call it, that music; cannot, will not know!

Someone laughs.

I open my throat, to be silent, breathing like this, breathing like running up a kilometer of steps … the door moves. It is Massoni. I will kill him very soon now. It may be that for one man to dry up the music in this country is like drying up the River Po with a spoon, but oh, this one drop of music, this Massoni, surely I will scoop him up and scatter him on the bank; for if I hate (and I do), and if I hate the gurgling men call music (and I do), and if I hate policemen (and before God I do that) then in all the world I hate this maestro-detective most of all, aside and apart and above all other things. Now I know I have been a child, with my breaking here, wrecking there. Guido will be *Guido* after this killing, so now—

But the door swings open and I see Massoni is not alone, and I sink down again quiet, and watch.

He is bringing a child, an eight-year-old boy with a dirty pale face and eyes shiny-black as that damned record. They both stop as the door swings shut and listen to it, both their silly mouths agape as if they each tried to make another ear of it to hear better. And now Massoni puts down the covered can and snatches up the violin; now again he makes the chatter and yammer of notes fly up at me, along with the violin on the record, and the boy watches, slowly moving his hands together until they hold each other, slowly making his eyes round. Massoni's face sleeps while the one hand swoops, the other crawls, then for a moment he looks down at the boy and winks at him and smiles a little and lets the face doze off again, playing notes the way a hose throws water-drops.

Then like slipping into warmth out of the snow, like the sudden taste of new bread to the starving, a silence falls over the room and I slump, weak and wet with sweat.

The boy whispers, 'Ah-h-h, Signor Massoni, ah-h-h …'

Massoni puts down the violin and touches it with his fingertips, as if it were the hair of a beloved instead of a twisted box with a long handle on it, says, 'But Vicente, it's easy you know.'

'Easy for you, Signor …'

Massoni laughs. He gets covered can, opens. Puts ground coffee into cookpot, pours in boiling water, sets kettle aside, puts cookpot on stove, lowers flame, stirs with long spoon, talks.

I lie limp, wet in the dark, smelling the coffee, watching them.

Massoni says, smiling, 'Yes, if you like, easy for me, impossible for you. But it will be easy for you, Vicente. You have two lessons now – tonight, three, and already what you do is easy for you. When you have been playing for as many years as I have, you will not play as well as I; you will play better; you will not be good, you will be great.'

'No, Signor, I could never—'

Massoni laughs and sweeps away the black bubbles on his coffee with his spoon. He lifts it off the burner and turns out the flame, and sets the pot on the table to settle. Says, 'I tell you, small one, I know what is good and what is great and what is hopeless. I know better than anybody. I am a policeman, glad of what I do, and not a good violinist eating out my heart wanting greatness, because I know what greatness is. Take up the violin, Vicente. Go on, take it.'

The boy takes the violin from the table and sets the ebony under his cheek and chin. He is afraid of it and he is past speech, and on him the violin looks the size of a 'cello.

'There,' Massoni says, 'there before you play a note, it is to be seen. Your feet placed so, to balance you when your music tilts the world. Your chest full like the beginning of a great voice which will be heard all over the earth. Throat, chin, belonging to the violin and it grown to you … Put up the bow, Vicente, but don't play yet. Ah … there is what the violinist calls the Auer arm, and you in your eighth year, your third lesson! Now put the violin down again, boy, and sit, and we will talk while I have my coffee. I have embarrassed you.'

I, Guido, watch from above with the bitter black wonder of the coffee smell pressing deep in the bridge of my nose, watch the child put down the violin exquisitely, like some delicate thing sleeping lightly. He sits before Massoni, who has poured a little coffee and much milk for him in a large cup, and is ladling in sugar like an American.

Massoni drinks his black and looks through the steam at the boy, says, 'Vicente, such a gift as yours is a natural thing and you must never feel you are different because of it … there are those who will try to make it so; pity them if you like, but do not listen to them. A man with talent eats, sweats, and cares for his children like any other. And if talent is a natural thing, remember that water is also, and fire, and wind; therefore flood and holocaust and hurricane are as natural as talent, and can consume and destroy you … You do not understand me, Vicente? Then … I shall tell you a story …

'There was a boy who had talent such as yours, or greater … oh, almost certainly greater. But he had no kind mother and father like yours, Vicente, no home, no sisters and brother. He was one of the wild ones who used to roam the hills after the war like dogs. Where he was born I cannot tell you, nor how he lived at all; perhaps some of the girls cared for him when he was a small baby. He was a year and a half old when he turned up at one of the UNRRA centers, starved, ragged, filthy.

'But you know what that baby could do, at a year and a half? He could whistle. Yes, he could. He would lie in his bundle of blankets and whistle, and people would stop and come and cluster around him.

'Perhaps if this happened today he would be cared for just for this one thing. But then, all was confusion; he was put with one family where the man died, and then into an orphanage which burned: these were unhappy accidents, but purely accidents. They could not quench the thing that was in him. Before he was three he knew a thousand melodies; he could sing words he did not understand, before he could speak; he could whistle the themes of any music he had once heard. He was full of music, that boy, full to bursting.'

(Above, listening, I, Guido, thought, now Massoni, who is filling you with such fairy-tales as this?)

Massoni puts his hands around the big cup as if to warm them, searches down into the black liquid as if to find more of his story, says, 'Now a natural thing like talent, like pure cool mountain water, if you put it in a closed place, cover it tight, set a fire under it, nothing happens, and nothing happens, and nothing … until *blam!* it breaks the prison and comes out. But what comes out is no longer pure cool kind water, but a blistering devil ready to scald, soak, smash whatever is near enough. You have changed it, you see, by what you have done to it.

'So. There is this small boy, three or four years old, with more music than blood in his body. And then something happens. He is taken into the family of a Corfu shepherd and not seen for six years. When we next hear of him he is a devil, just such a blistering devil as that gout of tortured mountain water. But he is not a jet of water, he is a human being; his explosion is not over in a second, but is to go on for years.

'Something has happened to him in the shepherd's house in those six years, something which put the cover down tight over what was in him, and heated it up.'

Vicente, the boy, asks, 'What was it?'

Massoni says nothing for a long time, and then says he doesn't know. Says, 'I mean to find out some day … if I can. The shepherd is dead now, the wife disappeared, the other children gone, perhaps dead too. They lived alone in a rocky place, without neighbors, fishing and herding sheep and perhaps other things … anyway, they are gone. All but this unhappy demon of a boy.'

(I, Guido, feel a flash of rage. Who's unhappy?)

Massoni says, 'So you see what can happen if a talent big enough is held back hard enough.'

Vicente, the boy, says, 'You mean to live apart from all music did such a thing to this child?'

Massoni shakes his head, says, 'No, that would not be enough by itself. It must have been something more – something that was done to him, and done so thoroughly that this has happened.'

'What things does he do?'

'Cruel, vicious things. They say meaningless things; but they are not meaningless. He beat an old beggar one night and broke his legs. He set fire to a print shop. He cut the hydraulic brake tube on a parked bus. He threw a big building-stone through the stained glass of St Anthony's. He destroyed the big loud-speaker over the door of a phonograph shop with the handle of a broom. And there are dozens of small things, meaningless until one realizes the single thread that runs through them all. Knowing that, one can understand why he does these things (though not why he wants to). One can also know, in the long list of small crimes, cruelties and ruinations a city like this must write each day, each week, which are done by this unfortunate boy and which are not.'

'Has no one seen him?' asks Vicente.

'Hardly. He took a toy from a child and smashed it under his foot, and we got a description; but it was a five-year-old child, it was after dark, it happened very quickly; it was not evidence enough to hold him. There was a witness when he wrecked the loud-speaker, and when he pushed a porter's luggage-truck on to the tracks at the railroad station, but again it was dark, fast, confused; the witnesses argued with one another and he went free. He moves like the night wind, appears everywhere, strikes when he is safe and the act is unexpected.'

(Ah now, Massoni, you are beginning to tell the truth.)

The boy Vicente wants to know how one may be sure all these things are really the work of this one boy.

Massoni says, 'It is the thread that runs through all his acts. In the shrine, St Anthony's, a choir was practicing. The toy he smashed was a harmonica. On the luggage truck were instrument cases, a trombone and a flügelhorn. The damaged bus carried members of an orchestra and their instruments (and a driver who had his wits about him, tried his brakes even as he began to move, or all might have been killed). The destruction of the loud-speaker speaks for itself. Always something about music, something against music.'

'The beggar?'

'A mad old man who sang all the time. You see?'

'Ah,' says the boy Vicente sadly.

'Yes, it is a sad thing. If music angers him so, his days and his nights must be a furnace of fury, living as he does in the most musical land on earth, with every voice, whistle, bell, each humming, singing, plunking, tinkling man, woman and child reaching him with music ... music reaches him, you see, as nothing can reach you and me, Vicente; it reaches him more than rain; it splashes on his heart and bones ... Ah, forgive me, forgive me, boy; I am using your lesson time on a matter of police business. Yet – it is not time wasted, if you gain from it something about the nature of talent, and how so natural a thing can break a block of stone to thrust one tender shoot into the sun, as you have seen a grass-blade do. And remember, too, that a great talent is not a substitute for work. A man of small skill, or even good skill like mine, must practice until his fingers bleed to bring his talent to flower; but if your talent is great, why then you must work even harder. The stronger the growth, the more tangled it can become; we want you to make a tall tree and not a great wide bramble-patch. Now enough of talk. Take up the violin.'

... So again I Guido descend into hell, while Massoni coaxes and goads the boy who goads and coaxes the instrument to scratch, squawk, squeak and weep. In between noises is advice and learning: 'A little higher with the bow arm, Vicente – so; now if there is a board resting on wrist, elbow, shoulder, I may set a brimming glass there and never spill. And to this level you must always return.' ... 'Na, na, get the left elbow away from the body, Vicente. Nobody scrunches up arm and fingers that way to play ... except Joseph Szigeti, of course, and you are not going to be the second Szigeti but the first Vicente Pandori.'

From my hole in the ceiling I Guido watch, and then strangely cease to watch ... as if watching was a thing to do, to try to do and a thing I could do or not do ... and as if I ceased trying to do this thing and became instead something not-alive, like a great gaping street-sewer, letting everything pour into me. A few minutes ago I am ready to shout, to come out, to kill – anything to stop this agony. Now I am past that. I am beaten into a kind of unconsciousness ... no; a sleep of the will; the consciousness is open and awake as never before. Along with it a kind of blindness with the eyes seeing. I see, but I am past seeing, past understanding what I see. I do not see them finish. I do not see them go. I am, after a long time, aware of what seems to be the sound of the violin, when the big low G string is touched by one single soft bounce of the bow, scraping a little under the boy's fledgling fingers. Hearing this, over and over, I begin to see normally again, and see only the dark room with a single band of light across it from a street-lamp outside the wide slit of window. Massoni is gone. Vicente is gone. The violin is gone. Yet I hear it, that soft scraping *staccato*, over and over.

It hurts my throat.

Hcoo ... hcoo ...

It hurts each time, the quiet sound, as if I am the violin being struck softly, and being so tender, hurting so easily, I softly cry out ...

And then I understand that it is not a violin I hear; I am sobbing up there in the dark. Enraged, I swallow a mouthful of sour, and stop the noise.

CHAPTER 5

'So – whaddaya want?'

The Medusa told him what it wanted, incredulously, as one explaining the utter and absolute obvious, and drew a blank from Gurlick. There was a moment of disbelief, and then a forceful repetition of the demand.

And Gurlick still did not understand. Few humans would, for not many have made the effort to comprehend the nature of the hive-mind – what it must be like to have such a mind, and further, to be totally ignorant of the fact that any other kind of mind could exist.

For in all its eons of being, across and back and through and through the immensities of space it occupied, the Medusa had never encountered intelligence except as a phenomenon of the group. It was aware of the almost infinite variations in kind and quality of the *gestalt* psyche, but so fused in its experience and comprehension were the concepts 'intelligence' and 'group' that it was genuinely incapable of regarding them as separable things. That a single entity of any species was capable of so much as lucid thought without the operation of group mechanisms, was outside its experience and beyond its otherwise near-omniscience. To contact any individual of a species was – or had been until now – to contact the entire species. Now, it pressed against Gurlick, changed its angle and pressed again, paused to ponder, came back again and, puzzling, yet again to do the exploratory, bewildered things a man might do faced with the opening of, and penetration through, some artifact he did not understand. There were tappings and listenings, and (analogously) pressures this way and that as if to find a left-hand thread. There were scrapings as for samples to analyze, prod-dings and pricks as for hardness tests, polarized rayings as if to determine lattice structures. And in the end there was a – call it a pressure test, the procedure one applies to clogged tubing or to oxide-shorts on shielded wire: blow it out. Take what's supposed to be going through and cram an excess down it.

Gurlick sat on the floor of the abandoned truck, disinterestedly aware of the distant cerebration, computation, discussion and conjecture. A lot of gabble by someone who knew more than he did about things he didn't understand. Like always.

Uh!

It had been a thing without sight or sound or touch, but it struck like all three, suffused him for a moment with some unbearable tension, and then receded and left him limp and shaken. Some mighty generator somewhere had shunted in and poured its product to him, and it did a great many things inside him somehow; and all of them hurt, and none was what was wanted.

He was simply not the right conduit for such a force. He was a solid bar fitted into a plumbing system, a jet of air tied into an electrical circuit; he was the wrong material in the wrong place and the output end wasn't hooked up to anything at all.

Spectacular, the degree of mystification which now suffused the Medusa. For ages untold there had always been some segment somewhere which could come up with an answer to anything; now there was not. That particular jolt of that particular force ought to have exploded into the psyche of every rational being on earth, forming a network of intangible, unbreakable threads leading to Gurlick and through him to Medusa itself. It had *always* happened that way – not almost always, but always. This was how the creature expanded. Not by campaign, attack, seige, consolidation, conquest, but by contact and influx. Its 'spores,' if they encountered any life-form which the Medusa could not control, simply did not function. If they functioned, the Medusa flowed in. *Always*.

From methane swamp to airless rock, from sun to sun through two galaxies and part of a third flickered the messages, sorting, combining, test-hypothesizing, calculating, extrapolating. And these flickerings began to take on the hue of fear. The Medusa had never known fear before.

To be thus checked meant that the irresistible force was resisted, the indefensible was guarded. Earth had a shield, and a shield is the very next thing to a weapon. It *was* a weapon, in the Medusa's lexicon; for expansion was a factor as basic to its existence as Deity to the religious, as breath or heart beat to a single animal; such a factor may not, must not be checked.

Earth suddenly became a good deal more than just another berry for the mammoth to sweep in. Humanity now had to be absorbed, by every measure of principle, of gross ethic, of life.

And it must be done through Gurlick, for the action of the 'spore' within him was irreversible, and no other human could be affected by it. The chances of another being in the same sector at the same time were too remote to justify waiting, and Earth was physically too far from the nearest Medusa-dominated planet to allow for an attack in force or even an exploratory expedition, whereby expert mind might put expert hands (or palps or claws or tenacles or cilia or mandibles) to work in the field. No, it had to be done through Gurlick, who might be – must be – manipulated by thought emanations, which are nonphysical and thereby exempt from physical laws, capable of skipping across a galaxy and back before a light-ray can travel a hundred yards.

Even while, after that blast of force, Gurlick slumped and scrabbled dazedly after his staggering consciousness, and as he slowly rolled over and got to his knees, grunting and pressing his head, the Medusa was making a thousand simultaneous computations and setting up ten thousand more. From the considerations of a space-traveling culture deep in the nebula came a thought in the form of an analogy: as a defense against thick concentrations of cosmic dust, these creatures had designed space-ships which, on approaching a cloud, broke up into hundreds of small streamlined parts which would come together and reunite when the danger was past. Could that be what humanity had done? Had they a built-in mechanism, like the chipmunk's tail, the sea-cucumber's ejectible intestines, which would fragment the hive-mind on contact from outside, break it up into two and a half billion specimens like this Gurlick?

It seemed reasonable. In its isolation as the only logical hypothesis conceivable by the Medusa, it seemed so reasonable as to be a certainty.

How could it be undone, then, and humanity's total mind restored? Therein lay the Medusa's answer. Unify humanity (it thought, reunify humanity) and the only problem left would be that of influx. If that influx could not be done through Gurlick directly, other ways might be found: it had never met a hive-mind yet that it couldn't enter.

Gasping, Gurlick grated, 'Try that again, you gon' kill me, you hear?'

Coldly examining what it could of the mists of his mind, the Medusa weighed that statement. It doubted it. On the other hand, Gurlick was, at the moment, infinitely valuable. It now knew that he could be hurt, and organisms which can be hurt can be driven. It realized also that Gurlick might be more useful, however, if he could be enlisted.

To enlist an organism, you find out what it wants, and give it a little in a way that indicates promise of more. It asked Gurlick then what he wanted.

'Lea' me alone,' Gurlick said.

The response to that was a flat negative, with a faint stirring of that wrenching, explosive force it had already used. Gurlick whimpered, and the Medusa asked him again what he wanted.

'What do I want?' whispered Gurlick. He ceased, for the moment to use words, but the concepts were there. They were hate and smashed faces, and the taste of good liquor, and a pile of clothes by the bank of a pond: she saw him sitting there and was startled for a moment; then she smiled and said, 'Hello, Handsome.' What did he want? ... Thoughts of Gurlick striding down the street, with the people scurrying away before him in terror and the bartenders standing in their open doors, holding shot-glasses out to him, calling, pleading. And all along South Main Street, where the fancy restaurants and clubs are, with the soft-handed hard-eyed big shots who never in their lives had an empty belly, them and their clean sweet-smelling women, Gurlick wanted them lined up and he would go down the line and slit their bellies and take out their dinners by the handful and throw it in their faces.

The Medusa at this point had some considerable trouble interrupting. Gurlick, on the subject of what Gurlick wanted, could go on with surprising force for a very long time. The Medusa found it possible to understand this resentment, surely the tropistic flailing of something amputated, something denied full function, robbed, deprived. And of course, insane.

Deftly, the Medusa began making promises. The rewards described were described vividly indeed, and in detail that enchanted Gurlick. They were subtly implanted feedback circuits from his own imaginings, and they dazzled him. And from time to time there was a faint prod from that which had hurt him, just to remind him that it was still there.

At last, 'Oh, sure, sure,' Gurlick said. 'I'll find out about that, about how people can get put together again. An' then, boy, I gon' step on their face.'

So it was, chuckling, that Daniel Gurlick went forth from his wrecked truck to conquer the world.

CHAPTER 6

Dimity Carmichael sat back and smiled at the weeping girl. 'Sex,' she told Caroline, 'is, after all, so *unnecessary*.'

Caroline knelt on the rug with her face hidden in the couch cushion, her nape bright red from her weeping, the end strands of her hair wet with tears.

She had come unexpectedly, in mid-afternoon, and Dimity Carmichael had opened the door and almost screamed. She had caught the girl before she could fall, led her to the couch. When Caroline could speak, she muttered about a dentist, about how it had hurt, how she had been so sure she could make it home but was just too sick, and, finding herself here, had hoped Dimity would let her lie down for a few minutes ... Dimity had made her comfortable and then, with a few sharp unanswerable questions ('What dentist? What is his name? Why couldn't you lie down in his office? He wanted you out of there as soon as he'd finished, didn't he? In fact, he wasn't a dentist and he didn't do the kind of operations dentists do, isn't that so?'), she had reduced the pale girl to this sodden sobbing thing huddled against the couch. 'I've known for a long time how you were carrying on. And you finally got caught.'

It was at that point, after thinking it out in grim, self-satisfied silence, that Dimity Carmichael said sex was after all so unnecessary. 'It certainly has done you no good. Why do you give in, Caroline? You don't *have* to.'

'I did, I did ...' came the girl's muffled voice.

'Nonsense. Say you wanted to, and we'd be closer to the truth. No one *has* to.'

Caroline said something – *I love* (or *loved*) *him so*, or some such. Dimity sniffed. 'Love, Caroline, isn't ... *that*. Love is everything else there can be between a man and a woman, without *that*.'

Caroline sobbed.

'That's your test, you see,' explained Dimity Carmichael. 'We are human beings because there are communions between us which are not experienced by – by rabbits, we'll say. If a man is willing to make some great sacrifice for a woman, it might be a proof of love. Considerateness, chivalry, kindness, patience, the sharing of great books and fine music – these are the things that prove a *man*. It is hardly a demonstration of manhood for a man to prove that he wants what a rabbit wants as badly as a rabbit wants it.'

Caroline shuddered. Dimity Carmichael smiled tightly. Caroline spoke.

'What? What's that?'

Caroline turned her cheek to rest it in her clenching hand. Her eyes were squeezed closed. 'I said … I just can't see it the way you do. I can't.'

'You'd be a lot happier if you did.'

'I know, I know …' Caroline sobbed.

Dimity Carmichael leaned forward. 'You can, if you like. Even after the kind of life you've lived – oh, I know how you were playing with the boys from the time you were twelve years old – but that can all be wiped away, and this will never bother you again. If you'll let me help you.'

Caroline shook her head exhaustedly. It was not a refusal, but instead, doubt, despair.

'Of course I can,' said Dimity, as if Caroline had spoken her doubts aloud. 'You just do as I say.' She waited until the girl's shoulders were still, and until she lifted her head away from the couch, turned to sit on her calves, look sideways up at Dimity from the corners of her long eyes.

'Do what?' Caroline asked forlornly.

'Tell me what happened – everything.'

'You know what happened.'

'You don't understand. I don't mean this afternoon – that was a consequence, and we needn't dwell on it. I want the cause. I want to know exactly what happened to get you into this.'

'I won't tell you his name,' she said sullenly.

'His name,' said Dimity Carmichael, 'is legion, from what I've heard. I don't care about that. What I want you to do is to describe to me exactly what happened, in every last detail, to bring you to *this*,' and she waved a hand at the girl, and her 'dentist,' and all the parts of her predicament.

'Oh,' said Caroline faintly. Suddenly she blushed. 'I – I can't be sure just wh-which time it was,' she whispered.

'That doesn't matter either,' said Dimity flatly. 'Pick your own. For example the first time with this latest one. All right? Now tell me what happened – every last little detail, from second to second.'

Caroline turned her face into the upholstery again. 'Oh … why?'

'You'll see.' She waited for a time, and then said, 'Well?' and again, 'Look, Caroline; we'll peel away the sentiment, the bad judgment, the illusions and delusions and leave you free. As I am free. You will see for yourself what it is to be that free.'

Caroline closed her eyes, making two red welts where the lids met. 'I don't know where to begin …'

'At the beginning. You had been somewhere – a dance, a club …?'

'A … a drive-in.'

'And then he took you …'

'Home. His house.'

'Go on.'

'We got there and had another drink, and – and it happened, that's all.'
'*What* happened?'
'Oh, I can't, I can't talk about it! Not to you! Don't you see?'
'I don't see. This is an emergency, Caroline. You do as I tell you. Forget I'm me. Just talk.' She paused and then said quietly, 'You got to his house.'

The girl looked up at her with one searching, pleading look, and, staring down at her hands, began speaking rapidly. Dimity Carmichael bent close to listen, and let her go on for a minute, then stopped her. 'You have to say exactly how it was. Now – this was in the parlor.'

'L-living room.'

'Living room. You have to see it all again – drapes, pictures, everything. The sofa was in front of the fireplace, is that right?'

Caroline haltingly described the room, with Dimity repeating, expanding, insisting. Sofa here, fireplace there, table with drinks, window, door, easy-chair. How warm, how large, what do you mean red, *what* red were the drapes? 'Begin again so I can see it.'

More swift and soft speech, more interruption. 'You wore what?'

'The black faille, with the velvet trim and that neckline, you know ...'

'Which has the zipper—'

'In the back.'

'Go on.'

She went on. After a time Dimity stopped her with a hand on her back. 'Get up off the floor. I can't hear you. Get up, girl.' Caroline rose and sat on the couch. 'No, no; lie down. Lie down,' Dimity whispered.

Caroline lay down and put her forearms across her eyes. It took a while to get started again, but at last she did. Dimity drew up an ottoman and sat on it, close, watching the girl's mouth.

'Don't say *it*,' she said at one point. 'There are names for these things. Use them.'

'Oh, I ... just *couldn't*.'

'Use them.'

Caroline used them. Dimity listened.

'But what were you feeling all this time?'

'F-feeling?'

'Exactly.'

Caroline tried.

'And did you say anything while this was going on?'

'No, nothing. Except—'

'Well?'

'Just at first,' whispered the girl. She moved and was still again, and her concealing arms clamped visibly tighter against her eyes. 'I think I went ...' and her teeth met, her lips curled back, her breath hissed in sharply.

Dimity Carmichael's lips curled back and she clenched her teeth and sharply drew in her breath. 'Like that?'

'Yes.'

'Go on. Did he say anything?'

'No. Yes. Yes, he said, "Caroline. Caroline. Caroline,"' she crooned softly.

'Go on.'

She went on. Dimity listened, watching. She saw the girl smiling and the tears that pressed out through the juncture of forearm and cheek. She watched the faint flickering of white-edged nostrils. She watched the breast in its rapid motion, not quite like that which would result from running up stairs, because of the shallow shiver each long inhalation carried, the second's catch and hold, the gasping release. 'Ah-h-h-h!' Caroline screamed suddenly, softly. 'Ahh ... I thought he loved me, I did think he loved me!' She wept, and then said, 'That's all.'

'No, it isn't. You had to leave. Get ready. Hm? What did he say? What did you say?'

Finally, when Caroline said, '... and that's all,' there were no questions to ask. Dimity Carmichael rose and picked up the ottoman and placed it carefully where it belonged by the easy-chair, and sat down. The girl had not moved.

'Now how do you feel?'

Slowly the girl took down her arms and lay looking at the ceiling. She wet her lips and let her head fall to the side so she could look at Dimity Carmichael, composed in the easy-chair – a chair not too easy, but comfortable for one who liked a flat seat and a straight back. The girl searched Dimity Carmichael's face, looking apparently for shock, confusion, anger, disgust. She found none of these, nothing but thin lips, dry skin, cool eyes. Answering at last, she said, 'I feel ... awful.' She waited, but Dimity Carmichael had nothing to say. She sat up painfully and covered her face with her hands. She said, 'Telling it was making it happen all over again, almost real. But—'

Again a silence.

'– but it was like ... doing it in front of somebody else. In front of—'

'In front of me?'

'Yes, but not exactly.'

'I can explain that,' said Dimity. 'You did it in front of someone – *yourself. You were watched.* After this, every time, every single time, Caroline, you will always be watched. You will never be in such a situation again,' she intoned, her voice returning and returning to the same note like some soft insistent buzzer, 'without hearing yourself tell it, every detail, every sight and sound of it, to someone else. Except that the happening and the telling won't be weeks apart, like this time. They'll be simultaneous.'

'But the telling makes it all so ... cheap, almost ... funny!'

'It isn't the telling that makes it that way. The act is itself ridiculous, ungraceful, and altogether too trivial for the terrible price one pays for it. Now you can see it as I see it; now you will be unable to see it any other way. Go wash your face.'

She did, and came back looking much better, with her hair combed and the furrows gone from her brows and the corners of her long eyes. With the last of her makeup gone, she looked even younger than usual; to think she was actually two years older than Dimity Carmichael was incredible, incredible ... She slipped on her jacket and took up her top coat and handbag. 'I'm going. I ... feel a lot better. I mean about ... things.'

'It's just that you're beginning to feel as I do about ... things.'

'Oh!' Caroline cried from the door, from the depths of her troubles, her physical and mental agonies, the hopeless complexity of simply trying to live through what life presented. 'Oh,' she cried, 'I wish I were like you. I wish I'd always been like you!' And she went out.

Dimity Carmichael sat for a long time in the not-quite-easy chair with her eyes closed. Then she rose and and went into the bedroom and began to take off her clothes. She needed a bath; she felt proud. She had a sudden recollection of her father's face showing a pride like this. He had gone down into the cesspool to remove a blockage when nobody else would do it. It had made him quite sick, but when he came up, unspeakably filthy and every nerve screaming for a scalding bath, it had been with that kind of pride. Mama had not understood that nor liked it. She would have borne the unmentionable discomforts of the blocked sewer indefinitely rather than have it known even within the family that Daddy had been so soiled. Well, that's the way Daddy was. That's the way Mama was. The episode somehow crystallized the great difference between them, and why Mama had been so glad when he died, and how it was that Dimity's given name – given by him – was one which reflected all the luminance of wickedness and sin, and why Salomé Carmichael came to be known as Dimity from the day he died. No cesspools for her. Clean, cute, crisp was little Dimity, decent, pleated, skirted and cosy all her life.

To get from her bedroom into the adjoining bath – seven steps – she bundled up in the long robe. Once the shower was adjusted to her liking, she hung up the robe and stepped under the cleansing flood. She kept her gaze, like her thoughts, directed upward as she soaped. The detailed revelation she had extracted from Caroline flashed through her mind, all of it, in a second, but with no detail missing. She smiled at the whole disgusting affair with a cool detachment. In the glass door of the shower-stall she saw the ghost-reflection of her face, the coarse-fleshed, broad nose, the heavy chin with its random scattering of thick curled hairs, the strong square clean yellow teeth. *I wish I were like you, I wish I'd always been like you!* Caroline had said that, slim-waisted, full-breasted Caroline, Caroline with the mouth which, in relaxation, pouted to *kiss me,* Caroline with the skin of a peach, whose eyes were long jewels of a rare cut, whose hair was fine and glossy and inwardly ember-radiant. *I wish I were like you* ... Could Caroline have known that Dimity Carmichael had yearned all her life for those words spoken that way by Caroline's kind of woman? For were they not the words Dimity herself repressed as she turned the pages of magazines, watched the phantoms on the stereophonic, technicolored, wide deep unbearable screen?

It was time now for the best part of the shower, the part Dimity looked forward to most. She put her hand on the control and let it rest there, ecstatically delaying the transcendent moment.

... *Be like you* ... perhaps Caroline would, one day, with luck. How good not to *need* all that, how fine and clear everything was without it! How laughingly revolting, to have a man prove the power of a rabbit's preoccupations with his animal strugglings and his breathy croonings of one's name, 'Salomé, Salomé, Salomé ...' (I mean, she corrected herself suddenly and with a shade of panic, 'Caroline-Caroline-Caroline.')

In part because it was time, and partly because of a swift suspicion that her thoughts were gaining a momentum beyond her control and a direction past her choice, she threw the control hard over to *Cold,* and braced her whole mind and body for that clean (surely sexless) moment of total sensation by which she punctuated her entire inner existence.

As the liquid fire of cold enveloped her, the lips of Dimity Carmichael turned back, the teeth met, the breath was drawn in with a sharp, explosive sibilance.

CHAPTER 7

Gurlick sank his chin into his collarbones, hunched his shoulders, and shuffled. 'I'll find out,' he promised, muttering. 'You jus' let me know what you want, I'll find out f'ya. Then, boy, look out.'

At the corner, sprawled out on the steps of an abandoned candy store, he encountered what at first glance seemed to be an odorous bundle of rags. He was about to pass it when he stopped. Or was stopped.

'It's on'y Freddy,' he said disgustedly. 'He don't know nothin' hardly.'

'Gah dime, bo?' asked the bundle, stirring feebly, and extending a filthy hand which flowered on the stem of an impossibly thin wrist.

'Well, sure I said somebody oughta know,' growled Gurlick, 'but not him, f'godsakes.'

'Gah dime, bo? Oh … it's Danny. Got a dime on ya, Danny?'

'All right, all right, I'll ast 'im!' said Gurlick angrily, and at last turned to Freddy. 'Shut up, Freddy. You know I ain't got no dime. Listen, I wanna ast you somethin'. How could we get all put together again?'

Freddy made an effort which he had apparently not considered worth while until now. He focused his eyes. 'Who – you and me? What you mean, put together?'

'I *tole* you!' said Gurlick, not speaking to Freddy; then at the mingled pressure of threat and promise, he whimpered in exasperation and said, 'Just tell me can we do it or not, Freddy.'

'What's the matter with you, Danny?'

'You gon' tell me or aincha?'

Freddy blinked palely and seemed on the verge of making a mental effort. Finally he said, 'I'm cold. I been cold for three years. You got a drink on you, Danny?'

There wasn't anybody around, so Gurlick kicked him. 'Stoopid,' he said, tucked his chin down, and shuffled away. Freddy watched him for a while, until his gritty lids got too heavy to hold up.

Two blocks farther, Gurlick saw somebody else, and immediately tried to cross the street. He was not permitted to. 'No!' he begged. 'No, no, no! You can't ast every single one you see.' Whatever he was told, it was said in no uncertain terms, because he whined, 'You gon' get me in big trouble, jus' you wait.'

Ask he must: ask he did. The plumber's wife, who stood a head taller than he and weighed twice as much, stopped sweeping her stone steps as he shuffled toward her, head still down but eyes up, and obviously not going to scuttle past as he and his kind usually did.

He stopped before her, looking up. She would tower over him if he stood on a box; as it was, he was on the sidewalk and she on the second step. He regarded her like a country cousin examining a monument. She looked down at him with the nauseated avidity of a witness to an automobile accident.

He wet his lips, and for a moment the moment held them. Then he put a hand on the side of his head and screwed up his eyes. The hand fell away; he gazed at her and croaked, 'How can we get together again?'

She kept looking at him, expressionless, unmoving. Then, with a movement and a blare of sound abrupt as a film-splice, she threw back her head and laughed. It seemed a long noisy while before the immense capacity of her lungs was exhausted by that first great ring of laughter, but when it was over it brought her face down again, which served only to grant her another glimpse of Gurlick's anxious filthy face, and caused another paroxysm.

Gurlick left her laughing and headed for the park. Numbly he cursed the woman and all women, and all their husbands, and all their forebears.

Into the park the young spring had brought slim grass, tree buds, dogs, children, old people and a hopeful ice-cream vendor. The peace of these beings was leavened by a scattering of adolescents who had found the park on such a day more attractive than school, and it was three of these who swarmed into Gurlick's irresolution as he stood just inside the park, trying to find an easy way to still the demand inside his head.

'Dig the creep,' said the one with *Heroes* on the back of his jacket, and another: '*Or-bit!*' and the three began to circle Gurlick, capering like stage Indians, holding fingers out from their heads and shrilling, 'Bee-beep! Bee-beep!' satellite signals.

Gurlick turned back and forth for a moment like a weathervane in a williwaw, trying to sort them out. 'Giddada year,' he growled.

'Bee-beep!' cried one of the satellites. 'Stand by fer *re-yentry!*' The capering became a gallop as the orbits closed, swirled around him in a shouting blur, and at the signal, 'Burnout!' they stopped abruptly and the one behind Gurlick dropped to his hands and knees while the other two pushed. Gurlick hit the ground with a *whoosh*, flat on his back with his arms and legs in the air. Around the scene, one woman cried out indignantly, one old man's mouth popped open with shock, and everyone else, everyone else, laughed and laughed.

'Giddada year,' gasped Gurlick, trying to roll over and get his knees under him.

One of the boys solicitously helped him to his feet, saying to another, 'Now, Rocky, ya shoonta. Ya shoonta.' When the trembling Gurlick was upright and the second of the trio – the 'Hero' – down on his hands and knees behind him again, the solicitous one gave another push and down went Gurlick again. Gurlick, now dropping his muffled pretenses of threat and counterattack, lay whimpering without trying to rise. Everybody laughed and laughed, all but two, and they didn't do anything. Except move closer, which attracted more laughers.

'Space Patrol! Space Patrol,' yelled Rocky, pointing at the approaching blue uniform. 'Four o'clock high!'

'*Esss-cape* velocity!' one of them barked; and with their antenna-fingers clamped to their heads and a chorus of shrill *beep-beeps* they snaked through the crowd and were gone.

'Bastits. Lousy bastits. I'll killum, the lousy bastits,' Gurlick wept.

'Ah right. *Ah* right! Break it up. Move it along. Ah right,' said the policeman. The crowd broke it up immediately ahead of him and moved along sufficiently to close the gap behind, craning in gap-mouthed anticipation of another laugh ... laughter makes folks feel good.

The policeman found Gurlick on all fours and jerked him to his feet, a good deal more roughly than Rocky had done. 'Ah right, you, what's the matter with you?'

The indignant lady pushed through and said something about hoodlums. 'Oh,' said the policeman, 'hoodlum, are ye?'

'Lousy bastits,' Gurlick sobbed.

The policeman quelled the indignant lady in mid-protest with a bland, 'Ah right, don't get excited, lady; I'll handle this. What you got to say about it?' he demanded of Gurlick.

Gurlick, half suspended from the policeman's hard hand, whimpered and put his hands to his head. Suddenly nothing around him, no sound, no face, pressed upon him more than that insistence inside. 'I don't care there *is* lotsa people, don't make me ast now!'

'What'd you say?' demanded the policeman truculently.

'A'right! A'right!' Gurlick cried to the Medusa, and to the policeman, 'All I want is, tell me how we c'n get together again.'

'What?'

'All of us,' said Gurlick. 'Everybody in the world.'

'He's talking about world peace,' said the indignant woman. There was laughter. Someone explained to someone else that the bum was afraid of the Communists. Someone else heard that and explained to the man behind him that Gurlick was a Communist. The policeman heard part of that and shook Gurlick. 'Don't you go shootin' your mouth off around here no more, or it's the cooler for you. Get me?'

Gurlick sniveled and mumbled, 'Yessir. Yessir,' and sidled, scuttled, cringing away.

'Ah right. Move it along. Show's over. Ah right, there ...'

When he could, Gurlick ran. He was out of breath before he began to run, so his wind lasted him only to the edge of the park, where he reeled against the railing and clung there to whimper his breath back again. He stood with his hands over his face, his fingers trying to press back at that thing inside him, his mouth open and noisy with self-pity and anoxia. A hand fell on his shoulder and he jumped wildly.

'It's all right,' said the indignant woman. 'I just wanted to let you know, everybody in the whole world isn't cruel and mean and – and – mean and cruel.'

Gurlick looked at her, working his mouth. She was in her fifties, round-shouldered, bespectacled, and most earnest. She said, 'You go right on thinking about world peace. Talking about it, too.'

He was not yet capable of speaking. He gulped air; it was like sobbing.

'You poor man.' She fumbled in an edge-flaked patent leather pocketbook and found a quarter. She held it and sighed as if it were an heirloom, and handed it to him. He took it unnoticing and put it away. He did not thank her. He asked, 'Do you know?' He pressed his temples in that newly developed compulsive gesture. 'I got to find out, see? I got to.'

'Find out what?'

'How people can get put back together again.'

'Oh,' she said. 'Oh dear.' She mulled it over. 'I'm afraid I don't know just what you mean.'

'Y'see?' he informed his inner tormentor, agonized. 'Ain't nobody knows – nobody!'

'Please explain it a little,' the woman begged. 'Maybe there's *someone* who can help you, if I can't.'

Gurlick said hopelessly, 'It's about people's brains, see what I mean, how to make all the brains go together again.'

'Oh, you poor man …' She looked at him pityingly, clearly certain that his brains indeed needed putting together again, and *Well, at least he realizes it, which is a sight more than most of us do.* 'I know!' she cried. 'Dr Langley's the man for you. I clean for him once a week, and believe me, if you want to know somebody who knows about the brain, he's the one. He has a machine that draws wiggly lines and he can read them and tell what you're thinking.'

Gurlick's vague visualization of such a device flashed out to the stars, where it had an electrifying effect. 'Where's it at?'

'The machine? Right there in his office. He'll tell you all about it; he's such a dear kind man. He told *me* all about it, though I'm afraid I didn't quite—'

'Where's it at?' Gurlick barked.

'Why, in his office. Oh, you mean, where. Well, it's 13 Deak Street, on the second floor; look, you can almost see it from here. Right there where the house with the—'

Without another word Gurlick put down his chin and hunched his shoulders and scuttled off.

'Oh, dear,' murmured the woman, worriedly, 'I do hope he doesn't bother Dr Langley too much. But then, he wouldn't; he *does* believe in peace.' She turned away from her good deed and started home.

Gurlick did not bother Dr Langley for long, and he did indeed bring him peace.

CHAPTER 8

Mbala slipped through the night, terrified. The night was for sleep, for drowsing in the kraal with one of one's wives snoring on the floor and the goats shifting and munching by the door. Let the jungle mutter and squeak then, shriek and clatter and be still, rustle and rush and roar; it was proper that it should do all these things. It was full of devils, as everyone knew, and that was proper too. They never came into the kraal, and Mbala never went into the dark. Not until now.

I am walking upside down, he thought. The devils had done that. The top of him had forgotten how to see, and his eyes stretched round and protuberant against the blackness. But his feet knew the trail, every root and rock of it. He sidled, because somehow his feet saw better that way, and his assegai, poised against – what? – was more on the ready.

His assegai, blooded, honorable, bladed now for half its length ... he remembered the day he had become a man and had stood stonily to receive it, bleeding from the ceremony, sick from the potions which had been poured into him and which, though they bloated his stomach, did nothing to kill the fire-ants of hunger that crawled biting inside him. He had not slept for two nights and a day, he had not eaten for nearly a week, and yet he could remember none of these feelings save as detached facts, like parts of a story told of someone else. The single thing that came to him fine and clear was his pride when they pressed his assegai into his hand and called him man. His slender little assegai, with its tiny pointed tip, its long unmarked shaft. He thought of it now with the same faint leap of glory it always brought him, but there was a sadness mixed with it now, and an undertone of primal horror; for although the weapon which slanted by his neck now was heavy steel, beautiful with carvings, it was useless ... useless ... and he was less of a man than that young warrior with his smooth tipped stick, he was less of a man than a boy was. In the man's world the assegai was never useless. It might be used well or ill, that was all. But this was the devil's world, and the assegai had no place or purpose here save to comfort his practiced hand and the tight-strung cords of his ready shoulder and back. It became small comfort, and by the moment smaller, as he realized its uselessness. His very manhood became a foolishness like that of old Nugubwa, whose forearm was severed in a raid, who for once did not die but mended, and who carried the lost limb about with him until there was nothing left of it but a twisted bundle like white sticks.

A demon uttered a chattering shriek by his very ear and scampered up into the darkness; the fright was like a blaze of white light in his face, so that for long seconds the night was full of floating flashes inside his eyeballs. In the daytime such a sound and scamper meant only the flight of a monkey; but here in the dark it meant that a demon had taken the guise of a monkey. And it broke him.

Mbala was frozen in the spot, in the pose of his fright, down on one knee, body arched back and to the side, head up, assegai drawn back and ready to throw at the source of his terror. And then—

He slumped, wagged his head foolishly, and climbed to his feet like an old old man, both hands on the staff of the spear and its butt in the ground. He began to trudge forward, balanced no longer on the springs of his toes, no longer sidewise and alert, but walking flat-footed and dragging his assegai behind him like a child with a stick. His eyes had ceased to serve him so he closed them. His feet knew the way. Beside him something screamed and died, and he shuffled past as if he had heard nothing. He dimly realized that he was in some way past fear. It was not any kind of courage. It was instead a stupidity marching with him like a ring of men, a guard and a barrier against everything. In reality it was a guard against nothing, and a gnat or a centipede would penetrate it quite as readily as a lion. But through such a cordon of stupidity, Mbala could not know that, and so he found a dim content. He walked on to his yam patch.

With Mbala's people, the yam patch was a good deal more than a kitchen garden. It was his treasure, his honor. His women worked it; and when it yielded well and the bellies of his kin were full, a man could pile his surplus by his door and sit and contemplate it, and accept the company of the less fortunate who would come to chat, and speak of anything but yams while the yearning spittle ran down their chins; until at last he deigned to give them one or two and send them away praising him; or perhaps he would give them nothing, and at length they would leave, and he could sense the bitter curses hiding in the somber folds of their impassive faces, knowing they could sense the laughter in his own.

Tribal law protecting a man's yam patch was specific and horrifying in its penalties, and the taboos were mighty. It was believed that if a man cleared a patch and cultivated it and passed it on to his son, the father's spirit remained to watch and guard the patch. But if a man broke some taboo, even unknowingly, a devil would drive away the guardian spirit and take its place. That was the time when the patch wouldn't yield, when the worms and maggots attacked, when the elephant broke down the thorn trees … and when the grown yams began to disappear during the night. Obviously no one but a demon could steal yams at night.

And so it was that misfortune, grown tall, would mount the shoulders of misfortune. A man who lost yams at night was to be avoided until he had cleansed himself and propitiated the offended being. So when Mbala began to lose yams at night, he consulted the witch doctor, who at considerable cost – three links of a brass chain and two goats – killed a bird and a kid and did many mumbling things with stinking smokes and bitter potions and spittings to the several winds, and packed up his armamentarium and hunkered down to meditate and at last inform Mbala that no demon was offended, except possibly the shade of his father, who must be furious in his impotence to guard the yams from, not a devil, but a man. And this man must be exorcized not by devil's weapons but by man's. At news of this, Mbala took a great ribbing from Nuyu, his uncle's second son. Nuyu had traveled far to the east and had sat in the compound of an Arab trader, and had seen many wonders and had come back with a lot less respect than a man should have for the old ways. And Nuyu said among howls of laughter that a man was a fool to pay a doctor for the doctor's opinion that the doctor could not help him; he said that he, Nuyu, could have told him the same thing for a third the price, and any unspoiled child would have said it for nothing. Others did not – dared not – laugh aloud like Nuyu, but Mbala knew well what went on behind their faces.

Well, if a man stole his yams at night, he must hunt the man at night. He failed completely to round up a party, for though they all believed the doctor's diagnosis, still night marches and dealings with demon's work – even men doing demon's work – were not trifles. It was decided after much talk that this exorcism would bring great honors to anyone so brave as to undertake it, so everyone in the prospective hunting party graciously withdrew and generously left the acquisition of such honors to the injured party, Mbala. Mbala was thereby pressured not only into going, but also into thanking gravely each and every one of his warrior friends and kinsmen for the opportunity. This he did with some difficulty, girded himself for battle, and was escorted to the jungle margin at evening by all the warriors in the kraal, while his wives stood apart and wept. The first three nights he spent huddled in terror in the tallest solid crotch he could find in the nearest tree out of sight of the kraal, returning each day to sit and glower so fiercely that no one dared ask him anything. He let them think he had gone each night to the patch. Or hoped they thought that. On the fourth morning he climbed down and turned away from the tree to be greeted by the smiling face of his cousin Nuyu, who waved his assegai and walked off laughing. And so at last Mbala had to undertake his quest in earnest. And this was the night during which the demons scared him at last into the numbness of impenetrable stupidity.

He reached his patch in the blackest part of the night, and slipped through the thorns with the practiced irregular steps of a modern dancer. Well into the thickest part of the bush which surrounded his yams – a bush his people called *makuyu* and others astralagus vetch – he hunkered down, rested his hands on his upright spear and his chin on his forearms. So he was here – splendid. Bad luck, thievery, shame and stupidity had brought him to this pinnacle, and now what? Man or devil, if the thief came now he would not see him.

He dozed, hoping for some lightening of the leaden sky, for a suspicious sound, for anything that would *give* him a suggestion of what to do next. He hoped the demons could not see him crouched there in the vetch, though he knew perfectly well they could. He was stripped of his faith and his courage; he was helpless and he did not care. His helplessness commanded this new trick of stupidity. He hid in it, vulnerable to anything but happily unable to see out. He slept.

His fingers slipped on the shaft of the assegai. He jolted awake, peered numbly around, yawned and let the weapon down to lie across his feet. He hooked his wide chin over his bony updrawn knees, and slept again.

CHAPTER 9

'You Doctor Langley?'

The doctor said, 'Good God.'

Dear kind man he might be to his cleaning lady, but to Gurlick he was just another clean man full of knowledges and affairs which Gurlick wouldn't understand, plus the usual foreseeable anger, disgust and intolerance Gurlick stimulated wherever he went. In short, just another one of the bastits to hate.

Gurlick said, 'You know about brains?'

The doctor said, 'Who sent you here?'

'You know what to do to put people's brains together again?'

'What? Who are you? What do you want anyway?'

'Look,' said Gurlick, 'I got to find this out, see. You know how to do it, or not?'

'I'm afraid,' said the doctor icily, 'that I can't answer a question I don't understand.'

'So ya *don't* know anything about brains.'

The doctor sat tall behind a wide desk. His face was smooth and narrow, and in repose fell naturally into an expression of arrogance. No better example in all the world could have been found of the epitome of everything Gurlick hated in his fellow-man. The doctor was archetype, coda, essence; and in his presence Gurlick was so unreasonably angry as almost to forget how to cringe.

'I didn't say that,' said Langley. He looked at Gurlick steadily for a moment, openly selecting a course of action: Throw him out? Humor him? Or study him? He observed the glaring eyes, the trembling mouth, the posture of fear-driven aggressiveness. He said, 'Let's get something straight. I'm not a psychiatrist.' Aware that this creature didn't know a psychiatrist from a CPA, he explained, 'I mean, I don't treat people who have problems. I'm a physiologist, specializing on the brain. I'm just interested in how brains do what they do. If the brain was a motor, you might say I am the man who writes the manual that the mechanic studies before he goes to work. That's all I am, so before you waste your own time and mine, get that straight. If you want me to recommend somebody who can help you with whatev—'

'You tell me,' Gurlick barked, 'you just tell me that one thing and that's all you got to do.'

'What one thing?'

Exasperated, adding his impatience with all his previous failures to his intense dislike of this new enemy, Gurlick growled, 'I tole ya.' When this got no response, and when he understood from the doctor's expression that it would get no response, he blew angrily from his nostrils and explained, 'Once everybody in the world had just the one brain, see what I mean. Now they's all took apart. All you got to tell me is how to stick 'em together again.'

'You seem to be pretty sure that everybody – how's that again? – had the same brain once.'

Gurlick listened to something inside him. Then, 'Had to be like that,' he said.

'Why did it have to be?'

Gurlick waved a vague hand. 'All this. Buildin's. Cars, cloe's, tools, 'lectric, all like that. This don't git done without the people all think with like one head.'

'It did get done that way, though. People can work together without – thinking together. That is what you mean, isn't it – all thinking at once, like a hive of bees?'

'Bees, yeah.'

'It didn't happen that way with people, believe me. What made you think it did?'

'Well, it did, thass all,' said Gurlick positively.

A startled computation was made among the stars, and, given the axiom which had proved unalterably and invariably true heretofore, namely, that a species did not reach this high a level of technology without the hive-mind to organize it, there was only one way to account for the doctor's incredible statement – providing he did not lie – and Gurlick, informed of this conclusion, did his best to phrase it. 'I guess what happened was, everybody broke all apart, they on their own now, they just don't remember no more. I don't remember it, you don't remember it, that one time you and me and everybody was part of one great big brain.'

'I wouldn't believe that,' said the doctor, 'even if it were true.'

'Sure not,' Gurlick agreed, obviously and irritatingly taking the doctor's statement as a proof of his own. 'Well ... I still got to find out how to stick 'em all together again.'

'You won't find it out from me. I don't know. So why don't you just go and—'

'You got a machine, it knows what you're thinkin',' said Gurlick suddenly.

'I have a machine which does nothing of the kind. Who told you about me, anyway?'

'You show me that machine.'

'Certainly not. Look, this has been very interesting, but I'm busy and I can't talk to you any more. Now be a good—'

'You got to show it to me,' said Gurlick in a terrifying whisper; for through his fogbound mind had shot his visions (she's in the water up to her neck, saying, *Hello, Handsome,* and he just grins, and she says, *I'm coming out,* and he says, *Come on then,* and slowly she starts up toward him, the water down to her collarbone, to her chest, to—) and a smoky curl of his new agony; he had to get this information, he *must.*

The doctor pressed himself away from his desk a few inches in alarm. 'That's the machine over there. It won't make the slightest sense to you. I'm not trying to hide anything from you – it's just that you wouldn't understand it.'

Gurlick sidled over to the equipment the doctor had pointed to. He stood looking at it for a moment, flashing a cautious ratlike glance toward the doctor from time to time, and pulling at his mouth. 'What you call this thing?'

'An electroencephalograph. Are you satisfied?'

'How's it know what you're thinkin'?'

'It doesn't. It picks up electrical impulses from a brain and turns them into wavy lines on a strip of paper.'

Watching Gurlick, the doctor saw clearly that in some strange way his visitor was not thinking of the next question; he was waiting for it. He could see it arrive.

'Open it up,' said Gurlick.

'What?'

'Open it. I got to look at the stuff inside it.'

'Now look here, I—'

Again that frightening hiss: 'I got to see it.'

The doctor sighed in exasperation and pulled open the file drawer of his desk. He located a manual, slapped it down on the desk, leafed through it and opened it. 'There's a picture of it. It's a wiring diagram. If it makes any sense to you it'll tell you more than a look inside would tell you. I hope it tells you that the thing's far too complicated for a man without train—'

Gurlick snatched up the manual and stared at it. His eyes glazed and cleared. He put the manual down and pointed. 'These here lines is wires?'

'Yes.'

'This here?'

'A rectifier. It's a tube. You know what a tube is.'

'Like radio tubes. Electric is in these here wires?'

'This can't mean anyth—'

'What's this here?'

'Those little lines? Ground. Here, and here, and over here the current goes to ground.'

Gurlick placed a filthy fingertip on the transformer symbol. 'This changes the electric. Right?'

Dumfounded, Langley nodded. Gurlick said, 'Regular electric comes in here. Some other kind comes in here. What?'

'That's the detector. The input. The electrodes. I mean whatever brain the machine is hooked up to, feeds current in there.'

'It ain't very much.'

'It ain't,' mimicked the doctor weakly, 'very much.'

'You got one of those strips with the wavy lines?'

Wordlessly the doctor opened the drawer, found a trace, and tossed it on top of the diagram. Gurlick pored over it for a long moment, referring twice to the wiring diagram. Suddenly he threw it down. 'Okay. Now I found out.'

'You found out what?'

'What I wanted.'

'Will you be kind enough to tell me just what you found?'

'God,' said Gurlick disgustedly, 'how sh'd *I* know?'

Langley shook his head, suddenly ready to laugh at this mystifying and irritating visitation. 'Well, if you've found it, you don't have to stick around. Right?'

'Shut up,' said Gurlick, cocking his head, closing his eyes. Langley waited.

It was like hearing one side of a phone conversation, but there was no phone. 'How the hell I'm supposed to do *that?*' Gurlick demanded at one point, and later, 'I gon' need money for anything like that. No, I can't. I can't, I tell ya; you just gon' git me in th' clink ... What you think he's gon' be doin' while I take it?'

'Who are you talking to?' Langley demanded.

'I dunno,' said Gurlick. 'Shut up, now.' He fixed his gaze on the doctor's face, and for seconds it was unseeing. Then suddenly it was not, and Gurlick spoke to him: 'I got to have money.'

'I'm not giving any handouts this season. Now get out of here.'

Gurlick, showing all the signs of an unwelcome internal goading, came around the desk and repeated his demand. As he did so, he saw for the very first time that Doctor Langley sat in a wheel chair.

That made all the difference in the world to Gurlick.

CHAPTER 10

Henry was tall. He stood tall and sat tall and had a surprisingly adult face, which made him all the more ridiculous as he sat through school day after day, weeping. He did not cry piteously or with bellows of rage and outrage, but almost silently, with a series of widely spaced, soft, difficult sniffs. He did what he was told *(Get in line ... move your chairs, it's story time ... fetch the puzzles ... put away the paints)* but he did not speak and would not play or dance or sing or laugh. He would only sit, stiff as a spike, and sniff. Henry was five and kindergarten was tough for him. Life was tough for him. 'Life is tough,' his father was fond of saying, 'and the little coward might as well learn.'

Henry's mother disagreed, but deviously. She lied to everyone concerned – to her husband, to Henry's teacher, to the school psychologist and the principal and to Henry himself. She told her husband she was shopping in the mornings but instead she was sitting in the corner of the kindergarten room watching Henry crying. After two weeks of this the psychologist and the principal corralled her and explained to her that the reality of home involved having her at home, the reality of school involved *not* having her at school, and Henry was not going to face the reality of school until he could experience it without her. She agreed immediately, because she always agreed with anyone who had a clear opinion about anything, went back to the room, told the stricken Henry that she would be waiting just outside, and marched out. She completely overlooked the fact that Henry could see her from the window, see her walk down the path and get into her car and drive away. If he had any composure left after that it was destroyed after a few minutes when, having circled the block and concealed her car, she crept back past the *Keep Off the Grass* sign, and spent the rest of the morning peeping in the window. Henry saw her right away, but the teacher and the principal didn't catch on to it for weeks. Henry continued to sit stiffly and hiss out his occasional sobs, wondering numbly what there was about school so terrifying as to make his mother go to such lengths to protect him, and, whatever it was, feeling a speechless horror of it.

Henry's father did what he could about Henry's cowardice. It pained him because, though he was certain it didn't come from his side, other people might not know that. He told Henry ghost stories about sheeted phantasms which ate little boys and then sent him up to bed in the dark, in a room where there was a hot-air register opening directly into the ceiling of the room below. The father had troubled to spread a sheet over the register and when he heard the boy's door open and close, he shoved a stick up through the register and moaned. The white form rising up out of the floor elicited no sound or movement from Henry, so the father went upstairs, laughing to see the effect he had not heard. Henry stood as stiff as ever, straight and tall, motionless in the dark, so his father turned on the light and looked him over, and then gave him a good whaling. 'Five years old,' he told the mother when he got back downstairs, 'and he wets his pants yet.'

He jumped out shouting at Henry from around corners and hid in closets and made animal noises and he gave him ruthless orders to go out and punch eight-and ten-year-olds in the nose and warmed his seat for him when he refused, but he just couldn't seem to make the dirty little sissy into anything else. 'Blood will tell,' he used to say knowingly to the mother who had never stood up to anyone in her life and had manifestly tainted the boy. But he clung to the hope that he could do something about it, and he kept trying.

Henry was afraid when his parents quarreled, because the father shouted and the mother wept; but he was afraid when they did not quarrel too. This was a special fear, raised to its peak on the occasions when the father spoke to him pleasantly, smiling. Undoubtedly the father himself did not realize it, but his pattern for punishing the boy was invariably a soft-voiced, smiling approach and a sudden burst of brutality, and Henry had become incapable of discriminating between a genuine pleasantry and one of these cheerful precursors to punishment. Meanwhile his mother coddled and cuddled him secretly and unsystematically, secretly violated his father's deprivations by contrabanding to him too much cookies and candy, yet all the while turned a cold and unresponsive back to any real or tacit plea for help in the father's presence. Henry's natural curiosity, along with his normal rebelliousness, had been thoroughly excised when they first showed themselves in his second and third years, and at five he was so thoroughly trained that he would take nothing not actually handed to him by a recognized authority, go nowhere and do nothing unless and until clearly instructed to do so. Children should be seen and not heard. Do not speak unless spoken to. 'Why didn't you poke that kid right in the nose? Why? *Why?*'

'Daddy, I—'

'Shaddup, you little yellow-belly. I don't want to hear it.'

So tall little, sad little Henry sat sniffing in kindergarten, and was numbly silent everywhere else.

CHAPTER 11

After clubbing Dr Langley with the floor-lamp, Gurlick rummaged around as ordered, and, bearing a bundle, went shopping. The Medusa permitted him to shop for himself first, quite willing to concede that he knew the subtleties of his own matrix better than it did. He got a second-hand suit from a hockshop in the tenderloin district, and a shave and a trim at the barber college. Esthetically the improvement was negligible; socially it was enormous. He was able to get what he wanted, though none of it was easy, since he personally knew the names of none of the things he was compelled to buy. Probably the metal samples were hardest of all to acquire; he had to go into an endless succession of glassy-eyed silences before a bewildered lab supply clerk undertook to show him a periodic table of the elements. Once he had that, things moved more rapidly. By pointing and mumbling and asking and trancing, he acquired lab demonstration samples of nickel, aluminum, iron, copper, selenium, carbon and certain others. He asked for but could not afford deuterium, four-nines pure tantalum, and six-nines silver. The electrical-supply houses frustrated him deeply on the matter of small-gauge wire with a square cross-section, but someone at last directed him to a jewelry-findings store and at last he had what he wanted.

By now he was burdened with a wooden crate rigged by an accommodating clerk into something approximating a foot-locker in size and shape, with a rope handle to carry it by. His destination was decided after a painful prodding session by the Medusa, which dug out of Gurlick's unwilling brain a memory that Gurlick himself had long ago let vanish – a brief and unprofitable stab at prospecting, or rather at carrying the pack for a friend who was stabbing at it, years ago. The important facet of the memory was an abandoned shack miles from anywhere, together with a rough idea of how to get there.

So Gurlick took a bus, and another bus, and stole a jeep and abandoned it, and at last, cursing his tormentors, slavering for his dream, and wailing his discomfort, he walked.

Heavy woods, an upland of scrub pine and dwarf maple, then a jagged rock ridge – that was it; and the roofless remnant of the shack like a patch of decay between and against the stained tooth-roots of the snaggly ridge.

Gurlick wanted more than water, more than food or to be left alone, Gurlick wanted rest, but he was not allowed it. Panting and sniffling, he fell to his knees and began to fumble with the ropes on his burden. He took out the mercury cells and the metal slugs and the wire and tube-sockets, and began to jumble them together. He didn't know what he was doing and he didn't have to. The work was being done by an aggregate of computing wills scattered across the heavens, partly by direct orders, partly by a semi-direct control, brain to neurone, by-passing that foggy swamp which comprised Gurlick's consciousness. Gurlick disliked the whole thing mightily, but except for a lachrymose grumble, no protest was possible. So he blubbered and slaved, and did not, could not, let up until it was finished.

When it was finished, Gurlick was released. He stumbled away from it, as if a rope under tension had tied him and was suddenly cut. He fell heavily, reared up on his elbows to blink at the thing, and then exhaustion overcame him and he slept.

When he fell asleep it was a tangle of wires and components, a stack of dissimilar metals strangely assembled, and with … capabilities. While he slept, the thoughts from the stars operated it, directly at last, not needing his blunt fumbling fingers. Within one of the circlets of square wire, a small mound of sand began to smoke. It rose suddenly and drifted down, rose again and drifted down, and lay finally smooth and flat. A depression of an unusual shape appeared in it. A block of Invar tumbled end over end from the small pile of metals and dropped into the sand. It slumped, melted, ran and was cast. Another piece was formed, then another, and with a swirl like the unpredictable formation of a dust-devil, the pieces whirled and fell together, an assembly. A coil of enameled copper wire rolled to the sand bed and stopped rolling … but continued to rotate, as its free end crawled outward to the assembly, snaked here, there, around a prong. A faint smell of burning, and the wire was spot-welded in seven places, and burned through where it was not needed.

Now Gurlick's original conglomeration began to shed its parts, some being invisibly shoved aside, others being drawn in to join the growing aggregate. Sometimes there was a long pause as if some inhuman digestive process were going on within the growing machine; then it would shudder as if shaken more tightly together, or it would thrust out a new sub-assembly to one side, which in turn would erect a foot-high T-shaped mast which would begin to swing from side to side as if seeking. Or there would be a flurry of activity as it tried and rejected materials in rapid succession; after one such scurry, its T-headed mast aimed at the rock near-by. There was a tense moment, a flicker of violet corona discharge; a great bite appeared in the rock, and a cold cloud of rock-dust which drifted over to the new machine and was absorbed into it – traces of silver, traces of copper, and certain borosilicates.

And when it was finished, it was … it was what Gurlick had built. However, it bore the same relation to the original as a superheterodyne receiver does to a twenty-cent home-rigged crystal set. Like its predecessor, it began, on the instant of its completion, to build another, more advanced version of itself.

CHAPTER 12

Tony Brevix and his wife and their four kids and the cat were moving. Tony drove the truck, a patched, rusted, flap-fendered quarter-ton panel truck with an immense transmission, a transmogrified rear end, and a little bitty motor that had rated 42 horsepower American when it was new, which was certainly not recently. In the truck were almost all of their household goods, carefully not packed in boxes, but stacked, folded, wadded and rodded down until the entire truck body was solid as a rubber brick. With Tony rode one and occasionally two of the children, who for children's mysterious reasons counted it a privilege to be subjected to the cold, the oil-smoke from the breather which came up through the holes under the floorboard, and the vehicle's strange slantwise gait as it carried its eightfold overload on only three ancient shock-absorbers. The cat did not ride in the truck, as there was no glass in the side windows.

Atty Brevix (her name, infuriatingly, was Beatitude, which made Batty and Titty and even, in the midst of an argument, Attitude) drove the station wagon, a long, hushed, low, overpowered this-year's dream-boat with lines as clean as those of a baseball bat and an appetite like a storm sewer. She drove with great skill and even greater trepidation, since she had misplaced her driver's license some weeks earlier and was convinced that this information was marked on the sides of their caravan as in neon lights. It had grown dark at the end of their second day on the road; they had taken a wrong turning and were miles away from their chosen track, although still going in the desired direction, and they began bitterly to regret their decision to make the remaining eighty miles in one jump rather than stop at a motel again. Nerves were raw, bladders acreak; two of the children were whining, two screaming, and four-year-old Sharon, who was always either talking or sleeping, blissfully slept. The cat set up a grating reiteration of one note, two of them every three seconds, while at a dead run it made the rounds of all glass areas of the station wagon, of which there were many. Every time it ran across Atty's shoulders she bit down on her back teeth until her jaw ached. The baby had wriggled clear of his lashing and was trying to stand up in the car-bed, so Atty drove with one hand on the wheel and one on his chest. Every time he sat up she pushed him down, and every time she pushed him down he screeched. In the truck Tony drove grimly, squinting through a windshield so spiderwebbed with scratches that oncoming lights made the whole thing totally opaque.

Carol, five and one of the weepers, and Billy, eight and a whiner, were the pair privileged to ride the truck, and while Billy described in incessant detail the food he wasn't getting, Carol cried steadily. It was a monotone bleat, rather like that of the cat, from whom she had probably learned it, and denoted no special sorrow but only an empty stomach. She would cease it completely at the first loom of light from an oncoming car, and announce the obvious: 'Here comes another one. Summon a *bish*. Summon a *bish*.'

And Billy would cease his listings ('Why *can't* I have a chocklit maltit? I bet I could drink three chocklit maltits. I bet I could drink four chocklit maltits. I bet I could drink five …') to say, 'Carol shoon't say summon a bish, Pop. Hey, *Pop!* Carol's sayin' summon a bish.'

And Tony would say, 'Don't say that, Carol,' whereupon the lights of the oncoming vehicle would be upon him, and in dedicated attention he would slit his eyes, set his jaw, and say precisely what Carol was trying to repeat.

Tony led, the car followed, it being somehow the male responsibility to find the right road. (They were not on the right road.) For some time he had been aware of the station wagon's headlights flashing on and off in his rear-view mirror. Each time he noticed it he cheerily flashed his own lights in acknowledgment, and kept going. After about an hour, the station wagon whisked by him like a half-heard insult and pulled in front, glaring at him with angry brake-lights. He did his best to stop in time, but Atty, though an excellent driver, had overlooked the detail of the load he was carrying, and the fact that stopping the wheels of the truck, and stopping the truck itself, were consecutive and not concurrent circumstances. In short, he ran into the back of the station wagon.

There was a moment of total cacophony. Tony closed his eyes, covered his ears, and let it pass him. He was then aware of an urgent tugging at his sleeve, and 'Pop! Pop!'

'Yes, Billy. Carol, shut up a minute.' Carol was wailing.

'You run into the station wagon, Pop.'

'I noticed that,' said Tony with heroic control.

'Pop …'

'Yes, Billy.'

'Why did you run into the station wagon?'

'Just felt like it, I guess.' He got out. 'You stay here and see if you can make Carol happy.'

'Okay, Pop.' To Carol, 'Shut up, mudface.' Carol's wail became an angry screech. Tony sighed and walked to the front of the truck. There was no breakage, just 'Bendage,' he murmured, and walked up to the driver's side of the station wagon. Atty was unpinning the baby. He thumped on the window and she rolled it down. She said something but he couldn't hear it. The noise in there was classic.

'What?' he shouted.

'I said, why didn't you stop?'

He glanced back vaguely at the crumpled front end of the truck. 'I *did*.'

'Here, hold him.' He held the baby under the armpits while she relieved him of several soggy fabrics. 'You might have killed all of us. Would you believe it, Sharon's still asleep. What do you think I was blinking my lights for?'

'I thought you just wanted to say hello.'

'I told you at the gas station to find some place along the road to stop so we could eat. Now everything's cold. Linda, you're six years old so *stop* that yelling!'

'What do you mean cold?'

'Our *din*ner. There's a sweet big boy, now you feel *much* better.' The baby screamed *much* louder.

'I didn't know we had any dinner. You must've bought it while I had Carol in the men's room. What'd you want me to take her in the men's room for anyway? It was awful. There was a guy pounding on the—'

'Hey, Mom!' This from Billy, who had ranged up behind Tony. 'You know what? Pop ran spang into the station wagon!'

'Get back in the truck.'

'Stay here, Billy. It's Sharon's turn to ride in the truck anyway. We're going to eat right here, right now.'

'Aw, gee, I didn't get to ride but a little tiny bit. Did you buy some choclit maltits, Mom? I bet I could drink seven—'

'Gosh, honey,' said Tony, 'let's go on at least until we find a place with some hot coffee and—'

'Is there a bathroom here?' demanded Linda at the top of her voice. 'I got to—'

'Yeh, and a bathroom,' finished Tony.

'I will not drive another inch with this hungry baby and these screaming children and my *back* hurts.'

'Well, I say let's go on,' said Tony firmly, and then wheedled, 'Come on, honey. You know you'll be glad you did.'

At that moment the cat, having reversed his orbit, caromed off the windshield and shot out the window as if he had been launched with boosters.

'You win,' said Tony. 'It'll take an hour to round him up. Where's that dinner?'

'Right here,' said Atty composedly. She reached back of the seat and '*Oh!*'

She gingerly lifted out a square white cardboard box and opened it. Tony said, 'What did you get?'

'Cheeseburgers,' said Atty in stricken tones, 'two with catchup and relish. Milk. Tomato juice. Dill pickles. Black coffee and rice pudding. And' – she peered down – 'blueberry pie. Here, dear. I'm not hungry.'

Tony thrust his head in a little farther and, in the glow from the dome light, gazed into the box. It took a moment for his eyes to orient, as sometimes happens with an unexpected close-up on a TV screen: what *is* that? and then he found himself looking down on what looked like the relief map of some justifiably forgotten, unwanted archipelago. In a sea of cold curdled milk and tomato juice was a string of hamburger islands on whose sodden beaches could be seen the occasional upthrust prow of a wrecked and sunken dill pickle. Just under the surface blueberries bobbed, staring up at him like tiny cataracted eyeballs. Over to the northeast, a blunt island of rice pudding gave up its losing battle and, before his eyes, disappeared under the waves.

'I'm not hungry either,' Tony said. Atty looked at him and tears started from her lids.

'I put it on edge,' she said, tapping the limp box. 'It seemed to take up so much room lying flat.' And suddenly she began to laugh.

'Whatcha got? Whatcha got?' demanded Billy, and when, wordless, his father had brought out the box, he happily plunged in with both grimy hands. 'Boy, oh boy, pickles ...'

They left it with him and began the complex process of getting the company's bladders wrung out in the roadside bushes.

The four-year-old, Sharon, woke contentedly in the back of the station wagon. She unwound her blanket and stretched. She was content; it had been a happy dream. She couldn't remember it, but it must have been a happy one because of the way she felt now. She lay drowsily listening to sounds near and far.

A wild scream, and 'Mommy! *Mom-meeee!* Billy frowed sand on my bottom!'

'Billy!'

Protestingly, 'No I din't she's a liar and I din't throw nothing I kicked it a little.'

Daddy: 'Honey, where's that little pack of Kleenex?'

Mommy: 'Carol's got it, dear. In the bushes.'

Daddy: 'Are you out of your MIND? The truck registration's in there!'

'Puss-puss-puss! Here, puss ...' Bang bang with a spoon on the cat's aluminum feeding dish.

Sharon became aware of the clean cool smell of fresh air, and the open tailgate near by. She slid silently out so that mean old Billy wouldn't see her and, clutching Mary Lou (an eyeless, naked, broken-footed, mattress-haired doll which was, above all things on earth, Sharon's most beloved), she slid into the dark bushes. 'Don't be 'fraid,' she told Mary Lou. 'It's the *friendly* dark.' She pressed on, stopped once to look back and be comforted at the beacon-like glow from the lights of the car and the truck, and then slipped over a ridge into velvety shadow, so dark that it seemed to be darkness itself that swallowed almost all sound from the road.

'Now that ol' Billy never find us,' said Sharon to Mary Lou.

At the road, Atty said to Tony, 'I don't feel tired, dear, just numb. Let's go all the way and get it over with.'

'Yeah. Maybe we can slide into a dog-wagon and get a hot cup of coffee while the kids sleep.'

'I wouldn't risk it,' said Atty positively. 'They'll sleep now and it will be quiet, and for the sake of a little quiet I can stand an empty stomach. I've had a belly full.'

'Yes, dear,' said Tony. 'So we'll drive all the way. Next stop, the new house.'

Later, in the truck, Linda said sleepily, 'Isn't it Sharon's turn with me in the truck, Daddy?'

And Tony squinted into the windshield and said, 'Hmm? Sharon? Oh, she slept through the whole thing.'

And in the station wagon, Billy called, 'Hey, Mom, where's Sharon?'

Atty said, 'Shh. The baby's asleep. It's Sharon's turn to ride with Daddy. Go to sleep.'

At which time Sharon stood on the ridge, turning round and round and looking for the guiding loom of lights. There was none, not anywhere but in the changing canyons of the cloudy sky where the stars peeped through. Turning and turning, Sharon lost the road, and herself was lost.

'Reely, it's the friendly dark,' she shakily assured her doll. In the friendly (oh please be friendly) dark, she began to walk carefully, and after a while she heard running water.

CHAPTER 13

When Gurlick fell asleep, the thing he had built was a tangle of components, possessing (to any trained terrestrial eye) a certain compelling symmetry and an elaborate uselessness (but how useless would a variable frequency oscillator seem to a wise bushman or a savage from Madison Avenue?); but when he awoke, the picture was different. Very different.

What Gurlick had built was not, in actuality, a matter receiver, although it acted as if such a thing were a possibility. It was, rather, a receiver and amplifier for a certain 'band' in the 'thought spectrum' – each of these terms being analogous and general. The first receiver, and its be-Gurlicked attachments, turned information into manipulation, and constructed from the elemental samples Gurlick had supplied it a second and much more efficient machine of far greater capacity. This in turn received and manipulated yet a third receiver and manipulator; and this one was a heavy-duty device. The process was, in essence, precisely that of the sailor who takes a heaving-line to draw in a rope which brings him a hawser. In a brief span of hours, machines were making machines to use available matter to make machines which would scout out and procure locally unavailable matter, which was returned to the site and used by other machines to make yet others, all specialized, and certain of these in immense numbers.

Gurlick came unbidden out of that dream, where he sat on the bank on the pile of clothes, shiny black and red and an edge of lacy white, and was greeted *(Hello, Handsome)* by her who so boldly (after he refused to go away) began to come up out of the water, slowly and gleaming in the sunlight, the water now down to her waist, and as she began to smile – he awoke in the midst of an incredible clanking city. Around him were row upon row of huge blind machines, spewing forth more machines by the moment: tanklike things with long snake necks and heads surrounded by a circlet of trumpets; silver balls ten feet in diameter which now and then would flick silently into the air, too fast to be believed, too silent; low, wide, massive devices which slid snail-like along roads of their own making, snouted with projectors which put out strange beams which would have been like light if they were not cut off at the far end as if by an invisible wall; and with these beams sniffing along the rocks, some of which trembled and slumped; and then there would be a movement up the beam to the machine, and from behind the machine silvery ingots were laid like eggs while fine cold dust gouted off to the side.

Gurlick awoke surrounded by this, blinking and staring stupidly. It was some minutes later that he realized where he was – atop a column of earth, ten feet in diameter and perhaps thirty feet high. All around for hundreds of yards the ground had been excavated and ... used. At the edge of his little plateau was a small domed box which, when his eye fell on it, popped open and slid a flat bowl of hot, mushlike substance toward him. He picked it up and smelled it. He tasted it, shrugged, grunted, raised the bowl to his lips and dozed its contents into his mouth with the heel of his hand. Its warmth in his belly was soothing, then puzzling, then frightening, the way it grew. He put his hands to his belt-line, and abruptly sat down, staring at his numb and disobedient legs. Dazed, he looked out across the busy scene and saw approaching him a stilted device with endless treads for feet and a turtlelike housing, perhaps a dozen feet in diameter. It straddled his imprisoning column of earth, achieving a sort of mechanical tiptoe, and the carapace began to descend over him and all his perch like a great slow candle-snuffer. He now could not speak, nor could he sit up any longer; he fell back and lay helpless, staring up and silently screaming ...

But as the device, its underside alive with more wriggling tool-tipped limbs than has a horseshoe crab, slowly covered him he was flooded with reassurance and promise, a special strength (its specialty: to make him feel strong but in no wise be strong) and the nearest thing to peace that he had ever known. He was informed that he was to undergo a simple operation, and that it was good, oh, good.

CHAPTER 14

Who has sent me to Massoni, and Massoni to me, Guido? Is all my life, everything in it lost, glad, hungry, weary, furious, hopeful, hurt – is it planned to lead me to Massoni and Massoni to me? Who has curved the path he treads, all the places he has been and things he has done, to meet mine and travel it?

Why could he not be a policeman like other police, who begin with a crime and follow the criminal forward to his arrest, instead of backward and backward until the day he was born? He has asked and asked, smelling my cold, old footprints from here to Ancona and from Ancona to Villafresca and from there back and back to the house of the Corfu shepherd, Pansoni. He will find nothing there because the house is gone, Pansoni dead, the sheep slaughtered, the trail cold. But, finding nothing there, he has leaped backward in time to find me arriving there as an infant, and back and back through the orphanage and everywhere else, until he sees me carried whistling out of the bomb ruins near Anzio.

Perhaps he needs to find nothing more about me. He has found what no one else has known … I may not have known it myself … the thread that runs through all I have done. Who could have known that cutting the hard black hose by the bus wheel, stamping the old man's legs against the curbstone, throwing the kerosene rags into the print shop – all were … acts of … music?

I moan and hump myself backward to the dark climbing space behind the wall, and fall scrabbling down and backward to floor level. I press aside the loose plywood and stand shaking, aching in the room. I am caked with dried sweat and dirt; cold, hungry, frightened. I hobble to the door, beginning to sob again, that soft bouncing *staccato*. It frightens me more. The iron door is locked. I am still more frightened. I shake the door and then run away from it and sink down on my knees by the bed, looking up, right, left, to see what is after me.

What could be after me?

I look under the bed. It is there, the black leather cheek of the violin case. The violin is after me.

Kill it, then.

I put my hand under the bed, a thumb-tip at the bottom, fingertips at the top, just enough to hold, as if the thing were going to be hot. I draw it out. It is not hot. The sound it makes, scraping along the rough concrete floor, is like the last water shouting and belching down a drain, and when it stops I hear the strings faintly ringing.

I open a steel clasp at the side. Once I am running from someone and hide in a dark cellar; I go around a heap of fallen timbers and back into a dark corner; behind me a rat squeaks once and leaps at me and, as I duck, scratches my shoulder and neck and I hear its yellow fangs come together as it squeaks again: *squeak-click!* all at once. Now in the dark silence the clasp of the violin case squeak-clicks just the same, and I feel the same blinding flash of terror. I kneel limp by the bed, wait until the heart-thunder goes out of my ears.

I do not want to see this violin; with all my soul I do not, and like someone watching a runaway truck bear down on a dog in the street, helpless and horrified, I kneel there and watch my hands lift the case and set it on the bed, open the other two clasps, turn back the lid.

Sheep gut, horse hair, twigs and shingles.

I put out a finger, slip it under the neck, lift the violin up far enough to rest half out of the case, take away my finger and look at it. It weighs nothing. It makes a sound as I lift it, like the distant opening of a door. I look at the pegs, and they take my eye along to the scroll, down, up, around, around again, around to spin dizzily somewhere down in the shining wood. I put my hands over my face and kneel there shaking.

Guido moves like the night wind – Massoni said it himself. Guido is a natural thing, like holocaust, like hurricane, and no one knows where he will strike next. Guido fears nothing.

Then why crouch here like a fascinated bird staring into the jaws of a serpent? The violin will not bite. The violin is nothing to fear. It is mute now; it is only when it makes music that—

Is music something to fear?

Yes, oh yes.

Music is a pressure inside, welling up and ready to burst out and fill the room, fill the world; but let a note of it escape and *blam!* the hard hand of Pansoni, the Corfu shepherd, bruises the music back into the mouth, or clubs down hard on the nape, so that you pitch forward and lie with your mouth full of sand and speckles of pain dancing inside the eyeballs. Pansoni can hear music before it is born, lying like too much food just under the solar plexus; and there he will kick you before ever a note can escape. Be six years old, seven, and tend the sheep in the rocky hills, you alone with the stones and the wind and the soft filthy silly sheep; sit on a crag and sing all the notes he has crushed in his hut, and he will come without a sound and slip up behind you and knock you spinning and sliding down the mountain.

And in time you learn. You learn that to hum is to ask for that ready hard hand, to whistle a note is to be thrown out into the cold night and to cower there until daylight without a crust to eat. You feel the music rising within you and before it can sound its first syllable you look up and his bright black eyes are on you, waiting. So ... you learn that music is fear, music is pain ... and deep, deep underneath, waiting until you are tall as a man and almost strong as a man, music is revenge; music is anger. You understand Pansoni, why he does these things. Pansoni knows that the music in you is remarkable – that is to say, noticeable, and there is that about Pansoni which strikes down whatever is noticeable as soon as it shows itself. Pansoni will not risk rumors in the countryside of the shepherd's boy who can sing any aria from any opera, whistle an entire violin concerto after hearing it once. Pansoni is a smuggler. Pansoni and his sheep and his boy Guido cannot be seen against the brown rocks and shadows of the seaside hills, and he will naturally extinguish, in this music-dyed map on which we crawl, the mighty beacon of melody which waits in the breast and brain of his ragged, beaten Guido.

Never look back, never look back, and damn you, Massoni, damn you, violin, you have made me look back!

I take my hands from my face and look at the violin. It has not moved nor spoken, nor has the scroll unfurled, nor the strings loosed themselves to reach for me like tentacles. My one finger lifted it and put it so, half out of its bed. It is only obedient, and ... and beautiful ...

I get to my feet. How long have I knelt there? My knee hurts, my foot is asleep. I take up the violin. It weighs nothing. My hand on its neck is at home; the smooth wood snugs down into my palm like part of the flesh. I squeeze it; it is strong and unyielding, not at all as fragile as it ought to be.

Squeezing it has brought the sound-box end close to me; I let it come and it touches my shoulder, throat, chin. Someone has intimately known the curve of my chin and left jaw; I turn my head a fraction, raise the fingerboard a fraction, and my chin and the ebony rest are one. I stand holding the violin like this for a long time, overcome with amazement, so much that there is no room for fear. I become aware of my chest, expanded as if to utter a note to be heard round the earth, my feet placed apart and ready to balance me when with my music I tilt the world. It is a sort of flight; my weight diminishes, my strength increases.

I take up the bow, thumb here, here the index and second fingers, the little finger straight and rigid and angling down as a prop to bear all the weight of the bow. Up elbow, down shoulder a bit ... there: so if there is a plank across shoulder, elbow, wrist and a full glass on it, not a drop is spilled.

I balance there a long time, until the muscles of shoulder and back begin to pain me. It comes to me that this is the hurting of weariness but not of strain, and to me, strangely, this knowledge is a glory.

I take down the bow, I take down the violin, I stand with one in each hand looking at them. I have not made a sound with them, but I will. A door has opened and let in music. A door has opened and let out fear. I need not make a note with this instrument to discover whether or not the dead hand of Pansoni will strike. If it took a note of music to be sure, then I would not be sure; I would fear him still. I have become *that* free: it need not be tested.

Massoni has given me the lesson, Massoni has given me my freedom. I am grateful to Massoni now, and will do him this service: since the prevention of my crimes and the release of my terror of anything musical are things which come first with him (for is he not first a thinking policeman and only second a violinist?) I shall permit him to give me also his violin. Thank you, Massoni: thank you; it is a wondrous change you have brought about in Guido.

I find a stiff sharp knife among Massoni's things, and a piece of iron wire, and in time – more time than this usually takes me, but then I am not as I was – I get the door unlocked.

I put the violin in its case and put the case under my flapping old trench coat, and I take my leave of Massoni and all things which have brought him into my life. For this violin, this spout for the music which boils within me, I have exchanged all other things I have been and done.

I shall kill anyone who tries to take it away from me.

CHAPTER 15

The spore, the 'raisin' which Gurlick had eaten, had been life or its surrogate. It had traversed space physically, bodily, and it had finished its function and its capabilities with its invasion of Gurlick. But the transfer of the life-essence of all the Medusa into all of humanity was something that earth-built machines – even if built on earth by others – could not accomplish. Only life can transmit life. A very slight alteration indeed – an adjustment of isotopes in certain ionized elements in Gurlick's ductless glands – would make the membership of humanity in the corpus of the Medusa a certainty. The machines now abuilding would effectively restore (the Medusa still unswervingly operated from a conviction that this was a restoration) the unity of the human species, its hive-mind, so that each 'person' could reach, and be reached by, all persons; but the fusion with the Medusa would be Gurlick's special chore, and would take place on the instant that his seed married with the ovum of a human female. As the machine slowly closed over him, its deft limbs already performing the first of a hundred delicate manipulations, it caught up his dream and congratulated him on it, and gave it detail and depth which his creative poverty had never made possible to him before, so that he lived it realer than real, from the instant of approach (and a degree of anticipation which might have destroyed him had he felt it earlier) to the moments of consummation, so violent they shook the earth and sent the sky itself acrinkle with ripples of delighted color. And more: for in these tactile inventions there was no human limitation, and it was given to him to proceed again, and yet again, without exhaustion or dulling familiarity, either through the entire episode or through any smallest part of it, whether it be the thrill of seeing the clothes (shiny black and scarlet, and the tumbled frosting of lace-edged white) or the pounding, fainting climax. Always, too, was the laughing offhand promise that *any* conquest of Gurlick's would be such a peak, or a higher one; let him wallow in his dream because he loved it, but let him understand also that it was only one of many, the symbol of any, the quality of all.

So while it built its machines to fuse ('again') the scattered psyche of humanity, it got Gurlick – good – and – ready.

CHAPTER 16

The warrior Mbala caught his thief perhaps an hour after he fell asleep squatting in the inky shadows of the astralagus vetch which encircled his yam patch. His assegai had fallen across his legs, and he was deep in that vulnerable torpor taught him by fear and weariness, so perhaps it really was the shade of his father, watching over the yam garden, who made the capture. Or that other powerful ghost men call Justice. Whatever the instrument, the thief walked out of the yam patch in the impenetrable dark and stepped so close to the sleeping warrior that his foot landed under the horizontal butt of Mbala's assegai. His other foot swung past the end of the shaft, and the first foot left the ground and caught the spear with its instep. The thief went flat on his face and the assegai snapped up and with great enthusiasm rapped Mbala painfully on the bridge of the nose.

In unison the two men squalled in terror, and then training dictated the outcome. The thief, who for most of his years had lifted nothing but other people's property, and that at irregular intervals, scrambled and slipped and fell flat again. Mbala, whose reflexes always placed action before conjecture, was up out of a sound sleep and a remaining cloud of stupidity-withdrawal, uttering a curdling battle screech, and plunging his assegai into his prostrate enemy's back before he was at all consciously aware. The prone man shrieked in agony, but it was the wrong shriek, as well as the wrong impact felt by Mbala's schooled hands. Apparently there had been enough stupidity left in that blazing moment to cause Mbala to handle his weapon as it lay, so that it was not the wide, long blade which presented itself to the thief's shoulders, but the bruising end of the shaft.

'Mbala! Mbala! Don't kill me! I am your brother, Mbala!'

Mbala, about to whirl his weapon end for end and settle the matter, checked himself and drove the haft down again. His prisoner, attempting to rise, fell flat again.

'Nuyu!'

'Yes, Nuyu, your own brother, your own dear brother. Let me up, Mbala! I haven't done anything to you!'

'I'm standing on a bag of yams,' growled Mbala. 'For that you die, Nuyu.'

'No! No, you can't! I am the son of the brother of your father! Your father wants me spared!' Nuyu screamed. 'Did he not turn your spear wrong-end-to when you first struck at me? Well, didn't he?' Nuyu insisted when Mbala seemed to hesitate.

Fury and disillusion made Mbala say, 'My father is gone from here.' He shifted suddenly, literally vaulting from his stance beside the prone man to one astride him, facing the feet, with his own heelbones pressing the fleshy part of the armpits flat to the ground. In pitch darkness it was done with amazing accuracy. In the moment when the warrior's weight was on the spear and pivoting, Nuyu uttered a short shrill scream, thinking his moment had come. As the rock-hard heels captured his armpits he grunted and arched his back and began flailing his legs.

'Uncle! Uncle! *Uncle!*'

Mbala reversed his spear at last. 'Hold still,' he said irritably. 'You know I can't see.'

'U-Un – cle!'

'*Now* you call on him. *Now* you fear the demon. *Now* you believe, eh, thief?' Mbala taunted. By touch alone, he drew the needle point across the man's kidneys, barely enough to part the skin. Nuyu squalled abominably and began to weep. 'Uncle, uncle ...' he sobbed and then abruptly was silent and motionless.

Mbala knew that trick well and was prepared for it, but when he began to see his shadow stretching away, lumping across the vetch and lost in the thorns, he forgot about trickery.

'Uncle ...' Nuyu moaned ... There was a new note to his weeping; hope, was it? And something else?

Nuyu lay with his head toward the yam patch, Mbala stood with his back to it. The patch was roughly circular, with the tubers scattered randomly in it. A thick rim of the vetch bushes bordered it back to the thorns. Almost exactly at the four midpoints of the compass stood four ship's prow monoliths. The mound on which the patch lay must at one time have been an almost conical rock mount, before some forgotten cataclysm split it exactly in two, northeast to southwest, and again in two, northwest to southeast. Settling and erosion had widened the crossed canyons until they took the form which Mbala's dead father had found. In the native language the place was called Giant's Mouth, and it was said that a man's shout from the center of the yam patch could be heard for a day's journey in every direction.

'Uncle, oh uncle,' Nuyu wept, with such a passion in his voice that Mbala bent curiously to look at him. He was bending his head back and up at an almost impossible angle, and his eyes strained at the roofs of their sockets. His dark face was ... silver.

Mbala sprang away from him, whirling about in the air. He came down crouching, staring up at the silver ball which floated down the sky. It halted perhaps ten feet above the center of the yam patch and stayed motionless.

Nuyu made a sound. Mbala glanced quickly down at him and, without understanding why, without trying to, he bent and helped the other man to his feet. They stood close together, watching.

'Like a moon,' Mbala murmured. He glanced at the silvered landscape and back again to the object. It had a brilliant, steady radiance, which fantastically left no after-image on the retina.

'He came,' said the thief. 'I called him and he came.'

'It might be a demon.'

'You doubt your own father?'

Mbala said, 'Father …' And the sphere sank to the center of the yam patch. Then it opened.

There were doors completely around the object, all hinged at their upper edges, so that when they opened they formed a sort of awning all around the sphere. A beam of light fanned out to the north, but it was like no light Mbala had ever seen. It was mauve with flickers of green, and though the air was clear and the walls of the crossed canyons brilliantly lighted by the sphere, it was impossible to see through the beam. Not only that, but the beam did not fade or spread from the source outward, and terminated as sharply as if it played on a wall, which it did not. This odd square end of the light beam pressed outward from the ship until it reached the margin of vetch, and nosed into it. There was a sound like water over rapids, hissing, churning, crackling. There almost seemed to be something moving back up the light beam into the ship, but one could not be sure.

The light pressed slowly outward through the vetch to the edge of the surrounding thorn trees and stopped. No, not stopped. It was scything away from them, moving slowly, and the square end was adjusting itself to the encroachments and retreats of the thorn.

Where it had passed the vetch was gone, and where it had been the bare ground was powdered with a white substance unlike anything they had ever seen. After a few minutes it changed and the ground seemed moist.

'Can you doubt now?' murmured Nuyu. 'Who but your father would clear your land?'

They stood in awe, watching the sphere clear the land. When it seemed reasonable to get out of its way they backed to the thorn and slipped through. If the sphere and its beam noticed them or their going, it made no sign. It just went on collecting and processing astralagus vetch, a weed with a high affinity for selenium. When it had all it could get from this pocket, it clicked shut, took a picture of the site, and leaped into the sky, where at ten thousand feet it switched on its sensors, located another patch of vetch to the north, and flashed away after the only thing it knew how to care about – selenium, from astralagus.

Mbala and Nuyu crept cautiously out on the new ground and looked around in the paling dawnlight. Nuyu touched the ground with his hand. It was wet, and cold. He saw some of the white material in a hole and picked it up. It disappeared in his hand leaving only a few drops of water. He grunted and wiped his hand on his kilt. What was another miracle at a time like this?

Mbala was still staring at the sky. Nuyu said, 'Will you kill me?'

Mbala brought his gaze down from the disappearing stars and gave it to Nuyu's face. He looked at it for a long while, and from all Nuyu could see there was no change in Mbala's expression at all; he looked at him as one will at distant lights. 'I lost my father,' he said at last, 'because he let my yarns be stolen. So I did not believe. But you believed, and he saved you, and he came back again. I will not kill you, Nuyu.'

'I died,' Nuyu breathed. 'Nuyu the unbeliever died when he saw your father.' He bent and picked up the sack of yams and extended them to Mbala.

'Nuyu the thief died,' said Mbala. 'The yams are yours and mine, forever in tomorrow and forever in yesterday. There has been no thief, then, Nuyu.'

They went back to the kraal to tell the women they would have a lot of new work tomorrow. As Nuyu passed the witch doctor, the old man reached out unseen and touched Nuyu's kilt. Then the witch doctor held the touching hand in his other, and hugged them against his chest. What he got from Nuyu he could have gotten from his mere presence. He knew that, but nevertheless he touched the kilt. The touch was a symbol the old man needed, and so he took and treasured it. He said to Mbala, 'Your demon is dead, then.'

At that Mbala and Nuyu smiled at one another, the devout and the convert, richly content with faith, and full of wonder.

CHAPTER 17

Gurlick lay hooded and unaware, passive under the submicroscopic manipulations of the machine which brought his special membership in the Medusa to his seed. So he did not observe the change in the mighty operations around him, when the egg-laying snail-gaited miners drew in and darkened the snouts of light, and fell neatly apart to have their substance incorporated in other, more needed machines; and these in turn completed their special tasks and segmented and dispersed to others which still needed them, until at last there remained only the long-necked, tank-treaded, trumpet-headed ones, and enough silver spheres to carry them, in their multi-thousands, to their precisely mapped destinations. There was no provision for failure, for there would be no failure. The nature of the electroencephalograph, and of its traces, clearly showed to the transcendent science of the Medusa exactly what was lacking in the average mind which kept it from being a common mind. The net would be comparatively simple to cast and draw shut, for it found the potent base of the hive mentality alive and awaiting it, showing itself wherever humans blindly moved in the paths of other humans, purely because other humans so moved; wherever friends apart impulsively sat down to write one another simultaneous letters, wherever men in groups (cartels, committees, mobs, and nations) divided their intelligence by their numbers and let that incredible quotient chart their course. The possible or probable nature of a human hive, once (re)established, was a question hardly explored, because it was hardly important. Once united, humanity would join the Medusa, because the Medusa always (not almost, not 'in virtually every case,' but *always*) infused the hives it touched.

So the factory-area rumbled to silence, and the noiseless spheres swept over the storage yard and scooped up their clusters of long-necked projectors, fell away up with them, flashed away to all the corners of earth, ready to place the projectors wherever their emanations (part sound, part something else) would reach masses of humans. They could not reach all humans, but they would reach most, and the established hive would then draw in the rest. No human would escape, none could; none would want to. Then, somewhere in this flawless, undivided, multi-skilled entity, Gurlick would plant a tiny fleck of himself, and at the instant of fusion between it and a living ovum, the Medusa would spread through it like crystallization through a supersaturated solution.

CHAPTER 18

Sharon Brevix squatted on the dry part of a stony stream bed, dying. It was the second night, and she hadn't come to the ocean or a city or any people at all. Billy had told her that lost people just have to find a river and go downstream and they'll be all right, because all the rivers flow into the sea and there's always a town or people there. She had started downstream as soon as it was light on the first morning. It never occurred to her to stay where she was until she heard a car, because she must certainly still be near the road, and a car had to come by eventually. She did not reason that when she traveled the stream bed for the first hour and it did not bring her to the road, it must therefore be leading her away from it.

She was, after all, only four years old.

By ten in the morning she was aching hungry, and by noon it was just awful. She whimpered and stopped for a while to cry hard, but after a time she got up again and kept on. The ocean couldn't be terribly far away after a person walks so far. (It was another twelve hundred miles, but she could not know that.) In the afternoon she had slept for a while, and when she awoke she found some wild raspberries on a bush. She ate all she could find until she was stung by a yellowjacket and ran away screaming. She found her little stream again and kept on going until it was dark.

Now it was very late and she was dying. She felt better than she had, because she felt nothing at all very much, except hungry. The hunger had not diminished with her other sensations, but it had the virtue of blanketing them. Fear and cold and even loneliness were as unnoticeable, in the presence of that dazzle of hunger, as stars at noon. In the excitement of packing, and on the two days of traveling, she had eaten little, and she had rather less to fall back on than most four-year-olds, which is little enough.

It was after midnight, and her troubled sleep had long since turned into a darker and more dangerous condition. Cramped limbs no longer tingled, and the chilly air brought no more shivers. She slept squatting, with her back and side against a nook of rock. Later, she might topple over, very possibly too weak to move again at all but for some feeble squirmings. Yet—

She heard a sound, she raised her head. She saw what at first she thought was a Christmas tree ornament, a silver ball with a dangle of gewgaws under it, in midair a few inches from her face. She blinked and resolved it into something much larger, much farther away, coming down out of the night sky. She heard a snarling howl. She looked a little higher, and was able to identify the running lights of a small airplane streaking down out of the high overcast.

Sharon rose to her feet, holding the rock wall to steady herself while her congealed blood began to move. She saw the globe about to land on clear ground at the top of a knoll three miles away. She saw the airplane strike it dead center while it was still thirty feet off the ground, and then plane, globe, and cargo were a tangled, flaming ruin on the hill. She watched it until it died, and then lay down to finish her own dying.

CHAPTER 19

Just another rash of saucer-sightings, thought the few observers, and recipients of their observations, in the brief minutes left to them to think as they had always thought. Some of the military had, in these minutes, a harrowing perplexity. Anything tracked at such speeds as the radars reported, must, with small variations, appear somewhere along an extrapolated path; the higher the speed, the finer the extrapolation. The few recordings made of the flick and flash of these objects yielded flight-paths on which the objects simply did not appear. It was manifestly impossible for them to check and drop straight to their destinations at such velocities; they did, however, and before the theoreticians could finish their redefinition of 'impossible,' they and all their co-workers, colleagues, acquaintances, cohabitants, heirs and assigns were relieved of the necessity to calculate. It happened so quickly, one minute a heterogenous mass of seething noncommunicants; the next, the end of Babel.

Henry, five years old, slept as usual flat on his back and face straight up, arms rigid, fists clenched under, and pinned down by his buttocks, and his ankles together. He was having a nightmare, soundlessly, of being surrounded by gentle smiling fathers, some of whom wore the masks of the other kids in his class, and storekeepers, and passing puppy dogs, but who were really just smiling fathers, dressed up and being gentle at the very verge of exploding in his face; and between him and all the fathers was a loving goddess with soft hands full of forbidden lollipops and raisin-bread peanut-butter sandwiches to be passed to little boys in the dark when they had been sent to bed without their suppers because they were little cowards; this goddess was there to care for him and protect him, but when the explosion came, with this breath or the next or the one after, the puppies and children and grocers and fathers would whisk through to him as if the goddess weren't there at all; and while they did what they would do to him, she would still be there smiling and ready with guilty lollipops, not knowing what the fathers were doing to him ... And under this nightmare was the color of hopelessness, the absolute certainty that to awake from it would be to emerge into it; the dream and the world were one now, fused and identical.

CHAPTER 20

These were people, these are anecdotes, dwelt upon for their several elements of the extraordinary. But each man alive has such a story, unique unto himself, of what is in him and of its molding by the forces around him, and of his interpretations of those forces. Here a man sees a machine as a god, and there a man sees God as an argument; and another uses men's argument quite as if it were a tool, a machine of his own. For all his ability to work in concert with his fellows, and to induce some sympathy in their vibrations, man remains isolated; no one knows *exactly* how another feels. At the very climax of sensation, man approaches unconsciousness ... unconsciousness of what? Why, of all around him; never of himself.

These were people, there are anecdotes of the night the world ended; this the night when people the world over thought their thoughts and lived their lives and at long, long last were wrong in thinking that tomorrow was the front part of today, yesterday the back, and that the way to go on was to go on as before.

This was the night, and the very moment, when Paul Sanders rose from the couch, lifted Charlotte Dunsay in his arms, and said, 'Well if it isn't now, it never will be.' ...

When young Guido strode a pre-dawn Rome, his very bones aching with music and a carven miracle under his arm, waiting the ardent reach of his unshackled talent. No lover, no miser, no acolyte on earth loved money or woman or Master more than Guido loved this violin; no whelping fox or wounded water-buffalo so watchful for an enemy ...

When the cousins Mbala and Nuyu, the redeemed backslider and the convert, turned into a new and glorious day of faith and many yarns ...

When Henry, who was five, lay stiffly in his bed and sniffled through a dream of smiling cruelties in a place quite like all other places to him, where he was despised ...

When Dimity Carmichael's dutiful alarm preceded the sunrise and she rose in her sensible cotton gown and made ready, eyes averted, to take her morning shower ...

When Sharon Brevix entered the dusk and the dark of her second lost day without shelter or food ...

Only motes among the millions, remarked upon for that about them which is remarkable, yet different only insofar as each is different *from*, or is different *within*, the pattern of qualities possessed two and three quarter billion living times under this sun.

CHAPTER 21

He stood motionless with the girl in his arms, ready to put her down on the sofa; and then, without a start, without a word of wonderment, Paul Sanders set her on her feet and stood supporting her with a firm arm around her shoulders until her head cleared and she could stand alone.

There was nothing said, because there was in that moment nothing to be said. In a split second there was orientation of a transcendent nature – nothing as crude as mutual mind-reading, but an instant and permeating acknowledgment of relationships: I to you, we to the rest of the world; the nature of a final and overriding decision, and the clear necessity of instant and specific action. Together Paul Sanders and Charlotte Dunsay left her apartment. The hallway was full of people in all stages of dress – all moving wordlessly, purposefully. No one paid Charlotte, in her transparent gown, the slightest attention.

They walked to the elevator bank. She paused before it with a half dozen other people, and he opened the door of the fire stairs and sprang up them two at a time. Emerging on the roof, he went to the kiosk which sheltered the elevator motor and cables, twisted off the light padlock with one easy motion, opened the door, and entered. He had never been here before in his life; yet without hesitation he reached to the left and scooped up a five-foot slice-bar which lay across the grating, and ran with it back down the fire stairs.

Without glancing at floor numbers, he left the fire stairs on the fourth floor, turned left and ran down the hall. The last door on the right opened as he reached it; he did not glance at the old lady who held it for him, nor did she speak. He sped through a foyer, a living room, and a bedroom, opened the window at the far right and climbed out.

There was a narrow ledge on which he could barely keep his balance and carry the heavy bar as well, yet he managed it. The chief enemy of a balancing man is the poison of fear which permeates him: I'll fall! *I'll fall!* but Paul felt no fear at all. He made a rapid succession of two-inch sidewise shuffles until he reached the big eyebolt from which there thrust, out and down, the huge chain supporting one end of a massive theater marquee. Here he turned sidewise and squatted, brought his bar up over his shoulder, and, reaching down, thrust the tip through the fourth link of the chain. Then he waited.

The street below – what he could see of it – seemed at first glance to be normally tenanted, with about as many people about as one might expect at this hour of a Saturday night. But then it could be seen that nobody *strolled – everyone* walked briskly and with purpose; one or two people ran, the way they ran indicating running to, not from anything. He saw Charlotte Dunsay across the street, swinging along on her bare feet, and enter a showroom where computing machines were on display. Though the place had been closed since noon, it was now open and lighted, and full of people silently and rapidly working.

There came a sound, and more than a sound, a deep pervasive ululation which seemed at first to be born in all the air and under the earth, sourceless. But as it grew louder, Paul heard it more from his left, and finally altogether from the corner of the building. Whatever was making that sound was crawling slowly up the street to take its place at the intersection, a major one where three avenues crossed. Patiently, Paul Sanders waited.

CHAPTER 22

From his soundless nightmare, Henry soundlessly awoke. He slid out of bed and trotted out of his room, past his parents' open door – they were awake, but he said nothing, and if they saw him, they said nothing either. Henry padded down the stairs and out into the warm night. He turned downtown at a dog-trot, and ran for three blocks south, one west, and two south. He may or may not have noticed that while the traffic lights still operated, they were no longer obeyed by anyone, including himself. Uncannily, cars and pedestrians set their courses and their speeds and held them, regardless of blind corners, passing and repassing each other without incident and with no perceptible added effort.

Henry had been aware for some time of the all but subsonic hooting and of its rapid increase in volume as he ran. When he reached the big intersection, he saw the source of the sound on the same street he ran on, but past the corner where the theater stood. It was a heavy tanklike machine, surmounted by a long flexible neck on top of which four horns, like square megaphones or speakers, emitted the sound. The neck weaved back and forth, tilting the horns and changing their direction in an elaborate repetitive motion, which had the effect of adding a slow and disturbing vibrato to the sound.

Henry dashed across the street and under the side-street marquee. He came abreast of the thing just as it was about to enter the intersection. Without breaking stride, Henry turned and dove straight into the small space between the drive-spindle of the machine's tread and its carrier rollers. His blood spouted, and on it the spindle spun for a moment; the other track, still driving, caused the machine to swerve suddenly and bump up on the sidewalk under the marquee.

Paul Sanders, at the very instant the child had leapt, and before the small head and hands entered the machine's drive, leaned out and down and jammed the chisel point of his slice-bar hard through the fourth link of the chain. Plunging outward, his momentum carried the bar around the chain and, as his weight came upon it, gave the chain a prodigious twist. The eyebolt pulled out of the building wall with a screech, and the corner of the marquee sagged and then, as the weight of the chain came upon it, and Paul Sanders's muscular body with it, the marquee let go altogether and came hammering down on the machine. In a welter of loose bricks, sheet-tin, movie-sign lettering and girders, the machine heaved mightily, its slipping treads grating and shrieking on the pavement. But it could not free itself. Its long neck and four-horned head twitched and slammed against the street for a moment, and then the deep howl faded and was gone, and the head slumped down and lay still.

Four men ran to the wreckage, two of them pushing a dolly on which rode an oxyacetylene outfit. One man went instantly to work taking measurements with scale, micrometer and calipers. Two others had the torch going in seconds and fell to work testing for a portion of the machine which might be cut away. The fourth man, with abrasive rasps and a cold chisel, began investigating the dismantling of the thing.

And meanwhile, in unearthly silence and with steady determination, people passed and repassed, on foot, in cars, and went about their business. No crowd collected. Why should it? Everybody *knew*.

The entire village population, with Mbala and Nuyu at their head and the witch doctor following, were within two hundred yards of Mbala's yam patch when the thing came down from the sky. It was broad daylight here, so the ghostly-luminous moonlit effect was missing; but the shape of the projector as it dangled by invisible bonds from the sphere was unprecedented enough to bring a gasp of astonishment and fear from the villagers. Mbala stopped and bowed down and called his father's name, and all the people followed suit.

The sphere dropped rapidly to the yam patch, which, judging from the photograph taken by the selenium miner, seemed an ideal position for a projector to land, to send forth its commanding, mesmerizing waves.

The sphere set down its burden and started up again without pause, swift as a bouncing ball. The projector began its wavering bass hooting which swept out through the echoing clefts of the great split rock, rolled down upon the villagers, and silenced their chant as if it had blotted it up.

There was a moment – mere seconds – of frozen inaction, and then half the warriors turned as one man and plunged away through the jungle. The rest, and all the women and children, drew together, over four hundred of them, and poured swiftly up the slope toward the yam patch. No one said a word or made a sound; yet when they choked the space between two of the stone steeples, half the people ran into the clearing, skirting its edge, while half squatted where they were, blocking their avenue from side to side. The runners reached the north opening, filled it, and also squatted, wordless and waiting.

Directly across from the first group, in the westward opening, there was movement as one, two, a dozen, a hundred heads appeared, steadily and quietly approaching. It was the Ngubwe, neighboring villagers with whom there was a tradition, now quiescent, of wife-stealing and warfare going back to the most ancient days. Mbala's people and the Ngubwe, though aware of each other at all times, were content to respect each other's privacy and each cultivate his own garden, and for the past thirty years or so there had been room enough for everybody.

Now three openings to the rock-rimmed plateau were filled with squatting, patient natives. Even the babies were silent. For nearly an hour there was no sound but the penetrating, disturbing howl of the projector, no motion but its complex, hypnotic pattern of weavings and turnings. And then there was a new sound.

Blast after shrill blast, the angry sound approached, and the waiting people rose to their feet. The women tore their clothes to get bright rags, the men filled their lungs and emptied them, and filled them again, getting ready.

Through the open southern gateway four warriors erupted, howling and capering. Hard on their heels came a herd of furious elephants, three, four – seven-nine in all, one old bull, two young ones, four cows and two calves, distraught, angry, goaded beyond bearing. The fleeing warriors separated, two to the right, two to the left, sprinted to and disappeared in the crowds waiting there. The big bull trumpeted shrilly, wheeled, and charged to the right, only to face nearly two hundred shrieking, capering people. He swerved away, his momentum carrying him along the rock wall and to the second opening, where he met the same startling cacophony. The other elephants, all but one young bull and one of the calves, thundered along behind him, and when he drew up as if to wheel and attack the second group, he was pounded and pressed from behind by his fellows. By now quite out of his mind, he put up his trunk, turned his mighty shoulders against those who pressed him, and found himself glaring at this noisy, shining thing in the center of the clearing.

He shrieked and made for it. It moved on its endless treads, but not swiftly enough, nor far enough, nor in enough places at once to avoid the tons of hysteria which struck it. The elephants tore off its howling head and its neck in three successive broken bits, and shouldered it over on its side and then on its back. The howling stopped with deafening suddenness when the head came off, but the tracks kept treading the air for minutes after it was on its back.

Elephants were used in Berlin, too, on the machine which landed in the park near the famous zoo, though this was a more disciplined performance by trained animals who did exactly as they were told. In China a projector squatted in a cleft in the mountains under a railroad trestle, and began hooting into the wind. An old nomad with arthritis hobbled out of the rocks and pulled two spikes, shifted one rail. A half mile down the track, the engineer and fireman of a locomotive pulling a combination passenger-freight train with over four hundred people aboard, wordlessly left their posts, climbed back over the tender, and uncoupled the locomotive from the first car. There was, on the instant, a man at every handwheel on the train. It coasted to a stop, while far ahead the locomotive thundered over the edge of the trestle and was crushing the projector before the alien machine could move a foot.

In Baffin Land a group of Eskimo hunters stood transfixed, watching a projector squatting comfortably on mounded and impassable pack ice and, in the crisp air, bellowing its message across the wastes to the ears of four and possibly five widely scattered settlements. The hunters had not long to wait; high above the atmosphere a mighty Atlas missile approached, and, while still well below their horizon, released a comparatively tiny sliver, the redoubtable Hawk. The little Hawk came shrieking out of the upper air, made a wide half-circle to kill some of its excess velocity, and then zeroed in on the projector with the kind of accuracy the old-time Navy bombardiers would brag about: 'I dropped it right down his stack.'

From then on missiles got most of the projectors, though in crowded areas, other means were found. In Bombay a projector took its greatest toll – one hundred and thirty-six, when a mob simply overran one of the machines and tore it to pieces with their bare hands. And in Rome one man despatched four of them and came out of it unscathed.

(A man?)

(Unscathed?)

CHAPTER 23

I am Guido, walking the back ways and the dark paths leading out of the city, to a place where this glossy glory of a violin can make itself known to me. No human soul will hear me coax a squeak out of it, or I will kill him for knowing of it. I will kill anyone who harms it, or who tries to take it from me. This city will no longer know Guido or see Guido, and it must get along for a while without Guido's small protests against music. Against music ... Listen now, someone is singing under the sliver of moon, far away, a little drunk ... No, God, that's the shift whistle at the auto place. Now wait, wait, stop and listen ...

I stop and look down the hill, across to the other hill, and I listen as I have never listened before, and I make a great finding, one of those large things you come to know while realizing that others have always known it. How many, many times have I heard a man say wind *sings* in the wires, a *musical* waterfall, the *melody* in certain laughter. But in fighting music all these years, I have not known, I have not let myself hear all these words, nor the music which is their meaning.

I hear it now, because through owning this violin, something has happened to me. I hear the city singing while it sleeps, and I hear a singing which would sweetly cry among these hills if the city had never existed, and will cry here when it is gone.

It is as if I have new ears, yes, and a new mind and heart to go with them. I think, in the morning, when this world wakes, oh, I shall hear, I shall hear ... and I lose the thought for its very size, thinking about what I am to hear from now on.

I go on to my hiding place. Guido's studio, I think, laughing. When they built the new highway into the city, they cut away the end of a crooked, narrow little street which used to climb the hill. Right at the top were two small houses, built Italian land style, four square stone walls which they filled with earth, then lay a four-sided dome of plaster on the earth, then dug away the earth when the plaster was hardened. These little houses will stand for a thousand years. The two I know of were buried by the embankment of the new road, where it comes near the hilltop on its stilts and curves across to the other hill. I found the houses when I escaped once from the police. I leaped from the police car and off the road, and down the embankment I put my leg in a hole, and the hole was a window. The second house is behind the first, buried completely, but there is a door between them. Two rooms in a hillside, and nobody knows but Guido.

I walk the new road, where it sweeps up to the hilltop, looking out over the city and hearing the city sing, and hearing that other music which will play, city or not, and it is all for me, for Guido. There is one thing which is not changed now: the world has always been against Guido, or Guido against the world; everything moved around Guido as its center. It still does, but while it does, it makes music. I laugh at this, waiting at the top of the slope for a gap in the traffic; always careful, I will not be seen dropping over the rail to the embankment below. I –

– hear a note and all sound, all singing stops for a moment; sight too, I think, and touch; a wave, a wrench, a great peace, and then I am back on the high road, holding the rail, clamping my violin case under my coat, looking at the sky. I am different. The ... meaning of 'I' is different ...

All across the city, like distant thunder heard in a high wind, there is a whisper of breaking metal, a twinkling of explosion and fire, and no music. To none of this do I pay attention; I am watching that which is slipping down out of the sky. A silver ball, and under it, four machines like tanks, their four long necks twined together, their four heads stacked neatly one on the other. But for the deep hooting which comes from these heads, they fall silently.

I take off my trench coat and let it fall. I open the violin case, take out the violin, strike the railing once with it, pull out the four pegs, clear away the strings with two quick swipes, until I hold only the smooth neck and fingerboard, which ends in the widening curled scroll.

I run downhill as fast as I can, faster than I have ever run before. I know I shall be met, by whom, how, and exactly when. It is an old Hispano-Suiza with wide flaring fenders and big yellow headlights, driven by a woman. I see the car coming, run straight down the middle of the road. She slows but does not stop. I leap to the front of the car, turn, hook a knee over the headlight brace, grasp the radiator ornament. She is already howling up the hill; faster she goes, and faster, all that mighty automobile can put out.

Acceleration pressure lessens and frees me; I move myself, get one foot on the hood and the other on the radiator, still holding with one hand to the headlight brace. It has all happened quickly; I have been riding perhaps twenty, twenty-five seconds. We are back to the top of the slope and traveling eighty, ninety kilometers ... who has made these observations and calculations as to our speed, the slope, the rate of descent of the globe and its machines, how close they must pass the rail? No matter who ... it has been done, and every slightest pull of her wrists, each lean and striving of my body against the wind, is part of those calculations; I know it, know it is right, without wonder and without astonishment ... for I have calculated it all; I know how; it must be right, I know so very well how. (And 'I' means something new now.)

She turns to the left and the front wheels shudder over the curb. I let go the brace and put my feet side by side on the radiator, and as the front of the car reaches the railing I spring up and out, flying as men have in their hearts always wished to fly … up and up into the dark. With my ears I know my speed, air rushing past, diminishing as I reach the top of my arc and begin to descend; it is in this poised moment that I meet the machines from the sky, with my left arm and both legs taking those intertwined metal necks. Below me the Hispano is turning end over end down the embankment.

I reach up with my violin neck, holding it by the flat protruding lower end of the ebony fingerboard, and find that with the other end, the hard curved polished scroll, I can reach the open trumpet mouth of the topmost head. It accepts the slight curve of the carving exactly; I ram it home, extract it, repeat the motion on the second, third, fourth, crushing some delicate something in the joined throats of each.

Then that pervasive hooting is gone, and we drift silently for a second – but only a second; we are on the ground near and between two of the stilts which support the road. A sort of curtain hangs there; as we touch earth, this curtain topples outward and falls across the globe. There are people – three women, four men. One of the men is old, and wears nothing but a wooden leg strapped to his thigh. One of the women wears an ermine jacket; the tall heels are broken off her shoes. They seize a rope and run, and drop a steel hook into the girders of the stilt. On the other side, a girl and a man, an impossibly fat man, place a hook on the other side. The hard fabric of the curtain smashes at me as I struggle free – it is one of those enormous woven mats of steel-cored hempen cable they use to cover rocks when dynamiting in the city. They have captured the globe with it, casting it like a net over birds! And the globe fights; it fights, plunging upward, making no sound. The net holds, the ropes hold; I hear the steel hooks crackle in the girders as they slip and grab. The plunging stops; the globe presses upward, trying and trying to break free. The anchor ropes hum, the net rustles with strain. I feel a warmth, a heat, from the globe; it drops abruptly, plunges upward once more, but weakly, and suddenly falls to the ground with the rope mat shrouding it and smoking. The four tanklike machines have not moved since they landed; with their voices gone they have no function.

The woman in ermine and the fat man run to a two-wheeled dolly standing under the roadway. I run to help them. Nobody speaks. It is an acetylene set. We drag it to the dead sphere and light it. We begin to cut the sphere open so that I – this new, wide, deep, all-over-the-world 'I' – can see what it is, how it works.

I – and 'I,' now, think as I work of what is happening – a different kind of thinking than any I have ever known ... if thinking was seeing, then all my life I have thought in a hole in the ground, and now I think on a mountaintop. To think of any question is to think of the answer, if the answer exists in the experience of any other part of 'I.' If I wonder why I was chosen to make that leap from the car, using all my strength and all its speed to carry me exactly to that point in space where the descending machines would be, then the wonder doesn't last long enough to be called that: I *know* why I was chosen, on the instant of wondering. Someone had measured the throat of one of the tank machines; someone knew what tool would fit it exactly and be right to destroy it most easily. The neck and scroll of my violin happened to be that tool, and I happened to be on the high road with it. I might have died. The woman driving the Hispano did die. These are things that do not matter; one will unhesitatingly break a fingernail in reaching to snatch a child from the fire.

Yet, as all knowledge of the greater 'I' is available to me, so is all feeling. The loss of my violin before I had made the first single note with it is a hurt beyond bearing; its loss in so important an action does not diminish the hurt at all. But to think of the hurt is to know all hurts, everywhere, of all of us who are now so strangely joined. Now there was a little boy in America, who when it was time threw himself into the drive of one of the tank machines because 'I' required that the drive slip just so much, just at that second. It is known to me now that the child Henry wanted hungrily to live, more than ever in his little life before, because he had, within the hour, experienced a half second of real peace. It hurt him, dying; knowing him as I (as 'I') do, it hurts to have him dead. Near him died a man, Paul, unhesitatingly, feeling the most pointed loss of a woman he desired to the moment he died, and whom he had almost possessed a moment before. There are many such deaths at this moment, all over the world, and not one which 'I' cannot feel; all are known to me – the helpless, so many of whom lie this minute crushed in their cars and houses, who crawl numbly away from the fires, not fast enough to get away. These are dying too, and hurting, and even these know Guido and Guido's loss; *Unfair, unfair,* they cry as they bleed and die; *you should not have lost your violin so soon!* All, all add themselves to me; all, all understand. I belong, belong; I, Guido, belong!

We have struck back with whatever would do the job, wherever it could be found, regardless of the cost, because no cost is too great to combat what has come upon us.

We will take care of our own; 'I' will defend 'myself.' And meanwhile the pressure of Guido's music floods 'me' and enriches the species, and Guido is enriched in numberless ways to an infinite degree. This is thinking as never before; this is living as never before; this is a life to be defended to a degree and in ways never before realized on this earth ... I wonder if anyone will ever speak again?

CHAPTER 24

Sharon Brevix thought, *I can see all over the world.* And she thought, *They've found me.*

You're four and you're lost: what bothers you? Hunger, cold, but mostly disorientation – detachment: not knowing where to go or where 'they' all are. Sharon awoke where she had dozed off ... rather, where she had slipped so very far over the slippery edge of the forever-dark. It was slippery no longer. She was hungry, she was cold, certainly; but *she wasn't lost.*

Suppose her mother were here – what would she do? *Are you all right?* Well, she was all right. Nothing broken, no cuts; no encounters with the bestial in any form. Her mother knew that and Sharon knew she knew that. The closeness she felt to her mother and to Billy and the other kids wasn't quite as nice as having them here, and being warm and having something to eat. But there were new ways, other ways, that were nicer – nicer than anything she had ever known. Billy now – see how glad he was, how afraid he'd been. How much he cared. It made her feel very good to know that Billy cared so much. It had always been his best-kept secret.

She knew she must sleep for an hour, so she closed her eyes and slept. It was quite a different thing from that other sleep.

When she awoke for the second time, it was instantly and with instant motion. She bounced to her feet no matter how stiff she felt and marked time, double-time, on a flat rock, banging her feet until they stung, and breathing deeply. Three minutes of that and she struck off purposefully into the still-dark underbrush, skipped on two stepping-stones across the brook, and unhesitatingly went to a fallen log where, the night before, she had seen a bright orange shelf fungus. She broke off large greedy pieces and crammed her mouth full of them. It was delicious, and safe, too, because although most people did not know it, someone, somewhere did know that this particular pileus was edible.

She trotted back to the half-cave where she had spent the night and got Mary Lou, her broken-footed doll, and fed her some of the fungus and a few drops of water from the brook. Then, cautioning the doll not to say a word, she set off through the woods.

In less than an hour, and while the light was still gray, she found herself at the edge of a meadow. She raised a warning finger at Mary Lou, and then stood still as a tree-trunk – an unnatural act for any child before now – and peered through the dawn-light until she saw a rabbit. It was aware of her and fear-frozen into exactly her immobility. Sharon outwaited it, let it move, let it move again, let it nibble on young clover and stare at her again and at last move curiously closer. When it was close enough, she pounced, not at the rabbit but at the place where the rabbit would be when she moved. The rabbit was there.

She transferred her grasp on the dew-damp, kicking creature to a one-handed grip just over the joints of the hind legs and stood up, lifting the rabbit clear of the ground. As it hung upside down, it immediately swung its head up and forward (as someone, somewhere, knew it would). Sharon brought the edge of her left hand down with a single smart chop, and broke its neck. She squatted down, and unhesitatingly nibbled a hole in the animal's throat with her sharp front teeth. She drank as much blood as she needed, offered some to Mary Lou (who didn't want any) wiped her mouth daintily with a handful of moist grass, picked up her doll and went her purposeful way. She knew which way to go. She knew where the road was and where a railroad was and where three farmhouses and a hunting lodge were. She also knew which one to go to, and that Daddy would come to pick her up, and that she would be at the meeting place before Daddy would, and which cellar window she was allowed to break to get in, and where the can opener was and how to prime the pump to get water. It was pretty wonderful. All she had to do was to need to know something, and if anyone knew it, she knew it.

She walked along happily, for a while sharing a stomach-shrinking thrill with some child, somewhere, who was riding a roller-coaster, and for a while doing a new kind of talking with her father. It was a tease; he'd have said to her, before: 'I thought you were in the station wagon and Mummy thought you were in the truck. Good thing we were wrong. There'd've been two of you, and then who'd wear the pink dress?' But now it came out as a kind of picture, or maybe a memory of two Sharons screeching at each other and pulling at the party dress, while two broken-footed Mary Lous looked on. It was funny and she laughed. It was more than a memory. It was all the relieved anxiety and deep fondness and self-accusation her Daddy felt over almost losing his Princess-Wicked-wif'-the-fickles-on-her-nose.

She reached the lodge and got in all right. After about an hour she looked out the window and saw a bush rattlesnake in the bare patch by the shed. She ran to the gun-cabinet and then to the bookcase for the box of .32 cartridges, and loaded the revolver and put it down and got the window open a crack and picked up the gun and braced it against the sill and got it lined up until she, or somebody, knew it was just right. Then she squeezed off a single shot that eliminated the snake's head. She unloaded the gun and ran a swab through it and put it away, and put the shells away, and then built a playhouse out of overturned furniture and sofa cushions, in which she and Mary

Lou fell fast asleep until Tony Brevix got there. All in all, she had a wonderful time. She never once had to wonder whether she was allowed to do this or that – she *knew*. Most important, she was by herself and in a new place, but she wasn't lost. She would never be lost again. If only nothing spoiled this, no one in the world would ever be lost again, no, nor wonder if somebody really loved them, or think they'd gone away and left them because they didn't want them.

It had always been thus between Sharon and Mary Lou, because Mary Lou knew Sharon loved her even when she accidentally left her out in the rain or threw her down the stairs. Now the children understood that kind of thing as well as the dolls, and never again would a child wonder if anyone cared, or grow up thinking that to be loved is a privilege. It's a privilege only to adults. To any child it's a basic right, which if denied dooms the child to a lifetime of seeking it and an inability to accept anything but child-style love. The way things were now, never again would a child be afraid of growing up, or hover anxiously near half-empty coffers so very easy to fill.

I know your need, the whole world was saying to 'I,' while 'I' everywhere could understand the justice of 'my' needs, and the silliness of so many wants.

When Tony Brevix came into the lodge he found her asleep. He knew she was aware of him and he knew that her awareness would not interrupt her slumber, not for a second. She slept smiling while he carried her out to the station wagon.

CHAPTER 25

There she stands the water beading her bright body her head to one side the water sparking off her hair, she smiles, says All Right Handsome What Are You Going To Do About It?

Crash!

A soft rumble and a glare of light: sky. Crash! A brighter, unbearable flash of light on light, a sharp smell of burning chemicals, a choking cloud of dust and smoke and the patter-patter of falling debris. Confusion, bewilderment, disorientation and growing anger at the deprivation of a dream.

The sharp command to every sentience, mechanical or not, on the entire hilltop: *Get Gurlick out of here!*

A flash of silver overhead, then a strange overall sticky, pore-choking sensation, like being coated with warm oil, and underneath, the torn hill dwindles away. There are still hundreds of projectors left, row on row of them, but from the size of the terraces where they are parked, there must have been hundreds of thousands more. *Crash!* A half dozen of the projectors bulge skyward and fall back in shatters and shards. Look there, a flight of jets. See, two silver spheres, dodging, dancing: then the long curve of a seeking missile points one out, and the trail and the burst make a bright ball on a smoky string, painted across the sky. *Crash! Crash!* Even as the scarred hill disappears in swift distance, the parked projectors can be seen bursting skyward, a dozen and a dozen and a score of them, pressing upward through the rain of pieces from those blasted a breath or a blink ago; and *cra—*

No, not *crash* this time, but a point, a porthole, a bay-window looking in to the core of hell, all the colors and all too bright, growing, too, too big to be growing so fast, taking the hilltop, the hillside, the whole hill lost in the ball of brilliance.

And for minutes afterward, hanging stickily by something invisible, frighteningly in midair under the silver sphere, but not feeling wind or acceleration or any of the impossible turns as the sphere whizzes along low, hedge-hopping, ground-hugging, back-tracking and hovering to hide; for minutes and minutes afterward, through the drifting speckles of overdazzled eyeballs, the pastel column can be seen rising and rising flat-headed over the land, thousands and thousands of feet, building a roof with eaves, the eaves curling and curling out and down, or are they the grasping fingers of rows and rows of what devils who have climbed up the inside of the spout, about to put up *what* hellish faces?

'Bastits,' Gurlick whimpered, 'tryin' to atom-bomb *me*. You tell 'em who I am?'

No response. The Medusa was calculating, for once, to capacity – even to its immense, infinitely varied capacity. It had expected to succeed in unifying the mind of humanity – it had correctly predicted its certainty of success and the impossibility of failure. But success like *this?*

Like this: In the first forty minutes humanity destroyed seventy-one per cent of the projectors and forty-three percent of the spheres. To do this it used everything and anything that came to hand, regardless of the cost in lives or materiel; it put out its fire by smothering it with its mink coat. It killed its cobra by hitting it with the baby. It moved, reactive and accurate and almost in reflex, like a man holding a burning stick, and as the heat increases near one finger, it will release and withdraw and find another purchase while he thinks of other things. It threw a child into the drive of a projector because he fit, he contained the right amount of the right grade of lubricant for just that purpose at just that time. It could understand in microseconds that the nearest thing to the exact necessary tool for tearing the throat out of a projector would be the neck and scroll of a violin.

And like this: Beginning in the forty-first minute, humanity launched the first precision weapon against the projectors, having devised and produced a seeking mechanism which would infallibly find and destroy projectors (though they did not radiate in the electromagnetic spectrum, not even infrared) and then made it compact enough to cram into the warhead of a Hawk, and, further, applied the Hawk to the Atlas. And this was only the first. In the fifty-second minute – that is, less than an hour after the Medusa pushed the button to unify the mind of man – humanity was using hasty makeshifts of appalling efficiency, devices which reversed the steering commands of the projectors (like the one which under its own power walked off the Hell Gate Bridge into eighty feet of water) and others which rebroadcast the projectors' signals 180 degrees out of phase, nullifying them. At the ninety-minute mark humanity was knocking out two of every three flying spheres it saw, not by accurate aiming (because as yet humanity couldn't tool up to countermeasure inertia-less turns at six miles per second) but by an ingenious application of the theory of random numbers, by which they placed proximity missiles where the sphere wasn't but almost certainly would be – and all too often was.

The Medusa had anticipated success. But, to sum up: success like *this?* For hadn't the humans stamped out every operable instrument of the Medusa's invasion (save Gurlick, about whom they couldn't know) in just two hours and eight minutes?

This incredible species, uniquely possessed of a defense against the Medusa (the Medusa still stubbornly insisted) in its instant, total fragmentation at the invader's first touch, seemed uniquely to possess other qualities as well. It would be wise – more: it was imperative – that Earth be brought into the fold where it would have to take orders. Hence – Gurlick.

It swept Gurlick back into its confidence, told him that in spite of the abruptness of his awakening, he was now ready to go out on his own. It described to him his assignment, which made Gurlick snicker like an eight-year-old behind the barn, and assured him that it would set up for him the most perfect opportunity its mighty computers could devise. Speed, however, was of the essence – which was all right with Gurlick, who spit on his hands and made cluck-cluck noises from his back teeth and wrinkled up half his face with an obscene wink, and snickered again to show his willingness.

The sphere hovered now at treetop level over heavily wooded ground, keeping out of sight while awaiting the alien computation of the best conceivable circumstances for Gurlick's project. This might well have proved lengthy, based as it was on Gurlick's partial, mistaken, romantic, deluded and downright pornographic information, and might even have supplied some highly amusing conclusions, since they would have been based on logic, and Gurlick's most certainly were not. These diverting computations were lost, however, and lost forever when the sphere dropped dizzyingly, released Gurlick so abruptly that he tumbled, and informed him that he was on his own – the sphere was detected. Growling and grumbling, Gurlick sprawled under the trees and watched the sphere bullet upward and away, and a moment later the appearance of a Hawk, or rather its trail, scoring the sky in a swift reach like the spread of a strain-crack in window glass.

He did not see the inevitable, but heard it in due course – the faint distant thump against the roof of the world which marked the end of the sphere's existence – and very probably the end of all the Medusa's artifacts on earth. He said an unprintable syllable, rolled over and eyed the woodlands with disfavor. This wasn't going to be like flying over it like a bug over a carpet, with some big brain doing all your thinking for you. On the other hand … this was the payoff. This was where Gurlick got his – where at long last he could strike back at a whole world full of bastits.

He got to his feet and began walking.

CHAPTER 26

Full of wonder, the human hive contemplated itself and its works, its gains, its losses and its new nature.

First, there was the intercommunication – a thing so huge, so different, that few minds could previously have imagined it. No analogy could suffice; no concepts of infinite telephone exchanges, or multi-sideband receivers, could hint at the quality of that gigantic cognizance. To describe it in terms of its complexity would be as impossible – and as purblind – as an attempt to describe fine lace by a description of each of its threads. It had, rather, *texture*. Your memory, and his and his, and hers over the horizon's shoulder – all your memories are mine. More: your personal orientation in the framework of your own experiences, your I-in-the-past, is also mine. More: your skills remain your own (is great music made less for being shared?) but your sensitivity to your special subject is mine now, and your pride in your excellence is mine now. More: though bound to the organism, Mankind, as never before, I am I as never before. When Man has demands on me, I am totally dedicated to Man's purpose. Otherwise, within the wide, wide limits of mankind's best interests, I am as never before a free agent; I am I to a greater degree, and with less obstruction from within and without, than ever before possible. For gone, gone altogether are individual man's hosts of pests and devils, which in strange combinations have plagued us all in the past: the They-don't-want-me devil, the Suppose-they-find-out devil, the twin imps of They-are-lying-to-me and They-are-trying-to-cheat-me; gone, gone is I'm-afraid-to-try, and They-won't-let-me, and I-couldn't-be-loved-if-they-knew.

Along with the imps and devils, other things disappeared – things regarded throughout human history as basic, thematic, keys to the structures of lives and cultures. Now if a real thing should disappear, a rock or a tree or a handful of water, there will be thunder and a wind and other violence, depending upon what form the vanished mass owned. Or if a great man disappears, there is almighty confusion in the rush to fill the vacuum of his functions. But the things which disappeared now proved their unreality by the unruffled silence in which they disappeared. Money. The sense of property. Jingoistic patriotism, tariffs, taxes, boundaries and frontiers, profit and loss, hatred and suspicion of humans by humans, and language itself (except as part of an art) with all the difficulties of communication between languages and within them.

In short, it was abruptly possible for mankind to live with itself in health. Removed now was mankind's cess-gland, the secretions of which (called everything from cussedness to Original Sin) had poisoned its body since it was born, distorting decencies like survival and love into greed and lust, turning Achievement ('I have built') into Position ('I have power').

So much for humanity's new state of being. As to its abilities, they were simply based, straightforward. There are always many ways to accomplish anything, but only one of them is really best. Which of them is best – that is the source of all argument on the production of anything, the creator of factions among the designers, and the first enemy of speed and efficiency. But when humanity became a hive, and needed something – as for example the adaptation of the swift hunting missile Hawk to the giant carrier Atlas – the device was produced without considerations of pride or profit, without waste motion, and without interpersonal friction of any kind. The decision was made, the job was done. In those heady first moments, anything and everything available was used – but with precision. Later (by minutes) fewer ingenious stopgaps were used, more perfect tools were shaped from the materials at hand. And still later (by hours) there was full production of new designs. Mankind now used exactly the right tool for the jobs it had to do ...

And within it, each individual flowered, finding freedoms to be, to act, to take enrichment and pleasure as never before. What were the things that Dimity (Salomé?) Carmichael had always needed, wanted to do? She could do them now. An Italian boy, Guido, packed taut with talent, awaited the arrival of the greatest living violinist from behind a now collapsed Iron Curtain; they would hereafter spend their lives and do their work together. The parents of a small stiff boy named Henry contemplated, as all the world contemplated, what had happened to him and why, and how totally impossible it would be for such a thing ever to happen again. Sacrifice there must be from time to time, even now; but never again a useless one. Everyone now knew, as if in personal memory, how fiercely Henry had wanted to live in that flash of agony which had eclipsed him. All Earth shared the two kinds of religious experience discovered by the Africans Mbala and Nuyu, wherein one had become confirmed in his faith and the other had found it. What, specifically, had brought them to it was of no significance; the fact of their devotion was the important thing to be shared, for it is in the finest nature of humanity to worship, fight it as he sometimes may. The universe being what it is, there is always *plus ultra, plus ultra* – powers and patterns beyond understanding, and more beyond these when these are understood. Out there is the call to which faith is the natural response and worship the natural approach.

Such was humanity when it became a hive – a beautiful entity, balanced and fine and wondrously alive. A pity, in a way, that such a work of art, such self-sufficiency, was to exist in this form for so brief a time ...

CHAPTER 27

Gurlick, alone of humans insulated from the human hive, member of another, sensed none of this. Driven, hungry through a whole spectrum of appetites, full of resentment, he shuffled through the woods. He had been vaguely aware of the outskirts of a town not far from where the silver sphere had set him down; he would, he supposed, find what he wanted there, though wanting it was the only thing quite clear to him. How he was to get it was uncertain; but get it he must. He was aware of the presence within him of the Medusa, observing, computing, but – not directing, cognizant as it was of the fact that the fine details of such an operation must be left to the species itself. Had it had its spheres and other machines available, there might have been a great deal it could do to assist Gurlick. But now – he was on his own.

He was in virgin forest now, the interlocked foliage overhead dimming the mid-morning sunshine to an underwater green, and the footing was good, there being little underbrush and a gentle downslope. Gurlick gravitated downhill, knowing he would encounter a path or a road sooner or later, and monotonously cursed his empty stomach, his aching feet, and his enemies.

He heard voices.

He stopped, shrank back against a tree trunk, and peered. For a moment he could detect nothing, and then, off to the right, he heard a sudden musical laugh. He looked toward the sound, and saw a brief motion of something blue. He came out of hiding, and, scuttling clumsily from tree to tree, went to investigate.

There were three of them, girls in their mid-teens, dressed in halters and shorts, giggling over the chore of building a fire in a small clearing. They had a string of fish, pike and lake trout, and a frying pan, and seemed completely and hilariously preoccupied.

Gurlick, from a vantage point above them, chewed on his lower lip and wondered what to do. He had no delusions about approaching openly and sweet-talking his way into their circle. It would be far wiser, he knew, to slip away and go looking elsewhere, for something surer, safer. On the other hand ... he heard the crackle of bacon fat as one of the girls dropped the tender slivers into the frying pan. He looked at the three lithe young bodies, and at the waiting string of fish, half of which were scaled and beheaded, and quietly moaned. There was too much of what was wanted, down there, for him to turn his back.

Then a curl of fragrance from the bacon reached him and toppled his reason. He rose from his crouch and in three bounds was down the slope and in their midst, moaning and slavering. One of the children bounded away to the right, one to the left. The third fell under his hands, shrieking.

'Now you jus' be still,' he panted, trying to hold his victim, trying to protect himself against her hysterical slappings, writhings, clawings. 'I ain't goin' to hurt you if you jus'—'

Uh! He was bowled right off his feet by one of the escapees who had returned at a dead run and crashed him with a hard shoulder. He rolled over and found himself staring up at the second girl who had run away as she stood over him with a stone the size of a grapefruit raised in both hands. She brought it down; it hit Gurlick on the left cheekbone and the bridge of his nose and filled the world with stars and brilliant tatters of pain. He fell back, wagging his head, pawing at his face, trying to get some vision back and kick away the sick dizziness; and when at last he could see again, he was alone with the campfire, the frying pan, the string of fish.

'Li'l bastits,' he growled, holding his face. He looked at his hand, on which were flecks of his own blood, swore luridly, turned in a circle as if to find and pursue them, and then squatted before the fire, reached for two cleaned fish, and dropped them hissing into the pan.

Well, he'd get that much out of it, anyway.

He had eaten four of the fish and had two more cooking when he heard voices again, a man's deep, 'Which way now? Over here?' and a girl's answer, 'Yes, where the smoke's coming from.'

Jailbait ... of course, of *course* they'd have gone for help! Gurlick cursed them all and lumbered down-slope, away from the sound of voices. Boy, he'd messed up, but good. The whole hillside would be crawling with people hunting him. He had to get out of here.

He moved as cautiously as he could, quite sure he was being watched by hundreds of eyes, yet seeing no one until he glimpsed two men off to his left and below him. One had binoculars on a strap around his neck, the other a shotgun. Gurlick, half-fainting with terror, slumped down between a tree trunk and a rock, and cowered there until he could hear their voices, and while he heard them, and after he heard them, with their curt certain syllables and their cold lack of mercy. When all was quite quiet again, he rose, and at that moment became aware of an aircraft sound. It approached rapidly, and he dropped back into his hiding place, trembling, and peeped up at the glittering patches of blue in the leafy roof. The machine flew directly overhead, low, too slowly – a helicopter. He heard it thrashing the air off to the north, downhill from him, and for a while he could not judge if it was going or coming or simply circling down there. In his pride he was convinced that its business was Gurlick and only Gurlick, and in his ignorance he was certain it had seen him through the thick cover. It went away at last, and the forest returned to its murmuring silence. He heard a faint shout behind and above him, and scuttled from cover and away from the sound. Pausing, a moment later, for breath, he caught another glimpse of the man with the shotgun off to his left, and escaped to the right and down.

And, thus pursued and herded, he came to the water's edge.

There was a dirt path there, and no one in sight; and it was warm and sunny and peaceful. Slowly Gurlick's panic subsided, and, as he walked along the path, there was a deep throb of anticipation within him. He'd gotten away clean; he had outdistanced his enemies and now, enemies, beware!

The path curved closer to the bank of the lake. Alders stood thick here, and there was the smell of moss. The path turned, and the shade was briefly darker here at the verge of the floods of gold over the water. And there by the path it lay, the little pile of fabric, bright red, shiny black, filmy white with edges iced with lace …

Gurlick stopped walking, stopped breathing until his chest hurt. Then he moved slowly past this incredible, impossible consolidation of his dream, and went to the bushes at the water's edge.

She was out there – *she*.

He made a sharp wordless sound and stood forward, away from the bushes. She turned in the water and stared at him, her eyes round.

Emancipated now, free to be what she had always wished to be, and to do what she needed to do without fear or hesitation; swimming now naked in the sun, sure and fearless, shameless; utterly oriented within herself and herself within the matrix of humanity and all its known data, Salomé Carmichael stood up in the water, under the sun, and said, 'Hello, Handsome.'

CHAPTER 28

So ended humanity within its planetary limits; so ended the self-contained, self-aware species-hive which had for such a brief time been able to feel, to the ends of its earth, its multifarious self. The end came some hours after the helicopter – the same one which had set her down by the pond – had come for Salomé Carmichael, which it had the instant Gurlick quit the scene. Gurlick had seen it from where he crouched guiltily in the bushes. After it had gone away he slowly climbed to his feet and made his way back to the pond. He hunkered down with his back to a tree and regarded the scene unwinkingly.

It had been right there, on the moss.

Over there had lain the pretty little heap of clothes, so clean, so soft, so very red, shiny black, the white so pretty. The strangest thing that had ever happened to him in his whole life had happened here, stranger than the coming of the Medusa, stranger than the unpeopled factory back there in the mountains, stranger, even, than the overwhelming fact of this place, of her being here, of the unbelievable coincidence of it all with his dream. And that strangest thing of all was that once, when she was here, she had cried out, and he had then been gentle. He had been gentle with all his heart and mind and body, for a brief while flooded, melted, swept away by gentleness. No wrinkled raisin from out of space, no concept like the existence of a single living thing so large it permeated two galaxies and part of a third, could be so shockingly alien to him, everything he was and had ever been, as this rush of gentleness. Its microscopic seed must have lain encysted within him all his life, never encountering a single thing, large or small, which could warm it to germination. Now it had burst open, burst him open, and he was shocked, shaken, macerated as never before in his bruised existence.

He crouched against the tree and regarded the moss, and the lake, and the place where the red and the black and the lace had lain, and wondered why he had run away. He wondered how he could have let her go. The gentleness was consuming him, even now ... he had to find somewhere to put it down, but there wouldn't be anyone else, anyone or anything, for him to be gentle to, anywhere in the world.

He began to cry. Gurlick had always wept easily, his facile tears his only outlet for fear, and anger, and humiliation, and spite. This, however, was different. This was very difficult to do, painful in the extreme, and impossible to stop until he was racked, wrung out, exhausted. It tumbled him over and left him groveling on the moss. Then he slept, abruptly, his whipped consciousness fleeing away to the dark.

CHAPTER 29

What can travel faster than light?

Stand here by me, friend, on this hillside, under the black and freckled sky. Which stars do you know – Polaris? Good. And the bright one yonder, that's Sirius. Look at them now: at Polaris, at Sirius. Quickly now: Polaris, Sirius. And again: Sirius, Polaris.

How far apart are they? It says in the book, thousands of light-years. How many? Too many: never mind. But how long does it take you to flick your gaze from one to the other and back? a second? A half-second next time, then a tenth? … You can't say that nothing, absolutely nothing, has traveled between the two. Your vision has; your attention has.

You now understand, you have the rudiments of understanding what it is to flick a part of yourself from star to star, just as (given the skill) you may shift from soul to soul.

With such a shift, down such a path, came the Medusa at the instant of its marriage to humanity. In all the history of humanity, the one instant (save death) of most significance is the instant of syngamy, the moment of penetration by the sperm of the ovum. Yet almost never is there a heralding of this instant, nor a sign; it comes to pass in silence and darkness, and no one ever knows but the mindless flecks of complex jelly directly involved.

Not so now; and never before, and never again would marriage occur with such explosion. A microsecond after that melding, Gurlick's altered seed to the welcoming ovum of a human, the Medusa of space shot down its contacting thread, an unerring harpoon carrying a line to itself, and all of its Self following in the line, ready to reach and fill humanity, make of it a pseudopod, the newest member of its sprawling corpus.

But if the Medusa's bolt can be likened to a harpoon, then it can be said that the uprushing flood it met was like a volcano. The Medusa had not a micro-microsecond in which to realize what had happened to it. It did not die; it was not killed any more than humanity would have been killed had the Medusa's plan been realized. Humanity would have become a 'person' of the illimitable creature. Now …

Now, instead, humanity became the creature; flooded it, filled it to its furthermost crannies, drenched its most remote cells with the Self of humankind. Die? Never that; the Medusa was alive as never before, with a new and different kind of life, in which its slaves were freed but its motivations unified; where the individual was courted and honored and brought special nutrients, body and mind, and where, freely, 'want to' forever replaced 'must.'

And all for want of a datum: that intelligence might exist in individuals, and that dissociated individuals might co-operate and yet not be a hive. For there is no structure on earth which could not have been built by rats, were the rats centrally directed and properly motivated. How could the Medusa have known? Thousands upon thousands of species and cultures throughout the galaxies have technological progress as advanced as that of Earth, and are yet composed of individuals no more highly evolved than termites, lemurs, or shrews. What slightest hint was there for the Medusa that a hive-humanity would be a different thing from a super-rat?

Humanity had passed the barriers of language and of individual isolation on its planet. It passed the barriers of species now, and of isolation in its cosmos. The faith of Mbala was available to Guido, and so were the crystal symphonies of the black planets past Ophiuchus. Charlotte Dunsay, reaching across the world to her husband in Hobart, Tasmania, might share with him a triple sunrise in the hub of Orion's great Nebula. As one man could share the *being* of another here on earth, so both, and perhaps a small child with them, could fuse their inner selves with some ancient contemplative mind leeched to the rocks in some roaring methane cataract, or soar with some insubstantial life-forms adrift where they were born in the high layers of atmosphere around some unheard-of planet.

So ended mankind, to be born again as hive-humanity; so ended the hive of earth to become star-man, the immeasurable, the limitless, the growing; maker of music beyond music, poetry beyond words, and full of wonder, full of worship.

CHAPTER 30

So too ended Gurlick, the isolated, alone among humankind denied membership in the fusion of humans, full of a steaming fog, aglow with his flickerings of hate and the soft shine of corruption, member of something other than humankind. For while humanity had been able to read him (and his dream) and herd him through the forest to its fulfillment, it had never been able to reach his consciousness, blocked as it was by the thought-lines of the Medusa.

These lines, however, were open still, and when humanity became Medusa, it flooded down to Gurlick and made him welcome. *Come!* it called, and whirled him up and outward, showing and sharing its joy and strength and pride, showering him with wonders of a thousand elsewheres and a hundred heres; it showed him how to laugh at the most rarefied technician's joke and how to feel the structure of sestinae and sonnets, of bridges and Bach. It spoke to him saying *We* and granting him the right to regard it all and say: *I*. And more: he had been promised a kingship, and now he had it, for all this sentient immensity acknowledged to him its debt. Let him but make the phantom of a wish of a thought, and his desires would be fulfilled. *Come!* it called. *Come!*

But the weight of the man o' war was on his mind. *Hide!* he thought. Don't attract attention. If he got out of line, the man o' war would squash him like a bug. But humanity, which had become Medusa, insisted, it beat down upon him, and finally Gurlick could withstand its force no longer. He turned and faced humankind as it had become, all-transcending, all-inclusive, all-knowing, pervasive – faced humankind as he had never faced it before in his life.

Humankind had changed.

His first reaction was *My God, it's full of people!*

Which was strange, because he found himself at the edge of a purple cliff which overlooked a valley with a silver river in it. Not silver like the poets say, which only means the reflection of sky-white; this one was metallic silver color, fluid, fast. He was aware without surprise that he sat on the tip of his spine, which was long, black and tapering, with two enormous hind legs, kneed in the middle like broken straws and pretty nearly as slender, forming the other two points of his tripod. He was chewing on a stone, holding it to black marble lips (which opened sidewise) with four hands (having scorpion-nippers for fingers) and he found it delicious. He turned his head around (all the way, without effort) and saw Salomé Carmichael behind him, and she was beautiful beyond belief, which was odd because she looked like a twelve-foot, blue-black praying mantis. But then, so did he.

She spoke, but it was not speech really, but a sort of semaphore of the emotions. He felt himself greeted, and made joyfully welcome *(Hello, oh hello, Danny, I knew you'd come, you had to come)* and then there was an invitation: *to the place to watch that game.* She moved close to him so that their bodies touched, and somehow he knew just exactly what to do to stay with her; in a blink they were somewhere else, on the top of a swaying green tree (the bark was the green part) and he had a round blunt front end like a bull-frog and four gauzy wings, and two long legs with webbed feet like a water-bird. Salomé was there too, of the same species and utterly lovely; and together they watched the game, understanding it as completely in all its suspensions and convolutions as any Earthside hockey or baseball or chess fan might follow his favorite. The teams were whole hives, and they could, all together, create sound-waves and focus them; at the focal point danced a blue-green crystal, held spinning in midair by the beam of sound. There were three hive-teams, not two, and if two should focus together on the crystal it would shatter musically, and that was a foul, and the third team won the point, and could have the playing field to dance in. And when the dance was over (there were points for the dance too) then another crystal would be projected high in the rosy air …

To a swimming place, tingling, refreshing, Gurlick knowing somehow that where they swam under a blue-black rock ceiling, the temperature was over a thousand degrees centigrade, and the gleaming bony paddles and sleek speckled flanks with which he swam and on which he felt the tingling were no flesh he had ever learned of. And to a flying place where all the people, welcoming as everywhere, and some known to him as people he had met on Earth, all these people were cobweb-frail, spending their lives adrift in the thin shifts of air with the highest mist peaks of a cloud-shrouded planet as their floor …

And Salomé gave him her story of envy and of her need to have others depend on her.

These two were ideal antagonists, ideal weapons in the conflict between Medusa and mankind. Medusa had won the battles; mankind had won the war. And it had all begun with Gurlick …

Somewhere in this communion between them, the whole thing was talked out. It was probably in the first couple of seconds of their first meeting, there over the silver river. If it were rendered into words it was Gurlick's complete wounding by the discovery (in his loneliness) that what had happened by the lake was no affair of his at all, but only a strategic move in a war between a giant and a behemoth; with it, all he had ever been in his tattered life, how there was nothing within him with a whole soul to give in exchange for accidental kindness; how he was unashamed to have far, far passed the point where he could keep clean and think well and be a man ... in short, the entire Gurlick, with all the reasons why, in one clear flash.

Gurlick, numb and passive as he tossed like a chip on their ocean of wonders, had at last a wish, and had it, and had it.

True, none of this could have come about without him. This result could not have been with anyone else in his place, so – true enough – he was owed a debt. Pay it, then.

Pay the debt ... You do not reward a catalyst by changing it, the unchanging, into something else. When a man is what Gurlick is, he is that because he has made himself so; for what his environment has done to him, blame the environment not so much as the stolid will that kept him in it. So – take away hunger and poverty (of body and soul), deprivation and discomfort and humiliation, and you take away the very core of his being – his sole claim to superiority.

You take away his hate. You take away from him all reason to hate anyone or anything – like the wet, like the cold.

So don't ask him to look out among the stars, and join in the revelries of giants. Don't thank him, don't treat him, and above all, do not so emasculate him as to take away from him his reasons to hate: they have become his life.

So they paid him, meticulously to the specifications he himself (though all unknowing) set up.

And as long as he lived, there was a city-corner, drab streets and fumes, sullen pedestrians and careless, dangerous aimers of trucks and cabs; moist unbearable heat and bitter cold; and bars where Gurlick could go and put in his head, whining for a drink, and bartenders to send him out into the wet with his hatred, back to a wrecked truck in a junk-yard where he might lie in the dark and dream that dream of his. 'Bastits,' Gurlick would mutter in the dark, hating ... happy: 'Lousy bastits.'

VENUS PLUS X

*Utterly aside from the
subject matter*
To
GERTRUDE
and her Isaac

'Charlie Johns,' urgently cried Charlie Johns: 'Charlie Johns, Charlie Johns!' for that was the absolute necessity – to know who Charlie Johns was, not to let go of that for a second, for anything, ever.

'I *am* Charlie Johns,' he said argumentatively, and plaintively, he said it again. No one argued, no one denied it. He lay in the warm dark with his knees drawn up and his arms crossed and his forehead pressed tight against his kneecaps. He saw dull flickering red, but that was inside his eyelids, and he was Charlie Johns.

C. Johns once stencilled on a foot-locker, written in speed-ball black-letter on a high-school diploma, typed on a pay-check. *Johns, Chas.* in the telephone book.

The name, all right. All right, fine, okay, but a man is more than a name. A man is twenty-seven years old, he sees the hairline just so in his morning mirror and likes a drop of Tabasco on his eggs (over light: whites firm, yolks runny). He was born with one malformed toe and a strabismus. He can cook a steak drive a car love a girl run a mimeograph go to the bathroom brush his teeth, including the permanent bridge, left upper lateral incisor and bicuspid. He left the house in plenty of time but he is going to be late to work.

He opened his eyes and it wasn't dull flickering red at all, but grey – a cold sourceless silver, grey like snail trails on the lilac leaves – a springtime thing, that. Spring it was, oh that springtime thing; it was love last night, Laura, she –

When daylight saving time is new, the daylit evening is forever, and you can do so much. How he *begged* Laura for the chance to get her screens up; if Mom could have seen that, now! And down in Laura's stinking cellar, shuffling through the half-dark with the screens under his arm, he had walked into the cruel point of the dangling strap-hinge of a discarded shutter, torn a hole in his brown tweed pants, punched a red blood-bruise (with warp and woof stamped on it) on his thigh. And worth it, worth it, all that forever-evening, with a girl, a real girl (she could prove it) for all the long end of the evening; and all the way home love! of here and of now, and spring of course, and oh of course *love!* said the tree-frogs, the lilacs, the air, and the way sweat dried on him. (Good – this is good. Good to be a part of here and of now, and spring of course, and oh of course, love; but best of all, to remember, to know it all, Charlie.) Better than love just to remember home, the walk between high hedges, the two white lamps with the big black 61 painted on each (Mom had done that for the landlord; she was clever with her hands) only they were pretty weathered by now, yes the hands too. The foyer with the mottled brass wall-full of mailboxes and discreet pushbuttons for the tenants, and the grille of the house phone that had never worked since they moved here, and that massive brass plate solidly concealing the electric lock, which for years he had opened with a blow of his shoulder, never breaking stride … and get closer, closer, because it is so important to remember; nothing remembered is important; it's remembering that matters; you can! you can!

The steps from the ground floor had old-fashioned nickel-plated nosings over carpet worn down to the backing, red fuzz at the edges. (Miss Mundorf taught first grade, Miss Willard taught second grade, Miss Hooper taught fifth. Remember *everything*.) He looked around him, where he lay remembering in the silver light; the soft walls were unlike metal and unlike fabric but rather like both, and it was very warm … he went on remembering with his eyes open: the flight from the second floor to the third had the nickel nosing too, but no carpeting, and the steps were all hollowed, oh, very slightly; mounting them, you could be thinking about anything, but that clack clack, as a change from the first flight's flap flap, put you right there, you knew where you were …

Charlie Johns screamed, 'Oh God – *where am I?*'

He unfolded himself, rolled over on his stomach, drew up his knees, and then for a moment could move no more. His mouth was dry and hot inside as pillowslips creasing under Mom's iron; his muscles, leg and back, all soft and tight-tangled like the knitting basket Mom was going to clean out some day …

… love with Laura, spring, the lights with 61, the shoulder on the lock, up the stairs flap flap, clack clack and – surely he could remember the rest of the way, because he had gone in gone to bed gotten up left for work … hadn't he? Hadn't he?

Shakily he pressed himself up, knelt, weakly squatted. His head dropped forward and he rested, panting. He watched the brown fabric of his clothes as if it were a curtain, about to open upon unknown but certain horror.

And it did.

'The brown suit,' he whispered. Because there on his thigh was the little rip (and under it the small hurtful bulge of the checkered bruise) to prove that he had not dressed for work this morning, had not even reached the top of the second flight. Instead, he was – here.

Because he could not stand just yet, he hunched around, fists and knees, blinking and turning his unsteady head. Once he stopped and touched his chin. It had no more stubble than it should have for a man coming home from a date he had shaved for.

He turned again and saw a tall oval finely scribed into the curved wall. It was the first feature he had been able to discover in this padded place. He gaped at it and it gave him Nothing.

He wondered what time it was. He lifted his arm and turned his head and got his ear to his watch. It was, thank God, still running. He looked at it. He looked at it for a long time without moving. He seemed not to be able to read it. At last he was able to understand that the numerals were the wrong way round, mirror-reversed; 2 was where 10 should be, 8 where 4 should be. The hands pointed to what should have been eleven minutes to eleven, but was, if this watch really were running backwards, eleven minutes past one. And it was running backwards. The sweep second-hand said so.

And do you know, Charlie, something under the terror and the wonderment said to him, do you know, all you want to do, even now, is remember? there was the terrible old battleax you got for Algebra 3 in high school, when you'd flunked Algebra 1 and had to take it over, and had gone through Algebra 2 and Geometry 1 on your belly, and flunked Geometry 2 and had to take it over – remember? and then for Algebra 3 you got this Miss Moran, and she was like IBM, with teeth. And then one day you asked her about something that puzzled you a little and the way she answered, you had to ask more … and she opened a door for you that you never knew was there, and she herself became something … well, after that, you watched her and knew what the frozen mein, the sharp discipline, the sheer inhumanity of the woman was for. She was just waiting for someone to come and ask her questions about mathematics a little beyond, a little outside the book. And it was as if she had long ago despaired of finding anyone that would. Why it meant so much to her was that she loved mathematics in a way that made it a pity the word 'love' had ever been used for anything else. And also that from minute to minute she never knew if some kid asking questions would be the last she'd ever know, or open a door for, because she was dying of cancer, which nobody never even suspected until she just didn't show up one day.

Charlie Johns looked at the faint oval in the soft silver wall and wished Miss Moran could be here. He also wished Laura could be here. He could remember them both so clearly, yet they were so many years apart from each other (and how many, he thought, looking at his wrist watch, how many years from me?) He wished Mom could be here, and the Texas redhead. (She was the first time for him, the redhead; and how would she mix with Mom? For that matter, how would Laura mix with Miss Moran?)

He could not stop remembering; dared not, and did not want to stop. Because as long as he kept remembering, he knew he was Charlie Johns; and although he might be in a new place without knowing what time it was, he wasn't lost, no one is ever lost, as long as he knows who he is.

Whimpering with effort, he got to his feet. He was so weak and muzzy-headed that he could only stand by bracing his feet wide apart; he could only walk by flailing his arms to keep his balance. He aimed for the faint oval line on the wall because it was the only thing here to aim for, but when he tried to go forward he progressed diagonally sidewise; it was like the time (he remembered) at the fun house at Coney Island, where they get you in a room and close it up and unbeknownst to you they tilt it a little to one side, you with no outside reference; and only green mirrors to see yourself in. They used to have to hose it out five, six times a day. He felt the same way now; but he had an advantage; he knew who he was, and in addition he knew he was sick. As he stumbled on the soft curved part where the floor became wall, and sank on one knee on the resilient silver, he croaked, 'I'm not myself just now, that's all.' Then he heard his own words properly and leapt to his feet: 'Yes I am!' he shouted, 'I am!'

He tottered forward, and since there was nothing to hold on the oval – it was only a thin line, taller than he was – he pushed against it.

It opened.

These was someone waiting outside, smiling, dressed in such a way that Charlie gasped and said, 'Oh, I beg your pardon ...' and then pitched forward on his face.

Herb Raile lives out in Homewood, where he has a hundred and fifty feet on Begonia Drive, and two hundred and thirty feet back to where Smitty Smith's begins its two-hundred-and-thirty-foot run to its one-hundred-fifty-foot frontage on Calla Drive. Herb Raile's house is a split-level, Smith's a rancher. Herb's neighbors to the right and left have splits.

Herb wheels into the drive and honks and puts his head out. 'Surprise!'

Jeanette is mowing the lawn with a power mower and with all that racket, the car horn makes her jump immoderately. She puts her foot on the grounding-plate and holds it down until the mower stops, and then runs laughing to the car.

'Daddy, Daddy!'

'Daddy, daddy, dad*eee!*' Davy is five, Karen three.

'Oh, honey, why are you *home!*'

'Closed the Arcadia account, and the great man says, Herb, he says, go on home to your kids. You look cool.' Jeanette is in shorts and a T-shirt.

'I was a good boy, I was a good boy,' Davy shrills, poking in Herb's side pocket.

'I was a good boy too,' shrieks Karen.

Herb laughs and scoops her up. 'Oh, what a man you'll grow up to be!'

'Shush, Herb, you'll get her all mixed up. Did you remember the cake?'

Herb puts down the three-year-old and turns to the car. 'Cake *mix*. Much better when you bake it yourself.' Stilling her moan, he adds, 'I'll do it, I'll do it. I can slam up a better cake than you any old day. Butter, toilet paper.'

'Cheese.'

'Damn. I got talking to Louie.' He takes the parcel and goes in to change. While he is gone, Davy puts his foot where Jeanette put her foot when she stopped the mower. The cylinder head is still hot. Davy is barefoot. When Herb comes out again Jeanette is saying, 'Shh. Shh. Be a man.'

Herb is wearing shorts and a T-shirt.

It wasn't maidenly modesty that made Charlie Johns keel over like that. Anything could have done it – a flashlight in the face, the sudden apparition of steps going down. And anyway, he'd thought it was a woman dressed like that. He hadn't been able to think of anyone else but women since he found himself in that tank – Laura, Mom, Miss Moran, the Texas redhead. He could see why a flash glance at this character would make anyone think so. Not that he could really see anything at the moment; he was lying flat on his back on something resilient but not so soft as the tank – rather like those wheel tables they have in hospitals. And someone was gently working on a cut high on his forehead, while a cool wet cloth smelling remotely like witch hazel lay blissfully across the rest of his forehead and his eyes. But whoever it was was talking to him, and though he couldn't understand a word, he didn't think it was a woman's voice. It was no *basso profundo*, but it wasn't a woman's voice. Oh brother, what a get-up. Imagine a sort of short bathrobe, deep scarlet, belted, but opening sharply away above and below. Above it was cut back behind the arms, and back of the neck a stiff collar stood up higher than the top of the head; it was shaped like the back of an upholstered chair and was darn near as big. Below the belt the garment cut back and down just as sharply to come together in a swallow-tail like a formal coat. In front, under the belt, was a short silky arrangement something like what the Scot wears in front of his kilt and calls a sporran. Very soft-looking slipper-socks, the same color as the robe, and with sharp-cut, floppy points front and back, came up to about mid-calf.

Whatever the treatment was, it killed the throb in his forehead with almost shocking suddenness. He lay still a moment, afraid that it might rear up and bash him as suddenly, but it didn't. He put up a tentative hand, whereupon the cloth was snatched away from his eyes and he found himself looking up into a smiling face which said several fluid syllables, ending in an interrogative trill.

Charlie said, 'Where am I?'

The face shrugged its eyebrows and laughed pleasantly. Firm cool fingers touched his lips, and the head wagged from side to side.

Charlie understood, so said, 'I don't understand you either.' He reared up on one elbow and looked around him. He felt much stronger.

He was in a large, stubbily T-shaped chamber. Most of the stem of the T was taken up by the – call it padded cell he had left; its door stood open still. Inside and out, it gleamed with that sourceless, soft, cold silver light. It looked like a huge pumpkin with wings.

The whole top of the T, floor to ceiling and from end to end, was a single transparent pane. Charlie thought he may have seen one as large in a department-store show-window, but he doubted it. At each end of the T were drapes; he presumed there were doors there.

Outside it was breathtaking. A golf-course can sometimes present rolling green something like that – but not miles, square miles of it. There were stands of trees here and there, and they were tropical; the unmistakable radiance of the *flamboyante* could be seen, nearly felt, it was so vivid; and there were palms – traveler's, cabbage, and coconut palms, and palmettos; tree-ferns and flowering cacti. On a clump of stone ruins, so very picturesque they might almost have been built there for the purpose of being picturesque ruins, stood a magnificent strangler fig nearly a hundred feet high, with its long clutching roots and multiple trunks matching the arch and droop of its glossy foliage.

The only building to be seen – and they were up quite high – twelve or fourteen stories, Charlie guessed, and on high ground at that – was impossible. Take a cone – a dunce cap. Taper it about three times as tall as it ought to be. Now bend it into a graceful curve, almost to a quarter circle. Now invert it, place its delicate tip in the ground and walk away, leaving its heavy base curving up and over and supported by nothing at all. Now make the whole thing about four hundred feet high, with jewel-like groups of pleasantly asymmetrical windows, and oddly placed, curved balconies which seemed to be of, rather than on the surface, and you have an idea of that building, that impossible building.

Charlie Johns looked at it, and at his companion, and, open-mouthed, at the building and back again. The man looked, and did not look human. The eyes were almost too far apart and too long – a little more of both, and they'd have been on the sides rather than the front of his face. The chin was strong and smooth, the teeth prominent and excellent, the nose large and with nostrils so high-arched that only a fraction of arc spared them from belonging to some horse. Charlie already knew that those fingers were strong and gentle; so was the face, the whole mein and carriage. The torso was rather longer, somehow, than it ought to be, the legs a little shorter than, if Charlie were an artist, he would have drawn them. And of course, those clothes …

'I'm on Mars,' quavered Charlie Johns, meaning to be funny somehow, and sounding pitiably frightened. He made a useless gesture at the building.

To his surprise, the man nodded eagerly and smiled. He had a warm and confident smile. He pointed to Charlie, to himself, and to the building, took a step toward the enormous window and beckoned.

Well, why not? ... yet Charlie cast a lingering glance back at the door of the silver cell from which he had emerged. Little as he liked it, it was the only thing here which was remotely familiar to him.

The man sensed his feeling, and made a reassuring, sort of U-turn gesture toward the distant building and back to the cell.

With a half-hearted smile, Charlie agreed to go.

The man took him briskly by the arm and marched off, not to the draped ends of the room, but straight to the window, straight *through* the window. This last he did by himself. Charlie dug in his heels and fled back to the wheeled table.

The man stood outside, firmly on thin air, and beckoned, smiling. He called to Charlie too, but Charlie only saw that; there was no sound. When one is in an enclosed place, one feels it – actually, one hears it – in any case, one knows it, and Charlie *knew* it. Yet that bright-robed creature had stepped through whatever enclosed it, leaving it enclosed, and was now impatiently, though cheerfully, calling to Charlie to join him.

There is a time for pride, thought Charlie, and this is it, and I haven't got any. He crept to the window, got down on his hands and knees, and slowly reached toward the pane. It *was* there, to ear, to spatial feel, but not to his hand. He inched outward.

The man, laughing (but laughing *with*, not laughing *at*, Charlie was certain) walked outdoors on nothing and came to him. When he made as if to take Charlie's hand, Charlie snatched it back. The man laughed again, bent and slapped hard against the level which unaccountably carried his feet. Then he stood up and stamped.

Well, obviously he was standing on *something*. Charlie, remembering (again) remembered seeing an old West Indian woman at San Juan airport, coming for no one knows what reason off her first flight, meeting her first escalator. She backed and filled and touched and jumped, until finally the husky young man with her picked her up bodily and plunked her on it. She grasped the rail and shrieked all the way up, and at the top, continued her shrieks; they were, they had been all along, shrieks of laughter.

Well, crawl he might, but he wouldn't shriek. Pale and hollow-eyed, he put a hand through where the pane wasn't, and slapped where the man had slapped.

This one he could feel.

Crawling on one hand and two knees, paddling ahead of him with the other hand, eyes slitted and head back so he would see out but not down, he passed through the nothing-at-all which so adequately enclosed the room, out upon the nothing-at-all which waited outside.

The man, whose voice he could suddenly hear again, laughingly beckoned him farther out, but Charlie was as far out as he intended to be. So to his horror the man suddenly swooped on him, lifted him bodily, and bumped his right hand down on a midair nothing about waist high to him – a handrail!

Charlie gazed at his right hand, apparently empty but grasping a blessed something; he could see the flattened flesh at the side of his grip, the whitening knuckles. He placed his other hand beside it and looked across the breeze – there was quite a breeze – at the other, who said something in his singing tongue and pointed downward. Reflexively Charlie Johns looked down, and gasped. It was probably no more than two hundred feet, but they looked to him like miles. He gulped and nodded, for obviously the man had said something cheerful like 'Helluva drop, hey?' Too late, he realized that the man had said the equivalent of, 'Shall we, old boy?' and he had gone and nodded his head.

They dropped. Charlie shrieked. It was not laughter.

The Bon Ton Alleys are – is – a complex, consisting of, naturally, bowling alleys, and of course an adjoining bar; but a good deal has been added. To the tissue-dispensers, for example, a second teensy-weensy dispenser for teensy tissues for milady's lipstick. To the bar, as well, foamy cottage curtains and a floor-length skirt around the pretzel-and-egg stand. The barmaid has become somehow a waitress. No one has traced the evolution from beer out of cans to pink ladies and even excuse-the-expression vermouth and soda. The pool tables are gone and are replaced by a gifte shoppe.

Here sit Jeanette Raile and her neighbor, Tillie Smith, over a well-earned (Tillie, especially, is getting to be a first-line, league-type bowler) crème de menthe frappé, and get down to the real business of the evening, which is – business.

'Accounting is accounting,' says Jeanette, 'and copy is copy. So why does old Beerbelly keep throwing his weight around in the copy department?'

Tillie sips and delicately licks. 'Seniority,' she says, a word which explains so much. Her husband works in the public relations department of Cavalier Industries.

Jeanette frowns. Her husband works for the agency that has the Cavalier account. 'He can't push *us* around.'

'Oh,' yawns Tillie, whose husband is a little older and doubtless, in some ways, a good deal sharper than Herb, 'those adding-machine people are easy to handle, because they're so awfully good at seeing what's in front of them.'

'What could be not in front of them?'

'Like that old Trizer that used to be with Cavalier,' Tillie said. 'One of the boys – now don't ask me which one – wanted a little more room in the office, so he had a chat with the Great Man – you know, funny funny – and made a bar-bet sort of thing that he could pad up the old expense account right through the ceiling and old Trizer would never catch it.' She sips, she laughs lightly.

'What happened?' asks Jeanette, agog.

'Why, old Trizer knew my – uh, this boy was after him, so when the heavy swindle-sheets started coming in, he quietly began to collect them until he had a stack heavy enough to drop on this boy's head. But the boy fed them out so carefully that it took a while. Meanwhile, of course, the Great Man was getting copies each time he did it, just to keep the funny funny gag alive. So by the time Trizer had his bomb ready to drop, five weeks had gone by and that was too long for the Great Man to think it was funny any more. So now they kicked old Trizer upstairs to the rear ranks of the Board of Directors where his seniority can't hurt anyone but himself.'

'Just deserts,' says Jeanette.

Tillie laughs. 'Sounds like a good name for a high-class bakery.'

'Just Desserts ... Oh yes,' says Jeanette brightly, for she hadn't thought of it until now, 'Herb's using that line to head up a new presentation to snag the Big-Bug Bakeries account. Be a dear and don't tell anyone.' Meanwhile she will tell Herb, but with the grasshopper speech – jump, boy, jump.

They stood on springy turf, Charlie with buckled knees, his companion's arm around him, holding him up. Charlie shook himself and stood, and when he could, he looked up. He then shuddered so hard that the arm tightened around him. He made an immense effort and grinned and threw off the arm. His companion made a small speech, with gestures for up, for down, for fast, for the bump on Charlie's head, for a matrix of humilities which probably included 'I'm sorry.' Charlie grinned again and feebly clapped him on the back. He then cast another worried look upward and moved away from the building. Not only was it altogether too big, much too high; the bulk of it seemed to be hanging over him like a fist. It was as wild a piece of architecture as the other, though more spindle-shaped than conical, more topple than top.

They moved across the turf – there seemed to be no roads or paths   and if Charlie had thought his companion's odd garb might attract attention, he was disabused. He himself was much more of an oddment. Not that the people peered, or crowded about: by no means. But one could sense by their cheerful waves and quickly averted eyes that they were curious, and further, that curiosity was out of place.

Rounding the building, they came upon perhaps fifty of them splashing in the pool. For bathing suits they wore only the soft silky sporran things, which clung to them without visible means of support; but by this time this was a category he was prepared to accept. They were, without exception, gravely polite in greeting him with a wave, a smile, a word, and apparently happy to see his companion.

Away from the pool, they wore a great many kinds and styles of clothes – often two by two, though he failed to catch the significance, if any, of this. It might be as little as a vivid, all but fluorescent ribbon of orange about the biceps – plus, of course, the sporran – or it might be as much as baggy pantaloons, tremendous winglike collars, steeple hats, platform sandals – there was no end to them, and, except for the ones who walked in pairs, there was no similarity between any of them except in the beauty of their colors and the richness and variety of the fabrics. Costume was obviously adornment to them, nothing more; unlike any people he had ever encountered or read about, they seemed to have no preoccupation with any particular part of their bodies.

He saw no women.

A strange place. The air was peculiarly invigorating, and the sky, though bright – with, now that he looked at it, a touch of that silvery radiance he had seen in the 'padded cell' – was overcast. Flowers grew profusely, some with heady, spicy scents, many quite new to him, with color splashed on with a free and riotous hand. The turf was as impossible as the buildings – even and springy everywhere, completely without bald patches or unwanted weeds, and in just as good shape here, near the buildings, where scores of people milled about, as it was far off.

He was led around the building and through an archway which leaned inexplicably but pleasantly to the left, and his companion took him solicitously by the arm. Before he could wonder why, they dropped straight down about sixty feet, and found themselves standing in an area vaguely like a subway station, except that instead of waiting for a train they stepped – rather, the native stepped; Charlie was hauled – off the edge of the platform and had to go through the unpleasant experience of flexing his legs to take a drop that just wasn't a drop – for the pit was bridged from side to side by the invisible substance which had levitated them down the building.

Halfway across, they stopped, the man gave Charlie a querying look, Charlie braced himself for anything at all and nodded; and, just how, Charlie couldn't see – it seemed to be some sort of gesture – they were flying through a tunnel. They stood still, and there was little sensation of starting or stopping; whatever it was they stood on whisked them away at some altogether unlikely speed until, in a very few minutes, they were stopped again at another platform. They walked into a sort of square cave at the side and were flicked up to ground level under the conical building. They walked away from the subway while Charlie concentrated on swallowing his heart and decided to let his stomach follow them whenever it had a mind to.

They crossed to what appeared to be a cave-like central court, all around the walls of which the natives were flashing up, flashing down, on their invisible elevators; they were a pretty sight with their bright clothes fluttering. And the air was filled with music; he thought at first it was some sort of public address system, but found that they *sang*; softly, moving from place to place, into the public hall and out of it, in beautiful harmonies, they hummed and trilled.

Then, just as they approached a side wall, he saw something that so dumbfounded him he barely noticed the experience of being flipped two hundred feet up like a squirted fruit-seed; he stood numb with astonishment, letting himself be pushed here, led there, while his whole sense of values somersaulted.

Two of the men who strolled past him in the central court were pregnant. There was no mistaking it.

He looked askance at his smiling companion – the strong face, the well-muscled arms and sturdy legs … true, the chin was very smooth, and – uh – he had very prominent pectoral muscles. The areola was considerably larger than those on a man … on the other hand, why not? The eyes were slightly different, too. What's so … now let's see. If 'he' were a woman, then they were all women. Then where were the men?

He recalled the way sh – h – the way he had been plucked up on the first lift, in those arms, like a sack of soda crackers. Well, if that's what the women could do – what could the men do?

First he pictured giants – real twelve, fifteen-foot behemoths.

Then he pictured some puny little drone chained up in a – a service station some place in the sub-basement …

And then he began to worry about himself. 'Where are you taking me?' he demanded.

His guide nodded and smiled and took him by the forearm, and he had the choice of walking or falling flat on his face.

They came to a room.

The door opened … dilated, rather; it was an oval door, and it split down the middle and drew open with a snap as they approached it, and it snapped enthusiastically closed behind them.

He stopped and backed up to the door. He was permitted to. The door felt solid enough for ten like him, and not even a knob.

He looked up.

They all looked back at him.

Herb Raile goes over to see Smitty. The kids are asleep. He has an electronic baby-sitter about the size of a portable radio. He knocks, and Smitty lets him in.

'Hi.'

'Hi.'

He crosses to the sideboard in the dining area of Smitty's living room, puts down the sitter and plugs it in. 'Whatch' doin'?'

Smitty scoops up the baby he had put on the couch when he went to answer the door. He hangs it on his shoulder where it attaches itself like a lapel. 'Oh,' he says, 'just generally mindin' the shop till the boss gets back.'

'Boss hell,' says Herb.

'You the boss in your house?'

'You know, you're kiddin',' says Herb, 'but I'll give you a straight answer in case that was a question.'

'Give me a straight answer in case.'

'Our kind of people, there is no boss in the house any more.'

'Yeah, I did think things were gettin' out of hand.'

'That's not what I mean, bonehead!'

'So what do you mean, headbone?' Smitty asks.

'It's a team, that's what I mean. There's a lot of yammering going on about the women taking over. They're not taking over. They're moving in.'

'Interestin' thought. You're a good, good boy,' he says, fatuously and with a sort of croon.

'I'm a what?'

'The baby, ya dumb bastard. He just burped.'

'Le's see him. Years since I picked up a little one like that,' says the father of three-year-old Karen. He takes the baby from Smith and holds it not quite at arm's length. 'Dather dather dather.' He flaps his tongue far out with each *th* sound. 'Dather dather.'

The baby's eyes get round and, held so under the armpits, its shoulders hunch up until its wet chin disappears in its bib. 'Dather dather.' The baby's eyes suddenly get almond-shaped, and it delivers a wide, empty smile with a dimple on the left, and a happy, aspirated buzz from the back of the throat. 'Dather dather hey he's smiling,' says Herb.

Smith ranges around behind Herb Railes where he can see. Impressed, 'Goddam,' he says. He puts his face next to Herb's. 'Dather dather.'

'You got to stick out your tongue far enough so he can see it move,' says Herb. 'Dather dather.'

'Dather dather dather.'

'Dather dather.' The baby stops smiling and looks quickly from one to the other. 'You're confusing him.'

'So shut up,' says the baby's father. 'Dather dather dather.' This so delights the baby that he crows and gets the hiccups.

'Scheiss,' says Smith. 'Come on in the kitchen while I get his water.'

They go in the kitchen, Herb carrying the baby, and Smith gets a four-ounce bottle out of the refrigerator and drops it in an electric warmer. He takes the baby from Herb and hangs it on his shoulder again. The baby hiccups violently. He pats it. 'Goddam, I told Tillie I'd pick up in here.'

'I'll be the boy-scout. You got your hands full.' Herb takes dishes from the counter-top, scrapes them into a step-on can, stacks them in the sink. He flips on the hot water. It is all very familiar to him because this sink and his sink and the sinks in the houses to right and to left and beyond and behind all are the same kind of sink. He picks up the can of liquid detergent and looks at it, pursing his lips. 'We never get this any more.'

'Whuffo?'

'Plays hell with your hands. Lano-Love, that's what we get now. Costs a little more but,' he says, ending his sentence with 'but.'

'"Two extra-lovely hands for two extra little pennies,"' says Smith, quoting a television commercial.

'So it's a commercial but just this once.' Herb turns on the hot water, tempers it with a little cold, picks up the spray head and one by one begins hot-rinsing the dishes.

There were Four of them, besides the one that had brought him. Two were in identical clothes – a vivid green sort of belly-band, and on the hips, the pannier parts of a full panniered skirt. But without the skirt. The tallest one, directly in front of Charlie, wore a subverted bathrobe somewhat like that of Charlie's companion, but dyed a firelit orange. The fourth wore something cut on the lines of the lower half of an 1890 man's bathing suit, in electric blue.

As Charlie's startled gaze turned to each, each smiled. They were all sprawled, posed, lounging on low benches and some hummocky hassocky things which seemed to have grown up out of the floor. The tall one was seated at a kind of desk which seemed to have been built before and around him (her) after the seating. Their warm friendly smiles, and their relaxed posture, were heartening, and yet he had the transient feeling that these amenities were analagous to the hearty rituals of modern business, which might do anything to a stranger before it was done with him, but which began, 'Sit down. Take off your shoes if you want – we're all buddies here. Have a cigar and don't call me mister.'

One of the green ones spoke in this people's bird-like (if the bird were a dove) tones to the orange one, gesturing toward Charlie, and laughed. Like his companion's laugh, it didn't seem to have too much laugh *at* in it. Said companion now spoke up, and there was general merriment. The next thing Charlie knew, his erstwhile guide, red bathrobe and all, was hunkered down, eyes squinched closed, feeling about frantically on the floor. Then he began to crawl on his knees and one hand, poking the other fearfully ahead, and wearing on his face an excruciating mask of comic terror.

They howled.

Charlie felt his ear-lobes getting hot, a phenomenon which was, in him, a symptom of either anger or alcohol, and he was very sure which one it wasn't, 'So let me in on the joke,' he rumbled. Still laughing, they looked at him perplexedly, while Red-robe kept on with his imitation of a 20th-century man meeting his first invisible elevator.

Something snapped in Charlie Johns, who had been pushed, pulled, prodded, dropped, flung, amazed, embarrassed, and lost just exactly as much as he could stand plus a straw's weight. He punted the red-clad rump with all the education of a high-school varsity toe, and sent the creature skidding across the room on its mobile face, almost to the foot of the yellow one's big desk.

Utter silence fell.

Slowly the red-robed one got up, turned to face him, while tenderly fondling the bruised backside.

Charlie pressed his shoulders a little harder against the unyielding door and waited. One by one he met five pairs of eyes. In each was no anger, and very little surprise; just sorrow; and he found that more ominous than fury. 'Well God damn it,' he said to the red robe, 'You asked for it!'

One of them cooed, and another chortled an answer. Then the red-robed one came forward and made a much more elaborate version of the series of moans and gestures which Charlie had seen before: the 'O I'm a swine, I didn't mean to hurt your feelings' message. Charlie got it, but was vexed by it; he wanted to say, well if you feel it was so wrong, why were you stupid enough to do it?

The yellow one rose, slowly and imposingly, and somehow got disentangled from the embrace of the desk. With a warm and pitying expression, he uttered a three-syllable word and gestured behind him, where a door opened, or rather a part of the wall dilated. There was a soft ululation of assent, and they all nodded and smiled and beckoned and waved toward it.

Charlie Johns moved forward just far enough to enable him to see through the doorway. What he saw was, as he had expected, heavily loaded with the unfamiliar, but none of the svelte, oddly unbalanced, interflowing gadgetry he saw could conceal the overall function of the flat padded table in its pool of light, the helmet-shaped business at one end, the clamp-like devices where arms and legs might go; this was some sort of operating room, and he wanted no part of it.

He stepped sharply backwards, but there were three people behind him. He whipped up a fist and found it gripped and held, high and helpless, just where it was. He tried to kick, and a bare leg flashed and locked knees with him, and it was a very strong leg indeed. The one in the orange robe came smiling apologetically and pressed a white sphere the size of a ping-pong ball against his right biceps. The ball clicked and collapsed; Charlie filled his lungs to yell but could never remember thereafter whether he had managed a sound.

'See this?' Herb says. They are in Smith's living room. Herb is idly turning the pages of the newspaper. Smitty is feeding the water to the baby skilfully spread out along his forearm, and says, 'What?'

'Brief briefs – but for men.'

'You mean underwear?'

'Like a bikini only less. Knit. My God they can't weigh more'n a quarter ounce.'

'They don't. Best thing to come along since the cocktail onion.'

'You got?'

'You damn bet I got. How much there?'

Herb consults the advertisement in the newspaper. 'Dollar'n a half.'

'You stop by Price Busters Discount over on Fifth. Two for two seventy-three.'

Herb looks at the illustration. 'Comes in white, black, pale yellow, pale blue and pink.'

'Yup,' Smitty says. Carefully he withdraws the nipple; the baby, hiccups corrected, is now asleep.

'Come on, Charlie – Wake up!'

Oh Mom just four more minutes I won't be late honest to pete I got in nearly two o'clock and I hope you never find out how pooped I was never mind what time. Mom?

'Charlie ... I can't tell you how sorry I am ...' *Sorry, Laura? But I wanted it to be perfect.* So who in real life ever makes it together the very first time? Come on, come on ... it's easy to fix; we just do it again ... *Oh-h-h ... Charlie ...*

'Charlie?' *Your name Charlie? Just call me Red.*

... once when he was fourteen (he remembered, remembered), there was this girl called Ruth and there was a sort of kiss-the-pillow kid's party, and no kidding, they played post office. The post office was the kind of airlock afforded by the double outside doors and double, heavily curtained inside doors of the old-fashioned house on Sansom Street, and all during the party Charlie kept looking at Ruth. She had that special kind of warm olive skin and sleek glossy short blue-black hair. She had a crooning whispery voice and a prim mouth and shy eyes. She was afraid to look at you for more than a second, and under that olive skin you could barely see a blush but without seeing anything you knew a blush made it warmer. And when the giggling and pointing and pointless chuckling chatter led around to Charlie's name being called, and then Ruth's, so that he and she would have to go into the post office and shut the door, something in him said only, 'Well, of course!' He held the door for her and she went in with her eyes cast down so they seemed closed; with her long lashes right on her warm cheeks; with her shoulders rounded with tension and her two hands hard-holding her two wrists; with her little feet making little steps; and to the yawping gallery making catcalls and kissing noises, Charlie winked broadly and then shut the door ... inside she waited silently, and he was a brash and forward little rooster known for it and needing to be known for it, and he took her firmly by the shoulders. Now for the first time she uncurtained her wise shy eyes and let him fall into the far dark there, where he swam unmoving for years-long seconds; so he said, this is all I want to do with you, Ruth; and he kissed her very carefully and very lightly in the middle of her smooth hot forehead and drew back again to totter into those eyes: because, Ruth, he said, it's all I should do with you. *You understand me, Charlie,* she breathed, *you do, you do understand me.*

'You understand me, Charlie. You do, you do understand me.'

He opened his eyes and fogs fled. Someone leaned close not Mom not Laura not Red not Ruth not anybody but that *thing* in the red cutaway bathrobe, who said again, 'You understand me now, Charlie.'

Now the words were not English, but they were as clear to him as English. He even knew the difference. The structure was different; transliterated, it would run something like 'You [second person singular, but of an alternative form denoting neither intimacy nor formality, but friendship and respect, as to a beloved uncle] understand [in the simple sense of verbal, rather than emotional or psychic understanding] me [a 'me' of helpful guidance and friendliness, as from a counsellor or guide, and not that of a legal-or-other superior] Charlie.' He was completely aware of all alternative words and their semantic content, although not of any cultural system which had made them that way, and he was aware that had he wanted to reply in English, he could have done so. Something had been added; nothing taken away.

He felt ... fine. He felt as if he had done without a little sleep, and he also felt a little sheepish, from a new inner knowledge that his earlier indignation was as pointless as his fear had been; these people had not meant to ridicule him and gave no indication of wishing to harm him.

'I am Seace,' said the red-robed one. 'Can you understand me?'

'Sure I can!'

'Please – speak Ledom.'

Charlie recognized the name – it was the term for the language, the country, and the people. Using the new tongue, he said, in wonder, 'I can speak it!' He was aware that he did so with an odd accent, due probably to his physical unfamiliarity with it; like every language, it contained sounds rather more special to it than to others, like the Gaelic glottal stop, the French nasal, the Teuton guttural. Yet it was a language well designed for the ear – he had a flash recollection of his delight, when he was just a kid, of seeing a typewriter with a script type-face, and how the curly tail of each letter joined with the one following – and the Ledom syllable, aurally speaking, joined just as cleverly to the next. It filled the mouth, too, more than does modern English, just as Elizabethan English was more sonorous an instrument. It would hardly be possible to speak Ledom with the lips open and the jaw shut, as many of his contemporaries did with English, which, in its evolution, seems bound to confound the lip-reader. 'I can speak it!' cried Charlie Johns, and they all cooed their congratulations; he had not felt so good about anything since the day he was seven and was cheered by all the boys on the float at a summer camp, when he swam his first strokes.

Seace took him by the upper arm and helped him to sit. They had him dressed in the almost exact equivalent of a hospital gown anywhere. He looked at this Seace (he recalled now that the 'I am Seace' phrase had occurred a number of times since he 'arrived,' but that previously his ear had not been able to separate one phoneme from another) and he smiled, really smiled, for the first time in this strange world. This elicited another happy murmur.

Seace indicated the native in the orange garments. 'Mielwis,' he introduced. Mielwis stepped forward and said, 'We are all very glad to have you with us.'

'And this is Philos.' The one in the ludicrous blue pants nodded and smiled. He had sharp humorous features, and a quick and polished glitter in his black eyes that might hide a great deal.

'And these are Nasive and Grocid,' said Seace, completing the introductions.

The green-clad ones smiled their greeting, and Grocid said, 'You're among friends. We want to make sure you know that, above anything else.'

Mielwis, the tall one, whom the other seemed to surround with some intangible aura of respect, said, 'Yes, please believe that. Trust us. And … if there's anything you want, just ask for it.'

Harmoniously, they all chorussed a ratification.

Charlie, warming toward them, wet his lips and laughed uncertainly. 'Mostly, I guess … information is what I want.'

'Anything,' said Seace. 'Anything at all you want to know.'

'Well, then, first of all – where *am* I?'

Mielwis, waiting for the other to defer to him, said, 'In the Medical One.'

'This building is called the Medical One,' Seace explained. 'The other one, the one we came from, is the Science One.'

Grocid said reverently, 'Mielwis is head [the word meant 'organizer' and 'commander' and something more subtle and profound, like 'inspirer'] of the Medical One.'

Mielwis smiled as if acknowledging a compliment, and said, 'Seace is head of the Science One.'

Seace deprecated what was apparently also a compliment, and said, 'Grocid and Nasive are heads of the Children's One. You'll want to see that.'

The two be-panniered ones accepted the accolade, and Grocid cooed, 'I hope you will come soon.'

Charlie looked from one to the other bewilderedly.

'So you see,' said Seace (and the 'see' was the 'comprehend' expression; it was like 'now you know all'), 'we're all here with you.'

The exact significance of this escaped Charlie, though he had the impression that it was something large – it was as if someone presented to you, at one and the same time, the Queen, the President and the Pope. He therefore said the only thing he could think of, which was, 'Well, thanks …' which seemed to please them, and then he looked at the one unidentified person left – Philos, the one in the pants. Surprisingly, Philos winked at him. Mielwis said off-handedly, 'Philos here is for you to study.'

Which is not precisely what he said. The sentence was formed with a peculiar grammatical twist, somewhat like the way a man says 'Onions don't like me,' when he means 'I don't like onions.' (Or shouldn't …) In any case, Philos did not seem to merit special honors and congratulations for being what he was, as did the heads of the Medical One, the Science One, and the Children's One. Maybe he just worked here.

Charlie put it away for future reference, and then looked around at their faces. They looked back attentively.

Charlie asked again, 'Yes, but where *am* I?'

They looked at one another and then back at him. Seace said, 'What do you mean, where are you?'

'Oh,' said Seace to the others, 'he wants to know *where* he is.'

'Ledom,' said Nasive.

'So where is Ledom?'

Again the swapped glances. Then Seace, with a the-light-is-dawning expression on his face, said, 'He wants to know where Ledom is!'

'Look,' said Charlie with what he thought was a reasonable amount of patience, 'Let's start right from the beginning. What planet is this?'

'Earth!'

'Good. Now we – *Earth?*'

'Yes, Earth.'

Charlie wagged his head. 'Not any Earth I ever heard about.'

Everybody looked at Philos, who shrugged and said, 'That's probably so.'

'It's some trick of this language,' Charlie said, 'If this is Earth, I'm a …' He could not, in this place, with these people, think of a simile fantastic enough. 'I know!' he said suddenly, 'There would be a word meaning Earth – the planet I live on – in any language! I mean, the Martian word for Mars would be Earth. The Venerian word for Venus would be Earth.'

'Remarkable!' said Philos.

'Nevertheless,' said Mielwis, 'this is Earth.'

'Third planet from the sun?'

They all nodded.

'Are you and I talking about the same sun?'

'Moment to moment,' murmured Philos, 'nothing is ever the same.'

'Don't confuse him,' said Mielwis in a tone stiff as an I-beam. 'Yes, it's the same sun.'

'Why won't you tell me?' Charlie cried. His emotion seemed to embarrass them.

'We did. We are. We mean to,' said Seace warmly. 'How else can we answer? This is Earth. Your planet, ours. We were all born on it. Though at different times,' he added.

'Different times? You mean ... time travel? Is that what you're trying to tell me?'

'Time travel?' echoed Mielwis.

'We all travel in time,' Philos murmured.

'When I was a kid,' explained Charlie, 'I used to read a lot of what we called science fiction. Do you have anything like that?'

They shook their heads.

'Stories about – well, mostly the future, but not always. Anyway, a lot of them were written about time machines – gadgets that could take you into the past or future.'

They all regarded him steadily. No one said anything. He had the feeling that no one *would*. 'One thing for sure,' Charlie said at length, shakily, 'this isn't the past.' Abruptly, he was terrified. 'That's it, isn't it? I'm ... I'm in the future?'

'Remarkable!' Philos murmured.

Mielwis said gently, 'We didn't think you'd come to that conclusion quite so soon.'

'I t told you,' said Charlie, 'I used to read—' And to his horror, he sobbed.

The baby is asleep, and from the electronic intercom, the mate to which is on a bracket in the doorway between Karen's and Davy's rooms in the other house, nothing comes but a soft 60-cycle hum. Their wives have not yet returned from bowling. It is peaceful there. They have drinks. Smitty sprawls half-off a couch. Herb is watching the television set, which happens to be turned off, but the easy-chair in which he is enfolded is so placed that it is a physical impossibility comfortably to look anywhere else. So on the blank screen he is looking at his thoughts. Occasionally he voices one ... 'Smitty?'

'Uh.'

'Say certain words to a woman, everything goes black.'

'... talkin' about?'

'"Differential",' says Herb.

Smitty rotates on a buttock far enough to get both feet on the floor and almost far enough to be sitting up.

'"Transmission",' Herb murmurs. '"Potential."'

'Transmission *what*, Herb?'

'"Frequency" is another one. What I mean, you take a perfectly good woman, good sense and everything. Runs an Italian finesse in bridge without batting an eye. Measures formula to the drop and sterilizes it to the second. Maybe even got an automatic timer in her head, can take out a four-minute egg at exactly four minutes without a clock. What I mean, has intuition, intelligence, plenty.'

'So okay.'

'Okay. Now you start explaining something to her that has one of these blackout words in it. Like here at last you can buy a car with a gadget on it that locks both rear wheels in such a way that they turn together, so you can pull out of a spot where one wheel is on ice. So maybe she's read about it in an ad or something, she asks you about it. You say, well, it just cuts out the differential effect. As soon as you say the word you can see her black out. So you tell her the differential is nothing complicated, it's these gears at the back of the drive shaft that make it possible for the rear wheel at the outside of a turn to rotate faster than the wheel at the inside. But all the while you're talking you can see she is blacked out, and she will stay blacked out until you get off the subject. Frequency, too.'

'Frequency?'

'Yeah, I mentioned it the other day and Jeanette like blacked out, so for once I stopped and said hey, just what is frequency anyway. Know what she said?'

'No; what she said?'

'She said it was part of a radio set.'

'Well, hell, women.'

'You don't get what I'm shootin' at, Smitty. Well hell women, hell! You can't dismiss it like that.'

'I can. It's a lot easier.'

'Well, it bothers me, that's all. Word like "frequency" now; it's good English. It says what it means. "Frequent" means often, "frequency" means how often something happens. "Cycles" – that's another blackout word – means what it says too: from the top around to the top again. Or maybe from forth to back to forth again, which amounts to the same thing. But anyway, you say a frequency of eight thousand cycles per second to a woman and she blacks out twice in a row simultaneously.'

'Well they just don't have technical minds.'

'They don't? Did you ever hear them talking about clothes, the gores and tucks and double french seams and bias cuts? Did you ever see one of them working one of those double-needle switch-back oscillating-bobbin self-fornicating sewing machines? Or in the office for that matter, running a double-entry bookkeeping machine?'

'Well, I still don't see what's so wrong if they don't bother to think through what a differential is.'

'Now you got your finger on it, or near it anyway! "They don't bother to think it through." They don't want to think it through. They can – they can handle much more complicated things – but they don't *want* to. Now, *why?*'

'Guess they think it's unladylike or something.'

'Now why the hell should that be unladylike? They got the vote, they drive cars, they do a zillion things men used to do.'

'Yours not to reason why,' Smitty grunts, and unfolding from the couch, he picks up his empty glass and comes for Herb's. 'All I know is, if that's the way they want it, let'm. You know what Tillie got yesterday? Pair desert boots. Yeah, exactly like mine. What I say is, let'm have their goddam blackout words. Maybe then by the time my kid grows up, that'll be the way he can tell which one is his father, so *vive la différence.*'

They brought him from the operating room to a place which they assured him was his own, and bade him good-bye in a way so ancient it preceded the phrase itself; it was the 'God be with you' from which good-bye evolved. It was Charlie's first encounter with their word for God and their way of using it, and he was impressed.

He lay alone in a rather small room, tastefully decorated in shades of blue. One entire wall was window, overlooking the park-like landscape and the uneasily-tottering Science One. The floor was a little uneven, like many of those he had seen here, slightly resilient and obviously waterproof, so designed that it obviously could be cleaned by flooding. At the corner, and in three places about the room, the floor reached upward in mushroom, or soft boulder contours to form seating arrangements, and the corner one could be altered by pressure on a small panel to be wider, narrower, higher, or possessed of any number of bumps, grooves and protuberances, in case one should want a prop under the shoulders or knees. Three vertical golden bars by this 'bed' controlled the lights; a hand placed between the first two, and raised or lowered, controlled the intensity, and a hand similarly slid between the second two ran the whole spectrum of color. An identical arrangement was placed near the door – or more properly, the unbroken wall which had in it a segment which dilated open when one gestured at a distinctive squiggle in the swirling design imprinted on the surface. The bed wall leaned inward, the opposite one out, and there were no square corners anywhere.

He appreciated their understanding thoughtfulness in giving him this needed privacy in which to pull himself together; he was grateful, angry, comfortable, lonesome, scared, curious and indignant, and such a stew must cool before anything could precipitate.

It was easy at first to whistle a whimsy in this dark: he had lost a world, and good riddance; what with one thing and another, he'd been getting pretty sick of it, and if he had ever thought there was a way of getting out of it alive, he might have wished for it.

He wondered what was left of it. Did we get the war? What lives in the Taj Mahal now – termites or alpha particles? Did that clown win the election after all, God forbid?

'Mom, did you die?'

Charlie's father had been so proud when he was born, and he had planted a redwood tree from seed. A redwood tree in Westfield, New Jersey! in the midst of a chicken-run, job-lot, shingle-and-lath type of developement project, fiendishly designed to be obsolescent ten years before the mortgage could be paid off; he had visualized it towering three hundred feet high over the ruins. But then he had inexcusably dropped dead, with his affairs in such a mess and his life-insurance premiums unpaid, that Charlie's mother had sold the few spoonsful of equity he had built up in it, and had moved away. And when Charlie was seventeen, he had gone back, moved by he knew not what, on a sort of pilgrimage; and though he had never known his father, finding the house still there, finding it a slum as his father had predicted, and finding the tree alive and growing, he had done a strange thing; he had touched the tree and he had said, 'It's all right, Dad.' Because Mom had never known need or a day of worriment while he lived, and had he lived, she might never have known them; but in some way she seemed convinced that he knew, trouble by trouble, scrape by scrape, humiliation by hardship, what she was going through, and inside, she seemed to feel as a woman might whose man was steadily beating the love out of her and all the tolerance. So in some vague way Charlie felt he had to go and say that to the tree, as if his father lived in it like a god damned hamadryad or something; he found it very embarrassing to remember the thing at all, but he remembered, he remembered.

Because that tree could be big now. Or if enough time had gone by, it could be dead … If the Texas redhead was a wart-nosed old madam in some oil seaport by now, the tree would be pretty darn big, and if Ruth (what the hell ever happened to Ruth?) was dead and gone, the tree might be the biggest thing in the whole North Jersey complex.

All right; now he knew one of the things he had to find out. *How far? How long ago?* (Not that it would make too much difference. Would it be twenty years, and the world changed and hostile but still too much the same, like Rip van Winkle's? Or if it were a hundred, or a thousand, what real difference would that make to him?) Still: the first thing he had to find out was, *How far?*

And the next thing had to do with he, himself, Charlie Johns. As far as he had been able to find out so far, there was nothing like him here, only those Ledom, whatever the hell they were. And – what were they?

He remembered a thing he had read somewhere: was it Ruth Benedict? Something about no item of man's language, or religion, or social organization, being carried in his germ cell. In other words you take a baby, any color, any country, and plank it down anywhere else, and it would grow up to be like the people of the new country. And then there was that article he saw containing the same idea, but extending it throughout the entire course of human history; take an Egyptian baby of the time of Cheops, and plank it down in modern Oslo, and it would grow up to be a Norwegian, able to learn Morse code and maybe even have a prejudice against Swedes. What all this amounted to was that the most careful study by the most unbiassed observers of the entire course of human history had been unable to unearth a single example of human evolution. The fact that humanity had come up out of the caves and finally built an elaborate series of civilizations was beside the point; say it took them thirty thousand years to do it; it was a fair bet that a clutch of modern babies, reared just far enough to be able to find their own food and then cast into the wilderness, might well take just as long to build things up again.

Unless some evolutionary leap, as huge as the one that had produced homo sap. in the first place, had occurred again. Now, he knew nothing yet about the Ledom – nothing to speak of; yet it was clear a) that they were humans of some sort and b) they were drastically unlike any humans of his time. The difference was more than a social or cultural difference – much more than the difference, say, between an Australian aborigine and an agency executive. The Ledom were physically different in many ways, some subtle, some not. So say they evolved from humanity; was that a clue to Item One: *How far?* Well, how long does a mutation take?

He didn't know that, but he could look out of his window (staying a respectful three paces away from it) and see some scores of bright flecks moving about in the parkland below; they were, or seemed to be, adults, and if their generations were the thirty years or so one thought of when one thought of generations, and if they did not lay eggs like a salmon and then hatch them all, why, they seemed to have been around for quite a while. To say nothing of their technology: how long does it take to get the bugs out of a design like the Science One yonder? ... That was a much harder question to answer. He remembered reading an ad in a magazine listing ten quite common items on a shopping list, aluminum foil, an anti-biotic ointment, milk in cartons, and the like, and pointing out that not a single one of these things could be had twenty years ago. If you lived in a technology like that of the mid-twentieth century, you were there to see the vacuum tube displaced by the transistor and that by the tunnel diode, while in one ten-year period the artificial satellite moved from the area of laughable fantasy to a hunk of hardware broadcasting signals from the other side of the sun. Maybe he was as funny as the West Indian lady on the escalator, but he shouldn't overlook the fact that her first escalator, strange as it was to her, wasn't even a product of her future.

So hang on to that, he told himself urgently. Be not too amazed. There were a lot of people living in his time who never did latch on to the idea that the curve of technological progress was not a flat slanting line like a diving board, but a geometrical curve like a ski-jump. These wistful and mixed-up souls were always suffering from attacks of belated conservatism, clutching suddenly at this dying thing and that, trying to keep it or bring it back. It wasn't real conservatism at all, of course, but an unthought longing for the dear old days when one could predict what would be there tomorrow, if not next week. Unable to get the big picture, they welcomed the conveniences, the miniaturization of this and the speed of that, and then were angrily confused when their support of these things changed their world. Well he, Charlie Johns, though he made no pretense of being a bigdome, seemed always to have been aware that progress is a dynamic thing, and you had to ride it leaning forward a little, like on a surfboard because if you stood there flat-footed you'd get drowned.

He looked out again at the Science One, and its unlikely stance seemed like an illustration of what he had been thinking. You'll have to lean strange ways to ride this one, he told himself ... which brought him back to the formulation of Question Two.

He mustn't waste his time now wondering *how* it had been done – how he had been snatched from the worn wooden steps between the second and third floors of 61 North 34th St, in his 27th year. *How* was certainly a matter of their technology, and he couldn't be expected to figure that out. He could hope to learn how, but not to deduce it. What he had to know was – *why?*

That broke itself down into a couple of compartments. He had a right to be biased, and assume that getting him here was a large and important undertaking – but it was a fair assumption. Finagling with space and time could hardly be small items. So there was this to consider: why had this large and important thing been done? that is to say, what were the Ledom getting out of it? … Well, it could be purely a test of their equipment: you got a new fish-lure, you try it out just to see what it will catch. Or: they needed a specimen, any old specimen, from exactly or about his portion of time and space, so they dredged it and it happened to be Charlie Johns. *Or:* they wanted Charlie Johns and no other, so they upped and got him. And this last, though logically the least likely, he unabashedly found easiest to believe. So Question Two resolved itself: *Why me?*

And Question Three followed as a corollary: *With me, what?* Charlie Johns had his faults, but he had, as well, a fairly balanced estimate of himself. He hadn't been snatched for his beauty nor his strength nor his intelligence, he was sure, because the Ledom could have done better in any or all departments, right there in his neighborhood. Nor was it for any special skill; Charlie used to say of himself that the only reason he wasn't a bum was that he worked all the time, and maybe he was a bum anyway. He had left high school in the tenth grade one time when Mom got sick, and what with one thing and another he never went back. He had sold ladies' underwear, refrigerators, vacuum cleaners and encyclopedias door to door; he had been a short order cook, elevator operator, puddler in a steel mill, seaman, carnival shill, bulldozer operator, printer's devil and legman for a radio station. In between times he had swamped on tractor-trailers, sold papers, posted outdoor advertising, painted automobiles, and once, at a world trade fair, he had made a living for a while smearing soft-fried egg-yolk on dishes so a demonstration dishwashing machine could wash it off. He had, always, read everything and anything he could get his hands on, sometimes at wild random and sometimes on the recommendation, knowingly or not, of someone he had been talking to; for furiously, wherever he went, he struck up conversations and picked people's brains. His erudition was wide and also full of holes, and sometimes his speech showed it; he would use words he had read and not heard, and was always barking his tongue on them. For example he had for years pronounced the word 'misled' as 'mizzled,' for a reason which demonstrates the clarity of his logic if nothing else: as a child he had seen on a box of English biscuits the picture of a trumpeter, from whose instrument came a staff of music with the staff drawn in wavy lines, probably to convey the idea of a fanfare *in vibrato*. Directly under and beside the staff was the legend 'Don't be misled'; to Charlie, 'mizzled' meant to be sort of wobbly and confused, like those lines. It was amazing how many people, for how long, caught his meaning when he used this word.

So … he was what he was, and for that, or for some of it, he had been reeled out of his world into this one. And that compartmented, too:

Either their purpose was to get him here, or – it was to get him away from there!

He mused on this. What had he been, or what had he been doing – or about to do – that the future didn't want him to be or do?

'Laura!' he cried aloud. It was just beginning, it was real, it was forever. Could that be it? Because if it was, he was going to find a way and then he was going to wreck this world, if he had to blow it up like a balloon and stick a hole in it.

Because look: If he were in the future, brought there to prevent something he was about to do in the past, and if it involved Laura, then the thing they wanted to prevent was probably any more Laura; and the only way that could have been worth their while was if Laura and he had a child or children. Which meant (he had read enough science fiction to be able easily to follow such a conjecture) that in *some* existence, some time-stream or other, he had in fact married Laura and had children by her; and it was this they had decided to interfere with.

'Oh God, Laura!' he cried ... she had not-quite red, not-quite blonde hair so that if you said apricot it would be too bright a name for the color; her eyes were brown, but so light in shade that it was the brown you use for gold when you haven't got gold paint. She defended herself fairly and clean, without any coyness or come-on, and when she surrendered it was with all her heart. He had wanted a lot of girls since he had discovered there was more to them than giggling, tattling and shrieks. He had loved a few. He had had more than a few – more than his share, he sometimes thought – of the ones he had wanted. But he had never (until Laura) had a girl he loved. It was like that thing with Ruth, when he was only fourteen. Something always happened. At these times – there had been a number of them – he had wanted the girl he loved more than anything else in life, except one thing, and that was: not to spoil it ... He had had fantasies, from time to time, about that, about a gathering of the four or five girls with whom this had happened, how they got their heads together to figure out why, loving them – and they knew he did, each one of them – why he had backed off. And how they would never, never be able to figure it out. Well, girls, that was the answer, take it or leave it, the simple answer: I didn't want to spoil it.

Until now.

'Now!' he cried aloud, startling himself. What the hell did 'now' mean?

... until Laura, until that kind of whole-hearted surrender. Only you couldn't call that surrender, because he surrendered too; they both did, all at once, altogether. Just that once; and then on the way home, on the stairs ...

Question Two was *why me?* 'You better have a damn good reason,' he muttered to the distant, tilted Science One. And it led to Question Three: *With me, what?* and its breakdown: he must go on, somehow, in this place – and he felt that that would almost certainly be it – or he would be able to go back. He had to find out about that.

He had to start finding out right now. He put his hand across all three of the bars that controlled the lights, and the door dilated.

Off-screen an imp-chorus shouts 'Goozle Goozle' in unison, and then with what sounds like ashcan lids, goes Wham Wham. On screen is a face: smooth, shiny-full-lipped, thick arch eyebrows, and arch is the word but (and 'but' here is unavoidable) sideburns down to *here*, and a thick muscular neck sticking out of the collar of an open black leather jacket.

    Goozle Goozle
        (Wham Wham)
    Goozle Goozle
        (Wham Wham)
    Goozle Goozle
        (Wham-) but instead of the *wham* for which one is tensed (Smitty's television has a sound system on it of immense authority, and that *wham* has a subsonic that scares you) the heavy fringe of lashes round the pale eyes comes up and the voice cuts in, an unhurried and unsexed voice, singing a tune. The words are something about Yee Ooo: I hold Yee Ooo, I kiss Yee Ooo, I love Yee Ooo, Ooo-Ooo. The camera dollies back and the singer is observed in a motion which one might explain by asserting that the singer, with infinite ambition, is attempting to grasp between his buttocks a small doorknob strapped to a metronome. An explosion of hysterical pipings causes the camera to cut to the front row of the audience, where a gaggle of girleens are speaking in tongues and shuddering from the internal impact of their own gender. Back to the singer who is (this must be the case) riding offstage upon an invisible model of that bicycle-like exercizing machine the handlebars of which go forward and back while the pedals go highstepping round and round and the saddle, the saddle goes up and down.

Smith casts a long arm, hooks the control, and twitches the TV set dead. 'Jesus.'

Herb Raile leans back in his big chair, closes his eyes, lifts his chin and says, 'Sensational.'

'What?'

'He's got something for everybody.'

'You *like* it!' Smith's voice cracks on the second word.

'I never said that,' says Herb. He opens his eyes and glares with mock ferocity at Smith. 'And don't you ever quote me I said I did, hear?'

'Well you said *something*.'

'I said he is sensational, which I allow you'll allow.'

'I'll allow.'

'And I said he's got something for everybody. The jailbait speaks for itself—'

'Squeaks.'

Herb laughs. 'Hey, I'm the copy expert here ... Squeak to me of love. Hey I can use that ... and those who are moved by feelings of overt or latent homosexuality, find an object. And the young bulls like his actions and his passions and are willing to copy the D.A. haircut and the jacket. And the women, especially the older ones, like him best of all; it's the baby face and the flower eyes that does it.' He shrugs. 'Something for everybody.'

'Forgot to mention your old neighbor buddy Smith,' says Smith.

'Well, everybody needs something to hate, too.'

'You're not really kiddin', Herb.'

'Not really, no.'

'You bother me, boy,' says Smith. 'When you get like this you bother me.'

'Like what?'

'Like you get all serious.'

'Is bad?'

'Man should take his work seriously. Shouldn't take himself seriously, how he feels and all.'

'What happens to the man?'

'He gets dissatisfied.' Smith looks at Herb owlishly. 'Man's in advertising, say, gets serious about products, say, does serious product research on his own time. Subscribes to, say, Consumer Reports. Gets feelings and takes them seriously. Gets an account, can't take his work seriously.'

'Put down the big gun, Smitty,' says Herb, but he is a little pale. 'Man picks up a new account, that's the most serious thing.'

'Everything else, kicks.'

'Everything else, kicks.'

Smith waves at the TV set. 'I don't like it and nobody's going to like it.'

It comes to Herb Raile then who sponsored that rock and roll show. A competitor. Smith's competitor Number One. Oh God me and my huge mouth. Wish Jeanette was here. She wouldn't have missed that. He says, 'I *said* it was a lousy show and I didn't like it.'

'So you got to say it *first*, Herbie, so you get understood.' He takes Herb's glass and goes away to build one more. Herb sits and thinks like an ad man should. One: the customer is always right. Two: but give me a single package from which comes all the odors of all the sins of all the sexes and I shall move the earth. And that – he glances at the great dead cataract of the dead TV eye – that was damn near it.

'I feel bad, real bad,' said Charlie Johns. He was aware that though in speaking Ledom, he did it the way one should speak in a foreign tongue – that is, to think in that language before speaking – his English idiom came through quaintly, like a Frenchman's engaging 'is it not?'s and 'but yes's.

'I understand,' said Philos. He came all the way into the room and poised near one of the built-in, or grown-on mushroom hassocks. He had changed to an orange and white striped arrangement like wings which sprang from his shoulders on stays of some sort; they swung free behind him. His well-knit body was, except for matching shoes and the ubiquitous silken sporran, otherwise uncovered. 'May I?'

'Oh sure, sit down, sit down … You do *not* understand.'

Philos raised a quizzical eyebrow. His eyebrows were thick and seemed level, but when he moved them, which was often, one could see that they were slightly peaked, each separately, like two furry almost flat ridged roofs.

'You're – *home*,' said Charlie.

He thought for an uncomfortable flash of time that Philos was going to take his hand in sympathy, and he stirred. Philos did not, but carried quite as much sympathy in his voice. 'You will be too. Don't worry.'

Charlie raised his head and looked carefully at him. He seemed to mean what he said, and yet … 'You mean I can go back?'

'I can't answer that. Seace—'

'I'm not asking Seace, I'm asking you. Can I be sent back?'

'When Seace—'

'I'll handle Seace when the time comes! Now you square with me: can I be sent back, or not?'

'You can. But—'

'But hell.'

'But you might not want to.'

'And why not?'

'Please,' said Philos, and his wings quivered with his earnestness, 'Don't be angry. Please! You have questions – urgent questions – I know that. And what makes them urgent is that you have in your mind the answers you want to hear. You will be more and more angry if you do not get those answers, but some can't be given as you would hear them, because they would not be true. And others … should not be asked.'

'Says *who?*'

'You! You! You will agree that some should not be asked, when you know us better.'

'I will like hell. But let's just try some out and get this ice broken. You will answer them?'

'If I can, of course.' (Here again was a grammatical shift. His 'If I can' meant almost the same as 'if I am able,' but there was a shadow of 'if I am enabled' in it. On the other hand – was he merely saying he would answer if he had the information? which after all is what 'enables' an answer.) Charlie put the thought aside, and gave him the urgent Question One.

'How far did you come? … How do you mean?'

'Just what I said. You took me from the past. How long ago was that?'

Philos seemed genuinely at a loss. 'I don't know.'

'You don't know? Or – no one knows?'

'According to Seace—'

'Up to a point,' said Charlie in exasperation, 'you're right; some of these questions will have to wait, at least until I see that Seace.'

'You're angry again.'

'No I'm not. I'm still angry.'

'Listen,' said Philos, leaning forward. 'We are a – well, a new people, we Ledom. Well, you'll learn all that. But you can't expect us to count time as you do, or continue some method of months and numbered years that has nothing to do with us … And how can it really matter – now? How can you care at all how long it has been, when your world is finished, and only ours is left to go on?'

Charlie turned pale. 'Did you say … finished?'

Sadly, Philos spread his hands. 'Surely you realized …'

'What could I realize!' Charlie barked; then, plaintively, 'But-but-but … I thought maybe somebody … even very old …' The impact wouldn't come all at once, but flickered about him in flashes of faces – Mom, Laura, Ruth – and changing massive chords of darkness.

Seace said gently, 'But I told you you could go back and be what you were born to be.'

Charlie sat numbly for a time, then slowly turned to the Ledom. 'Really?' he said, pleadingly, like a child promised the impossible – but promised.

'Yes, but then you'll be there knowing …' Philos made an inclusive gesture, 'all you'll know.'

'Oh hell,' said Charlie, 'I'll be home – that's the thing.' But something inside him was looking at a new-found coal of terror, was breathing on it, making it pulsate bright and brighter. To know about the end – when it was coming, how it was coming; to know, as man has never known before, that what was coming really was *the* end, was *it* … You lie down beside Laura's warm body knowing it. You buy Mom's lousy tabloid newspaper that she believes every word of, knowing it. You go to church (maybe pretty often, knowing it) and watch a wedding go by with the white-silk confection sitting so close to the button-busting groom midst a roaring sea of happy car-horns, knowing it. Now in this crazy off-balance place they wanted to tell him just when, just how.

'I tell you what,' he said hoarsely, 'you just send me back and just don't tell me when or how. Okay?'

'You are bargaining? Then will you do something for us?'

'I—' Charlie made a fumble at the sides of his hospital gown, but there were no pockets to turn out empty, '– I got nothing to bargain with.'

'You have a promise to bargain with. Would you make a promise, and keep it, to get that?'

'If it's that kind of promise I could keep.'

'Oh, it is, it is. It's just this: Know us. Be our guest. Learn Ledom from top to bottom – its history (there isn't much of that!), its customs, its religion and reason for being.'

'That could take forever.'

Philos shook his dark head, and in his black eyes, the lights gleamed. 'Not too long. And when we feel you really know us, we will tell you, and you'll be free to go back. *If you want to.*'

Charlie laughed. 'That's an *if?*'

Soberly, Philos answered him: 'I think it is.'

Just as soberly, Charlie Johns said, 'Let's look at the fine print, friend. The clause about "not too long" bothers me. You could claim that I didn't know all about Ledom when it turns out I haven't counted every molecule in every eyeball in the place.'

For the first time Charlie saw the flush of anger in a Ledom face. Philos said levelly, 'We would not do anything like that. We do not and I think we could not.'

Charlie felt his own anger stir. 'You're asking me to take a hell of a lot on faith.'

'When you know us better—'

'You want me to make promises *before* I know you better.'

Surprisingly, engagingly, Philos sighed and smiled. 'You are right – for you. All right then – no bargains now. But pay attention: I offer this, and Ledom will stand by it: if, during your examination of us and our culture, you find yourself satisfied that we are showing you everything, and that we are progressing with the disclosure fast enough to suit you, you may make the promise to see it through. And at the end, when we are satisfied that you have seen enough to know us as we would have you know us – then we will do whatever you wish about sending you back.'

'Hard to argue with a deal like that ... And just for the record, suppose I never do make that promise?'

Philos shrugged. 'You'll probably be returned to whence you came in any case. To us, the important thing is to have you know us.'

Charlie looked long into the black eyes. They seemed guileless. He asked, 'Will I be able to go anywhere, ask any question?'

Philos nodded.

'And get answers?'

'Any answer we are [enabled] to give.'

'And the more questions I ask, the more places I go, the more I see, the sooner I get to leave?'

'Exactly so.'

'I'll be damned,' said Charlie Johns to Charlie Johns. He rose, took a turn around the room, while Philos watched him, and then sat down again. 'Listen,' he said, 'before I called you in here I had myself a think. And I thought up three big questions to ask you. Mind you, in thinking them up, I didn't know what I know now – that is, that you were prepared to cooperate.'

'Try them, then, and be sure.'

'I mean to. Question One we have been over. It was, how long in the future – my future – did I come.' He held up a quick hand. 'Don't answer it. Aside from what you've said, which isn't much but which seems to be that Seace is the one to answer such questions, I don't want to know.'

'That's—'

'Shush a minute until I tell you why. First of all, it might be a tipoff as to when the end came, and I honestly don't ever want to know that. Second, now that I think of it, I can't see it would make any difference. If I go back – hey: are you sure I would go back to the very place and time I started from?'

'Very close to it.'

'Okay. If that's so, it can't matter to me whether that's a year or ten thousand years back. And in the meantime I'd as soon not think of my friends old or my friends dead, or any of that: when I go back I'll be with my friends again.'

'You'll be with your friends again.'

'All right: so much for Question One. Question Three is also answered; it was, What is going to happen to me here?'

'I'm glad it's answered.'

'All right; that leaves the one in the middle. Philos: *Why me?*'

'I beg your—'

'Why me? Why *me?* Why didn't you find someone else for your body-snatching? Or if it had to be me, why did you bother? Was it that you were testing your equipment and took what came? Or do I have some special quality or skill or something that you need? Or – did you, oh *damn* you! did you do it to stop me from doing something back then?'

Philos recoiled from him and his vehemence – not so much in fear, but in surprise and distaste, as one might step back from a burst sewer pipe.

'I shall try to answer all of those questions,' he said cooly, having given Charlie thirty seconds of silence to hear the unpleasant echoes of his own voice, and to be sure he was finished. 'First of all, it was you and only you we took, or could have taken. Second: yes, we were after you especially, for a special quality you have. The last part is, you'll surely agree with me, ridiculous, illogical and hardly worth your anger. For look: (the 'look' was 'Attend: reason this out. Observe: reflect.') In view of the fact that you have every chance of being returned to almost exactly whence you came, how could your removal possibly affect your subsequent acts? Very little time will have passed.'

Glowering, Charlie thought that over. 'Well,' he said at length, 'maybe you're right. But I'll be different, wouldn't you say?'

'From knowing us?' Philos laughed pleasantly. 'And do you really and truly believe that knowledge of us can seriously affect you as you were?'

In spite of his wishes, an answering grin tugged at the corner of Charlie's mouth. Philos had a good laugh. 'I guess it can't. All right.' Much more agreeably, he asked, 'Then would you mind telling me what's so special I've got that you need?'

'I do not mind at all.' (It was one of the times when Charlie's idiom came out sounding quaint, and Philos was clearly, but with friendliness, imitating him.) 'Objectivity.'

'I'm sore and I'm bewildered and I'm lost. What the hell kind of objectivity is that?'

Philos smiled. 'Oh, don't worry: you qualify. Look: did you ever have the experience of having an outsider – and not necessarily any kind of a specialist – say something about you that taught you something about yourself – something you couldn't have known without the remark?'

'I guess everyone has.' He was reminded of the time he heard the voice of one of his minor-episode girl-friends coming unmistakably through the thin partition of a bathhouse at South Beach – and she was talking about him! – saying, '– and the first thing he'll say to you is that he never went to college, and he long ago got so used to competing with college graduates that he doesn't bother to find out any more whether or not.' It was not a large thing nor too painfully embarrassing, but never again did he mention the matter of college to anyone; for he hadn't known he *always* said it, and he hadn't known how silly it sounded.

'Well, then,' said Philos. 'As I told you, we are a new race, and we make it our business to know everything we can about ourselves. We have tools for this purpose that I couldn't even describe to you. But the one thing, as a species, we can't have, and that is objectivity.'

'That may be all very well, but I'm no expert at observing races or species or cultures or whatever it is you're driving at.'

'You *are*, though. Because you're different. That alone makes you an expert.'

'And suppose I don't like what I observe?'

'Don't you see,' said Philos urgently, 'that does not matter? Liking or not liking us will be only facts among facts. We wish to know what becomes of what you see when it is processed by what you think.'

'And once you have it—'

'We know ourselves better.'

Wryly, Charlie said, 'All you'll know is what I think.'

Just as wryly, Philos said, 'We can always take exception …'

At last, they laughed together. Then, 'Okay,' said Charlie Johns. 'You're on.' He delivered a mighty yawn and excused himself. 'When do we start? First thing in the morning?'

'I thought we—'

'Look,' Charlie pleaded, 'I've had a long day, or whatever it was, and I'm beat.'

'You're tired? Oh well, then, I don't mind waiting while you rest some more.' Philos settled himself more comfortably in his seat.

After a moment of perplexed silence, Charlie said, 'What I mean is, I have to get some sleep.'

Philos sprang up. 'Sleep!' He put a hand to his head, struck it. 'I do apologize; I'd quite forgotten. Of course! … how do you do it?'

'Huh?'

'We don't sleep.'

'You don't?'

'How do you do it? The birds put their heads under their wings.'

'I lie down. I close my eyes. Then I just – lie there, that's all.'

'Oh. All right. I'll wait. About how long?'

Charlie looked at him askance: he could be kidding. 'Usually about eight hours.'

'Eight *hours!*' and immediately, courteously, as if ashamed for having shown either ignorance or curiosity, Philos moved toward the door. 'I'd better leave you alone to do it. Would that be all right?'

'That would be fine.'

'If you should want anything to eat—'

'Thanks, they told me about that when they told me how to work the lights, remember?'

'Very well. And you'll find clothes in the closet here.' He touched, or almost touched, a swirl in the wall-print opposite. A door dilated and slammed shut again. Charlie got a glimpse of shatteringly brilliant fabrics. 'Pick out what you like best. Ah …' he hesitated … 'you'll find them all … ah, concealing, but we've tried to design them as comfortably as possible in spite of that. But you see … none of the people have ever seen a male before.'

'You're – females!'

'Oh – no!' said Philos, waved and was gone.

Smith runs to Old Buccaneer, Herb Railes observes, standing in Smith's downstairs bathroom and looking into the medicine chest. The medicine chest is on the wall over the toilet, and there is another chest over the vanity shelf, which is beside the sink. All these houses have the two chests. In the prospectus they were labelled *His* and *Hers*. Jeanette called them *His* and *Ours*, and apparently Tillie Smith is (in Herb's earlier phrase) moving in as well, for one and a half of the four shelves are cluttered with feminalia. As for the rest, there is Old Buccaneer Erector Set, which makes the beard stand up before shaving, and Old Buccaneer Captain's Orders, which makes the hair lie down after combing. Also Old Buccaneer Tingle, a bath oil with added Vitamin C. (Herb one time got a huge yuk out of a dictionary definition of buccaneer: a sea robber, and said no wonder they have to put more of the stuff in it, but it was not the kind of joke that makes Smitty laugh.) Personally Herb is a little sorry for Smitty to be stuck with all that Old Buccaneer, because there is better stuff on the market. Sleek Cheek for example. Herb owes much of his altitude at the agency to the fact of having authored Sleek Cheek's slogan: a picture of a Latin American wolf (carefully continental, if your tastes were transatlantic) rubbing jowls with an ecstatic and mammariferous memsahib, over the legend *You wan' a sleek cheek?*

Well! Herb says, almost aloud. A tube of pile ointment.

Tranquilizers of course, buffered aspirins and a bottle of monstrous half-blue, half-yellow capsules. *One three times a day*. Achromycin, Herb is willing to bet. Carefully touching nothing, he leans forward to peer at the label. The date tells him that it was bought three months ago. Herb thinks back. That was about the time Smitty quit drinking for a while.

Prostate, hey?

Colorless lipstick – for chapped lips. Colorless nail polish. Touch stick. What the hell is a touch stick, No. 203 Brown? He leans closer. The fine print says *For temporary retouching between applications of TouchTone tint*. Time marches on, Smitty. Better yet delete the comma: Time marches on Smitty.

Charlie remembered (remembered, remembered) a chant he had heard in kindergarten. He had heard it from the big kids, the kids in second grade, the girls skipping rope:

> *Hutch-ess Putch-ess* bring the *Dutch-ess*
> *Mom*-my's *going* to *have* a *ba*-by
> Not a *boy*
> Not a *girl*
> But *just* a *lit-tle ba*-by.

Chanting silently, he fell asleep. He dreamed about Laura ... they had known each other such a little time, and yet forever; already they had a lover's language, little terms and phrases with meaning for them and for no one else: *That's a man thing, Charlie*. He could say, 'That's a woman thing, Laura,' even about her shrill small squeak when the June bug got caught in her apricot hair, and make her laugh and laugh.

Waking, he went through a strange zone, coming to a place of sensibility in which he knew clearly and coldly that Laura was separated from him by impenetrable barriers of space and time, but in which, simultaneously, his mother sat at the foot of the bed. And as he passed through this zone, it became clearer and clearer to him that he was in Ledom, so that there would be none of that traveler's disorientation on fully awakening; yet with it, the sense of his mother's presence became stronger and stronger, so that when he Opened his eyes and she was not there, it was as if he had seen her – she herself, not her image – disappear with an audible *pop*. Therefore, furious and injured, he awoke crying for his mother …

When he had his feet under him and his head at last on top, he walked to (but not too near) the window and looked out. The weather had not changed, and he seemed to have slept the clock around, for the sky, though still overcast, was quite as bright as it had been during his trip from the Science One. He was ravenous; and, remembering his instructions, he went to the shelf-bed on which he had slept, and pulled outward on the bottom of the first of the three golden bars. An irregular section of the wall (nothing was ever square, flat, vertical or exactly smooth around here) disappeared up and back rather like the cover of a rolltop desk, and as if the orifice were a comic mouth thrusting out a broad tongue, a kind of board slid outward. On it rested a bowl and a platter. In the bowl was a species of gruel. On the platter was a mound of fruit, exotically colored and exquisitely arranged to make the best artistic display of its improbable series of shapes. There were one or two honest bananas and oranges, and some grape-like things, but the others were bulging and blue, mottled, iridescent vermilion and green, and at least seven varieties of red. What he wanted more than anything else in the world, this or any other, was something cold to drink, but there was nothing like that. He sighed and picked up an orchid-colored globe, sniffed it – it smelled, of all things, like buttered toast – and tentatively bit into it. He then emitted a loud grunt of astonishment, and cast about him for something with which to wipe his face and neck. For though the fruit's skin was, to his lips, at room temperature, its juice, which emerged under considerable pressure, was icy cold.

He had to use his white gown to mop up with, after which he took up a second specimen of the orchid fruit and tried again, with gratifying results. The clear, cold juice was without pulp, and tasted like apples with an overtone of cinnamon.

He then looked at the gruel. He had never been fond of cooked cereals, but the aroma from this one was appetizing, though he could not place it. An object lay beside the bowl, a tool of some sort. In outline it was spoonlike, but actually it consisted only of a handle holding a bright blue, fine wire loop, rather like a miniature tennis racquet without strings. Puzzled, he held it by the handle and thrust the loop into the porridge. To his surprise the gruel mounded up over the wire loop as if it had had a solid spoon-bowl under it. Lifting it, he saw that the food mounded on the underside in the same way – not one bit more, and it didn't drip. Cautiously he mouthed it, and found it so delicious he could not be perturbed at the rubber-sheet texture of the invisible area inside the loop. He looked at it, true, and thrust an experimental finger through it (it resisted his finger only slightly) but all the while he was rejoicing, gland by salivary gland, at the savory, sweet-spicy, and downright muscular belly-filling nature of the gruel-like food. The flavor was utterly new to him, but, gobbling until the blue wire was distorting itself against the empty bottom of the bowl, he prayerfully wished to see it again some time soon.

Content, physically at least, he sighed and rose from the bed, whereupon the board with its cargo silently slid into the opening which immediately became part of the wall. 'Room service,' Charlie murmured, wagging his head in approval. He crossed to the closet Philos had shown him and palmed the squiggle in the wall design. The door dilated. The compartment was illuminated, again by that dull sourceless silver glow. Casting a wary eye on the edges of the irregular oval opening – for that thing could open and close with real enthusiasm – he peered inside, hoping to see his good brown normal United States pants. They were not there.

Instead was a row of constructions – that was the only word for it – of fabrics stiff and floppy, starched, filmy, opaque, and all of these in combinations; reds, blues, greens, yellows, fabrics which seemed all colors at once, with threads picking up one and another hue from those around them; and fabrics with no color at all, which subdued anything they overlaid. These were put together in panels, tubes, folds, drapes, creases and seams, and variously scalloped, fringed, embroidered, appliquéd and hemmed. As his eye and hand became inured to this dazzle, a certain system became manifest; the mélange could be separated, and certain internal systems removed to be inspected by themselves as garments. Some were as simple as a night-shirt – functionally speaking, though anyone sleeping in one would surely dream he was being sliced by a diffraction grating. There were nether garments too, in the form of floppy pantaloons, leotards, tight briefs, G-strings and loin-cloths, as well as kilts long and short, flowing and crinolined, skirts full and hobbled. But what was this glittering two-inch wide, eight-foot ribbon, built like a series of letter U's attached by their top ends? And how were you supposed to wear a perfect sphere of resilient black material – on your head?

He put it on his head and tried to balance it there. It was easy. He tipped his head to roll it off. It stayed where it was. He pulled at it. It wasn't easy. It was impossible. It was stuck to him. It didn't pull at his hair either; it seemed to be his scalp it was stuck to.

He went to the three gold bars, prepared to lay his hand across them to call Philos, and then paused. No, he'd get dressed before he called for help. Whatever these crazy mixed-up people turned out to be, he still felt he didn't want to resume the practice of having a woman help him get dressed. He'd quit that some years ago.

He returned to the closet. He quickly learned the knack of hanging clothes in it. They were not on hangers exactly, but if you took a garment and spread it the way you wanted it to hang, and touched it to the wall inside the door at the right, it stayed the way it was. Then you could shove it across the closet where it slid as if on a wire, only there was no wire. When you pulled it out, it collapsed and was simply an empty garment again.

He found a long piece of material shaped roughly like the outline of an hourglass, with a length of narrow ribbon at one end. The material was a satisfyingly sober navy blue, the ribbon a rich red. Now, he thought, that ought to diaper up into a pretty fair pair of trunks. He pulled off the white gown – fortunately it was open in the back, or he'd never have gotten it off over the black ball that bounced and nodded over his head with every move. He placed the ribbonless end of the blue material on his abdomen, pulled the rest between his legs and up the back, and getting hold of the ends of the ribbon, brought them around the sides, meaning to tie them together in front. But before he could do that they fused into one, with no sign of a join or seam. He tugged at the ribbon; it stretched, then came slowly back until it was snug around his waist, where it stopped contracting. Marveling, he tugged the free front end of the material up until it was tight enough to suit him in back and between the legs, then let the free end fall in a sort of apron in front. He turned and twisted, looking at it admiringly. It fitted like his own skin, and although his legs were, at the sides, bare up to the waist, with only a strip of red belting there, he was otherwise, as Philos had suggested, concealed.

As for the rest of him, he'd just as soon skip it, for, as he had learned in his brief outdoor experience, this was a tropical place. On the other hand, most of these people seemed to wear something on the top half, if only an armband or something on the shoulder blades. He mused at the clutter of finery in the closet and saw a patch of the same dark blue as the garment he was wearing. He pulled it out. It seemed to be a sort of coat or cloak, which appeared heavy but was actually feather-light, and not only was it an exact match, but it had a thin piping of the same red as the waistband of his breech-clout. Putting it on turned into a puzzle, until he realized that, like the red thing Seace had worn, it did not come over the shoulders but went under the arms instead.

It had the same stand-up collar in the back, and in the front it met just over his breastbone. There was no fastening there, but it needed none; it settled softly onto his pectoral muscles and clung there. The waist was fitted, though it did not meet in front; still, it was fitted and stayed that way. The skirt was not like Seace's, pulling back and down to a swallowtail, but was squared off at about knuckle length all the way around.

And there were shoes in the bottom of the closet; on a shelf he saw the irreducible minimum in shoes: shaped pads made to adhere to the ball of the foot and the toes, underneath, and others to fit only the heel, with nothing between. There were many others, too; thonged and buckled sandals, and sandals with ties and self-fusing ribbons and no apparent fastening at all; soft pliant knee boots of many colors, turned-up, Turkish style shoes, platforms, huaraches, and many, many others, excepting anything which might confine or cramp the foot. He let color be his guide, and sure enough, found a pair of almost weightless, chamois-like boots which exactly matched the predominantly navy, touched with crimson outfit he was wearing. He hoped they were his size … and they were, perfectly, beautifully; and then he realized that certainly all *these* shoes would naturally be his or anyone's size.

Pleased with himself, he tugged once again aimlessly at the ridiculous black bubble bobbing on his head, and then went to the bars and palmed them. The door dilated with a snap, and Philos walked in. (What – was he standing with his nose on it for the last eight hours?) He was wearing a spreading kilt of amaryllis yellow, matching shoes, and a black bolero, which he seemed to have put on backwards. But on him it didn't look bad. His eloquent dark face lighted up as he saw Charlie: 'Dressed already? Oh, fine!' and then indescribably puckered. It was a tight expression which Charlie couldn't quite fathom.

'You think it's all right?' he asked. 'I wish I had a mirror.'

'Of course,' said Philos. 'If I may …' He waited. Charlie sensed that in an offhand, ritualistic way, like 'Gesundheit,' he was responding to the request. But – with 'May I?'

'Well, sure,' said Charlie, and gasped. For Philos touched his hands together – and then Philos was gone! and instead someone else stood there, resplendent in deep navy with a high collar which excellently framed his rather long face, with well-fitting trunks with a nicely-draped apron in front of them, with very handsome shoes, and even with the bare shoulders which surmounted the full jacket, and the silly black ball bobbling on its head, the figure was a pretty snorky one. Except for the face, which unaccountably did not matter to him.

'All right?' The figure vanished and Philos reappeared; Charlie stood there openmouthed. 'How did you do that?'

'Oh, I forgot – you couldn't have seen that.' He extended his hand, on which he wore a ring of bright blue metal, the same glistening blue as the wire with which Charlie had eaten his breakfast. 'When I touch it with my other hand, it makes a pretty good mirror.' He did so, and the handsome figure with the silly ball on its head reappeared and then vanished.

'Now that is a *gadget*,' said Charlie, for he had always been fond of gadgetry. 'But why on earth do you carry a mirror around with you? Can you see yourself in it too?'

'Oh no.' Philos, though he still wore the puckered expression, managed to build a smile into it. 'It's purely a defensive device. We seldom quarrel, we Ledom, and this is one of the reasons. Can you imagine yourself getting all worked up and contorted and illogical (the word contained the concepts for 'stupid' and 'inexcusable') and then coming face to face with yourself, looking at yourself exactly as you look to everyone else?'

'Cool you down some,' agreed Charlie.

'Which is why one asks permission before using it on anyone before doing so. Just politeness. That's something that's as old as my kind of humanity and probably yours too. A person resents being shown himself unless he specifically wants it.'

'You have quite a toy-shop here,' said Charlie admiringly. 'Well ... do I pass muster?'

Philos looked him up and down and up, and the puckered expression intensified. 'Fine,' he said in a strained voice. 'Just fine. You've chosen very well. Shall we go?'

'Look,' said Charlie, 'you've got some trouble or other, haven't you? If there's anything the matter with the way I look, now's the time to tell me.'

'Oh well, since you ask ... do you,' (Charlie could see he was choosing his words carefully) '... do you care very much for that – ah – hat?'

'That, for God's sake. It's so light I almost forgot about it, and then you and the mirror thing – hell no! I touched it to my head somehow or other and I can't get it off no way.'

'That's no trouble.' Philos stepped to the closet, dilated it, reached inside and came out with something about the size and shape of a shoehorn. 'Here – just touch it with this.'

Charlie did so, and the black object tumbled to the floor where it bounced soggily. Charlie kicked it into the closet and replaced the shoe-horn thing. 'What is that?'

'The de-stator? It inactivates the biostatic force in the material.'

'And biostatic force is what makes these clothes stick to themselves and to me?'

'Well, yes, because this is not exactly non-living material. Ask Seace: I don't understand it myself.'

Charlie peered at him. 'You still got trouble. You'd better come out with it, Philos.'

The pucker increased, and Charlie had not thought it could. 'I'd rather not.

The last time anyone thought you were funny you booted him clear across Mielwis' central chamber.'

'I'm sorry about that. I was a lot more lost then than I am now … So – out with it.'

'Do you know what that was you were wearing on your head?'

'No.'

'A bustle.'

Shouting with laughter, they left the room.

They went to see Mielwis.

'Take their time bowling,' says Smith.

'Out on strike.'

'A funny funny copy man.' But Smith is not putting Herb down; he is laughing inside.

The silence falls. They are talked out. Herb knows that Smith knows that each knows the other is looking for something to say. Herb reflects that it's a funny thing people can't just be together without burping out words, any old words; but he does not say it aloud because Smith might think he's getting serious again.

'Cuffs going out again,' says Smith after a while.

'Yeah. Millions and millions of guys getting their pants altered. What you suppose the tailor does with all the cuffs? And what happens to all the cuff material the manufacturers don't use?'

'Make rugs.'

'Cost the same,' says Herb, meaning the new cuffless pants.

'*Oh* yeah.' Smith knows what he means.

That silence again.

Herb says, 'You got much wash-n-wear?'

'A few. Everybody does.'

'Who washes it and wears it?'

'Nobody,' says Smith, with a touch of indignation. 'Any good cleaner's got a special process by now, does a good job.'

'So why wash-n-wear?'

Smith shrugs. 'Why not?'

'I guess so,' says Herb, knowing when to get off a subject.

The silence.

'Ol' Farrel.'

Herb looks up at Smith's grunt, and sees Smith looking out and across through his picture window and the picture window of the split level house diagonally opposite. 'What's he doing?'

'TV, I guess. But dig the crazy chair.'

Herb rises, crosses the room. He carries an ashtray, puts it on the table, comes back. From a hundred and thirty feet away he doesn't seem to be staring. 'One of those contour chairs.'

'Yeah, but *red*. In that room, how can he get a red chair?'

'Just stick around, Smitty. He'll be remodeling.'

'?'

'Remember two years ago, all knotty pine and ranch type stuff, and then one day in come that big green chair of his. Inside of a week, voom. Early American.'

'Oh yeah.'

'So inside of a week, you watch.'

'Voom.'

'That's what I said.'

'How can he pop for two remodeling jobs in three years?'

'Maybe he got relatives.'

'You know him?'

'Me? Hell no. Never been in the place. Hardly said hello.'

'Thought he was hard up though.'

'Whuffo?'

'Car.'

'So he spends it on remodeling.'

'Queer people anyway.'

'What type queer?'

'Tillie saw her buy blackstrap molasses at the super.'

'Oh hell,' says Herb, 'it's like a cult, that stuff. No wonder about the car. Prob'ly don't even care who sees it's eighteen months old.'

The silence.

Smith says, 'Bout time painted this place.'

Herb says, 'Me too.'

White lights scythe the landscaping; Smith's station wagon wheels into the drive, into the carport and dies. Car doors slam like a two-syllable word. Female voices approach, two speaking simultaneuosly, neither missing a thing. The door opens, Tillie comes in, Jeanette comes in.

'Hi bulls, what's bulling?'

'Just man talk,' says Smith.

They walked undulating corridors and twice stepped harmlessly into bottomless pits and were whisked upwards. Mielwis, in a diagonal arrangement of wide ribbon wrapped to the right around his body and down his right leg, and wrapped to the left down around his left leg, yellow and purple, was alone and looked quite imposing. He greeted Charlie with grave cheerfulness and clearly, openly, audibly approved the navy-blue outfit.

'I'll leave you,' said Philos, to whom Mielwis had paid no attention whatever (which, thought Charlie, might have meant only acceptance) until he said this, nodded and smiled kindly. Charlie waved a finger, and Philos was gone.

'Very tactful,' said Mielwis approvingly. 'We have only one like Philos.'

'He's done his best for me,' said Charlie, and then added in spite of himself, 'I think …'

'Well now,' said Mielwis, 'Good Philos tells me you feel much better.'

'Let's just say I'm beginning to know how I feel,' said Charlie, 'which is more than I knew when I first got here.'

'Unsettling experience.' Charlie watched him carefully, in some way compelled to. He had no reference whatever as to the probable age of these people, and if Mielwis seemed older, it was probably the sum of that barely acknowledged respect which others gave him, and his slightly larger size, and fuller face, and the really extraordinary – even here – spacing of his eyes. But there was nothing about any of these people which bespoke aging as he had known it.

'So you want to find out all there is to know about us.'

'I certainly do.'

'Why?'

'That's my ticket home.' The phrase was so idiomatic that it was nearly meaningless in the language, and Charlie knew it as soon as he said it. There seemed no concept for 'payment' or 'pass' in the tongue; the word he had chosen for 'ticket' came out meaning 'label' or 'index card.' 'I mean,' he supplemented, 'I am told that when I have seen all you care to show me—'

'– and all you care to ask—'

'– and give you my reactions to it, you are prepared to put me back where I came from.'

'I am pleased to be able to ratify that,' and Charlie got the impression that without bragging, Mielwis was informing him that for him, Mielwis, to ratify it was a large measure. 'Let us begin.' Somehow that seemed like a witticism.

Charlie laughed puzzledly. 'I hardly know where.' Some words he had read somewhere – Charles Fort? Oh! How he'd have loved this setup! – Fort had said, 'To measure a circle, begin anywhere.' 'All right then. I want to know about … something personal about the Ledom.'

Mielwis spread his hands. 'Anything.'

Suddenly shy, he couldn't ask directly. He said, 'Philos said something last night – or anyway, just before I slept … Philos said you Ledom had never seen the body of a male. And I immediately thought he meant you were all females. But when I asked him, he said no. Now, either you're one or the other, right?'

Mielwis did not answer, but remained still, looking at him kindly from those wide eyes and keeping a poised, also kindly, half-smile on his lips. In spite of his embarrassment, which for some reason began to be acute, Charlie recognized the technique and admired it; he'd had a teacher once who did that. It was a way of saying 'Figure it out for yourself,' but it would never be used on anyone who had not all the facts. Sort of like the 'Challenge to the Reader' in an Ellery Queen whodunit.

Charlie jumbled together in his mind all the uneasy impressions he had had on the matter: the large (but not unusually large) pectoral development, and the size of the areolae; the absence of wide-shouldered, narrow-hipped individuals. As to other cosmetic characteristics, like the hair, worn in as many different ways as clothes, though predominantly short, and the clothes themselves with their wild variegation, he refused to be led astray.

Then he turned to the language, which so unaccountably (to him) he could speak with fluency, and yet which was constantly presenting him with mysteries and enigmas. He looked at the grave and patient Mielwis, and said to himself in Ledom: 'I am looking at him.' And he examined the pronoun 'him' by itself for the very first time, and found that it had gender only in his own reference; when he spoke the word it translated to 'him' in English because, for some reason of his own, Charlie preferred it that way. But in its own reference, in the Ledom tongue, it had no sexual nor gender meaning. Yet it was a *personal* pronoun; it would not be used in speaking of things. In English, 'it' is an impersonal pronoun; the word 'one' used as a pronoun is not, stilted though it may be: 'One would think one was in Paradise.' The personal pronoun – and there was only one! in Ledom was like that: personal and without gender. That Charlie had told himself it was 'he' was Charlie's own mistake, and now he knew it.

Did the pronoun's having no gender mean the Ledom then had no sex? For that would be one way to make Philos' extraordinary remark consistent: they had never seen a male, but they were not females.

The words and concepts 'male' and 'female' existed in the language … the alternative was: *both*. The Ledom, each of them, had both sexes.

He looked up into Mielwis' patient eyes. 'You're both,' he said.

Mielwis did not move or speak for what seemed a very long time. Then his half-smile broadened, as if he were pleased at what he saw in Charlie's upturned face. Gently, then, he said, 'Is that such a terrible thing?'

'I haven't thought whether or not it's terrible,' said Charlie candidly. 'I'm just trying to figure how it's possible.'

'I'll show you,' said Mielwis, and in his stately way he rose and came around his desk toward the stricken Charlie.

'Hi, bulls!' says Tillie Smith. 'What's bulling?'

'Just man talk,' says Smith.

Herb says, 'Hi, bowls. What's bowling?'

Jeanette says, 'Three strikes and I'm out.'

'Herb already used the gag,' Smith says in his leaden way, which isn't true.

Tillie tops them all: 'What's everybody saying highballs for? Let's all have a drink.'

'Not us,' says Herb quickly, clinking ice in an otherwise empty glass. 'I've had mine and it's late.'

'Me too,' says Jeanette because she gets the message.

'Thanks for the drinks and all the dirty jokes,' Herb says to Smith.

'Let's not tell 'em about the dancing girls,' says Smith.

Jeanette makes wide bowling gestures. ''Night, Til. Keep 'em rolling.'

Tillie also makes bowling gestures, causing Smith to reseat himself on his shoulderblades, where he much prefers to be in any case. The Railes gather up her bowling bag, Herb grunting dramatically as he hefts it, and the babysitter, which Jeanette unplugs and tucks under Herb's left arm while she inserts her handbag under his right, and because she is a lady, waits for him to open the door for her with his knee.

'Come this way,' Mielwis said, and Charlie rose and followed him into a smaller room. One whole end, floor to ceiling, was a pattern of slits with labels – some sort of filing system, he presumed; and Lord preserve us, even these were not in straight lines, but in arcs ... and come to think of it, they did resemble the arcs he had seen drawn on an assembly bench, once, by an efficiency expert: maximum reach of right hand, optimum reach of left hand, and so on. Attached to one wall was a flat white soft shelf – an examination table if ever he saw one. Mielwis, in passing, batted it gently and it followed him down the room, slowly sinking, until when it was within ten feet of the wall it was at chair height. 'Sit down,' Mielwis said over his shoulder.

Numbly, Charlie sat, and watched the big Ledom stand and glance over the labels. Suddenly, surely, he reached up. 'Here we are.' He hooked his slender fingertips in one of the slots and moved his hand downward. A chart began feeding out of the slot; it was about three feet wide and was very nearly seven feet long. As it came down the lights in the room slowly dimmed, while the picture on the chart brightened. Mielwis reached up and started a second chart and then sat beside Charlie.

The room was now totally dark, and the charts blazed with light In full color, they were the front and side views of a Ledom, clad only in the silky sporran which began perhaps an inch under the navel and fell, widening from perhaps a palm's breadth at the top, to its lower edge, which was roughly three inches above mid-thigh, and which extended from the front of one leg to the front of the other. Charlie had seen them, already, longer and shorter than this, and also red, green, blue, purple and snowy white, but he had yet to see the Ledom who went without one. It was obviously a tight taboo, and he did not comment.

'We shall dissect,' said Mielwis, and by means unperceived by Charlie Johns, he caused the chart to change: *blip!* And the sporran, as well as the superficial skin under it, were gone, exposing the fascia and some of the muscle fibres of the abdominal wall. With a long black pointer he magically produced, he indicated the organs and functions he described. The tip of the pointer was a needle, a circle, an arrow and a sort of half-parenthesis at his will, and his language was concise and intimately geared to Charlie's questions.

And Charlie asked questions! His unease had long since disappeared, and two of his most deep-dyed characteristics took over: one, the result of his omnivorous, undisciplined, indefatigable reading and picking of brains; second, the great gaping holes this had left in his considerable body of knowledge. Both appeared far more drastic than he had heretofore known; he knew ever so much more than he knew he knew, and he had between five and seven times as much misinformation and ignorance than he had ever dreamed.

The anatomical details were fascinating, as such things so often are, and for the usual reason which overwhelms anyone with the vestiges of a sense of wonder: the ingenuity, the invention, the efficient complexity of a living thing.

First of all, the Ledom clearly possessed both sexes, in an active form. First of all, the intromittent organ was rooted far back in what might be called, in homo sap., the vaginal fossa. The base of the organ had, on each side of it, an os uteri, opening to the two cervixes, for the Ledom had two uteri and always gave birth to fraternal twins. On erection the phallos descended and emerged; when flaccid it was completely enclosed, and it, in turn, contained the urethra. Coupling was mutual – indeed, it would be virtually impossible any other way. The testicles were neither internal nor external, but superficial, lying in the groin just under the skin. And throughout, there was the most marvellous reorganization of the nervous plexi, at least two new sets of sphincter muscles, and an elaborate redistribution of such functions as those of Bartholin's and Cowper's glands.

When he was quite, quite satisfied that he had the answers, and when he could think of no more, and when Mielwis had exhausted his own promptings, Mielwis flicked the two charts with the back of his hand and they slid up and disappeared into their slots, while the lights came up.

Charlie sat quietly for a moment. He had a vision of Laura – of all women … of all men. *Biology*, he remembered irrelevantly; *they used to use the astronomical symbols for Mars and Venus for male and female … What in hell would they use for these? Mars plus y? Venus plus x? Saturn turned upside down?* Then he heeled his eyes and looked up at Mielwis, blinking. 'How in the name of all that's holy did humanity get *that* churned up?'

Mielwis laughed indulgently, and turned back to the rack. He (and even after such a demonstration, Charlie found himself thinking of Mielwis as 'he' – which was still the convenient translation of the genderless Ledom pronoun) he began hunting up and back and down. Charlie waited patiently for new revelation, but Mielwis gave an annoyed grunt and walked to the corner, where he placed his hand on one of the ubiquitous, irregular swirls of design. A tiny voice said politely, 'Yes, Mielwis.'

Mielwis said, 'Tagin, where have you gone and filed the homo sap. dissections?'

Came the tiny voice, 'In the archives, under Extinct Primates.'

Mielwis thanked the voice and went round to a second bank of slots at the side. He found what he was looking for. Charlie rose when he beckoned, and came to him, and the bench followed obediently. Mielwis tapped down more charts, and seated himself.

The lights dimmed and went out; the charts flamed. 'Here are dissections of homo sap., male and female,' Mielwis began. 'And you described Ledom as churned up. I want to show you just how little real change there has been.'

He began with a beautiful demonstration of the embryology of the human reproductive organs, showing how similar were the prenatal evidences of the sexual organs, to the end of showing how really similar they remained. Every organ in the male has its counterpart in the female. 'And if you did not come from a culture which so exhaustively concentrated on differences which were in themselves not drastic, you would be able to see how small the differences actually were.' (It was the first time he had heard any of the Ledom make a knowledgeable reference to homo sap.) He went on with some charts of a pathological nature. He demonstrated how, with biochemicals alone, one organ could be made to atrophy and another actually perform a function when it itself had been vestigial to begin with. A man could be made to lactate, a woman to grow a beard. He demonstrated that progesterone was normally secreted by males, and testosterone by females, if only in limited amounts. He went on to show pictures of other species, to give Charlie an idea of how wide a variety there is, in nature, in the reproductive act: the queen bee, copulating high in midair, and thereafter bearing within her a substance capable of fertilizing literally hundreds of thousands of eggs for literally generation after generation; dragon-flies, in their winged love-dance with each slender body bent in a U, forming an almost perfect circle whirling and skimming over the marshes; and certain frogs the female of which lays her eggs in large pores in the male's back; seahorses whose males give birth to the living young; octopods who, when in the presence of the beloved, wave a tentacle the end of which breaks off and swims by itself over to the female who, if willing, enfolds it and if not, eats it. By the time he was finished, Charlie was quite willing to concede that, in terms of all nature, the variation between Ledom and homo sap. was neither intrinsically unusual nor especially drastic.

'But what happened?' he asked, when he had had a chance to mull all this. 'How did this come about?'

Mielwis answered with a question: 'What first crawled out of the muck and breathed air instead of water? What first came down out of the trees and picked up a stick to use as a tool? What manner of beast first scratched a hole in the ground and purposely dropped in a seed? It happened, that's all. These things happen …'

'You know more about it than that,' accused Charlie. 'And you know a lot about homo sap. too.'

With a very slight touch of testiness, Mielwis said, 'That's Philos' specialty, not mine. As far as the Ledom is concerned. As for homo sap., it was my understanding that you purposely wish not to know the time or nature of its demise. No one's trying to deny you information you really want, Charlie Johns, but does it not occur to you that the beginnings of Ledom and the end of homo sap. may have something to do with one another? Of course … it's up to you.'

Charlie dropped his eyes. 'Th-thanks, Mielwis.'

'Talk it over with Philos. He can explain if anyone can. And I'll allow,' he added, smiling broadly, 'that he knows where to stop better than I do. It isn't in my nature to withhold information. You go talk it over with him.'

'Thanks,' Charlie said again. 'I – I will.'

Mielwis' parting word was to the effect that Nature, profligate though she may be, generator of transcendant and complicated blunders, holds one single principle above all others, and that is continuity. 'And she will bring that about,' he said, 'even when she must pass a miracle to do it.'

'Oh, you know it's great,' Jeanette says to Herb as she makes a couple of nightcaps (anyway) and he is returning to the kitchen after looking at the children, 'it's great having neighbors like the Smiths.'

'Great,' says Herb.

'Like I mean interests in common.'

'Do any good tonight?'

'Oh yes,' she says, handing him the glass and perching against the sink. 'You've been working for seven weeks on a presentation for the Big Bug Bakeries to sell a promotion on luxury ice-cream and cake shoppes.' She pronounces it 'shoppies.'

'I have?'

'Name of store chain, *Just Desserts*.'

'Oh hey, purty purty. You're a genius.'

'I'm a scrounge,' she says, 'Tillie came out with it as a crack and maybe she'll forget she said it which is why you've been working on it for seven weeks.'

'Clever clever. Will do. Smitty put me down once tonight.'

'You punch him in the nose?'

'Sure. Middle-large wheel in big account. Fat chance.'

'Whoppen?'

He tells her about the TV show, how he said some things that sounded like compliments for it, and it sponsored by the competition.

'Oh,' she says. 'You fool you, but all the same he's a wick.' A wick is their personal idiom for anyone who does wicked things.

'I got out from under pretty good.'

'All the same, you want to get a bomb ready just in case.'

He glances out the window and across the lot. 'Awful dose for a bomb to go bang.'

'Only if they know who dropped it.'

'Aw,' he says, 'we don't want to bomb him.'

'Course not. We just want a bomb in case. Besides, I got a bombsite it would be a shame to waste.' She tells turn about old Trizer who got kicked upstairs and would be so happy to roll something down on Smitty.

'Get off him, Jeannette. He got prostate.'

'"And there he lay, prostate on the floor." He tell you?'

'No, I found out, that's all.' He adds, 'Piles too.'

'Oh goody. I'll twig Tillie.'

'You are the most vindictive female I ever heard of.'

'They put my little buddy-buddy-hubby down, and I won't let'm.'

'Besides, she'll think I told you.'

'She'll only wonder and wonder how it ever got out. I'll fix it, buddy-buddy-hubby. We're a team, that's what.'

He swirls his drink and watches it spin. 'Smitty said something about that.' He tells her about the desert boots and how Smitty thinks pretty soon the kids won't know which one is the father.

'Bother you?' she says brightly.

'Some.'

'You forget it,' she tell him. 'You're hanging on to somebody's dead hand from way back. What we are, we're a new kind of people, buddy-buddy. So suppose Karen and Davy grow up without this big fat Thing you read about, the father image, the mother image, all like that.'

'"The Story of my Life, by Karen Railes. When I was a lit-tul girrul I did-unt have a mom-my and dad-dy like the other lit-tul boys and girruls, I had a Committee."'

'Committee or no, gloomy-Gus, they have food drink clothes house and love, and isn't that supposed to be all of it?'

'Well yes, but that father image is supposed to be worth something too.'

She pats him on the cheek. 'Only if you way down deep feel you have to be big. And you're already sure you're the only one big enough to belong to this Committee, right? Let's go to bed.'

'How do you mean that?'

'Let's go to bed.'

Charlie Johns found Philos standing outside Mielwis' office, looking as if he had just arrived. 'How was it?'

'Huge,' said Charlie. 'It's, well, overwhelming, isn't it?' He looked carefully at Philos, and then said, 'I guess it isn't, not to you.'

'You want more? Or was that enough for now? Do you have to sleep again?'

'Oh no, not until night.' The word 'night' was there to be used, but like 'male' and 'female,' seemed to have a rather more remote application than he needed to express himself. He thought he ought to add to it. 'When it's dark.'

'When what is dark?'

'You know. The sun goes down. Stars, moon, all that.'

'It doesn't get dark.'

'It doesn't ... what are you talking about? The earth still turns, doesn't it?'

'Oh, I see what you mean. Oh yes, I imagine it still gets dark out there, but not in Ledom.'

'What is Ledom – underground?'

Philos cocked his head on one side. 'That isn't a yes or no kind of question.'

Charlie looks down the corridor and out one of the huge panes to the overcast bright silver sky. 'Why isn't it?'

'You'd better ask Seace about it. He can explain better than I can.'

In spite of himself, Charlie laughed, and in answer to Philos' querying look, he explained, 'When I'm with you, Mielwis can supply the answers. When I'm with Mielwis, he tells me that you're the expert. And now you send me to Seace.'

'What did he say I was an expert at?'

'He didn't say, exactly. He implied that you knew all there was to know about the history of Ledom. He said something else ... let's see. Something about you knowing when to stop giving information. Yes, that was it; he said you'd know where to stop, because it isn't in his nature to withhold information.'

For the second time Charlie saw a swift flush pass through Philos' dark enigmatic face. 'But it's my nature.'

'Oh, now, look,' said Charlie anxiously, 'I could be misquoting. I could have missed something. Don't make me a source of trouble between you and—'

'Please,' said Philos evenly, 'I know what he meant by it, and you haven't done any harm. This is one thing in Ledom which has nothing to do with you.'

'It has, it has! Mielwis said that the beginning of Ledom may well have something to do with the end of homo sap., and that's the one thing I want to steer clear of. It certainly does involve me!'

They had begun to walk, but now Philos stopped and put his hands on Charlie's shoulders. He said, 'Charlie Johns, I do beg your pardon. We're both – we're all wrong, and all right. But truly, there is nothing in this interchange that you're responsible for. Please let it go at that, for it was wrong of me to behave that way. Let my feelings, my problems, be forgotten.'

Slyly, Charlie said, 'What – and not know everything about Ledom?' And then he laughed and told Philos it was all right, and he would forget it.

He wouldn't.

In bed, Herb suddenly says, 'But Margaret don't love us.'

Contentedly, Jeanette says, 'So we'll bomb her too. Go to sleep. Margaret who?'

'Mead. Margaret Mead the anthropologist who had that article I told you about.'

'Why she don't love us?'

'She says a boy grows up wanting to be like his father. So when his father is a good provider and playmate and is as handy around the house as a washer-dryer combination or a garbage disposer or even a wife, why the kid grows up full of vitamins and fellow-feeling and becomes a good provider and playmate and etcetera.'

'So what's wrong with that?'

'She says from Begonia Drive can't come adventurers, explorers and artists.'

After a silence, Jeanette says, 'You tell Margaret to go climb Annapurna and paint herself a picture. I told you before – we're a new kind of people now. We're inventing a new kind of people that isn't all bollixed up with Daddy out drunk and Mommy with the iceman. We're going to bring out a whole fat crop of people who like what they have and don't spend their lives getting even with somebody. You better quit thinking serious thinks, buddy-buddy-hubby. It's bad for you.'

'You know,' he says in amazement, 'that's precisely exactly what Smitty told me.' He laughs. 'You tell it to me to set me up, he tells it to me to put me down.'

'I guess it's how you look at it.'

He lies there for a time thinking about his-and-her desert boots and my parent is a Committee and how dandy a guy can be with a dish cloth, until it starts to spin a bit in his head. Then he thinks the hell with it and says, 'Good night, honey.'

'Good night, honey,' she murmurs.

'Good night, sweetie.'

'G'night, sweetie.'

'God damn it!' he roars, 'Stop calling me all the time the same thing I call you!'

She is not scared exactly, but she is startled, and she knows he is working something out, so she says nothing.

After a time Herb touches her and says, 'I'm sorry, honey.'

She says, 'That's all right – George.'

He has to laugh.

It took only a few minutes by 'subway' – there was a Ledom name for it but it was a new one and has no direct English translation – for Philos and Charlie to get to the Science One. Emerging under that toppling-top of a structure, they made their way around the pool, where thirty or forty Ledom were splashing again (it could hardly be 'still') and they stood a moment to watch. There had been little talk on the way, both having apparently a sufficiency of things to think about, and it was through his own thoughts that Charlie murmured, watching the diving, wrestling, running: 'What in time keeps those little aprons on?' And Philos, reaching gently, tugged at Charlie's hair and asked, 'What keeps that on?'

And Charlie, for one of the very few times in his whole life, blushed.

Around the building and under the colossal overhang they went, and there Philos stopped. 'I'll be here when you're through,' he said.

'I wish you'd come up with me,' said Charlie. 'This time I'd like you to be around when somebody says, "Talk to Philos about it."'

'Oh, he'll say it all right. And I'll talk you blue in the face when the time comes. But don't you think you should know more about Ledom as it is before I confuse you with a lot of things about what it was?'

'What *are* you, Philos?'

'A historian.' He waved Charlie over to the base of the wall and placed his hand on the invisible railing. 'Ready?'

'Ready.'

Philos stepped back and Charlie went hurtling upward. By this time he was familiar enough with the sensation to be able to take it without turning off the universe; he was able to watch Philos walking back toward the pool. Strange creature, he thought. Nobody seems to like him.

He drifted to a silent stop in apparent midair before the great window, and boldly stepped toward it. And through it. And again he sensed that certainty of enclosure as he did so: what did it do, that invisible wall – withdraw its edges exactly around him, so that he formed part of the enclosure while passing through? It must be something like that.

He looked around. The first thing he saw was the padded cell, the silver winged pumpkin, the time machine, with its door open just as it had been when he emerged. There were the draped ends of the room, and some kind of oddly leaning equipment on a sort of heavy stand near the center of the room; some chairs, a sort of stand-up desk with a clutter of papers on it.

'Seace?'

No answer. He walked across the room a little timidly, and sat on one of the chairs, or hummocks. He called again, a little louder, with still no results. He crossed his legs and waited, and uncrossed them and recrossed them on the other side. After a time he rose again and went to peer into the silver pumpkin.

He hadn't known it would hit him so hard; he hadn't known it would hit him at all. But there, just there on that smooth soft curved silver floor, he had sprawled, more dead than anything, years and unknown miles away from everything that ever mattered, even with the precious sweat dried on his body. His eyes burned in a spurt of tears. Laura! Laura! Are you dead? Does being dead make you any nearer where I am? Did you grow old, Laura, did your sweet body wrinkle and shrivel up? When it did, were you suddenly glad I wasn't there to see it? Laura, do you know I'd give anything in life and even life itself to touch you once – even to touch you if you were old and I was not?

Or … did the end, the final, awful *thing* happen while you were young? Did the big hammer hit your house, and were you gone in a bright instant? Or was it the impalpable rain of poison, making you bleed inside and vomit and lift up your head and look at the lovely hair fallen out on the pillow?

How do you like me? he cried in a silent shout and a sudden soundless crash of gaiety; how do you like Charlie in navy-blue, red-piped diapers and a convertible coat with the top down? How about this crazy collar?

He knelt in the doorway of the time machine and covered his face with his hands.

After a while he got up and went looking for something to wipe his nose on.

Looking and looking, he said, 'I'm going to be with you when it happens, Laura. Or until it happens … Laura, maybe we can both die of old age, waiting …' Blinded by his own feelings, he found himself fumbling with the drapes at one end of the room without really knowing how he got there or what he was doing. Back there was nothing but wall, but there was a squiggle, and he palmed it. An opening like the one which had contained his breakfast appeared, only no long tongue came shoving out. He bent and peered into the illuminated interior, and saw a pile of roughly cubical transparent boxes stacked inside, and a book.

He took out the boxes, at first just curiously, then with increasing excitement. He took them out one by one, but carefully, one by one, he put them back as he had found them.

In a box was a nail, a rusty nail, with bright metal showing where it had been diagonally sheared.

In a box was a rain-faded piece of a book of matches, with the red from the match-heads staining the paper sticks. And he knew it, he knew it! He'd recognize it anywhere. It was only a fragment, but that was from Dooley's Bar and Grill over on Arch Street. Except that ... that the few letters that were left were reversed ...

In a box was a dried marigold. Not flamboyant, not one of Ledom's crossbred bastardized beautiful miracle blossoms, but a perky little button of a dried-up marigold.

In a box was a clod of earth. Whose earth? Was this earth that her foot had trodden? Did it come from the poor sooty patch of ground under the big white lantern with the fading 61 painted on it? Had the very tip of the time machine's front tooth bitten this up on an early try?

Finally, there was a book. Like everything else here, it refused to be a neat rectangle, being a casual circular affair about as precise in contour as an oatmeal cookie, and the lines inside were not-quite-regular arcs. (On the other hand, if you learned to write without shifting your elbow, wouldn't arced lines be better to write on?) But anyway it opened hingewise as a good book should, and he could read it. It was Ledom, but he could read it, which astonished him no more than his sudden ability to speak it; less, rather; he had already been astonished and that was that.

It consisted first of all of some highly technical description of process, and then several pages of columnar entries, with many erasures and corrections, as if someone had made here a record of some tests and calibrations. Then there were a great many pages each of which had received an imprint of four dials, like four clocks or instruments, minus their hands. Towards the end these were blank, but the first were scribbled and scrawled over, with the dial-hands marked in and odd notes: *Beetle sent, no return.* There were a lot of these *no return* entries, until he came to a page over which was scrawled a huge and triumphant Ledom-style exclamation point. It was Experiment 18, and shakily written was *Nut sent, Flower returned!* Charlie got out the box with the flower in it and, turning it over several times, finally located the number 18.

Those dials, those dials ... he turned suddenly and hurried to the leaning array of unfamiliar equipment near the center of the room. Sure enough, there were four dials on it, and around the rim of each, a knob, tracked to circle the dial. Let's see, you'd set the four knobs according to the book, and then – oh sure, there it was. A toggle switch is a toggle switch in any language, and he could read ON and OFF in this one.

Back he went to the corner, turned the pages frantically. Experiment 68 … the last one before the unfilled pages began. *Sent Stones. Return:* (In Ledom phonetics) *Charlie Johns.*

He clutched the book hard and began to read those settings off that paper and into his head.

'Charlie? You here, Charlie Johns?'

Seace!

When Seace, having entered from some invisible dilating doorway behind the time machine, came round the corner, Charlie had been able to return the book. But he wasn't able to find the squiggle in time, and there he stood, with the compartment open and the boxed dead marigold in his hand.

'What you doing?'

Herb opens his eyes and sees his wife standing over him. He says, 'Lying in a hammock of a Saturday noon a-talkin' to my broad.'

'I was watching you. You were looking very unhappy.'

'As Adam said when his wife fell out of the tree – Eve's dropping again.'

'Oh, you golden bantam you! … tell mama.'

'You and Smitty don't want me to talk serious.'

'Silly. I was asleep when I said that.'

'All right. I was thinking about a book I read one time which I wish I had to read over. *The Disappearance*.'

'Maybe it just disappeared, then. Oh God, it's Philip Wylie. Likes fish, hates women.'

'I know what you mean and you're wrong. He likes fish but hates the way women are treated.'

'That makes you look unhappy in a hammock?'

'I wasn't really unhappy. I was just trying awful hard to remember exactly what the man said.'

'In *The Disappearance*? I remember. It's about how all the women in the world disappeared one day, right off the earth. Spooky.'

'You did read it! Oh good. Now, there was a chapter in it that kind of set out the theme. That's what I want.'

'Oh-h-h-h … yes. I remember that. I started to read it and then I skipped it because I wanted to get on with the story. There was this—'

'The only thing I like about a copywriter that's better than a best-seller writer,' Herb interrupts, 'is that though they're both wordsmiths, a copywriter makes it his business to never let his words get between the customer and the product. That's what Wylie did with that chapter in that book. Nobody who needs it ever gets to read it.'

'You mean *I* need it?' she says defensively, then, 'What is it he's got I need?'

'Nothing,' says Herb miserably, and sinks back in the hammock with his eyes closed.

'Oh, honey, I didn't mean—'

'Oh, I'm not mad. It's just, I think he agrees with you. I think he knows why he does better than you do.'

'Agrees with *what*, for Pete's sake!'

Herb opens his eyes and looks past her at the sky. 'He says people made their first big mistake when first they started to forget the similarity between men and women and began to concentrate on the difference. He calls that *the* original sin. He says it has made men hate men and women too. He blames it for all wars and all persecutions. He says that because of it we've lost all but a trickle of the ability to love.'

She snorts. 'I never said any of that!'

'That's what I was thinking so hard about. You said we were a new kind of people coming up, like a Committee or a team. The way there are girl things to do, and boy things to do, and nowadays it doesn't much matter who does 'm; we both can, or either.'

'Oh,' she says. 'That.'

'Wylie, he even makes a funny. He says some people think that most men are stronger than most women because men have bred women selectively.'

'Do you breed women selectively?'

He laughs at last, which is what she wants; she can't bear to have him looking sad. 'Every damn time,' he says, and topples her into the hammock.

Seace, his head cocked to one side, came briskly down to Charlie. 'Well, my young booter-in-the-tail. What are you up to?'

'I'm sorry about that,' Charlie stammered. 'I was very mixed up.'

'You dug out the flower, hm?'

'Well, I came and – you were, I mean weren't—'

Surprisingly, Seace clapped him on the shoulder. 'Good, good; it's one of the things I was going to show you. You know what that flower is?'

'Yes,' said Charlie, almost unable to speak. 'It's a m-marigold.'

Seace fumbled past him and got out the book, and wrote down the name of the flower. 'Doesn't exist in Ledom,' he said proudly. He nodded toward the time machine. 'Never can tell what that thing will dredge up. Of course, you're the prize specimen. Chances are once in a hundred and forty three quadrillion of doing it again, if that makes any sense to you.'

'You … you mean that's all the chance I have of going back?'

Seace laughed. 'Don't look so woebegone! Milligram by milligram – I do believe, atom by atom – what you put in there, you take out. Question of mass. Have complete choice of what we shove in. What comes out—' He shrugged.

'Does it take long?'

'That's something I hoped to learn from you, but you couldn't say. How long do you think you were in there?'

'Seemed like years.'

'Wasn't years; you'd have starved to death. But this end, it's instantaneous. Shut the door, throw the switch, open the door, it's all over.' Calmly, he took the marigold from Charlie, and the book, slung them back in the hole, and palmed it shut. 'Now then! What d'you want to know? I'm told I'm to draw the line only at information about when and how homo sap. cuts its silly collective throat. Sorry. Don't take that personally. Where do you want to begin?'

'There's so much …'

'You know something? There's precious little. Let me give you an example. Can you imagine a building, a city, a whole culture maybe, running on the single technological idea of the electric generator and the motor – which is essentially the same thing?'

'I – well, sure.'

'And pretty amazing to someone who'd never known such a thing before. With just electricity and motors, you can pull, push, heat, cool, open, close, light – well, more or less, name it, you have it. Right?'

Charlie nodded.

'Right. All motion things, see what I mean? Even heat is motion when you get right down to it. Well, we have a single thing that does all that the electric motor can do, plus a whole range of things in the static area. It was developed here in Ledom, and it's the keystone to the whole structure. Called A-field. A is for Analog. A very simple-minded gadget, basically. 'Course, the theory—' He wagged his head. 'You ever hear of a transistor?'

Charlie nodded. This was a man with whom one could converse with one's neck-muscles.

Seace said, 'Now there's as simple-minded a device as a device can get. A little lump of stuff with three leads into it. Shove a signal in one wire, out comes the same signal multiplied by a hundred. No warm-up time, no filaments to break, no vacuum to lose, and almost no power to operate.

'Then along comes the tunnel diode and makes the transistor complicated, overweight, oversized and inefficient in comparison, and it's much smaller and, to the naked eye, a lot simpler. But the theory, God! I've always said that some day we'll reduce these things so far that we'll be able to do anything at all with nothing at all drawing no power – only nobody'll be able to understand the theory.'

Charlie, who had encountered the professorial joke before, smiled politely.

'All right: the A-field. I'll try to make it non-technical. Remember that spoon you used this morning? Yes? Yes. Well, in the handle is a sub-miniature force-field generator. The shape of the field is determined by guides made of a special alloy. The field is so small you couldn't see it, even if it was visible, which it isn't, with nine electron microscopes in series. But that blue wire around the edge is so composed that every atom in it is an exact analog of the subatomic particles forming the guides. And for reasons of spatial stress that I won't waste your time with, an analog of the field appears inside the loop. Right? Right. That's the gadget, the building block. Everything else around here is done by piling it up. The window – that's an analog loop. There's two of 'em holding up this building – you didn't think it was done with prayer, did you?'

'The building? But – the spoon was a loop, and I imagine the window is too, but I don't see any loops outside the building. It would have to be outside, wouldn't it?'

'It sure would. You have an eye, but you don't need an eye to see that. Sure, this heap is propped up two ways from the outside. And the loops *are* there. But instead of being made of alloy, they're standing waves. If you don't know what a standing wave is I won't bother you with it. See that?' He pointed.

Charlie followed his fingers and saw the ruins and the great strangler fig.

'That,' said Seace, 'is one of the props, or the outer end of it. Try to imagine a model of this building, held up by two triangles of transparent plastic, and you'll have an idea of the shape and size of the fields.'

'What happens when somebody walks into it?'

'Nobody does. Cut an arch in the ground-line of your piece of plastic, and you'll see why not. Sometimes a bird hits one, poor thing, but mostly they seem to be able to avoid it. It remains invisible because the surface isn't really a surface, but a vibrating matrix of forces, and dust won't sit on it. And it's perfectly transparent.'

'But ... doesn't it yield? The bowl of that spoon I used, it sagged under the weight of the food – I saw it. And these windows ...'

'You *have* got an eye!' Seace commended. 'Well, wood is matter, brick is matter, steel is matter. What's the difference between them? Why, what's in 'em, and how it's put together, that's all. The A-field can be dialled to be anything you want it to be – thick, thin, impermeable, what have you. Also rigid – rigid like nothing else has ever been.'

Charlie thought: That's just dandy as long as you pay your electric bill to keep the thing up there; but he didn't say it because the language had no word for 'electric bill,' or even 'pay.'

He looked out at the strangler fig, squinted his eyes, and tried to see the thing that was holding the building up. 'I bet you can see it when it rains,' he said at last.

'No you can't,' said Seace briskly. 'Doesn't rain.'

Charlie looked up at the bright overcast. 'What?'

Seace joined him and also looked up. 'You're looking at the underside of an A-field bubble.'

'You mean—'

'Sure, all of Ledom is under a roof. Temperature controlled, humidity controlled, breezes blowing when they're told to.'

'And no night ...'

'We don't sleep, so why bother?'

Charlie had heard that sleep was quite possibly an inbred tendency, inherited from cave-folk who of necessity crouched unmoving in caves during dark hours to avoid the nocturnal carnivore; according to the theory, the ability to lose consciousness and relax during those times became a survival factor.

He glanced again at the sky. 'What's outside, Seace?'

'Better leave that to Philos.'

Charlie began to grin, and then the smile cut off. This shunting from one expert to another seemed always to occur when he skirted the matter of the end of the human species as he had known it.

'Just tell me one thing, as – ah – a matter of theory, Seace. If the A-field is transparent to light, it would be transparent to any radiation, no?'

'No,' said Seace. 'I told you – it's what we dial it up to be, including opaque.'

'Oh,' said Charlie. He turned his eyes away from the sky, and he sighed.

'So much for static effects,' said Seace briskly. Charlie appreciated his understanding. 'Now: the dynamic. I told you, this stuff can do anything the electric motor and electricity can do. Want to move earth? Dial an analog field down so thin it'll slip between molecules, slide it into a hillside. Expand it a few millimeters, back it out. Out comes a shovel full – but the shovel is as big as you want it to be, and your analog can be floated anywhere you want it. Anything can be handled that way. One man can create and control forms for pouring foundations and walls, for example, remove them by causing them to cease to exist. And it isn't any sand-and-chemical mud you pour; the A-field can homogenize and realign practically anything.' He thumped the concrete-like curved pillar at the side of the window.

Charlie, who at one time had run a bulldozer, began to compliment himself on his early determination to be only impressed, but not amazed, by technology. He recalled one time on a drydock job, when he was driving an Allis-Chalmers HD-14 angledozer back to the tractor shop to have a new corner welded on the blade, and a labor foreman flagged him and asked him to backfill a trench. While the pick-and-shovel boys scrambled out of the way, he backfilled and tamped a hundred feet of trench on one pass, in about 90 seconds – a job which would have taken the 60-odd men the rest of the week. Given the gadgetry, one skilled man is a hundred, a thousand, ten thousand. It was difficult, but not impossible, to visualize the likes of the Medical One, four hundred feet high, being put up in a week by three men.

'And more on the dynamic side. The right A-field can make like an X-ray for such things as cancer control and genetic mutation effects – but without burns or other side effects. I suppose you've noticed all the new plants?'

All the new people too, said Charlie, but not aloud.

'That grass out there. Nobody mows it; it just lies there. With the A-field we transport everything and anything, process food, manufacture fabrics – oh everything; and the power consumption is really negligible.'

'What kind of power is it?'

Seace pulled at his horse-nostrilled nose. 'Ever hear of negative matter?'

'Is that the same thing as contraterrene matter – where the electron has a positive charge and the nucleus is negative?'

'You surprise me! I didn't know you people had come so far.'

'Some guys who wrote science fiction stories came that far.'

'Right. Now, know what happens if negative matter comes in contact with normal matter?'

'Blam. The biggest kind.'

'That's right – all the mass turns into energy, and with the tiniest particle of mass, that still turns out to be a whole *lot* of energy. Now: the A-field can construct an analog of anything – even a small mass of negative matter. It's quite good enough to make a transformation with normal matter and release energy – all you want. So – you construct the analog field with an electrical exciter. When it begins to yield, a very simple feedback makes it maintain itself, with plenty of energy left over to do work.'

'I don't pretend to understand it,' smiled Charlie. 'I just believe it.'

Seace smiled back, and said with mock severity, 'You came here to discuss science, not religion.' Brisk again, he went on, 'Let's call it quits on the A-field, then, right? Right. All I really wanted to point out to you was that it is, in itself, simple, and that it can do almost anything. I said earlier – or if I didn't I meant to – that all of Ledom has, as keystones, two simple things, and that's one of them. The other – the other has the made-up name of cerebrostyle.'

'Let me guess.' He translated the term into English and was going to say, 'A new fashion in brains?' but the gag wouldn't take in Ledom: 'Style' was indeed a word and concept in Ledom, but it was not the same word as the suffix (in Ledom) of 'cerebrostyle.' This second kind of style had the feeling of *stylus*, or writing implement. 'Something to write on brains with.'

'You've got the point,' said Seace, 'but not by the handle … It's something a brain writes on. Well … put it this way. Being impressed by a brain is its first function. And it can be used – and it is used – to impress things on brains.'

Confused, Charlie smiled, 'You'd better tell me what it is, first.'

'Just a little colloidal matter in a box. That, of course, is an over-simplification. And to continue the mistake of oversimplifying, what it does when it's hooked up to a brain is to make a synaptic record of any particular sequence that brain is performing. You probably know enough about the learning process to know that a mere statement of the conclusion is never enough to teach anything. To the untaught mind, my statement that alcohol and water interpenetrate on the molecular level might be taken on faith, but not in any other way. But if I lead up to it, demonstrate by measuring out a quantity of each, and mixing them, show that the result is less than twice the original measure, it begins to make some sense. And to go back even further, before that makes any sense, I must be sure that the learning mind is equipped with the concepts 'alcohol,' 'water,' 'measure,' and 'mix,' and further that it is contrary to the brand of ignorance known as common sense that equal quantities of two fluids should aggregate to less than twice the original amount. In other words, each conclusion must be preceded by a logical and consistent series, all based on previous observation and proof.

'And what the cerebrostyle does is to absorb certain sequences from, say, my mind and then transfers them to, say, yours; but it is not the mere presentation of a total, a conclusion; it is the instillation of the entire sequence which led up to it. It's done almost instantaneously, and all that's required of the receiving mind is to correlate it with what's already there. That last, incidentally, is a full-time job.'

'I'm not sure that I—' Charlie wavered.

Seace drove on. 'What I mean is that if, among a good many proven data, the mind contained some logically-arrived-at statement – and mind you, logic and truth are two totally different things – to the effect that alcohol and water are immiscible – that statement would ultimately find itself in conflict with other statements. Which one would win out would depend on how much true and demonstrable data were there to match it against. At length (actually, damn soon) the mind would determine that one of the statements was wrong. That situation will itch until the mind finds out *why* it's wrong – that is, until it has exhaustively compared each logical step, from premise to conclusion, of every relative step of every other conclusion.'

'A pretty fair teaching device.'

'It's the only known substitute for experience,' smiled Seace, 'and a sight faster. I want to stress the fact that this isn't just indoctrination. It would be impossible to impress untruth on a mind with the cerebrostyle, however logical, because sooner or later a conclusion would be presented which was contrary to the observed facts, and the whole thing would fall apart. And likewise, the cerebrostyle is not a sort of "mind probe" designed to dig out your inner secrets. We have been able to distinguish between the dynamic, or sequence-in-action currents of the mind, and the static, or storage parts. If a teacher records the alcohol-and-water sequence to its conclusion, the student is not going to get the teacher's life-history and tastes in fruit along with his lesson in physics.

'I wanted you to understand this because you'll be going out among the people soon and you'll probably wonder where they *get* their education. Well, they get it from the cerebrostyle, in half-hour sessions once each twenty-eight days. And you may take my word for it, for every other of those days they are working full time on the correlations – no matter what else they may be doing.'

'I'd like a look at that gadget.'

'I haven't one here, but you've already met it. How else do you suppose you learned an entire language in – oh, I guess it was all of twelve minutes?'

'That hood thing in the operating room behind Mielwis' office!'

'That's right.'

Charlie thought that over for a moment, and then said, 'Seace, if you can do that, what's all this nonsense about having me learn all I can about Ledom before you'll send me home? Why not just cook my head under that thing for another twelve minutes and give it to me that way?'

Seace shook his head gravely. 'It's your opinion we want. *Your* opinion, Charlie Johns. The one thing the cerebrostyle gives you is the truth, and when you get it, you *know* it's the truth. We want you to get your information through the instrument known as Charlie Johns, to learn the conclusions of that Charlie Johns.'

'I think you mean I'm not going to believe some of the things I see.'

'I know you're not. You see? The cerebrostyle would give us Charlie Johns' reaction to the truth. Your own observations will give us Charlie Johns' reaction to what he thinks is the truth.'

'And why is that so important to you?'

Seace spread his cool clever hands. 'We take a bearing. Check our course.' And before Charlie could evaluate that, or question him further, he hurried to sum up:

'So you see we aren't miracle-workers, magicians. And don't be surprised to find out that we're not, after all, primarily a technological culture. We can do a great deal, true. But we do it with only two devices which, as far as Philos is able to tell me, are unfamiliar to you – the A-field and the cerebrostyle. With them we can eliminate power – both man- and machine-power – as a problem; we have more than we'll ever need. And what you would call education no longer takes appreciable power or plant or personnel, or time. Likewise, we have no shortages of food, housing, or clothing. All of which leaves the people free for other things.'

Charlie asked, 'What other things, for God's sake?'

Seace smiled. 'You'll see ...'

'Mommy?' Karen demands. Jeanette is giving the three-year-old her bath.

'Yes, honey.'

'Did I reely reely come out of your tummy?'

'Yes, honey.'

'No I didn't.'

'Who says you didn't?'

'Davy says *he* came out of your tummy.'

'Well, he did. Close your eyes tight-tight-tight or you'll get soap in 'em.'

'Well, if Davy came out of your tummy why didn't I come out of Daddy's tummy?'

Jeanette bites her lip – she always tries her best not to laugh at her children unless they are laughing first – and applies shampoo.

'Well, Mommy, *why?*'

'Only mommies get babies in their tummies, honey.'

'Not daddies, ever?'

'Not ever.'

Jeanette sudses and rinses and sudses again and rinses again, and nothing more is said until the pink little face safely regains its wide-open blue eyes. 'I want bubbles.'

'Oh *honey!* Your hair's all rinsed!' But the pleading look, the I'm-trying-not-to-cry look, conquers, and she smiles and relents. 'All right, just for a while, Karen. But mind, don't get bubbles on your hair. All right?'

'Right.' Karen watches gleefully as Jeanette pours a packet of bubble-bath into the water and turns on the hot faucet. Jeanette stands by, partly to guard the hair, partly because she enjoys it. 'Well then,' says Karen abruptly, 'we don't need daddies then.'

'Whatever do you mean? Who would go to the office and bring back lollipops and lawnmowers and everything?'

'Not for that. I mean for babies. Daddies can't make babies.'

'Well, darling, they *help*.'

'How, Mommy?'

'That's enough bubbles. The water's getting too hot.' She shuts off the water.

'*How*, Mommy?'

'Well, darling, it's a little hard maybe for you to understand, but what happens is that a daddy has a very special kind of loving. It's very wonderful and beautiful, and when he loves a mommy like that, very very much, she can have a baby.'

While she is talking, Karen has found a flat sliver of soap and is trying to see if it fits. Jeanette reaches down into the bathwater and snatches her hand up and slaps it. 'Karen! Don't touch yourself *down there*. It's not *nice!*'

'Getting the hang of it?'

Charlie glanced thoughtfully at Philos, who had been waiting for him at the foot of the invisible lift, as always appearing as if he just happened to be there, as always with the alert dark eyes sparkling with some secret amusement … or perhaps just knowledge … or perhaps something quite different, like grief. 'Seace,' said Charlie, 'has the darndest way of answering every question you ask, and leaving you with the feeling he's concealing something.'

Philos laughed. As Charlie has noticed before, Philos had a good laugh. 'I guess,' said the Ledom, 'you're ready for the main part of it. The Children's One.'

Charlie looked across at the Medical One, and up at the Science One. 'These are pretty "main," I'd say.'

'No they're not,' said Philos positively. 'They're the parameters, if you like – the framework, the mechanical pulse, but for all that they're only the outer edge, and a thin one at that. The Children's One is the biggest of all.'

Charlie looked up at the tilting bulk over him and marveled. 'It must be a long way from here.'

'Why do you say that?'

'Anything bigger than this—'

'– you'd see from here? Well, there it is.' Philos pointed – at a cottage. It lay in a fold of the hills, surrounded by that impeccable greensward, and up its white, low walls, flaming flowering vines grew. Its roof was pitched and gabled, brown with a dusting of green. There were flower-boxes at the windows, and at one end, the white wall yielded to the charm of fieldstone, tapering up to be a chimney, from which blue smoke drifted.

'Mind walking that far?'

Charlie sniffed the warm bright air, and felt the green springiness under his feet. 'Mind!'

They walked toward the distant cottage, taking a winding course through the gently rolling land. Once Charlie said, 'Just that?'

'You'll see,' said Philos. He seemed taut with expectancy and delight. 'Have you ever had any children?'

'No,' said Charlie, and thought immediately of Laura.

'If you had,' said Philos, 'would you love them?'

'Well, I guess I would!'

'Why?' Philos demanded. Then he stopped and with great gravity took Charlie's arm and turned him to face him, and said slowly, 'Don't answer that question. Just think about it.'

Startled, Charlie could think of no response except, at last, 'All right,' which Philos accepted. They walked on. The sense of expectancy somehow increased. It was Philos, of course; the Ledom radiated something … Charlie remembered having seen a movie once, a sort of travelogue. The camera was placed on an airplane which flew low over plains country, over houses and fields, with the near land rushing past, and the musical background was as expectant as this. The film gave you no warning of the absolute enormity that was to come; for time and distance which seemed forever, there was only the flat country and the speed, and the occasional road and farm, but the music grew in tension and suspense, until with an absolute explosion of color and of perspective, you found yourself hurtling over the lip of the Grand Canyon of the Colorado.

'Look there,' said Philos.

Charlie looked, and saw a young Ledom in a yellow silken tunic, leaning against a rocky outcropping in a steep bank not far ahead. As they approached, Charlie expected anything but what actually happened; when one meets a fellow being, there is reaction, interaction of some kind, whether one is homo sap. or Ledom or beaver; but here there was none. The Ledom in yellow stood on one leg, back against the rock, one foot against the other knee, both hands clasped under the raised thigh. The rather fine-drawn face was averted, turned neither directly toward them nor away, and the eyes were half-closed.

Charlie said in a low voice, 'What's—'

'Shh!' hissed Philos.

They walked unhurriedly past the standing figure. Philos veered close and, signalling to Charlie to be silent, passed a hand back and forth close to the half-closed eyes. There was no response.

Philos and Charlie walked on, Charlie turning frequently to look back. All the while they were in sight, there was no movement but the gentle shifting of the silken garment in the light breeze. When at last a turn put a shoulder of the hill between them and the entranced creature, Charlie said, 'I thought you said the Ledom don't sleep.'

'That isn't sleep.'

'It'll do until the real thing comes along. Or is he sick?'

'Oh no! … I'm glad you saw that. You'll see it again, here and there. He's just – stopped.'

'But what's the matter with him?'

'Nothing, I tell you. It's a – well, call it a pause. It was not uncommon in your time. Your American Indians, the Plains Indians, could do it. So could some of the Atlas Mountain nomads. It isn't sleep. It's something that, doubtless, you do when you sleep. Did you ever study sleep?'

'Not what you might call study.'

'I have,' said Philos. 'One thing of especial interest is that when you sleep, you dream. Actually, you hallucinate. Sleeping regularly as you do, you perform this hallucination while you are sleeping, although sleep is here, as in many other ways, only a convenience; even you can do it without sleeping.'

'Well, there's what we called daydreaming—'

'Whatever you call it, it's a phenomenon universal to the human mind, and perhaps I shouldn't limit it to humanity. Anyway, the fact remains that if the mind is inhibited, or prohibited, from performing the hallucinations, for example by being wakened each time it slips into this state, it breaks down.'

'The mind breaks down?'

'That's right.'

'You mean if you had wakened that Ledom there, he'd have gone insane?' Brutally, he demanded, 'Are you all that delicately balanced?'

Philos laughed away the brutality; it was a sincere response to something ludicrous. 'No! Oh, never that! I was talking about a laboratory situation, a constant and relentless interruption. I can assure you that he saw us; he was aware. But his mind made a choice, and chose to pursue whatver it was that was going on in his head. If I had persisted, or if something so unusual as the sound of *your* voice' – the emphasis was slight but meaningful; it occurred then to Charlie that his voice here was a baritone horn among flutes – 'had snapped him out of it, he would have talked normally with us, forgiven us for the intrusion, waved us good-bye.'

'But why do it? What does he do it *for?*'

'What do you do it for? ... It seems to be a mechanism by which the mind detaches itself from reality in order to compare and relate data which in reality cannot be associated. Your literature is full of hallucinatory images of the sort – pigs with wings, human freedom, fire-breathing dragons, the wisdom of the majority, the basilisk, the *golem*, and equality of the sexes.'

'Now look—' Charlie cried angrily, and then checked himself. The likes of Philos could not be reached by rage; he sensed that, and said bluntly, 'You're playing with me, so it's a game. But you know the rules and I don't.'

Disarmingly, Philos cut it out, then and there; his sharp eyes softened and in complete sincerity, he apologized. 'I'm previous,' he added. 'My turn comes after you've seen the rest of Ledom.'

'Your turn?'

'Yes – the history. What you think of Ledom is one thing; what you will think of Ledom plus its history is another; what you will – but never mind that.'

'You'd better go on.'

'I was going to say, what you will think of Ledom plus its history plus *your* history is another matter altogether. But I won't say it,' declared Philos engagingly, 'because if I did I should only have to apologize again.'

In spite of himself Charlie laughed with him, and they went on.

A few hundred yards from the cottage, Philos turned him sharp right and they climbed a rather steep slope to its crest, and followed it until they came to a knoll. Philos, in the lead, stopped and waved Charlie up beside him. 'Let's watch them for a little while.'

Charlie found himself looking down on the cottage. He could now see that it was at the brink of a wide valley, part wooded, (or was that orchard? They *wouldn't* do anything in straight lines here!) and part cultivated fields. Around and between the fields and woods, the country was as parklike as it had been by the big buildings. Scattered throughout were more cottages, widely separated, each unique – timber, fieldstone, a sort of white stucco, plaster, even what looked like turf – and each widely separated from all the others, some by as much as half a mile. He could see more than twenty-five of the cottages from their vantage point, and there were probably more. Like scattered, diverse flower-petals, the bright garments of the people showed here and there through the woods and fields, on the green borders, and on the banks of the two small streams which wandered down the valley. The silver sky domed it all, falling to hills all about; it seemed then to be a dish-shaped mesa, and higher than anything around it, for he could see nothing beyond the gentle ramparts of the valley itself.

'The Children's One,' said Philos.

Charlie looked down past the growing thatch of the cottage below, to the yard and pond before it. He began to hear the singing, and he saw the children.

Mr and Mrs Herbert Raile are shopping for children's clothes in the dry-goods wing of an enormous highway supermarket. The children are outside in the car. It is hot out there so they are hurrying. Herb pushes a supermarket shopping cart. Jeanette fans through the stacks of clothes on the counters.

'Oh, look! Little T-shirts! Just like the real thing.' She takes three for Davy, size Five, and three for Karen, size Three, and drops them in the cart. 'Now, pants.'

She marches briskly off, with Herb and the shopping cart in her wake. He unthinkingly follows the international rules of the road: a vessel approaching from the right has the right of way; a vessel making a turn loses the right of way. He yields right of way twice on these principles and has to run to catch up. A wheel squeaks. When he runs it screams. Jeanette proceeds purposively right, straight ahead three aisles, and left two, and then stops dead. A little breathless, Herb and squeak regain her aura.

She demands, 'Now where are pants?'

He points. 'Over there where it says PANTS.' They had early passed within an aisle of it. Jeanette *tsks* in her haste and retraces her quick steps. Herb wheels and squeaks after her.

'Corduroy too hot. All the Graham kids in denim right now. You know Louie Graham didn't get his promotion,' murmurs Jeanette like one in prayer, and passes up the denim. 'Khaki. Here we are. Size Five.' She takes two pairs. 'Size Three.' She takes two pairs, and drops them into the cart, and hurries off. Herb squeaks, stops, screams, and squeaks after her. She takes two turns left, proceeds three aisles and stops. 'Where are children's sandals?'

'Over there where it says CHILDREN'S SANDALS,' pants Herb, pointing. Jeanette *tsks*, and sprints to the sandals. By the time he overtakes her she has picked out two pairs of red sandals with yellow-white gum soles, and drops them into the cart.

'*Stop!*' gurgles Herb, almost laughing.

'What is it?' she says in midstride.

'What do you want now?'

'Bathing suits.'

'Well look there then, where it says BATHING SUITS.'

'Don't nag, dear,' she says, moving off.

He maneuvers a stretch in which, briefly, he can wheel beside her close enough to be heard over the squeaks, and says, 'The difference between men and women is—'

'A dollar ninety-seven,' she says, passing a counter.

'– that men read directions and women don't. I think it's a matter of sexual pride. Take some out-and-out-genius of a packager, he dreams up a box for you to pinch it, tear back to dotted line, and then gives you a string to pull open the inner liner.'

'Leotards,' she says, passing a counter.

'Nine engineers bust their brains on the packaging machinery. Sixteen buyers go out of their heads finding enough of the right materials. Twenty-three traffic men answer two A.M. phone calls moving seventy thousand tons of material. And when you get it into your kitchen you open it with a ham slicer.'

'Bathing suits,' she says. 'What did you say, honey?'

'Nothing, honey.'

She rapidly scatters the contents of a bin called *Size* 5. 'Here we are.' She holds up a small pair of trunks, navy with red piping.

'Looks like a diaper.'

'It stretches,' she says; perhaps this is a *sequitur* but he does not investigate. He rummages through *Size* 3 and comes up with a similar pair of trunks, but about as large as his palm. 'Here it is. Let's beat it before those kids fry out there.'

'Oh *Herb!* silly: that's a *boy's* bathing suit!'

'I think it would look cute as hell on Karen.'

'But Herb! It hasn't any *top!*' she cries, rummaging.

He holds up the little trunks and looks ruminatively at them. 'What does Karen need a top for? Three years old!'

'Here's one. Oh dear, it's the same as Dolly Graham's.'

'Is there anybody in our neighborhood who is going to be aroused at the sight of a three-year-old's tit?'

'Herb, don't talk dirty.'

'I don't like the implication.'

'*Here* we are!' She displays her find, and giggles. 'Oh, how very, very *sweet!*' She drops it into the shopping cart, and they squeak swiftly toward the checkout, with their six T-shirts, four khaki shorts, two pairs of red sandals with yellow-white gum soles, one size 5 navy swimming trunks, one size 3 perfect miniature bikini.

The children, more than a dozen of them, were in and around the pond, and as they played, they sang.

Charlie had never heard such singing. He had heard much worse, and, as singing goes, some better; but he had never heard singing *like* this. It was something like the soft sound made by one of those tops which gives out an organ-toned chord, and then, slowing, shifts to another, related chord. Sometimes such toys are designed to issue a single constant note, which sounds as part of the two or even three chords as they modulate. These children, some in adolescence, some mere toddlers, sang that way; and the extraordinary thing about it was that, of the fifteen or so voices which at one time or another involved themselves, never more than four, or very occasionally five, sang at once. The chord of music hung over the group, sometimes bunched over a cluster of small brown bodies, then moving by degrees across the pond to the other side, then spreading itself out so that alto notes came from the left, soprano from the right. One could almost watch the chord as it condensed, rarefied, hovered, spread, leapt, changing its hues all the while in compelling sequences, tonic, then holding the keynote reinforced by two voices in unison while the background shifted to make it a dominant, one fell away to a seventh, and then, rather than drop back to the tonic, one voice would flat a halftone and the chord, turned blue, would float there as the relative minor. Then a fifth, a sixth, a ninth sweet discord and it would right itself as the tonic chord in another key – all so easy, so true and sweet.

Most of the children were naked; all were straight-limbed, clear-eyed, firm-bodied. To Charlie's as yet uneducated eye they all looked like little girls. They seemed not to concentrate at all on their music; they played, splashed, ran about, built with mud and sticks and colored bricks; three of them threw a ball amongst them. They spoke to each other in their dove-like language, called, squeaked as they ran and were almost caught, squealed too, and one cried like – well, like a child, when he fell (and was ever so quickly caught up by three others, comforted, kissed, given a toy, teased to laughter) but over it all hung that changing three-part, four-part, sometimes five-part chord, built by one and another in a pause, between breaths, in midair diving into the water, between spoken question and answer. Charlie had heard something like this before, in the central court of the Medical One, but not so bright, so easy; and he was to hear this chordal music wherever he went in Ledom, wherever the Ledom gathered in larger groups; it hung over the Ledom as the fog of their body-heat hangs over the reindeer herds in the frigid Lapland plains.

'Why do they sing like that?'

'They do everything together,' said Philos, eyes shining. 'And when they're together, doing different things, they do that. They can be together, feel together, singing like that no matter what else they may be doing. They feel it, like the light of the sky on their backs, without thinking about it, just – loving it. They change it for the pleasure of it, the way that one walks from the cold water to the warm stones, for the feeling on his feet. They keep it in the air, they take it from the air around them and give it back. Here, let me show you something.' Softly, but clearly, he sang three notes rapidly: *do, sol, mi* ...

And as if the notes were bright play-bullets, shot to each of three children, three children picked them up – one child for each note, so that the notes come in as arpeggio and were held as chord; then they were repeated, again as arpeggio and again held; and now one child – Charlie saw which one, too; it was one standing waist-deep in the pond – changed one note, so that the arpeggio was *do, fa mi* ... and immediately afterward *re, fa mi*, and suddenly *fa, do la* ... so it went, progressing, modulating, inverting; augmented, with sixths added, with ninths added, with demanding sevenths asking the tonic but mischievously getting the related minor instead. At length the arpeggio was lost as an arpeggio, and the music eased itself back to a steady, constantly changing chord.

'That's ... just beautiful,' breathed Charlie, wishing he could say it as beautifully as the beauty he heard, and disliking himself for his inability.

Philos said, gladly, 'There's Grocid!'

Grocid, a scarlet cloak ribboned about his throat, the rest of it airborne, had just emerged from the cottage. He turned and looked up, waved and sang the three notes Philos had sung (and again they were caught, braided, turned and tossed among the children) and laughed.

Philos said to Charlie, 'He's saying that he knew who it was the instant he heard those notes.' He called, 'Grocid! May we come?'

Grocid gladly waved them in, and they plunged down the steep slope.

Grocid snatched up a child and came to meet them. The child sat astride his shoulders, crowing with joy and batting at the billows of the cloak. 'Ah, Philos. You've brought Charlie Johns. Come down, come down! It's good to see you.' To Charlie's astonishment, Grocid and Philos kissed. When Grocid approached him, Charlie stiffly stuck out his hand; with instant understanding, Grocid took it, pressed it, let it go. 'This is Anaw,' said Grocid, brushing the side of the child's cheek with his hair. The youngster laughed, buried its face in the thick mass, extricated a laughing eye, and with it peeped at Charlie. Charlie laughed back.

They went together into the house. Dilating bulkheads? Concealed lighting? Anti-gravity tea-trays? Self-frosting breakfast food? Automatic floors? No.

The room was near enough to being rectangular as it needed to be to satisfy eyes which had become, Charlie suddenly realized, hungry for a straight line. The ceiling was low and raftered, and it was cool there – not the antiseptic and unemotional kiss of conditioned air, but the coolness of vine-awninged windows, low ceilings, and thick walls; it was the natural seepage of the earth itself s cool subcutaneous layers. And here were chairs – one of hand-rubbed wood, three of rustic design, with curves of tough liana and slats and spokes of whole or split tree-trunks. The floor was flagstone, levelled and ground smooth and grouted with, of all things, a glazed purple cement, and brilliant hand-tied rag rugs set it off. On a low table was a gigantic wooden bowl, turned from a single piece of hardwood, and a graceful but very rugged beverage set – a pitcher and seven or eight earthenware mugs. In the bowl was a salad, beautifully arranged in an elaborate star-pattern, of fruits, nuts, and vegetables.

There were pictures on the walls, mostly in true-earth colors – greens, browns, orange, and the yellow-tinted reds and red-tinted blues of flowers and ripe fruit. Most were representational and pleasingly so; some were abstract, a few impressionistic. One especially caught his eye; a scene of two Ledom, with the observation angle strangely high and askew, so that you seemed to be looking down past the shoulder of the standing figure to the reclining one below. The latter seemed to be broken in some unspecified way, ill and in pain; the whole composition was oddly blurred, and its instant impact was of being seen through scalding tears.

'I'm very glad you could come.' It was the other head of the Children's One, Nasive, standing by him and smiling. Charlie turned away from his contemplation of the picture and saw the Ledom, in a cloak exactly the same as Grocid's, extending his hand. Charlie shook it and let it slip away; he said, 'I am too. I like it here.'

'We rather thought you would,' said Nasive. 'Not too different from what you're used to, I'll bet.'

Charlie could have nodded and let it go, but in this place, with these people, he wanted to be honest. 'Too different from most of what I've been used to,' he said. 'We had some of this, here and there. Not enough of it.'

'Sit down. We'll have a bite now – just to keep us going. Leave some room, though; we'll be in on a real feast shortly.'

Grocid filled all-but-rimless earthenware plates and passed them around, while Nasive poured a golden liquid into the mugs. It was, Charlie discovered, a sharp but honey-flavored beverage, probably a sort of mead, cool but not cold, with a spicy aftertaste and a late, gentle kick. The salad, which he ate with a satin-finished hardwood fork which had two short, narrow tines and one broad long one with a very adequate cutting edge, was eleven ways delicious (one for each variety of food it contained) and it strained his self-control to the utmost not to *a*) gobble and *b*) demand more.

They talked; he did not join in very much, although aware of their courteous care to say that which might include or interest him, or at least not to launch into anything of length which might exclude him. Fredon had weevils over the hill there. Have you seen the new inlay process Dregg's doing? Wood in ceramic; you'd swear they'd been fireglazed together. Nariah wanted to put in for biostatic treatment of a new milkweed fiber. Eriu's kid broke his silly leg. And meanwhile the children were in and out, miraculously never actually interrupting, but simply flashing in, receiving a nut or a piece of fruit, hovering breathlessly to ask a favor, a permission, or a fact: 'Illew says a dragonfly is a kind of spider. Is it?' (No; none of the arachnids have wings.) A flash of purple ribbon and yellow tunic, and the child is gone, to be replaced instantly by a very small and coquettish naked creature which said clearly, 'Grocid, you got a funny face.' (You got a funny face too.) Laughing, the mite was gone.

Charlie, eating with effortful slowness, watched Nasive, crouched on a nearby hassock, deftly prying a splinter out of his own hand. The hand, though graceful, was large and strong, and seeing the point of a needle-like probe excavating below the base of the middle finger, Charlie was struck by the sight of the callouses there. The flesh of the palm and the inside of the fingers seemed as tough as a stevedore's. Charlie found himself making an effort to square this with flowing scarlet garments and 'art' furniture, and realized it wasn't his privilege, just now, to draw such balances. But he said, thumping the sturdy arm of the rustic chair, 'Are these made here?'

'*Right* here,' said Nasive cheerfully. 'Made it myself. Grocid and I did this whole place. With the kids, of course. Grocid made the plates and the mugs. Like 'em?'

'I really do,' said Charlie. They were brown and almost gold, swirled together. 'Is it a lacquer on earthenware, or is that A-field of yours a kiln for you?'

'Neither,' said Nasive. 'Would you like to see how we do it?' He glanced at Charlie's empty plate. 'Or would you like some—'

Regretfully, Charlie laid the plate aside. 'I'd like to see that.'

They rose and went toward a door at the back. A child half-hidden in the drapes at the back of the room darted mischievously at Nasive, who, without breaking stride, caught it up, turned it squealing upside down, very gently bumped its head on the floor, and set it on its feet again. Then grinning, he waved Charlie through the door.

'You're very fond of children,' said Charlie.

'My God,' said Nasive.

And here again the language was shaded so that a translation must lose substance. Charlie felt that what he meant when he said 'My God' was a direct response to his remark, and in no sense an expletive. Was the child his God, then? Or … was it the concept The Child?

The room in which they stood was a little higher than the one they had left, and wider, but utterly different from the harmonious, casual, comfortable living space. This was a workshop – a real working workshop. The floor was brick, the walls were planed but otherwise unfinished planks, milled shiplap fashion. On wooden pegs hung tools, basic tools: sledge and wedges, hammers, adze, spoke-shave, awl, draw-knife, hatchet and axe, square, gauge, and levels, brace and a rack of bits, and a set of planes. Against the walls, and here and there out on the floor, were – well, call them machine tools, but they were apparently hand-fashioned, sometimes massively, from wood! A table-saw, for example, was powered from underneath by treadles, and by a crank and connectingrod arrangement, caused a sort of sabresaw to oscillate up and down. A detachable, deep-throated frame was clamped to it, to guide the top end of the saw-blade, and was loaded with a *wooden* spring. There was a lathe, too, with clusters of wooden pulleys for speed adjustment, and an immense flywheel – it must have weighed five hundred pounds – made of ceramic.

But it was the kiln which Nasive had brought him to see. It stood in the corner, a brick construction with a chimney above and a heavy metal door, which stood up on brick pilings. Underneath was a firepot on casters – 'It's our forge, too,' Nasive pointed out as, with a muscular tug, he rolled it out and back under again and mounted on it, well to one side, was a treadle-operated bellows. The outlet from the bellows led to a great floppy object which looked like a deflated bladder, which in fact it was. Nasive pumped vigorously on the treadle and the wrinkled thing sighed, tiredly got up off its back, and wobbled upright. It then began to swell.

'I got the idea from a bagpipe one of the kids was learning to play,' said Nasive, his face glowing. He stopped pumping and pulled a lever a little way toward him; Charlie heard air hissing up through the grates. He pulled it a bit more, and the air roared. 'You have all the control you could possibly want and you don't have to tell some brawny adult to take a long trick at it; all the kids in the place can come in and each does as much as he can, even the little ones. They love it.'

'That's wonderful,' said Charlie sincerely, 'but – surely there's an easier way to do it.'

'Oh, surely,' said Nasive agreeably – and not by one word did he enlarge on it.

Charlie looked admiringly about him, at the neat stacks of lumber which had obviously been milled here, the sturdy bracing of the wooden machines, the – 'Look here,' said Nasive. He threw a clamp from the chuck end of the lathe ways and gave the ways a shove upward. Hinged at the tailstock end, it swung upright and latched into place – 'A drill press!' cried Charlie, delighted.

He pointed to the flywheel. 'That looks like ceramic. How did you ever fire anything that size?'

Nasive nodded toward the kiln. 'It'll take it. Just barely. Of course, it was in there for a while … we had to clear out the rest of the place and hold a feast and dancing until it was done.'

'With the people dancing on the treadle,' laughed Charlie.

'And everywhere else. It was quite a party,' Nasive laughed back. 'But you wanted to know why we made the flywheel of ceramic. Well, it's massive, and it was less work to cast it to run true than it would be to true up a stone one.'

'I don't doubt that,' said Charlie, looking at the flywheel but thinking of invisible elevators, time machines, a fingertip device which, he had been told, could take large bites out of hillsides and transport what it bit wherever it was wanted. The fleeting thought occurred to him that perhaps these people out here didn't know what they had back at the big Ones. Then he recalled that it was at the Medical One he had first seen Grocid and Nasive. So then the thought came to him that, knowing what they had at the Ones, they were denied these things, and must plod from cottage to field, and work up those case-hardened callouses, while Seace and Mielwis magicked ice-cold breakfast fruits from holes in the wall by their beds. Ah well. Them as has, gits. 'Anyway, that is really one large hunk of ceramic.'

'Oh, not really,' said Nasive. 'Come and look.'

He led the way to a door in the outside wall, and they stepped through into a garden. Four or five of the children were tumbling about on the grass, and one was up a tree. They shouted, cooed, crowed at the sight of Nasive, flew to him and away; while he talked he would tousle one, spin another around, answer a third with a wink and a tickle.

Charlie Johns saw the statue.

He thought, would you call this Madonna and Child?

The adult figure, with some material that draped like fine linen thrown loosely half around it, knelt, looking upward. The figure of the child stood, also looking upward, with a transcendant, even ecstatic expression on its face. The child was nude, but its flesh tones were perfectly reproduced, as were the adult's, whose garment was shot through with all colors possible to a wood fire.

The two remarkable features about this sculpture were, first, that the figure of the adult was three feet high, and that of the child over *eleven feet*!; second, that the entire group was one monstrous single piece of perfectly glazed, faultlessly fired terra cotta.

Charlie had to ask Nasive to repeat himself, saying something about kilns, as he was swept with wonderment at the beauty of this work of art, its finish, but most of all its symbolism. The small adult kneeling in worship of the giant child, rapt face fixed on the huge standing figure; and the child, in a rapture of its own, detached from the adult and aspiring upward ... somewhere ... higher in any case.

'*That* kiln I can't show you,' Nasive was saying.

Charlie, still spellbound, scanned the great lovely work, wondering if it had been fired in pieces and erected. But no; the glaze was flawless, without line or join from top to bottom. Why, even the base, made and colored like a great mass of flowers, a regular mound of petals, was glazed!

Well then! They did get a crack at that A-field magic after all!

Nasive said, 'It was sculpted right where it stands, and fired there too. Grocid and I did most of it, except the flowers; the children did the flowers. More than two hundred children screened all that clay, and worked it so it wouldn't fracture in the fire.'

'Oh ... and you built your kiln around it!'

'We built three kilns around it – one to dry it, which we tore down so we could paint it; one to set the color glazes, which we tore down to coat it, and one for the final glaze.'

'Which you tore down and threw away.'

'We didn't throw it away. We used the bricks for the new floor in the workshop. But even if we had thrown it away – it was worth it.'

'It was worth it,' said Charlie. 'Nasive ... what *is* it? What does it mean?'

'It's called The Maker,' said Nasive. (In the language, that was *creator*, and also *the one who accomplishes. The doer*.)

The adult adoring the child. The child in adoration of something ... else.

'The Maker?'

'The parent makes the child. The child makes the parent.'

'The child *what?*'

Nasive laughed, that full, easy, not 'at' kind of laugh which seemed to come so easily to these people. 'Come now: whoever became a parent without a child to make him so?'

Charlie laughed with him, but as they left, looked back over his shoulder at the gleaming terra cotta, he knew that Nasive might have said more. And indeed Nasive seemed to understand that, and his feelings about it, for he touched Charlie's elbow and said softly, 'Come. I think that later, you will understand better.'

Charlie wrenched himself away, but his eyes were full of that exquisite, devout pair shining in the garden. As they crossed the workshop, Charlie asked himself, But why is the child bigger than the parent?

… And knew he had asked it aloud when Nasive, stepping into the living room, and incidentally snatching the same youngster they had seen before delightedly cowering in the drapes, and as before scooping it up, turning it over and bumping its little head on the floor until it hiccupped with laughter: 'But – children are, you know.'

Well … in this language, as in English, 'bigger' could mean 'greater' … oh, he'd think about it later. With shining eyes, he looked at the faces in the room, and then felt a very real pang of regret. One ought not to see such a thing, and then have no one new to show it to.

Philos understood, and said, 'He's seen your statue, Grocid.' 'Charlie Johns, thank you.'

Charlie felt enormously pleased, but, not being able to see his own shining eyes, did not for the life of him know what he was being thanked for.

The Brute begins ominously, straddle-gaited, hunch-shouldered, to approach the bed against which She cowers in her negligee.

'Don't hurt me!' she cries in an Italian accent, whereupon the camera dollies in with the lurch of The Brute, becoming The Brute, and all the blood-and-flesh bugs within the steel-and-chrome beetles ranked up before the gargantuan screen of the drive-in theater, bat their eyes and thrum with the blood in their flesh. The very neon-stained air around the popcorn machines is tumid with it; hooded dead headlights in row upon row seem to bulge with it.

When the camera dollies in close enough to make it possible, for this season cleavage is 'in' but the areola is 'out,' The Brute's big hand darts in from off-camera, smites her ivory cheek stingingly (the straddle-gaited lumbering music stings too) and drops below the frame of the picture, whereupon we hear silk ripping. Her face, still close up, forty-three tinted feet six inches from tangled hair to dimpled chin, is carried backward by the camera or The Brute and pressed to the satin pillow, whereupon the dark shadow of The Brute's head begins to cover her face with the implacable precision of the studio sound-man's hand on a volume knob.

'Don't hurt me! Don't hurt me!'

Herb Raile, behind the wheel of his automobile, is at last made aware of a rhythmic wrestling going on beside him. Although Karen is fast asleep on the back seat, Davy, who at this hour is ordinarily dead to the world, is blaringly wide awake. Jeanette has a half-nelson on the boy and with her other hand is attempting to cover his eyes. Davy is chinning himself on her wrist as on a horizontal bar, and both of them are, in spite of and during this exercize, snatching what avid glances at the screen as they can.

Herb Raile, snatching what avid glances he can at the screen while analyzing this activity, says without turning his head, 'What's the *matter?*'

'Nothing for a *child* to see,' she hisses. She is a little out of breath from one or another of these stimuli.

'Don't hurt me!' screams shatteringly the She on the screen, then spasms her face and closes her eyes: 'Ah-h-h-h-h …' she moans, '… hurt me. Hurt me. Hurt me. Hurt me.'

Davy rips down the blinding hand: 'I wanna *see!*'

'You do as you're told or I'll—' Herb barks imperatively, watching the screen. Davy sharply nips his mother's forearm. She utters a small scream and says, 'Hurt me!'

In not less than seventy feet of super-polychrome three-and-a-quarter-to-one-aspect-ratio tumble-sounded explication, the screen rapidly and succinctly explains that due to an early misunderstanding She and The Brute were actually really and truly married the whole time, and when She has finished broken in passion and in English as well explaining to The Brute that the clear source of their excesses is the legality of their loving, the screen dissolves in a blare of light and a blaze of trumpets, leaving the audience limp and blinking in the here and now.

'You shouldn't've let him see all that,' says Herb accusingly.

'I didn't but he did. He bit me.'

There is an interlude wherein it seems to dawn on Davy that he has done something punishable; he need not know *what* to get it over with, which is done by weeping and being comforted by raspberry sherbet and a shrimp roll. The sherbet, initially on a stick, presents its own problem by leaving same; after a moment of watching it enfold his numb but apparently hot fingertips while it drips exactly on the crease of his trousers, Herb solves the problem by putting it entire into his mouth, which makes the bridge of his nose ache and by which Davy allows he has been robbed. This is not a crisis after all because the lights dim and the screen flares up again for the second feature.

'Something for Davy after all,' says Herb after the second minute. 'Why don't they run the Western first and spare our kids looking at that kind of you know.'

'Sit up on my knee, honey,' Jeanette says. 'Can you see all right?'

Davy sees all right the fight at the cliff edge, the falling body, the old man lying broken at the foot of the cliff, the evil cowpoke bending over him, the gush of good bright red blood from the old man's mouth: 'I'm … Chuck … Fritch … help me!'; the evil cowpoke's laughing, 'You're Chuck Fritch are you; that's all I want to know!'; his drawing of the .45, the roaring shots, the twitch of the old man's body as the slugs rip into him and his agonized grunts, the grin on the evil cowboy's face as he stomps the old man's face only they keep that specific off camera, but afterward you can watch him kick the body the rest of the way down into the canyon.

Flashback to a dirt street with duckboard sidewalks. Herb says thoughtfully, 'Yeah, I'll call 'em tomorrow, that's what I'll do, ask 'em why they don't put the Westerns on first.'

They went to Wombew's house, the dooryard of which was surrounded by strong and intricate basketwork, which was essentially nothing more than poles driven into the ground and vines woven around them; Wombew, a hawk-nosed young adult, showed Charlie how this was not merely a fence, but was integral with the house, for the walls were built of it too, and then plastered with a clayey mud from the neighborhood – the timeless mud-and-wattle construction – which when quite dry had been coated with a species of whitewash which was not white, but violet. The roof was thatched and planted with the thick-matted, mowing grass found all through Ledom. The house was lovely, especially in its interior planning, for mud-and-wattle need make no compromise with standard lumber lengths, and the more curved the walls, the more stable they are, just as a curved piece of paper may be stood on edge. Grocid and Nasive and their children came along and helped show Charlie Wombew's treasures.

They went to Aborp's house, which had been built of rammed earth, wooden forms having been set up and the moistened earth put between them and compacted by hand with the end of a heavy timber wielded by four strong Ledom standing on the top of the forms. Once it had dried, the forms could be removed. Like the wattle building, this too could be designed very flexibly. Grocid and Nasive and their children and Wombew's children and Wombew came along.

They went to Obtre's house, which was made of cut stone, built up in square modules. Each module had its domed roof, which was made with great simplicity. You fill the four walls right to the top with earth, mound it to suit, and lay on plaster until it is nearly a foot thick. Once it is set, you then dig out all the earth. It is said that this kind of house, with this roof, will stand a thousand years. Obtre and Obtre's children joined them as they went on.

Edec had a moss-chinked log house, Viomor lived right inside a hill, part shored and panelled with hand-rubbed wood, part cut from the living rock. Piante had a fieldstone house with a sod roof, and all the walls were covered with splendid tapestries – not draped, but applied flat so their marvellous pictures and designs could be read; and in the back, Charlie saw the handmade loom which had made them all, and for a while watched Piante and his mate work the loom, while two tiny children threw the shuttle. And Piante's children and Piante joined them, and his mate, and so did Viomor's family and Edec's; and as they crossed the park areas, people in their bright garments, windblown children and leggy adolescents, came out of the fields and orchards, dropping hoes and mattocks, pruning knives and machetes at the borders, and came along.

As the crowd grew, so grew the music. It was never louder; it grew larger instead.

So at last, visiting and gaining as it went, the multitude, and Charlie Johns, came to the place of worship.

Jeanette flings herself unhappily on the neat afternoon bed.

What makes me that way?

She has just turned away a home improvement services salesman. Which is all right in itself. Nobody asks these eager beavers to ring your doorbell and they have to take their chances. Nobody in her right mind is going to buy what she doesn't want, and nowadays you have to get it straight in your head what you don't want and stick to it, or they'll pull you down, bleed you.

It wasn't that; it was the way she had brushed the man off. She had acted this way before and doubtless she would again, and that is what is making her feel so rotten.

Did she have to be *that* abrupt?

Did she have to give the icy stare, the cold word, the not-quite-but-very-nearly slammed door? None of that was *her*, was Jeanette. Could she have done it – get rid of him, that is – acting like Jeanette instead of like some moving-picture parody of the hard life of a traveling salesman?

Sure she could have.

She sits up. Maybe this time she can think it through and it won't bother her ever again.

She *has* gotten rid of unwanted sales people, and gotten out of similar situations, many, many times before by being Jeanette. A smile, a little lie, something about the baby's waking up or I think I hear the phone; easy, and no harm done. My husband bought one just day before yesterday. Oh I wish you'd come around last week; I just won one in a contest. Who's to call her a liar? They go away and nobody's hurt.

But then, once in a while, like this one just now, she curls her lip and spits an icicle. And like just now, she stands by the not-quite-slammed door and bites her long coral thumbnail, and then goes to peer unseen through the marquisette curtain, being careful not to move it or touch it, and she watches the way he walks away; she can tell, by the way he walks down the path, that he's hurt. She's hurt and he's hurt, and who gets anything for it?

She feels rotten.

Why especially him? He wasn't offensive. Far from it. A nice-looking fellow with a good smile, strong teeth, neat clothes, and he wasn't about to shove his foot in the door. He treated her like a lady who might be helped by what he was selling; he was selling that, and not himself.

You know, she tells herself, if he had been a real crumb, a winking, eyebrow-waggling creep who'd goggle at the bottom end of your bra strap and make a kissing noise, you'd have told him off in the nice way – a fast, light, harmless brush.

Well, then, she tells herself, apalled, that's the answer. You liked him; that's why you threw the freeze.

She sits on the edge of the bed looking at that idea, and then she closes her eyes and lets her imagination get as foolish as it likes, imagining him coming in, touching her; imagining him right here with her.

And that rings no bell. It really doesn't. What she liked about the man wasn't anything like that at all.

'Now how can you like a man without wanting him?' she demands of herself aloud.

There is no answer. It is an article of faith with her. If you like a man, it has to be because you want him. Whoever heard of it any other way?

People just don't go around liking people on sight *unless*. And if she can't feel that she wants him, it's one of those subconscious whatcha-ma-callits; she's just not letting herself know it.

She doesn't want to want some other guy besides Herb, but she must. So she's rotten.

She falls back down on the bed and tells herself she ought to be hung up by the thumbs. She's rotten clear through.

The feast was on a mountain – at least, it was the highest hill Charlie had yet seen. Nearly a hundred Ledom were waiting there when Philos and Charlie and the great crowd arrived. In a grove of dark-leaved trees, on the faultless greensward, food was arrayed, laid out Hawaiian fashion on platters of woven fresh leaves and broad grasses. No Japanese flower-arranger ever did a more careful job than these gifted people with their food. Each platter and clever green basket was a construction in color and form, contrast and harmony; and the smells were symphonic.

'Help yourself,' smiled Philos.

Charlie looked around him dazedly. The Ledom were coming from every direction, filtering through the trees, greeting each other with glad cries. There were frequent embraces, kisses.

'Where?'

'Anywhere. It's all everybody's.'

They stepped through the swirling crowd and seated themselves under a tree. Before them were lovely mounds of food, laid up in graspable, bite-sized portions, and so beautifully arranged that until Philos reached, and disturbed a symmetry, Charlie hadn't the heart to begin.

A pretty child came by with a tray balanced on its head, and a half-dozen mugs apparently designed for the purpose; they were shaped like truncated cones with wide bases. Philos held out a hand and the child skipped toward them; Philos took two mugs and kissed the child, who laughed and danced away. Charlie took a mug and sipped; it was like cool applejuice with peach overtones. He began to eat with enthusiasm. The food tasted as good as it looked – a most extreme statement.

When he was able to slow down enough to look about again, he found the grove thick with a pleasant tension; perhaps it was the cloud of music which hovered over the people that exemplified it most, for it lay in a wide chordal whisper, surging with a pulsation that seemed to become more regular by the moment. One thing that struck Charlie was the fact that a great many people seemed to be feeding each other rather than themselves. He asked about it.

'They're just sharing. If you experience something especially good, don't you feel the need to share it with someone?'

Charlie recalled his odd touch of frustration in the realization that there had been, for him, no one to show the great terracotta statue to, and said, 'I – guess so.' He looked at his companion suddenly. 'Look – don't let me keep you from uh – joining your friends if you want to.'

A strange expression crossed Philos' face. 'That is most kind of you,' he said warmly. 'But I – wouldn't in any case. Not just now.' (Was that a slight rush of color in his neck and cheeks? And what was it? Anger? Charlie felt suddenly unwilling to pry.)

'A lot of people,' he commented after a while.

'All there are.'

'What's the occasion?'

'If you don't mind, I'd like you to tell me what you think, after it's over.'

Puzzled, Charlie said, 'Very well …'

They fell silent, listening. Softer and softer became the giant manifold music of the people, humming a series of close, and closely related chords. There crept into it a strange staccato, and looking about him, Charlie saw that some of them were gently tapping themselves, and sometimes their companions, on the base of the throat. It gave the voices a strange thrum, which at last took on a very definite rhythm, rapid but distinct. It seemed an eight-beat, with a slight emphasis on the first and fourth. On this was imposed a low four-tone melody, which cycled, cycled, cycled … everyone seemed to crouch, to lean forward a little, to tense …

Suddenly came the clarion of a powerful soprano voice, a very cascade of notes, bursting upward like a writhing firework from the drone of the bass melody, and subsiding. It was repeated either from far off in the grove, or from a small voice near by; it was impossible to tell. Two tenors, by some magic striking in a major third apart, repeated the explosion of notes in harmony, and as it faded and fell, another strong voice, a blue-cloaked Ledom seated near Charlie, caught it up and blew it skyward again, this time stripping it of its accidentals and graces and all its *glissandi*, giving it up in its purest form, six clear notes. There was an excited rustle all about, as of appreciation, and a half-dozen scattered voices repeated the six-note theme in unison, then again repeated it. On the second of the six notes, someone else was inspired to start the theme right there; it became fugal, and voice after voice took it up; it burst and fell, burst and fell, interwoven and complex and thrilling. All the while the bass susurrus, with its throat-thumping irregular rhythm, lay under the music, swelling and sighing, swelling greater and drawing back.

Then with a movement as explosive as that first soprano statement, a nude figure came spinning down toward them, weaving in and out between the tree-trunks and among the people; spinning so fast that the body contours were a blur, yet sure-footedly avoiding every obstacle. The spinning Ledom leapt high right by Philos, and came to earth kneeling, face and arms spread on the soft sward. Another came spinning, then another; soon the dark wood was alive with movement, with the swirl of the cloaks and headdresses some wore, with the flash of bodies and blurring limbs. Charlie saw Philos spring to his feet; to his amazement he found himself standing, crouching, buffeted by the rising current of sound and motion. It became an effort not to fling himself into it as into a sea. He drew back finally and clung to the bole of a tree, gasping; for he had an overriding fear that his unschooled feet would never stay under him in the whirling press; that they would be as inadequate to shift and change as were his ears to contain all that was happening in the air about, as were his bewildered eyes to absorb the rush and patterning of those bodies.

It became, for him, a broken series of partial but sharply focussed pictures; the swift turn of a torso; the tense, ecstatic lifting of a fever-blinded head, with the silky hair falling away from the face, and the body trembling; the shrill cry of a little child in transport, running straight through the pattern of the dance, arms outstretched and eyes closed, while the frantic performers, apparently unthinkingly, made way by hairsbreadth after hairsbreadth until a dancer swung about and caught up the infant, *threw* it, and it was plucked out of the air and whirled up again, and once more, to be set down gently at the edge of the dance. At some point unnoted by him, the bass drone had become a roar, and the rhythm, instead of resulting from the subtle tapping of the pharynx, had become a savage beat, furious fists on unnerved thorax and abdomen.

Charlie was shouting ...

Philos was gone ...

A wave of *something* was generated in the grove, and was released; he could feel it rush him and dissipate; it was as tangible as the radiation from an opened furnace door, but it was not heat. It was not anything he had ever felt, imagined, or experienced before ... except perhaps by himself ... oh never by himself; it was with Laura. It was not sex; it was a thing for which sex is one of the expressions. And at this its peak, the harmonious tumult altered in kind, though not at all in quality; the interweaving flesh of the Ledom became a frame encircling the children – so many, many children – who had somehow formed themselves into a compact group; they stood proud, even the tiniest ones, proud and knowing and deeply happy, while all about, the Ledom worshipped them, and sang.

They did not sing of the children. They did not sing to the children. It may be said in no other way but this: they sang the children.

Smitty has come out to chat over the back fence – actually, it is a low stone wall – with Herb. It happens that Smitty is sick furious with Tillie over something that does not matter really. Herb has been sitting on a lawn chair under a red and white umbrella with the afternoon paper, and he is furious also, but with somewhat less sickness and impersonally as well. Congress has not only passed a particularly stupid bill, but has underscored its particular stupidity by overriding a presidential veto. Seeing Smitty, he throws down the paper and strides to the back wall.

'How come,' he says, meaning it purely as a preliminary remark, 'the world is so full of dirty sons of bitches?'

'That's easy,' is the instant, dour remark. 'Every one of 'em was born out of the dirtiest part of a woman.'

Though in Ledom it never grew dark, it seemed darker with most of the people gone. Charlie sat on the cool green moss with his wrists on his kneecaps and his back against an olive tree, and bent his head to put his cheeks against the backs of his hands. His cheeks felt leathery, for there unaccountable tears had dried. At length he straightened up and looked at Philos, who waited patiently beside him.

Philos, as though to be sure not to utter a word lest it spoil something for his guest, acknowledged him with a soft smile and a peaking of his odd eyebrows.

'Is it over?' Charlie asked.

Philos leaned back against the tree, and with a motion of his head indicated a group of Ledom, three adults and a half-dozen children, far down the grove, who were cheerfully picking up the mess. Over them, like an invisible swarm of magic bees, hung a cloud of music, at that moment triads, minor thirds, winging neatly upwards in formation, hovering, fading, winging upwards again. 'It's never over,' Philos said.

Charlie thought about that, and the statue called *The Maker*, and about as much as he dared to think about what had passed in the grove, and about the sound which dwelt about these people wherever they gathered.

Philos asked, quietly, 'Do you want to ask me again what place this is?'

Charlie shook his head and got to his feet. 'I think I know,' he said.

'Come, then,' said Philos.

They walked to the fields, and through and by the fields and cottages, back toward the Ones, and they talked:

'Why do you worship children?'

Philos laughed. It was pleasure, mostly. 'First of all, I suppose it's because religion – and just to preclude argument, I'll define religion for this purpose as the supra-rational, or mystic experience – it's because religion seems to be a necessity to the species – but it would seem as well that the experience is not possible without an object. There is nothing more tragic than a person or a culture who, feeling the need to worship, has no object for it.'

'For the sake of no argument, as you say, I'll buy that,' said Charlie, aware of how quaint that sounded in Ledom. The word for 'buy' was 'interpenetrate' – a derivation of 'exchange' – but surprisingly, shy as he might from its overtones in this place, his meaning emerged. 'But why children?'

'We worship the future, not the past. We worship what is to come, not what has been. We aspire to the consequences of our own acts. We keep before us the image of that which is malleable and growing – of that which we have the power to improve. We worship that very power in ourselves, and the sense of responsibility which lives with it. A child is all of these things. Also ...' and he stopped.

'Go on.'

'It's something which you need a good deal of adjustment to absorb, Charlie. I don't think you can do it.'

'Try me.'

Philos shrugged. 'You asked for it: We worship the child because it is inconceivable that we would ever obey one.'

They walked in silence for a long time.

'What's the matter with obeying the God you worship?'

'In theory, nothing, I suppose, especially when along with the obedience goes the belief in a living – that is, current, and contemporaneously knowledgeable God.' Philos paused, choosing words. 'But in practice, more often than not, the hand of God in human affairs is a dead hand. His dictates are couched in the interperetations of Elders of one kind and another – past-drenched folk with their memories impaired, their eyes blinded, and all the love in them dried up.' He looked at Charlie, and his dark strange eyes were full of compassion. 'Haven't you been able to see yet that the very essence of the Ledom is – passage?'

'Passage?'

'Movement, growth, change, catabolism. Could music exist without passage, without progression, or poetry; could you speak a word and call it a rhyme without speaking more words? Could life exist … why, passage is very nearly a definition for life! A living thing changes by the moment and by each portion of each part of a moment; even when it sickens, even when it decays, it changes, and when it stops changing, it's – oh, it could be many things; lumber, like a dead tree; food, like a killed fruit; but it's not life any more … The architecture of a culture is supposed to express its state of mind, if not its very faith; what do the shapes of the Medical One and the Science One say to you?'

Charlie snickered; it was the laugh of unease, like embarrassment. '*Tim … ber!*' he cried in an imitation bellow, in English. Then he explained, 'That's what the loggers used to shout when they'd cut through a tree-trunk and it was about to fall: get out of the way!'

Philos laughed appreciatively and without rancor. 'Have you ever seen a picture of a man running? Or even walking? He is off balance, or would be if he were as frozen as the picture is. He could hardly run or walk if he weren't unbalanced. That is how you progress from any place to any other place – by beginning, over and over again, to fall.'

'And then it turns out they're propped up on invisible crutches.'

Philos twinkled, 'All symbols are, Charlie.'

Again, Charlie was forced to laugh. '"There's only one Philos."' He said it with unconscious mimicry. And again, he saw Philos flush darkly. Anger – for that matter, even mild irritation – was so rare here that it was more shocking than profanity. 'What's the matter? Did I—'

'Who said that? Mielwis, wasn't it?' Philos shot him a sharp glance, and read the answer from Charlie's face. He apparently read also the necessity for the end of anger, for with an obvious effort he put his down, and pleaded: 'Don't feel you've said anything wrong, Charlie. It isn't you at all. Mielwis …' He drew and released a deep breath. 'Mielwis occasionally indulges in a private joke.' Abruptly and, with evident purpose, changing the subject, he demanded, 'But about the architecture – don't you quarrel with the concept of dynamic imbalance in the face of these?' He swept his hand to indicate the cottages – mud-and-wattle, rammed earth, log and plaster and stone and hewn planks.

'Nothing tottery about that,' agreed Charlie, nodding toward the one they were passing – the Italian square-module one with the domed plaster roofs over each square.

'So they're not symbols. Or not in the sense that the big Ones are. They're the concrete results of our profound conviction that the Ledom will never separate themselves from the land – and I mean that in its widest possible sense. Civilizations have a pernicious way of breeding whole classes and generations of people who make their livings once removed – twice, ten, fifty times removed from the techniques of the hand. Men could be born, live, and die, and never move a spade of earth, or true a timber, or weave a swatch, or even see spade, adze or loom. Isn't that so, Charlie? Wasn't it so with you?'

Charlie nodded thoughtfully. He had had the same thought himself – he really had, one day when, city-bred as he was, he hired out to pick beans once when he needed the money and there was an ad in the paper. He had hated it, living in barracks with a filthy herd of human misfits, and working all day in cramping, crouching, baking, soaking labor for which he was untrained and in which – even in the matter of picking beans – he was unskilled. Yet it had come to him that just this once, when once he actually ate a bean, that he himself was taking from the womb of the soil that which it bore and which could in turn sustain him. He was putting his two naked hands to the naked earth, and between him and it was no complex of interchange, status, substitution, or intricate many-layered system of barter between goods and services. And it had come to him again more than once since, when the intimate, earthy matter of filling his belly was taken care of by making marks on paper, by scraping and stacking restaurant plates and scrubbing pots, by pulling steering clutches on a bulldozer or pushing buttons on an adding machine.

'Such men have an extremely limited survival value,' Philos was saying. 'They have, like good survival creatures, adapted to their environment – but that environment is a large and elaborate machine; there is very little about it which is as basic as the simple act of plucking a fruit or finding and cooking the proper grass. Should the machine be smashed, or should even some small but integral part of it stop working, everyone in it will become a hopeless dependant in precisely the length of time it take his stomach to empty itself. *All* the Ledom – every single one of us – though we might find ourselves with one or two real skills, have a working knowledge of agriculture and basic construction, weaving, cooking, and waste disposal, and how to make fire and mid water. Skilled or no – and no one is skilled in everything – an unskilled person with a working knowledge of necessities is better able to survive than a man who could, say, control a sheet-metal mill better than anyone else in the world but does not know how to join a rafter or save seedcorn or dig a latrine.'

'Oh-h-h,' said Charlie in tones of revelation.

'What is it?'

'I'm beginning to see something here ... I couldn't square all that push-button living in the Medical One with all the hand-made crockery. I thought it was a matter of privilege.'

'Those who work in the Ones eat out here as a privilege!' (Actually, the word 'privilege' here is not exact; it translated 'favor' or 'treat.') 'The Ones are first of all working places, and the only places where the work from time to time is so exacting and must be done with such precision that it is efficient to save time. Out here it is efficient to use time; we have so much of it. We do not sleep, and no matter how carefully you build or cultivate, the work keeps getting finished.'

'How much time do the children spend in school?'

'School – oh. Oh, I see what you mean. No, we don't have schools.'

'No schools? But … oh, that is good enough for people who only want to know how to plant and build do-it-yourself housing … is that what you mean? But – what about your technologists – you don't live forever, do you? What happens when one needs replacing? And what about books … and music manuscript … and – oh, all the things that people learn to read and write for? Mathematics – reference books—'

'We don't need them. We have the cerebrostyle.'

'Seace mentioned it. I can't say I understand it.'

'I can't say that either,' said Philos. 'But I can assure you it works.'

'And you use it for teaching, instead of schools.'

'No. Yes.'

Charlie laughed at him.

Philos laughed too, and said, 'I wasn't as confused as I sounded. The "no" was for your statement, we use the cerebrostyle for teaching. We don't *teach* our children the "book" kind of learning, we implant it with the cerebrostyle. It's quick – it's only a matter of selecting the right information block and throwing a switch. The (he here used a technical term for 'unused and available memory cells') and the synaptic paths to them are located and the information "printed" on the mind in a matter of seconds – one and a half, I think. Then the block is ready for the next person. But *teaching*, now; well, if there is any teaching done with this implanted information, you do it yourself, either by consciously thinking it through – much faster than reading, by the way – while you're working in the fields, or during a "pause" – remember the Ledom we saw standing alone just before we got to Grocid's house? … But even that process you can't call teaching. Teaching is an art that can be learned; learning from a teacher is an art that can be learned; anyone who tries – and we all try – can gain a certain competence in teaching; but a *real* teacher, now – he has a talent. He has a gift like a fine artist or musician or sculptor. Oh, we think highly of teachers, and of teaching. Teaching is part of loving, you know,' he added.

Charlie thought of cold, repellent, dying Miss Moran and understood in a great warm flash. He thought of Laura.

'We use the cerebrostyle,' said Philos, 'as we use the A-field; we don't depend on it. We don't, therefore, *need* it. We learn reading and writing, and we have a great many books; any Ledom who cares to may read them, although we generally like to have him put on the cerebrostyle "setter" while he reads, and make a new block.'

'These blocks – they can hold a whole book?'

Philos held up two thumbnails, side by side. 'In about that much space … And we know how to make paper and manufacture books, and if we ever had to, we would. You must understand that about us; we shall never, never be the slaves of our conveniences.'

'That's good,' said Charlie, thinking of many, many past things which were not good; thinking of whole industries crippled when the elevator operators went on strike in a central office building, thinking of the plight of a city apartment dweller during a power failure, without water, refrigeration, lights, radio, television; unable to cook, wash, or be amused. But … 'Even so,' he mused, 'there's something about it. I don't like. If you can do that you can select a block and implant a whole set of beliefs and loyalties; you could arrange a slavery that would make any of ours look like a practice hop in a sack race.'

'No we *can't!*' Philos said forcefully. 'To say nothing of the fact that we wouldn't. You don't love, nor gain love, by imprisonment or command, or by treachery and lies.'

'You don't?' asked Charlie.

'The parts of the mind are now clearly defined. The cerebrostyle is an information transfer device. The only way you could implant false doctrines would be to simultaneously shut off all other memory plus all the senses; because I assure you that whatever the cerebrostyle gives you is subject to review against everything you already know plus everything you experience. We could not teach inconsistencies if we tried.'

'Do you ever withhold information?'

Philos chuckled. 'You do hunt for flaws, now, don't you?'

'Well,' said Charlie, 'do you ever withhold information?'

The chuckle clicked off. Philos said soberly, 'Of course we do. We wouldn't tell a child how to prepare fuming nitric acid. We wouldn't tell a Ledom how his mate screamed under a rock-fall.'

'Oh.' They walked a while in silence … a Ledom and his mate … 'You do marry, then?'

'Oh yes. To be lovers is a happy thing. But to be married – that is happiness on a totally different level. It is a solemn thing among us, and we take it very seriously. You know Grocid and Nasive.'

A light dawned in Charlie's mind. 'They dress alike.'

'They do everything alike, or if not alike, then together. Yes, they're married.'

'Do you … do the people … uh …'

Philos clapped him on the shoulder. 'I know about your preoccupation in the matter of sex,' he said. 'Go on – ask me. You're among friends.'

'I'm *not* preoccupied with it!'

They walked on, Charlie sullenly, Philos humming softly, suddenly, in harmony with a distant melody that drifted down to them from some children in the fields. Hearing it, Charlie's sullenness abruptly lifted. He realized that these things are, after all, comparative; the Ledom genuinely were less preoccupied with sexual matters than he was, just as he was less preoccupied than, say, a Victorian housewife who would refer to the 'limbs' of a piano, and who would not put a book by a male author on a shelf next to one by a female author unless the two authors happened to be married.

And he was prepared to accept, as well, Philos' statement that he was among friends.

As conversationally as possible, he asked, 'What about children?'

'What about children?'

'Suppose one – ah – gets born and the – ah – parent isn't married?'

'Most of them are born that way.'

'And it makes no difference?'

'Not to the child. Not to the parent, either, as far as anyone else is concerned.'

'Then what's the point of getting married?'

'The point, Charlie, is that the whole is greater than the sum of its parts.'

'Oh.'

'The greatest occasion of sexual expression is a mutual orgasm, wouldn't you say?'

'Yes,' said Charlie as clinically as he could.

'And procreation is a high expression of love?'

'Oh yes.'

'Then if a Ledom and his mate mutually conceive, and each bears twins, does not that appear to be a fairly transcendant experience?'

'F-fairly,' said Charlie in a faint voice, overwhelmed. He put the transcendance away in the back of his mind, kneeing it down until it stopped making quite so large a lump. When he could, he asked, 'What about the other kind of sex?'

'*Other* kind?' Philos wrinkled his brow, and apparently went through some sort of mental card-file. 'Oh – you mean just ordinary expressive sex.'

'I suppose that's what I mean.'

'Well, it happens, that's all. Anything which is an expression of love can happen here, sex, or helping put on a roof, or singing.' Glancing at Charlie's face, he nodded to his invisible card-file and went on: 'I think I know what's perplexing you. You come from a place where certain acts and expressions were held in a bad light – frowned upon, even punished. Is that it?'

'I guess.'

'Then apparently this is what you want to know: There is no opprobrium connected with it here. It isn't regulated in any way. It can only happen when it's an expression of mutual affection, and if there isn't mutual affection, it doesn't happen.'

'What about the young?'

'What *about* the young?'

'I mean … kids, you know. Experimenting and all that.'

Philos laughed his easy laugh. 'Question: When are they old enough to do it? Answer: When they are old enough to do it. As for experimentation, why experiment with anything that's almost as commonly seen as the greeting kiss?'

Charlie gulped. Put this where he may, it still made a lump. Almost plaintively, he said, 'But – what about unwanted children?'

Philos stopped dead, turned, and looked at him, his dark face showing an almost comic succession of changes: shock, amazement, disbelief, question (Are you kidding? Do you mean what you just said?); and at length, of all things, apology. 'I'm sorry, Charlie. I didn't think you could shock me, but you did. I thought that after the amount of research I've done, I was proof against it, but I guess I never expected to stand here in the middle of Ledom and try to engage my mind with the concept of an *unwanted* child.'

'I'm sorry, Philos. I didn't mean to shock anybody.'

'*I'm* sorry. I am surprised that I was shocked, and sorry that I showed it.'

Then, through an orchard, Grocid hailed them, and Philos asked, 'You thirsty?' and they struck off toward the white cottage. It was good, for a while, to be able to get their attention away from one another. It was good to be able to go out and look at the terracotta again.

Herb stands in the moonstruck dark looking down at his daughter. He has slipped out of bed and come here because, on other occasions, he has found it a good place to be for the distraught, the confused, the hurt and puzzled mind. It is not easy to contain feelings of violence and unrest while, breathless, one leans close to examine by moonlight the meeting of the eyelids of a sleeping child.

His malaise began three days ago, when his neighbor Smith, in bitter casualness, tossed a remark over the back wall. The statement itself had seemed, at the time, to go by him like a bad odor; he had chatted about a political matter and the talk had then dwindled away to inconsequence. Yet since then he found he had taken the remark away with him; it was as if Smitty, having been plagued by some festering growth, had been able to drive it into his, Herb's flesh.

It is with him now and he cannot put it by.

Men are born out of the dirtiest part of a woman.

Herb dissociates the remark from Smith, a man who has his troubles and his especial background, for neither of which he is completely accountable. What is troubling Herb Raile is an issue far larger; he is wondering what it is about humanity, since it first came out of the trees, in all the many different things it has been and done, which makes it possible for even one man to say once a thing as filthy as that.

Or was it more than an obscene joke … is it true, or nearly true?

Is that what is meant by the inescapable taint of Original Sin? Is it men's disgust of women that makes so many of them treat women with such contempt? Is it that which makes it so easy to point out that the Don Juans and the Lotharios, for all their hunger for women, are often merely trying to see how many women they can punish? Is this the realization which makes a man, having like a good Freudian child passed into a period of mother-fixation, find a turning point and begin to hate his mother?

When did men begin to find womanhood despicable – when did they decree the menses unclean, and even to this day practice in their houses of worship the ritual known as 'churching of women' – the old post-natal purification ceremony?

Because I don't feel that way, he says silently and devoutly. I love Jeanette because she is a woman, and I love her all over.

Happily, Karen sighs in her sleep. The anger and terror and outrage of his thoughts tumble away, and he smiles over Karen, yearns over her.

Nobody, he thinks, ever wrote anything about father-love. Mother-love is supposed to be a magic expression of the hand of God or something, or maybe the activity of certain ductless glands; it depends on who's talking. But father-love … an awful funny thing, father-love. He's seen an otherwise mild and civilized man go clean berserk because 'somebody did something to my kid.' He knows from his own experience that after a while this father-love thing begins to spread out; you begin to feel that way, a little, toward all kids. Now where's that come from? The kid never inhabits the abdomen, doesn't pull on and feed off the body, as with women; mother-love makes sense, it figures; a baby grows on and of the mother's flesh like a nose. But the father? Why, it takes some pretty special circumstances to make a father even remember the particular two- or three-second spasm that did the job.

Why wouldn't it ever occur to anyone to say humanity was full of sons of bitches because it issued from the filthiest part of a man? It wouldn't, you know; not ever.

Because, it says here, man is superior. Man – mankind (and oh yes, women have learned this trick!) mankind has in it a crushing need to feel superior. This doesn't have to bother the very small minority who actually are superior, but it sure troubles the controlling majority who are not. If you can't be really good at anything, then the only way to be able to prove you are superior is to make someone else inferior. It is this rampaging need in humanity which has, since pre-history, driven a man to stand on the neck of his neighbor, a nation to enslave another, a race to tread on a race. But it is also what men have always done to women.

Did they actually find them inferior to begin with, and learn from that to try to feel superior to other things outside – other races, religions, nationalities, occupations?

Or was it the other way around: did men make women inferior for the same reason they tried to dominate the outsider? Which is cause, which effect?

And – isn't it just self-preservation? Wouldn't women dominate men if they had the chance?

Aren't they trying it right now?

Haven't they already done it, here on Begonia Drive?

He looks down at Karen's hand in the moonlight. He saw it first when it was an hour old, and was thunderstruck by the perfection of the fingernails, of all things; so tiny! so tiny! so perfect! And is this little hand to take hold of reins, Karen, or pull strings, Karen? Are you come into a world where down deep the world despises you, Karen?

The father-love suffuses him, and unmoving, yet he sees in a transported moment himself standing like a warrior between the slime-born sons of bitches and his child.

'Nasive …'

The Ledom, glowing with pleasure, stood before the terracotta group with Charlie, smiled and answered, 'Yes?'

'Can I ask you something?'

'Anything.'

'Confidential, Nasive. Is it wrong to ask you that?'

'I don't think so.'

'And if I step out of bounds in asking, you won't take it poorly? I'm a stranger here.'

'Ask me.'

'It's about Philos.'

'Oh.'

'Why is everyone here so hard on Philos? Let me take that back,' he amended quickly. 'That puts it too strongly. It's just that everyone seems to sort of … disapprove. Not so much of him, but of something about him.'

'Oh,' said Nasive, 'I don't think it's anything that matters very much.'

'You're not going to tell me, then.' There was a stiff silence. Then Charlie said, 'I'm supposed to be learning all I can about Ledom. Do you or do you not think I would gain some kind of insight by knowing something that was wrong in Ledom? Or am I supposed to judge you only by—' he nodded at the statue – 'what you like best about yourselves?'

As he had seen Philos do before, Charlie watched a Ledom instantly and completely disarmed. The impact of truth on these folk was, apparently, enormous.

'You couldn't be more right, Charlie Johns, and I shouldn't have hesitated. But – in all fairness to Philos, I must in turn ask *your* confidence. The matter is, after all, Philos' business and not mine nor yours.'

'I won't let him know I know.'

'Very well, then. Philos stands a little apart from the rest of us. For one thing, he has a secretiveness about him – which in a way is useful; he is given access to a great many things which the rest of us are better off without. But one feels that he … prefers it that way, while to the normal Ledom, that sort of thing might be a duty, but it would be an onerous one.'

'That doesn't seem reason enough to—'

'Oh, it isn't the prime discomfort he generates! The other thing about him – perhaps it is part of the same thing – is that he won't marry.'

'A person doesn't *have* to marry, does he?'

'Oh no indeed.' Nasive moistened his full lips and frowned. 'But Philos behaves as if he is still married.'

'*Still* married?'

'He was married to Froure. They were to have children. One day they walked out to the edge of the sky—' (Charlie comprehended the odd phrase) – 'and there was an accident. A rock-slide. They were buried for days. Froure was killed. Philos lost the unborn children.'

Charlie recalled that Philos had used 'screaming in a rock-slide' as a figure of speech.

'Philos grieved … well, we can all understand that. We love a great deal, we love many ways; our mates we love deeply indeed, and so we understand the nature of grief. But as basic with us as love itself is the necessity to love the living, not the dead. It makes us feel … uncomfortable … to have someone around who holds himself aloof from loving freely, to be faithful to someone who is gone. It's … pathological.'

'Maybe he'll get over it.'

'It happened many years ago,' said Nasive, shaking his head.

'If it's pathological, can't you treat it?'

'With his agreement, we could. And since his particular quirk presents nothing worse than a mild discomfort for a few of us, he is free to remain the way he is if that's what he wishes.'

'Now I understand that little joke of Mielwis.'

'What was that?'

'He said, "There's only one like him!" but he said it as a joke.'

'That was hardly worthy of Mielwis,' said Nasive sternly.

'Whatever it was, it's confidential.'

'Of course … And now do you feel you know us any better?'

'I don't,' said Charlie, 'but I feel I will.'

They exchanged smiles and returned to the house to join the others. Philos was deep in conversation with Grocid, and Charlie was certain they were talking about him. Grocid confirmed this by saying, 'Philos tells me you're almost ready to pass judgment on us.'

'Not exactly that,' laughed Philos. 'It's just that I've given you almost all I have. How long it takes you to draw your conclusions is up to you.'

'I hope it's a long time,' said Grocid. 'You're very welcome here, you know. Nasive likes you.'

It was the kind of remark which in Charlie's day might be made out of the subject's presence, but not in it. Charlie glanced swiftly at Nasive, only to find him nodding. 'Yes, I do,' said Nasive warmly.

'Well, thanks,' said Charlie. 'I like it here too.'

'Smith is a swine.'

Herb Raile, preoccupied, hears these words from Jeanette as she comes in the back door after a visit with Tillie, and he starts violently. He has shared none of his recent thoughts about Smith with her nor with anyone, though he feels a great need to unburden himself. He has checked over all possible recipients for his pressures – one of the girls, maybe, who hung around after the League of Women Voters meetings, or some of the folks at the Great Books gatherings, or the P.T.A., although as the father of a five-year-old he was only peripherally involved there as yet, likewise the local School Board Association. But he is afraid. Swine or no, Smith's advice was sound: A new account – that's serious. Anything else, kicks.

He is not getting any kicks at all out of this thing; it's too large for him and it is not crystallized. Surprised as he is over the confluence of Jeanette's remark to his thoughts, he is not even sure yet whether he thinks Smith is a swine. A pig among people is a pig, he tells himself, but a pig among pigs is people.

'What's he done?'

'You go over there, that's all. He'll show it to you. Tillie's just wild.'

'I wish I knew what you are talking about, honey.'
'I'm sorry, honey. It's a sign thing, a sort of plaque in the rumpus room.'
'Something like those urinary-type labels for the liquor bottles?'
'Much worse. You'll see.'

'What's next, Philos?'
'A good hard look at yourself,' said Philos, and then turned and took the edge off the words with a warm smile. 'A categorical "yourself," I mean. You wouldn't want to evaluate Ledom in a vacuum. Much better to be able to set it up against the other culture for contrast.'
'I already can, I think. In the first place—' but Philos was interrupting:
'You can?' he said, with such meaning that Charlie shut up.
They were walking the final mile between the Children's One and the Science One. A little petulantly, Charlie said, 'I know enough about my own people, I think, to—'
Again Philos sardonically interrupted, and said, 'You do?'
'Well, if you don't think so,' said Charlie with some heat, 'go ahead!'
'Go ahead and what?'
'Set me straight.'
'I am,' said Philos, taking no offense and, strangely, giving none. 'We're going to do it with the cerebrostyle. Quicker, easier, much more detailed, and,' he grinned, 'inarguable and uninterruptible.'
'I wouldn't interrupt and argue.'
'You would; you must. There is literally no subject ever encountered in the history of mankind so unsusceptible to objective study as that of sex. Countless volumes have been written about history and historical motivations with never a mention of sex. Entire generations, and scores of successive generations, of students have pored over them and taken them for the truth and the whole truth, and some have gone on to teach the same things in the same way – even when the importance of sex motivations to the individual had been revealed, even when the individual, in his daily life, was interpreting his whole world with them, filling his thoughts and his language with sex referents. Somehow history remained to a great majority of people a series of anecdotes about some strangers who performed acts and fulfilled desires strangely separated from the sexual behavior of their times – behavior which was at once the result and the cause of their acts. Behavior which produced both history and the blind historian … and, I suppose, his blindness as well. But I should be saying these things after you're through the course, and not before.'
'I think,' said Charlie a little stiffly, 'we'd better get to it.'
They walked round the Science One and took the subway to the Medical One, and Philos led Charlie through the nowfamiliar horizontal catacombs

and vertiginous flights of the huge building. Once they passed through a good-sized hall, rather like a railroad waiting room; it was full of the Ledom chordal hum and the soft cooing of their voices; Charlie was particularly struck by the tableau of two identically cloaked Ledom, each with a sleeping child on the knees, each nursing another ... 'What are they all waiting for?'

'I think I told you – everyone comes here every twenty-eight days for a checkup.'

'Why?'

'Why not? Ledom is small, you know – we haven't eight hundred people yet – and no one lives more than two hours' walk away. We have all the facilities, so – why not?'

'How thorough is the checkup?'

'Very.'

Near the top of the building Philos stopped in front of a doorslit. 'Palm it – there.'

Charlie did so, and nothing happened. Then Philos palmed it and it opened. 'My private preserve,' said Philos. 'The nearest thing to a lock you will find in all Ledom.'

'Why lock anything?' Charlie had noticed the absence of locks, especially throughout the Children's One.

Philos waved Charlie in, and the door snapped shut. 'We have very few taboos in Ledom,' he said, 'but one of them is against leaving highly contagious material around.' He was half-joking, Charlie knew; yet there was a strong serious element in what he said. 'Actually,' Philos explained, 'few Ledom would bother with this,' and he waved a hand carelessly at a half-dozen floor-to-ceiling bookshelves and a wall-rack of small stacked transparent cubes. 'We're infinitely more concerned with the future, and none of this matters much any more. Still ... "man, know thyself" ... It might make some folks pretty unhappy to know themselves this well.'

He went to the rack of cubes, consulted an index, and took down a cube. In purple, it bore a small line of numbers; he checked this against the index and then went to a low couch and, from one of the magically-appearing wall niches, drew a piece of apparatus. It was a bowl-shaped helmet supported by a jointed arm. 'The cerebrostyle,' he said. He tipped it up so Charlie could look inside the bowl. It showed nothing but a dozen or so rubbery nubbins, set into its crown. 'No electrodes, no probes. And it doesn't hurt a bit.'

He took his small numbered cube, opened a chamber near the top of the helmet, dropped the cube in, closed and clamped the lid. Then he lay on the couch, drew the helmet down and pressed it against his head. The instrument seemed to tilt a bit, forward and back, finding purchase, orienting.

It ceased to move, and Philos relaxed. He smiled up at Charlie, and said,

'Now excuse me a couple of seconds.' He closed his eyes, reached up and touched a stud at the edge of the helmet. The stud remained depressed; his hand fell limply away.

There was a deep silence.

The stud clicked, and instantly Philos opened his eyes. He pushed away the helmet and sat up. There was no sign of fatigue or strain. 'That didn't take long, did it?'

'What did you do?'

Philos pointed to the little hatchway into which he had dropped the cube. 'That's a little dissertation I prepared on certain aspects of homo sap.,' he said. 'It needed a little … editing. There are certain facts you say you do not wish to know, and besides, I wanted it to come to you from me, like a letter, rather than impersonally, like a textbook.'

'You mean you can alter these records, just like that?'

'It takes a little practice, and a deal of concentration, but – yes. Well – go ahead.' When Charlie looked at the helmet and hesitated, Philos laughed at him. 'Go on. It won't hurt, and it'll bring you that much closer to home.'

Boldly, then. Charlie Johns lay down. Philos swung the helmet over him and helped him place it over his head. Charlie felt the blunt little fingers inside touch his scalp, cling. The helmet moved, and then was still. Philos took his hand and guided it to the stud. 'Push this yourself, when you're ready. Nothing will happen until you do.' He stepped back. 'Relax.'

Charlie looked up at him. There was no spite or slyness in the strange dark eyes; only warm encouragement.

He pressed the stud.

Herb crosses the back yard, wondering how to ask Smitty about the plaque, or whatever it was, that had steamed Jeanette up so, without actually informing him that Jeanette is angry.

Smitty is poking at a border of marigolds, and when he sees Herb, he gets up, dusts off his knees, and solves the problem:

'Hi. Come on over; I want to show you something. Think you'll get a charge out of it.'

Herb vaults the low wall and goes with Smith into the house and down the steps. Smith has a nice rumpus room. The heater looks like a hi-fi set and the hi-fi set looks like a radiator. The washer-dryer looks like a television, the television looks like a coffee table, the bar looks like a bar, and the whole business is in knotty pine.

Over the bar in front-and-center position, well framed and glazed, in large gothic or black-letter script, so you have to read it slowly and it's all the funnier for that, is a quotation which declares itself (down at the end in fine print) vaguely as the work of 'a Middle Ages Philosopher':

> 𝔄 𝔊ood 𝔚oman (as an old philosopher observeth) is but like one 𝔈le put in a bagge amongst 500 𝔖nakes, and if a man should have the luck to grope out that one 𝔈le from all the 𝔖nakes, yet he hath at best but a wet 𝔈le by the taile.

Herb is prepared to join Jeanette in indignation, sight unseen, but the plaque takes him deliciously by surprise, and he roars, while Smitty chuckles in the background. Then Herb asks how Tillie likes it.

'Women,' Smitty pontificates, 'are squares.'

Philos had said it well: it was like a letter. 'Reading' it, however, was unlike anything he had ever experienced consciously before. He had pressed the stud, which emitted a soft *chuck!*, and then there was a passage of time which was measureless, in that the mental clock which tells a man, unthinking, whether a bell rang five seconds, five minutes, or five hours ago, was momentarily stopped or suspended. It could not have been very long, however, and there was, in any ordinary sense, no loss of awareness, for when the stud went *chuck!* again, Philos still stood over him, smiling. But he now felt precisely as if, at that very moment, he had put down, after an absorbed reading, a long and interesting letter from a friend.

He said, startled into English, 'Well, for *God's* sake!'

Charlie Johns, [the 'letter' had begun] you cannot be objective about this discussion. But try. Please try.

You cannot be objective about it because you have been indoctrinated, sermonized, drenched, imbued, inculcated and policed on the matter since first you wore blue booties. You come from a time and place in which the maleness of the male, and the femaleness of the female, and the importance of their difference, were matters of almost total preoccupation.

Begin, then, with this – and if you like, regard it as mainly a working hypothesis. Actually it is a truth, and if at the end it passes the tests of your own understanding, you will see that it is a truth. If you do not, the fault is not with you, but with your orientation:

There are more basic similarities than differences between men and women.

Read through an anatomy manual. A lung is a lung, a kidney a kidney in man or in woman. It may be that statistically, women's bone-structure is lighter, the head smaller, and so on and on; yet it is not impossible that mankind had, for many thousands of years, bred for that. But aside from such conjectures, the variations permissible to what is called 'normal' structure provide many examples of women who were taller, stronger, heavier-boned than most men, and men who were smaller, slighter, lighter than most women. Many men had larger pelvic openings than many women.

In the area of the secondary sexual characteristics, it is only statistically that we can note significant differences; for many women had more body hair than many men; many men had higher-pitched voices than many women ... I call again on your objectivity: suspend for a moment your conviction that the statistical majority is the norm, and examine the cases, in their vast numbers, which exist outside that probable fiction, that norm. And go on:

For even with the sex organs themselves, variations in development – and here, admittedly, we approach the pathological – have yielded countless cases of atrophied phalli, hypertrophied clitori, perforate rathes, detached labia ... all, viewed *objectively*, reasonably subtle variations from the norm, and capable of producing, on an initially male or female body, virtually identical urogenital triangles. It is not my intention to state that such a situation is or should be normal – at least, not after the fourth fetal month, though up to then it is not only normal but universal – but only to bring out to you that its occurrence is easily within the limits of what has been, since prehistory, possible to nature.

Endocrinology demonstrates a number of interesting facts. Both male and female could produce male and female hormones, and did, and as a matter of fact, the preponderance of one over the other was a subtle matter indeed. Then if you throw that delicate balance out, the changes which could be brought about were drastic. In a few months you could produce a bearded and breastless lady and a man whose nipples, no longer an atrophied insigne of the very point I am making here, could be made to lactate.

These are gross and extreme examples purely for illustration. There have been many women athletes who could exceed in strength, speed and skill the vast majority of men, but who were nonetheless what you might call 'real' women, and many men who could, say, design clothing – traditionally a woman's specialty – far better than most women, yet who were what you might call 'real' men. For when we get into what I might broadly term cultural differences between the sexes, the subtlety of sexual distinction begins to become apparent. What say the books:

Women have long hair. So have the Sikhs, whom some call the toughest breed of soldiers ever bred. So had the 18th-century cavaliers, and brocaded jackets and lace at throat and wrists as well. Women wear skirts. So does a kilted Scot, a Greek *evzone*, a Chinese, a Polynesian, none of whom could deserve the term 'effeminate.'

An objective scan of human history proliferates these examples to numbers astronomical. From place to place, and in any place from time to time, the so-called 'provinces' of male and female rise like the salinity of a tidal rivermouth, mingling, separating, ebbing and regrouping ... before your first

World War, cigarettes and wrist-watches were regarded as unquestionably female appurtenances; twenty years later both were wholeheartedly adopted by the men. Europeans, especially central Europeans, were startled and very much amused to see American farmers milking cows and feeding chickens, for never in their lives had they seen that done by any but women.

So it is easily seen that the sexual insignes are nothing in themselves, for any of them, in another time and place, might belong to both sexes, the other sex, or neither. In other words, a skirt does not make the social entity, woman. It takes a skirt plus a social attitude to do it.

But all through history, in virtually every culture and country, there has indeed been a 'woman's province' and a 'man's province,' and in most cases the differences between them have been exploited to fantastic, sometimes sickening extremes.

Why?

First of all, it is easy to state, and easy to dispose of, the theory that in a primitive, primarily hunting-and-fishing society, a weaker, slower-moving sex, occasionally heavy with child and forced frequently to pause to nurse her young, is not as well fitted to hunt and fight as the fleeter-footed, untrammeled, hard-muscled male. However, it may well be that the primitive woman was not that much smaller, slower, weaker than her mate. Perhaps the theory confuses cause and effect, and perhaps, if some other force had not insisted upon such a development, accepted it, even bred for it, the nonparous females might have hunted with the best of the men, while those men who happened to be slower, smaller, weaker, kept house with the pregnant and nursing women. And this has happened – not in the majority of cases, but many times nevertheless.

The difference existed – granted. But it was exploited. It was a difference which continued to exist long, long after there was any question of hunting or, for that matter, of nursing. Humanity has insisted upon it; made it an article of faith. Again:

Why?

It would seem that there *is* a force which widens and exploits this difference, and, isolated, it is a deplorable, even terrifying pressure.

For there is in mankind a deep and desperate necessity to feel superior. In any group there are some who genuinely are superior ... but it is easy to see that within the parameters of any group, be it culture, club, nation, profession, only a few are really superior; the mass, clearly, are not.

But it is the will of the mass that dictates the mores, initiated though changes may be by individuals or minorities; the individuals or minorities, more often than not, are cut down for their trouble. And if a unit of the mass wants to feel superior, it will find a way. This terrible drive has found expression in many ways, through history – in slavery and genocide, xenophobia and snobbery, race prejudice and sex differentiation. Given a man who, among his fellows, has no real superiority, you are faced with a bedevilled madman who, if superiority is denied him, and he cannot learn one or earn one, will turn on something weaker than himself and *make it inferior*. The obvious, logical, handiest subject for this inexcusable indignity is his woman.

He could not do this to anyone he loved.

If, loving, he could not have insulted this close, so-little-different other half of himself, he could never have done it to his fellow man. Without this force in him, he could never have warred, nor persecuted, nor in pursuit of superiority lied, cheated, murdered and stolen. It may be that the necessity to feel superior is the source of his drive, and his warring and killing have brought him to mighty places; yet it is not unconceivable that without it he might have turned to conquering his environment and learning his own nature, rising very much higher and, in the process, earning life for himself instead of extinction.

And strangely enough, man always wanted to love. Right up to the end, it was idiomatic that one 'loved' music, a color, mathematics, a certain food – and aside from careless idiom, there were those who in the highest sense loved things beyond anything which even a fool would call sexual. 'I could not love thee, dear, so much, loved I not honor more.' 'For God so loved the world, he gave his only begotten son ...' Sexual love is love, certainly. But it is more precise to say that it is *loving*, in the same way we might say that justice is loving, and mercy is loving, forbearance, forgiveness, and, where it is not done to maximize the self, generosity.

Christianity was, at the outset, a love movement, as the slightest acquaintance with the New Testament clearly documents. What was not generally known until just before the end – so fiercely was all knowledge of primitive Christianity suppressed – was that it was a charitic religion – that is, a religion in which the congregation participated, in the hope of having a genuine religious experience, an experience later called theolepsy, or seized of God. Many of the early Christians did achieve this state, and often; many more achieved it but seldom, and yet kept going back and back seeking it. But once having experienced it, they were profoundly changed, inwardly gratified; it was this intense experience, and its permanent effects, which made it possible for them to endure the most frightful hardships and tortures, to die gladly, to fear nothing.

Few dispassionate descriptions of their services – gatherings is a better term – survive, but the best accounts agree on a picture of people slipping away from fields, shops, even, palaces, to be together in some hidden place – a mountain glade, a catacomb, anywhere where they might be uninterrupted. It is significant that rich and poor alike mingled at these gatherings: male and female. After eating together – genuinely, a love feast – and invoking the spirit, perhaps by song, and very likely by the dance, one or another might be seized by what they called the Spirit. Perhaps he or she – and it might be either – would exhort and praise God, and perhaps the true charitic (that is, divinely gifted) expression would issue forth in what was called 'speaking in tongues,' but these exhibitions, when genuine, were apparently not excessive nor frenetic; there was often time for many to take their turn. And with a kiss of peace, they would separate and slip back to their places in the world until the next meeting.

The primitive Christians did not invent charitic religion, by any means; nor did it cease with them. It recurs again and again throughout recorded history, and it takes many forms. Frequently they are orgiastic, Dionysic, like the worship of the Great Mother of the Gods, Cybele, which exerted an immense influence in Rome, Greece and the Orient a thousand years before Christ. Or chastity-based movements like the Cathars of the Middle ages, the Adamites, the Brethen of the Free Spirit, the Waldenses (who tried to bring a form of apostolic Christianity into the framework of the Roman church) and many, many others appear all through history. They have in common one element – the subjective, participant, ecstatic experience – and almost invariably the equality of women, and they are all love religions.

Without exception they were savagely persecuted.

It seems that there is a commanding element in the human makeup which regards loving as anathema, and will not suffer it to live.

Why?

An objective examination of basic motivations (and Charlie! I *know* you can't be objective! but bear with this!) reveals the simple and terrible reason.

There are two direct channels into the unconscious mind. Sex is one, religion is the other; and in pre-Christian times, it was usual to express them together. The Judeo-Christian system put a stop to it, for a very understandable reason. *A charitic religion interposes nothing between the worshipper and his Divinity.* A suppliant, suffused with worship, speaking in tongues, his whole body in the throes of ecstatic dance, is not splitting doctrinal hairs nor begging intercession from temporal or literary authorities. As to his conduct between times, his guide is simple. He will seek to do that which will make it possible to repeat the experience. If he does what for him is right in this endeavor, he will repeat it; if he is not able to repeat it, that alone is his total and complete punishment.

He is guiltless.

The only conceivable way to use the immense power of innate religiosity – the need to worship – for the acquisition of human power, is to place between worshipper and Divinity a guilt mechanism. The only way to achieve that is to organize and systematize worship, and the obvious way to bring this about is to monitor that other great striving of life – sex.

Homo sapiens is unique among species, extant and extinct, in having devised systems for the suppression of sex.

There are only three ways of dealing with sex. It may be gratified; it may be repressed; or it may be sublimated. The latter is, through history, often an ideal and frequently a success, but it is *always* an instability. Simple, day-by-day gratification, as in what is called the Golden Age of Greece, where they instituted three classes of women: wives, *hetaerae* and prostitutes, and at the same time idealized homosexuality, may be barbaric and immoral by many standards, but produces a surprising degree of sanity. A careful look, on the other hand, at the Middle ages, makes the mind reel; it is like opening a window on a vast insane asylum, as broad as the world and as long as a thousand years; here is the product of repression. Here are the scourging manias, when people by the thousands flogged themselves and each other from town to town, seeking penance from excesses of guilt; here is the mystic Suso, in the fourteenth century, who had made for him an undergarment for his loins, bearing a hundred and fifty brass nails filed sharp; and lest he try to ease himself in his sleep, a leather harness to hold his wrists firmly against his neck; and further, lest he try to relieve himself of the lice and fleas which plagued him, he put on leather gloves studded with sharp nails which would tear his flesh wherever he touched it; and touch it it did, and when the wounds healed he tore them open again. He lay upon a discarded wooden door with a nail-studded cross against his back, and in forty years he never took a bath. Here are saints licking out lepers' sores; here is the Inquisition.

All this in the name of love.

How could such a thing so change?

The examination of one sequence clearly shows how. Take the suppression of the Agape, the 'love feast,' which seems to have been a universal and necessary appurtenance of primitive Christianity. It can be unearthed by records of edicts against this and that practice, and it is significant that the elimination of a rite so important to worship seems to have taken between three and four hundred years to accomplish, and was done by a gradualism of astonishing skill and efficiency.

First of all, the Eucharistic, the symbolic ritual of the body and blood of Christ, was introduced into the Agape. Next, we find the Agape better organized; there is now a bishop, without whom the Agape may not be held, for he must bless the food. A little later the bishop is traditionally kept standing through the meal, which of course keeps him separate, and above the others. After that, the kiss of peace is altered; instead of kissing one another, all the participants kiss the officiating priest, and later, they all kiss a piece of wood which is handed around and passed to the priest. And then, of course, the kiss is done away with altogether. In the year 363, the Council of Laodicaea is able to establish the Eucharist as a major ritual by itself, by forbidding the Agape within a church, thus separating them. For many years the Agape was held outside the church door, but by 692 (the Trullan Council) it was possible to forbid it altogether, under the penalty of excommunication.

The Renaissance cured many of the forms of insanity, but not the insanity itself. When temporal and ecclesiastical authorities still maintained control over basically sexual matters – morals, and marriage, for example (although it was very late in the game when the Church actually performed marriage; marriages in England at the time of Shakespeare were by private contract valid, and by Church blessing licit) guilt was still rife, guilt was still the filter between a man and his God. Love was still equated with passion and passion with sin, so that at one point it was held to be sinful for a man to love his wife with passion. Pleasure, the outer edge of ecstasy, was in the dour days of Protestantism, considered sinful in itself, wherever gained; Rome held specifically that any or all sexual pleasure was sinful. And for all this capped volcano produced in terms of bridges and houses, factories and bombs, it gouted from its riven sides a frightful harvest of neurosis. And even where a nation officially discarded the church, the same repressive techniques remained, the same preoccupation with doctrine, filtered through the same mesh of guilt. So sex and religion, the real meaning of human existence, ceased to be meaning and became means; the unbridgeable hostility between the final combatants was the proof of the identity of their aim – the total domination, for the ultimate satisfaction of the will to superiority, of all human minds.

Herb Raile goes in to say goodnight to the kids. He kneels on the floor by Karen's bed. Davy watches. Herb cradles Karen in his arms, tickles her tummy until she squeals, kisses the side of her neck and bites the lobe of her ear. Davy watches, big-eyed. Herb covers Karen's head with the blanket, quickly ducks out of sight so she can't see him when she pulls the blanket down. She searches, finds him, giggles wildly. He kisses her again, smooths the blanket over her, whispers 'Your daddy *loves* you,' says goodnight and turns to Davy, who watches, solemn.

Herb reaches out his right hand. Davy takes it. Herb shakes it. 'Good night, old man,' he says. He releases the hand. 'Good night, Dad,' says Davy, not looking at Herb. Herb turns out the light and leaves. Davy gets out of bed, wads up his pillow, crosses the room and whangs the pillow down as hard as he can on Karen's face.

'I can't,' says Herb quite a while later, after the tears are dried and the recriminations done with, 'understand whatever made him do that.'

We Ledom renounce the past.

We Ledom (continued the cerebrostyle 'letter') leave the past forever, and all products of the past except for naked and essential humanity.

The special circumstances of our birth make this possible. We come from a nameless mountain and as a species we are unique; as all species, we are transient. Our transience is our central devotion. Transience is passage, is dynamism, is movement, is change, is evolution, is mutation, is life.

The special circumstance of our birth include the blessed fact that in the germ-plasm is no indoctrination. Had homo sap. had the sense (it had the power) it could have shut off all its poisons, vanquished all its dangers, by raising one clean new generation. Had homo sap. had the desire (it had both sense and power enough) to establish a charitic religion and a culture to harmonize with it, it would in time have had its clean generations.

Homo sap. claimed to be searching for a formula to end its woes. Here is the formula: a charitic religion and a culture to go with it. The Apostles of Jesus found it. Before them the Greeks found it; before them, the Minoans. Since then the Cathars found it, the Quakers, the Angel Dancers. Throughout the Orient and in Africa it has been found repeatedly ... and each time it has failed to move any but those it touched directly. Men – or at least, the men who moved men – always found that the charitic is intolerant of doctrine, neither wanting it nor needing it. But without doctrine – presbyter, interpreter, officiator – the men who move men are powerless – that is to say, not superior. There is nothing to gain in charitism.

Except, of course, the knowledge of the soul; and everlasting life.

Father-dominated people who form father-dominated cultures have father-religions: a male deity, an authoritative scripture, a strong central government, an intolerance for inquiry and research, a repressive sexual attitude, a deep conservatism (for one does not change what Father built), a rigid demarcation, in dress and conduct, between the sexes, and a profound horror of homosexuality.

Mother-dominated people who form mother-dominated cultures have mother-religions: a female deity served by priestesses, a liberal government – one which feeds the masses and succors the helpless – a great tolerance for experimental thought, a permissive attitude toward sex, a hazy boundary between the insignes of the sexes, and a dread of incest.

The father-dominated culture seeks always to impose itself upon others. The other does not. So it is the first, the patrist culture which tends to establish itself in the main stream, the matrist which rises within it, occasionally revolts, more often is killed. They are not stages of evolution, but phases marking swings of the pendulum.

The patrists poison themselves. The matrists tend to decay, which is merely another kind of poison. Occasionally one will meet a person who has been equally influenced by his mother and his father, and emulates the best of both. Usually, however, people fall into one category or the other; this is a slippery fence on which to walk ...

Except for the Ledom.

We are liberal in art and in technological research, in expression of all kinds. We are immovably conservative in certain areas: our conviction, each of us, never to lose the skills of the hand and of the land. We are raising children who will emulate neither mother-images nor father-images, but parents; and our deity is the Child. We renounce and forego all products of the past but ourselves, though we know there is much there that is beautiful; that is the price we pay for quarantine and health; that is the wall we put between ourselves and the dead hand. This is the only taboo, restriction – and the only demand we have from those who bore us.

For, like homo sap., we were born of earth and of the creatures of earth; we were born of a race of half-beasts, half-savages; homo sap. birthed us. Like homo sap. we are denied the names of those from whom we sprung, though, like men, we have much evidence of the probabilities. Our human parents built us a nest, and cared for us until we were fledged, but would not let us know them, because, unlike most men, they knew themselves and therefore would not be worshipped. And no one but themselves, they and the mothers, knew of us, that we were here, that we were something new on the face of earth. They would not betray us to homo sap., for we were different, and like all pack, herd, hive animals, homo sap. believes in the darkest part of the heart that whatever is different is by definition dangerous, and should be exterminated. Especially if it is similar in any important way (oh how horrible the gorilla, how contemptible the baboon) and most especially if in some way it might be superior, possessing techniques and devices surpassing their own (remember the Sputnik Reaction, Charlie?) but with absolute and deadly certainty if their sex activities fall outside certain arbitrary limits; for this is the key to all unreason, from outrage to envy. In a cannibal society it is immoral not to eat human flesh.

The stud went *chuck!* and Charlie Johns found himself looking up into Philos' sardonic smiling eyes.

He said, startled into English, 'Well, for *God's* sake!'

'No bowling tonight, honey?'

'No, honey. I called Tillie Smith and begged off and she was glad and I was glad.'

'You gals tiffing?'

'Oh, no! Far from it. It's just that … well, Tillie's very touchy these days. She knows it and she knows I know it. She'd much rather skip bowling altogether than get huffy with me and she knows she would if she did so she won't.'

'Sounds like the old prostate acting up again!'

'Herb, you're gossiping. Besides, she hasn't got a prostate.'

'She hasn't got Smitty's prostate, so that's the trouble.'

'Oh, I guess so, Herb, you old scandal-monger you.'

'Sex … it's like pants.'

'Wh …? – oh dear, there you go getting philosophical again. All right – get it off your chest.'

'Not philosophical. More like what do you call making fables?'

'Fabulous.'

'So I'm fabulous. Sex is like pants. All right. I go from here down Begonia to the Avenue and walk two blocks and get cigarettes and walk back, pass a lot of people, nobody notices.'

'*Every*body notices, you great big handsome—'

'No wait – wait. Nobody really notices. You come along and ask all those people I passed, did they see me. Some say yes; most don't know. You get the ones said yes, ask 'em what type pants I was wearing. Now actually they could be chinos or dungarees or from the tux with black silk stripes or gabardine.'

'This isn't about sex.'

'Wait, wait. Now suppose I leave here to go to the drug store I don't wear any pants.'

'*Any* pants?'

'Uh-huh. Now who notices?'

'You wouldn't get as far as the avenue. Don't you dare try it, right past the Palmers.'

'Everybody notices – right! So – sex. Somebody get enough, it hardly even matters what kind, as long as it's not too funny-lookin', he goes about his business, don't think about it, don't bother anyone else. But when he has none, none at all, boy! From here to there, it's all he can think about, but *all*, and likewise he bothers everyone in sight. Tillie.'

'Oh, *that* wouldn't bother Tillie.'

'Not what I mean. I mean, that's the way with Tillie now. What's bothering her, you can't go bowling she's too jumpy.'

'I think you're right, you know that, about sex is like pants. Only don't go talking it around, people will say you said Tillie doesn't wear pants.' Jeanette laughs shrilly. 'What a thought. Any old pants.'

'Long as it covers the situation. Yuk. Something old, something new, something borrowed, something blue.'

'Yuk yourself, and don't you dare try it.'

Outside in the hall they met Mielwis, who said, 'How are you coming along, Charlie Johns?'

'I'm there,' said Charlie warmly. 'I think you're the most remarkable thing ever to hit this old planet, you Ledom. It's enough to make a fellow really religious, the business of a mutation like you coming along just when the rest of us were going up in smoke.'

'You approve of us, then.'

'Once you get used to the idea ... well, I should say I do! God, it's a pity there weren't a few of you around – ah – preaching or something. I mean it.'

Mielwis and Philos exchanged a glance. 'No,' said Philos, as it were across Charlie and out of his range, 'not yet.'

'Will it be soon?'

'I think we'll go out to the Edge,' said Philos. 'Just Charlie and I.'

'Why?' Mielwis asked.

Philos smiled, and the dark lights in his eyes flashed. 'It takes a while to walk back.'

Mielwis then smiled too, and nodded. 'I'm glad you think well of us, Charlie Johns,' he said. 'I hope you always do.'

'What else?' said Charlie, as he and Philos turned away down the corridor. They dropped down a shaft, and in the main court, Charlie demanded, 'Now what was that all about?'

'There's still something you don't know,' said Philos, waving at a child, who twinkled back at him.

'Something you're going to show me out at the Edge?'

'What I said to Mielwis,' replied Philos, obviously not answering the question, 'was, in effect, that after I tell you the rest of it, a good long walk might help you to shake it down.'

'Is it that hard to take?' laughed Charlie.

Philos did not laugh. 'It's that hard to take.'

So Charlie stopped laughing, and they walked out of the Medical One and struck off across the open land in a direction new to Charlie.

'I miss the dark,' said Charlie after a while, looking up at the silver sky. 'The stars ... what about astronomy, Philos, and geophysics, and things like that, that need a little more scope than olive groves and farm fields?'

'There's plenty of that in the cerebrostyle files, in case it gets important suddenly. Meanwhile,' said Philos, 'it'll wait.'

'For what?'

'For a livable world.'

'How long will that be?'

Philos shrugged. 'Nobody can tell yet. Seace thinks we should put up a satellite every hundred years or so to check.'

'Every hundred years or so? For God's sake, Philos – how long are you going to stay bottled up here?'

'As long as it takes. Look, Charlie, mankind has spent some thousands of years looking outward. There's a great deal more in the files about the composition of white dwarf stars than there is about the structure of the earth under our feet. It's a good analogy; we need to balance things up a bit by spending a while looking inward instead of outward. As one of your writers – Wylie, I think – said, we have to get away from the examination of the *object* and get to know the *subject*.'

'And meanwhile you're at a standstill!' cried Charlie, and waved an indicative hand at a distant Ledom patiently weeding with a hoe. 'What are you going to do – stand still for ten thousand years?'

'What is ten thousand years,' asked Philos equably, 'in the history of a race?'

They walked in silence for a time over the rolling land, until Charlie gave a small, almost embarrassed laugh and said: 'I guess I'm not used to thinking that big ... Listen, I'm still hazy about just how the Ledom got started.'

'I know,' said Philos reflectively. 'Well, with the first two, word was passed to a number of very intelligent and far-thinking people. As I told you in the 'style, they made it a point to conceal their identities from us, and you can be sure they were ten times as cautious with the rest of the world. Homo sap. wouldn't take kindly to the idea of being supplanted; am I right?'

'I'm afraid you are.'

'Even if the new species wasn't in direct competition,' nodded Philos. 'Well then: though we don't have any direct knowledge as to who they were, it's clear that they must have had very astute advice in a dozen different fields. They developed the first cerebrostyle, for example, and did most of the groundwork on the A-field, though I don't think the first field was actually generated until we were on our own. Whether they worked on us – for us – until they died, or brought the work to a certain point and then sealed us off, and went back to wherever they came from, I couldn't say. I only know for certain that there was a small colony of young Ledom in a large mountain cave which opened onto an otherwise inaccessible valley. The Ledom never set foot in that valley until the A-field was developed and it could be roofed over.'

'Then the air wasn't radioactive, or anything like that!'

'No, it wasn't.'

'Then the Ledom actually coexisted with homo sap. for a while!'

'Yes indeed. The only way they might have been discovered would be from the air. Of course, once the A-field was ready, that was no longer a problem.'

'What does it look like from the air?'

'I'm told,' said Philos, 'it looks like more mountains.'

'Philos, you Ledom all resemble one another pretty much. Are – were you all one family?'

'Yes and no. As I understand it, there were two of us at first, unrelated. The rest are descended from those.'

Charlie thought a moment, then decided not to ask the question which was in his mind. Instead he asked, 'Could anyone leave here?'

'No one would want to, would they?'

'But – *could* they?'

'I suppose so,' said Philos, in a mildly irritated tone. Charlie wondered if this was a conditioning or some such. It would be logical. 'How long have the Ledom been here?'

'I'll answer that,' said Philos, 'but not now.'

A little taken aback, Charlie trudged along for a while in silence. Then he asked, 'Are there any more Ledom settlements like this?'

'None.' Philos seemed to becoming more and more laconic.

'And isn't there anyone out there at all?'

'We presume not.'

'Presume? Don't you know?' When Philos would not respond, Charlie asked him point-blank, 'Is homo sap. really extinct?'

'Inescapably,' said Philos; and he had to be satisfied with that.

They had reached the edge of the valley, and were climbing foothills. The going was more difficult, but Philos seemed to want to go faster, seemed to be driven by something. Charlie noticed how he kept examining the rocks about them, kept looking back toward the looming Ones.

'You looking for something?'

'Just a place to sit down,' said Philos. They threaded their way between huge boulders and came at last to a steep dope, part solid rock, part talus. Philos glanced again toward the Ones – they were invisible from here – and said in a strange, taut voice, 'Sit down.'

Charlie, realizing that he had for many minutes been building up to something large, something unexpected, found himself a flat rock and crouched on it.

'This is where I ... lost ... my mate, my Froure,' said Philos.

Recalling that he had promised Nasive that he would not admit previous knowledge, Charlie, with no difficulty at all, put a sympathetic expression on his face and said nothing.

'It was a long time ago,' said Philos. 'I had just been given the history assignment. The overall idea was to see what would happen if one of us was drenched with it; if it was as poisonous as some people feared. And by some people, I mean some of the people who worked with us in the First Cave. They believed pretty strongly that we should cut all ties with homo sap., who seemed to have fumbled the ball pretty badly, and try not to emulate him in any way, even unconsciously. This would cost us his art, his literature, and a great deal of what was good in his evaluations; but at the same time they did not want us denied his pure sciences – you mentioned astronomy yourself – and some of the developmental data. It pays, you know, sometimes, to know what mistakes to avoid. It not only saves trouble; in a moral sense it makes some of the most appalling errors worth while, good for something. So ... try it on the dog first,' he said, with a bitter little smile.

'I'd gotten about as far along as you are in the study of the Ledom and of homo sap., though in a good deal more detail. Froure and I had been married only a short while, and I'd had to spend a lot of time alone. I thought it would be nice if Froure and I took a long slow walk, just to talk, to be together. We were both pregnant ... We sat down here and the ... the ...' Philos swallowed and began over. 'The ground opened up. That's the only way I can say it. Froure went right ... *down*. I jumped to—'

'I'm sorry,' said Charlie uselessly.

'Four days later they dug me out. They never found Froure. I lost both my babies. The only ones I'll ever have, I guess.'

'But surely you could—'

Philos interrupted the warm suggestion. 'But surely I wouldn't—' he said, pleasantly mocking. Seriously, then, 'I like you, Charlie Johns, and I trust you. I'd like to show you why I can't possibly marry, but you'll have to promise me your absolute confidence.'

'Certainly!'

Philos regarded him solemnly for a long moment, then touched his hands together. The mirror-field sprang into existence. He placed the ring, with the field still operating, on the ground, stepped back a yard, and gave a sharp pull at the edge of a flat rock. It tilted, discovering a dim hole or tunnel-mouth. The mirror, frameless and perfect, reflecting against the big boulder, would offer perfect camouflage to the hole behind it, should anyone approach from the Ones. Philos dropped into the hole, beckoned to Charlie, and passed out of sight.

Thunderstruck, Charlie followed.

Thirty people in the living room is a bit of a squeeze, but it's all friendly and informal and people don't mind sprawling around on the floor. The minister is a good man. He's a good man, thinks Herb, in any old way you want to use the words. When this Rev. Bill Flester was a chaplain in the army, he'd bet the church people said that and the brass and the GI's too. Flester has clear eyes and very good teeth, and iron-grey, crew-cut hair and a young ruddy face. His clothes are sober but not funereal, and his narrow tie and narrow lapels, like his words, speak their language. He has begun by stating a thesis like a text for a sermon, but it is not a Biblical text; it is a working phrase like what you'd run across on Madison Avenue or any place; it is, 'There's always a way, if you can only think of it.' The neighbors listen raptly. Jeanette watches the teeth. Tillie Smith watches the shoulders, which are broad, and the iron-grey crew-cut. Smitty, folded up on the end of a coffee table, leans forward and with his thumb and forefinger pulls his lower lip out so you can see clear to the floor of his mouth in front of his teeth, which is the Smith semaphore for 'This guy has something here.'

'Now our Jewish friends,' Flester is saying, with a filtered approval, 'have built themselves that very pretty little temple down on Forsythia Drive, and over on the other side of the development our Catholic buddies have themselves a nice little brick chapel. Now I've done a little reading and a lot of legwork, and I find there are twenty-two different Protestant churches within ten miles of here; people from this development go to eighteen different ones, and we have at least fifteen represented right here in this room. Now nobody's going to build fifteen or twenty or twenty-two different kinds of Protestant churches here. Now the school people know what to do about small scattered outlets, and so do the grocery people. They centralize.

'It just seems to me we ought to take a leaf from their book. A church has to look to efficiency, and product appeal, and rising costs just like any other operation. In a new situation, you find new ways to do business, like the idea of driving your car into a bank, like this shopping by television they talk about in the Sunday papers. We're all Protestants and we all want to go to church right here in the neighborhood. The only thing in our way is a question of doctrine. There are a lot of folks take their doctrine pretty seriously, and let's be frank, there have been quarrels about it.

'A lot has been done with the idea of uniting churches. You give a point, I give a point, we get together. But a lot of folks figure they have gotten together by losing something. That's the way it makes some folks feel: a compromise is when everybody loses something. We don't want that here.

'I think with all respect that some folks have hold of the wrong end of the stick. There must be a way to join together where nobody loses and everybody gains. There always *is* a way if you can only think of it.

'Now what I think, and I take no credit for it because any of you people would come up with the same answer if you had yourself involved in it like I have, I think we ought to get the people in from all the different churches, on the top level; what you would call a management group, an executive group, and I think we ought to kick around the idea of a little church for all of us. But instead of fighting about which brand to stock, let's load the shelves with all the brands, you know, top quality goods from all over. You go in there to God's supermarket with a need to fill, and it's there for you, and you wheel over and take it off the shelf.

'Now just for an example of what I mean, if one of you ladies has been loyal to Del Monte brand all your life, I wouldn't want you to hide it like a secret, I wouldn't want to hire a boy to go to work and rip off all the labels, I wouldn't want you to stop using it or stop telling all your girl-friends you think that's best. I just want you to have it and use it and be happy with it. And there's going to be no quarrel between you and the market, or between you and another customer, if she wants some other brand, because that brand is going to be right there on the same kind of shelf under good lighting and a fair display.

'If we can put this proposition to – heh – management from all over, like you might say the distributors, I don't think they will fight the idea of more distribution without disturbing consumer loyalty. I think they'll get just as enthusiastic about packaging and point-of-sale merchandizing as the store management will. Here'll be management dedicated to "service" in a new way.

'No one needs to go without anything he really needs – that's the American way. If you want your kiddies baptized by immersion, we'll have a font or pool big enough. If you want candles on the altar, fine; a Sunday is big enough to have services with them and without them. The candlesticks can be telescopic. Pictures and decorations? Put them in slots and hinges so they can be changed or slid out of sight or anything you like.

'I won't go into any more detail about it; it's *your* church and we'll set it up your way. Long as we're guided by the idea of service – and all that means is that we're not fixing to offend anybody. There are more similar ways of loving your God than different ways of loving your God, and it's high time and past time we moved along with the main currents of the American system and let our churches service us with self-service of the best kind, with plenty of parking space and a decent playground for the kiddies.'

Everybody applauds.

Philos set his shoulder against the slab and it swung up and shut. It was totally dark for a moment, and then there was a scrabbling sound and Philos unearthed a lump of coldly glowing material and set it in a cleft. 'There's one more important thing for you to learn about Ledom, and in an ugly sort of way,' said Philos, 'you couldn't have been given a better way to learn it. Mielwis himself hasn't the slightest notion how good. Put this on.' From some hidden hollow in the rock he drew a cloak; thick cobweb might describe such a material. He got a similar one and enveloped himself in the folds. Charlie, speechless, followed suit, while Philos went on, in driving, almost angry tones, 'Down Froure went, and in I plunged, and when Froure dug me out – Froure with a broken foot and four broken ribs, mind you – we found ourselves in here – it's what the geologists call a chimney. It wasn't quite this tidy. Digging out was past trying. We went *in*.'

He pushed past Charlie and seemed to crouch down in black shadows in the corner; then he was gone. Charlie followed, and found the black spot was a hole, a tunnel-mouth. In the dark, Philos took his hand. Charlie stumbled on the hem of the cloak and cursed. 'It's too hot.'

'Keep it on,' Philos ordered flatly. He moved forward purposively, all but dragging Charlie, who sidled and shuffled and did his best to keep up; and all the while Philos talked, short, sharp, hurried; what he said obviously hurt him to say. 'First thing I remember we were in a sort of blind cave back in here. Froure had managed some sort of light, and I felt I was turning inside out. The babies were lost then, my two. It took about three hours. The light held out, I'm … sorry to say. Watch your head, it's low here … about six and a half months along. Good well-formed youngsters.'

'Your kind of youngsters,' Philos' voice came out of the dark after a long shuffling pause. 'Homo sap. youngsters.'

'What?'

Philos stopped in the dark and there was a scrabbling. Again from a pile of loose rubble he drew a glowing block of material and set it up. They were in a smooth-walled cave which had at one time doubtless been a pressure-bubble in the magma of a volcano. 'Right here, it was,' Philos nodded. 'Froure tried to hide them from me. I get … upset when people try to hide things from me.

'We explored a bit. The whole hillside was honeycombed with these chimneys. It no longer is, by the way. We found a way back, a hole a hundred feet away from the rock-fall. But we found a way through, too – right through the hill, and it comes out past the "sky."

'I was hurt and grieved and more than a little angry. Froure too. We had a crazy idea. Froure's foot and ribs were only painful, not dangerous, and we Ledom can handle pain pretty well. But I had internal injuries and something had to be done about it. So we agreed that I should go back, and Froure would just – disappear for a while.'

'Why?'

'I had to find out. I'd lost two babies, and they were homo sap. Was it just me? Well, there was a way to find out. And if I found out what I was afraid of finding out, I wanted Froure and me away from Ledom – far enough, at least to be able to think it through …

'So I'd go back. Froure would stay. I'd get treatment, and hurry back as quickly as I could. Well … I crawled up the other chimney and we made another rock-fall, and the searchers found me all right, and they naturally dug where I told them, and naturally Froure was not found. But we made that second rock-fall a little too good. I was hurt again … it was longer, much longer, than I thought it would be when at last I was on my feet again. I hurried back here – they were oh, so understanding, and left me to grieve any way I wanted to – I hurried back, hoping against hope that I would be in time, and I was not in time. Froure, all alone, bore two babies, and one died.

'They were homo sap.'

'Philos!'

'Yes, homo sap. So we began to be sure. Somehow a baby had to be born in the Medical One to be born a Ledom. Does that sound like anything you ever heard about a mutation?'

'It sure doesn't.'

'There is no mutation, Charlie, and that's what Mielwis wanted you to know. And Froure is alive and here, and so is my homo sap. child, and that's what *I* wanted you to know.'

It was too much – much too much – for Charlie Johns to grasp all at once. He began to take it in little bites.

'Mielwis doesn't know this happened to you.'

'Right.'

'Your … Froure is here, alive?' (But Nasive said the rock-fall had been years ago!) 'How long, Philos?'

'Years. Soutin – the child – he's almost as big as you are.'

'But … why? Why? Cutting yourselves off from everyone—'

'Charlie, as soon as I could, I began finding out all I could about Ledom – things I'd never thought to ask before. The Ledom are an open and honest people – you know that – but they're human and they need privacy. Maybe that's the way they get it – they answer questions but they do not always volunteer. There are secrets in the Medical One and the Science One – not secrets in the sense of your ridiculous "classified" and "restricted" and "top secret" nonsense. But things, many things, that ordinarily it would never occur to anyone to ask about. No one ever thought to question total anesthesia for our monthly physical, for example, and we have that all our lives; no one wondered why our babies were "incubated" for a month before we ever saw them; who would think to ask about such a thing as experimentation in time travel? Why, it was almost an accident I stumbled across the Control Natural – as it was, I never saw him – and I'd have passed by the hint if it hadn't been for Soutin's birth.'

'What's the Control Natural?'

'A child hidden away in the Medical One. A homo sap. with his mind kept asleep; something they can check their work against. So you see our three that died, and Soutin, weren't the only homo saps. born here. It was when I found out about the Control Natural that we decided Soutin would stay hidden here – which of course meant Froure stayed too. When Soutin was born, he was a funny-looking little tyke – you'll forgive me, Charlie, but to us he was funny-looking – but we loved him. Everything that happened made us cherish him the more. Mielwis is never going to get Soutin.'

'But … what's going to happen? What are you going to do?'

'That's up to you, Charlie.'

'Me!'

'Will you take him back with you, Charlie?'

Charlie Johns peered through the dim silver light at the cloaked figure, the mobile, sensitive face. He thought about the doggedness, the pain, the care; the aching loneliness between two of these loving people forced to be so often apart, and all for the love they bore for their child. And he thought of the child – here a hermit-person, buried like a mole; in Ledom a freak or a laboratory animal; and back in his time – what? Without knowing the language, the customs … it could be worse than anything Mielwis could do.

He almost shook his head, but he couldn't, with the tearing anxiety showing on Philos face. Besides – Seace wouldn't allow it; Mielwis wouldn't allow it. (But remember – remember? He knew the settings for the machine, remember?)

'Philos … could you get us to the time machine in the Science One without anyone knowing?'

'I could if I needed to.'

'You need to. I'll take him.'

What Philos said was nothing special. The way he said it was one of the richest rewards Charlie Johns had ever known. With his dark eyes shining, Philos merely whispered, 'Let's go tell Froure and Soutin.'

Philos wrapped up snugly in the thick cloak, signalling Charlie to do the same, and then placed his hands flat on the far wall, one above the other. His fingers sank into hidden purchases, and he pulled outward. A section of the smooth rock, tall as a man, rotated into the chamber. It was hollow, and shaped in cross-section like a wedge of pie. From its triangular dark interior came a gout of frosty air. 'A kind of airlock,' said Philos. 'The "sky" ends back there; actually, we're outside of it now. I can't just keep an open tunnel or the constant air loss would make someone curious at the pressure station.' It was Charlie's first recognition that the warm, fresh air all over Ledom was not only conditioned, but pressurized as well.

'Is it winter now?'

'No, but it's almighty high up … I'll go first and wait to guide you.' He stepped into the wedge-shaped chamber and pressed against the inner wall. It rotated him out of sight, then swung back inside, empty. Charlie stepped in and pushed. Before him, the door-edge swung against solid rock; behind, it clipped at his heels as he pushed. And then he was standing on a hillside, under stars; he gasped from the thin sharp cold, but perhaps the gasp was more for the stars.

In the starlight, which was quite bright enough, they sprinted down the slope, dropped panting into a deep cleft in the rock, and in it, Philos found a door. He pushed it inward; warm wind blew on them. They stepped inside, and the wind blew the door shut. They went forward again, and opened a second door, and there, running toward them down a long low room, with a real wood fire cracking on a real stone hearth; running toward them gladly came Froure, limping but running, and running freely and gladly, Soutin.

Charlie Johns murmured a single word and pitched forward in a dead faint; and the word he said was 'Laura.'

*

'Sometimes when you look around you it scares you,' says Herb.

Jeanette is dipping popcorn in puddles of egg color in a muffin tin, so Davy can make himself an Indian necklace. Davy is only five but he is very good with a needle and thread. 'So don't look around. What are you looking at?'

'The radio, listen to that.' A voice is wailing in song. The discerning ear, if forced to listen (if not forced, the discerning ear would not listen) might recognize the theme as *Vesti la Giubba;* the lyric has to do with disappointment at the junior prom, and both lyric and theme are occluded by a piano playing octaves in the high treble: *Klingklingkling-Klingklingkling,* six quarter-notes to the measure. 'Who's that singing?'

'*I* don't know,' says Jeanette with a certain degree of annoyance. 'I can't be bothered with all this Somebody Brothers and Miltown Trios. They all sound alike.'

'Yeah, but who, who's that?'

She poises popcorn over the purple and stops to listen. 'It's that wall-eyed one night before last on television with the crooked teeth,' she guesses.

'No!' he says triumphantly. 'That was that backstreet Fauntleroy they call Debsie. Namely a boy type. *This* is a woman, girl type.'

'You don't say.' She listens while the voice glisses up the entire four-and-a-half-tone compass of its range and disappears behind the tire-chain-style piano-playing. 'You know, you're right.'

'I know I'm right, and it scares you.' Herb slaps the magazine he has been reading. 'I'm reading in here where Al Capp, you know, the cartoon Al Capp, says about magazine illustrating, at long last you can tell again in a magazine illustration which is the man and which is the woman. The prettiest one is the man. So just while I'm reading that along comes the radio and there's a girl singer with that special growl that makes her sound like a boy singer sounding like a girl.'

'And that scares you?'

'Well, things could get confusing,' he says jocosely. 'Goes on like this much longer, there's going to be a mutation, that like breeds true and you don't know is a boy or a girl.'

'Silly. You don't make mutations that way.'

'I know it. All I mean is, things go on this way, when the double-sex type mutation arrives, nobody'll notice it.'

'Oh, you're making too much of it, Herb.'

'Sure. But all the same and seriously, don't you have the feeling sometimes that there's some great force at work trying to make women into men and verse vicey? Not only this singer bit. Look at Soviet Russia. Never on earth has a great social experiment turned so many women into so huge a herd of pit ponies. Look at Red China, where at last the little China dolls have been liberated out of the slavery of the honky-tonks and get to wear overalls and shovel coal fourteen hours a day alongside their brothers. It's just the other side of that record we just heard.'

Jeanette dips the purple and drips it. 'Oh no,' she says, 'on the other side is *Stardust*.'

'You said "Laura," and—'

Charlie looked up at the beamed ceiling. 'I'm sorry,' he said faintly. 'Maybe I've been too long without sleep. I'm sorry.'

'What is a Laura?'

Charlie sat up, Philos assisting. He looked at the speaker, a brown-haired, grey-eyed Ledom with strong but fine-drawn features, and those rare, firm, sculptured lips which yet can smile readily. 'Laura was the one I loved,' he said, simply as a Ledom might say it. 'You must be Froure.' And then he looked again, looked again at the other.

Shy, yet standing beside, not behind the pillar which held the beam which held the rock ceiling. Cloaked, high-collared in the Ledom manner, with biostatic material drawn like his own, snug over the breast. But then cut down and back, leaving the lower body bare but for the sporran-like silk. A face ... a *nice* face, neither boyish nor too beautiful; and oh, it was not Laura; it's just that she had Laura's hair.

She.

'Soutin,' said Philos.

'Y-y-you kept saying *he!*' cried Charlie stupidly.

'About Soutin? Yes, of course – what else?'

And it came to Charlie, yes of course – what else! For Philos had told his story in the Ledom tongue, and he had always used the Ledom pronoun which is not masculine nor feminine but which also is not 'it'; it was he, Charlie himself, who had translated it 'he.'

He said to the girl, 'You have hair just like Laura's.'

She said, shyly, 'I'm glad you came.'

They wouldn't let him sleep – they couldn't; they had not the time – but they rested and fed him; Philos and Froure toured the house, half underground, half on the rim of a high mesa, inaccessible to any wingless thing, with broad acres of woodland behind, and meadowland where, they told him, Soutin had shot deer with a bow and arrow. Philos and Froure toured the house openly, they wept, they were prepared never to see it again. It was as late as this that Charlie found himself wondering what would become of them after he had taken Soutin away. What was the thing they were doing – treason? What was the penalty for treason? He could not ask. The language had no words for concepts like punishment.

They left the house, climbed the hill, entered the airlock. Inside, they buried the block of light. Through the tunnel into the chimney-top, and there they buried the other block. They discarded their cloaks there and hid them, and came out into the green land, under the steely sky of Ledom. Slowly they walked toward the Ones, two by two like lovers, for Philos and Froure were lovers and Charlie and Soutin must walk so, for she was terrified.

Nearing the Medical One, Froure dropped back and walked with Soutin and Charlie, while Philos walked ahead. Some few might remember Froure, but not seeing him alone. But if Philos, the solitary one, were seen walking like a lover—

And all the way, holding Soutin, whispering warnings and encouragements and sometimes direct orders; all the way, the thoughts curled and burned in the back of Charlie's mind.

'Don't scream,' he said to Soutin sternly as they approached the subway; he wished he had had someone to say that to him when he first saw it. Stepping into the dark entrance, he turned and caught her tight in his arms, forced her face into the cup of his shoulder. She was lithe as a lioness but as they dropped, rigid with terror. Scream! Why – she couldn't breathe!

And on the subway she simply held him; bruised him with her hard slim fingers, as she stood with eyes and lips sealed. But at the other end, when the invisible lift whisked her up, and she had her first experience of the motion that had so thoroughly de-stomached him – she laughed!

... And he was glad of her, parting him now and now again from the thoughts

– of love one another
– of man with grafted uterus coupling with man with grafted uterus
– of the knowing pride of children, worshipped
– of the hand of Grocid, and of Nasive, in burnished wood
– of the knives and needles stitching a manmade and inhuman newness into the bodies of babes
– and oh the distance between, or the fusion of, deity and a dirty joke.

They flung up the side of the tilting structure, Charlie smothering Soutin's wild laughter in his shoulder, and walked into the bright shuttered silence of Seace's laboratory. *He won't be there*, Charlie told himself urgently.

But he was there. He turned from some equipment at the end of the room and strode toward them, unsmiling.

Charlie sidled, drawing Soutin with him, making it necessary for Seace to pass him in order to speak to Philos.

Seace said, 'Philos, it is not your time to be here.'

Philos, pale, opened his mouth to speak, when *'Seace!'* cried Froure sharply.

Seace had not seen Froure, or had not looked at the long 'dead' Ledom. He turned to brush away the interruption, and then his gaze snapped, clamped, clung to Froure's finedrawn features. Froure smiled and touched his hands together, and the mirror-field sprang out; it was fiendish, it was exquisite in timing, for the scientist, given one clear glimpse of that unmistakable face, impossibly here and living, saw it replaced with his own image. At the very moment he was doubting his eyes, his eyes were denied him.

'Take it down,' he said hoarsely. 'Froure: is it Froure?' He came breathing up to the intangible plane of the mirror; Philos slipped beside Froure and took the ring; Froure slipped aside and Philos played Seace up the room like a hypnotized bird, then snapped it off and stood smiling. '*Seace!*' called Froure from behind him ...

And all the while Charlie Johns was working, working at the control dials of the time machine. He set them, one, two, three, four, thumbed the toggle, turned and flung Soutin through the open door of the machine, dove after her, hooking the door to in midair as he dove. The last thing he saw as the door swung was Seace, aware at last, flinging Froure roughly aside, leaping for the controls.

Charlie and Soutin fell together in a tangle. For a moment they stayed just as they were, and then Charlie got to his feet, knelt by the trembling girl, and put his arms around her.

'I wanted to say goodby to them,' she whispered.

'It's going to be all right,' he soothed. He stroked her hair. Suddenly – perhaps it was reaction – he laughed. 'Look at us!'

She did: at him, at herself, and turned frightened attentive eyes to him. He said, 'I was thinking what it will be like, on the stairs, when we arrive; me in the Superman outfit, you ...'

She pulled at her high-collared, swept-back garment. 'I won't know what to do. I'm so ...' She moved the silk of her 'sporran.' 'This,' she said, her voice cracking with the desperate courage of confessional, 'it isn't real; I couldn't ever grow ... Do you suppose they'll know, where we're going?'

He stopped laughing instantly. 'They'll never know,' he assured her soberly.

'I'm so frightened,' she said.

'You never need to be frightened again,' he told her. Nor I, he thought. Philos wouldn't have sent her back to the time when humanity lit the fuse. Or ... would he? Would he think it worth while to give her a year among her own kind, a month, even if she must die with them?

He wished he could ask Philos.

She said, 'How long will it take?'

He glanced at the hairline crack which was the door. 'I don't know. Seace said, instantaneous ... from the Ledom end. I suppose,' he said, 'the door wouldn't open while the machine is ...' he was going to say 'moving' and then 'traveling' and then 'operating' and they all seemed wrong. 'I guess if the door is unlocked, we'll have arrived.'

'Are you going to try it?'

'Sure,' he said. He didn't go near it, or look at it.

'Don't be frightened,' she said.

Charlie Johns turned and opened the door.

'God bless Mommy and Daddy and Grandma Sal and Grandma Felix and I guess Davy too,' sings Karen to her own tune. 'And—'

'Go on, dear. Was there someone else?'

'Mmm. And God bless God, ay-men.'

'Well, that's very sweet, dear. But why?'

Karen says through the translucent margins of slumber, 'I just always God-bless everybody that loves me, that's why.'

Charlie Johns opened the door into a blaze of light, a blaze of silver light, a silver blaze of overcast, a stretch of silver from here clear to the Medical One, point-down and tipped and filling the view.

'You forgot something,' said a voice. Mielwis.

Behind Charlie, a stricken sound. Not turning, 'Stay where you are!' he rapped. Instantly Soutin pushed past him, ran out of the machine, by the controls, by Mielwis, by Grocid, by Nasive, by Seace, all of whom stared at her while she flung herself down beside Philos and Froure, who lay side by side on the floor, their hands flat and neat on their abdomens, their feet too limp. For a moment nothing was heard but Soutin's hard inhalations; the sighs between were silent.

'If you've killed them,' Charlie said at last, in a voice full of hate, 'You've killed their child too.'

There was no comment, unless Nasive's dropped gaze was a comment. Mielwis said softly, 'Well?' Charlie knew he was referring to his earlier remark.

'I forgot nothing. I appointed Philos to report to you. As far as I made any promises at all, I kept them that way.'

'Philos is unable to report.'

'That's your doing. What about your end of the deal?'

'We keep our promises.'

'Let's get to it.'

'We want your reactions to Ledom first.'

What can I lose now? he thought forlornly, but there was no softening in him. He slitted his eyes and said carefully, 'You're the rottenest pack of perverts that ever had the good sense to hide in a hole.'

A sort of rustle went through them – movement, not sound. Finally, 'What changed you, Charlie Johns? You thought very well of us a few hours ago. What changed you?'

'Only the truth.'

'What truth?'

'That there is no mutation.'

'Our doing it ourselves makes that much difference? Why is what we have done worse to you than a genetic accident?'

'Just because you do it.' Charlie heaved a deep breath, and almost spit as he said, 'Philos told me how old a people you are. Why is what you do evil? Men marrying men. Incest, perversion, there isn't anything rotten you don't do.'

'Do you think,' said Mielwis courteously, 'that your attitude is unusual, or would be if the bulk of mankind had your information?'

'About a hundred and two percent unanimous,' Charlie growled.

'Yet a mutation would have made us innocent.'

'A mutation would have been natural. Can you say that about yourself?'

'Yes! Can you? Can homo sap? Are there degrees of "nature"? What is it about a gene-changing random cosmic particle that is more natural than the force of the human mind?'

'The cosmic ray obeys the laws of nature. You're abrogating them.'

'It was homo sap. who abrogated the law of the survival of the fittest,' said Mielwis soberly. 'Tell me, Charlie Johns: what would homo sap. do if we shared the world with them and they knew our secrets?'

'We'd exterminate you down to the last queer kid,' said Charlie coldly, 'and stick that one in a side-show. That's all I have to say. Get me out of here.'

Mielwis sighed. Nasive said suddenly, 'All right, Mielwis. You were right.'

'Nasive has held all along that we should share ourselves and the A-field and the cerebrostyle with homo sap. I feel you would try to do as you just said – and that you'd turn the field into a weapon and the 'style into a device for the enslavement of minds.'

'We probably would, to wipe you off the earth. Now crank up your time machine.'

'There isn't any time machine.'

Literally, Charlie's knees buckled. He turned and looked at the great silver sphere.

'*You* said it was a time machine. We didn't. You told Philos it was – he believed you.'

'Seace—'

'Seace arranged some scenery. A watch with backwards numerals. A book of matches. But it was you – you who believed what you wanted to believe. You do that, you homo sap. You let anyone help you, if he helps you believe what you want to believe.'

'You said you'd send me back!'

'I said we'd return you to your previous state, and we will.'

'You ... *used* me!'

Mielwis nodded, almost cheerfully.

'Get me out of this,' snarled Charlie. 'Whatever you're gibbering about.' He pointed to the grieving girl. 'I want Soutin as well. You've gotten along fine without Soutin so far.'

'I think that would be fair,' said Grocid.

'How soon do you want to—'

'Now! Now! Now!'

'Very well.' Mielwis held up a hand; somehow it made everyone stop breathing. Mielwis spoke a two-syllable word: 'Quesbu.'

Charlie Johns shuddered from head to foot, and slowly put up his hands and covered his eyes.

After a time, Mielwis said softly, 'Who are you?'

Charlie put down his hands. 'Quesbu.'

'Don't be alarmed, Quesbu. You're yourself again. Don't be afraid any more.'

Grocid, awed, breathed, 'I didn't think it could be done.'

Seace said rapidly, softly, 'His own name – a post-hypnotic command. He's really – but Mielwis will explain.'

Mielwis spoke: 'Quesbu: do you still remember the thoughts of Charlie Johns?'

The man who had been Charlie Johns said dazedly, 'Like ... a sort of dream or ... or a story someone told.'

'Come here, Quesbu.'

Trusting, childlike, Quesbu came. Mielwis took his hand, and against the young man's biceps he pressed a white sphere, which collapsed. Without a sound Quesbu collapsed. Mielwis caught him deftly and carried him over to the side, where Philos and Froure lay. He put Quesbu down beside them and looked into the frightened, lost eyes of Soutin.

'It's all right, little one,' Mielwis whispered. 'They're only resting. Soon you'll be together again.' He moved slowly, so as not to startle her, but with great sureness, and touched her with another of the little spheres.

Jeanette tells Herb about Karen: she says God bless God, because she God-blesses everybody who loves her.

'So does God,' says Herb flippantly; and as the words hang there it is not flippant any more.

'I *love* you,' says Jeanette.

... And at last the heads of Ledom may confer quietly among themselves.

'But there really was a Charlie Johns?' asked Nasive.

'Oh yes indeed there was.'

'It's ... not a happy thing,' said Nasive. 'When I took the position that we should share what we have with homo sap., it was a ... sort of unreal argument. There wasn't anything real involved, somehow; just words, just names of things.' He sighed. 'I liked him. He seemed to – to understand things, like our statue, *The Maker*, yes, and the feast ...'

'He understood all right,' said Seace with a touch of sarcasm. 'I'd like to have seen how much he understood if we'd told him the truth about ourselves before he saw the statue and the feast, instead of afterward.'

'Who was he, Mielwis?'

Mielwis exchanged a look with Seace, shrugged slightly, and answered, 'I might as well tell you. He was in a homo sap. flying machine that crashed in the mountains near here. It came apart in the air. Most of it burned and fell on the other side, far away. But that one part landed right on our "sky" and perched there. Charlie Johns was inside, very badly hurt, and another homo sap. who was already dead. Now, you know the "sky" looks just like mountains from above, but all the same it wouldn't be too good an idea to have search parties climbing around on it.

'Seace saw the wreckage up there in his instruments, and immediately put up an A-field carrier and snatched it down. I did my very best to save his life, but he was too badly hurt. He never regained consciousness. But I did manage to get a complete cerebrostyle record of his mind.'

Seace said, 'It's the most complete record we ever got of a mind.'

'Then it came to us, Seace and me, that we could use the record to find out what homo sap. would think of us if he knew about us. All we had to do was to suppress the id, the "me" part of someone by deep hypnosis, and replace it with Charlie Johns' cerebrostyle record. Having Quesbu, it was a simple matter.'

Grocid wagged his head in amazement. 'We didn't even *know* about Quesbu.'

'The Control Natural. No, you wouldn't. A research property of the Medical One. There has never been any reason to tell anyone about Quesbu. He's been well-treated – happy, even, I think, though he's never known anything but his own compound in the Medical One.'

'He has now,' said Nasive.

Grocid asked, 'What's to become of them – Quesbu and the other?'

Mielwis smiled. 'If it hadn't been for this incredible Philos and his hiding Froure and the child all these years – and hide them he did; I never in the world suspected a thing about it – I'd be hard put to it to answer that. Quesbu could hardly be confined again, after his stretch as Charlie Johns, even if he regards it as a dream. For a lot of his experience wasn't dream at all – he did, after all, personally and truly visit all the Ones. Yet he's too old now to be turned into a Ledom, except in a partial way; I wouldn't commit such a thing upon him.

'But the child Soutin gives us a new opportunity. Can you imagine what it might be?'

Grocid and Nasive shared a glance. 'We could build them a house?'

Mielwis shook his head. 'Not in the Children's One,' he said positively. 'They're too ... different. Any amount of care, of love, even, couldn't make up for it. It would be asking too much of them, and perhaps too much of us. Never forget who we are, Grocid – what we are, what we're for. Humanity has never attained its optimum ability to reason, its maximum objectivity, until now, because it has always plagued itself with its dichotomies. In us, the very concept of any but individual differences has been eliminated. And Quesbu and Soutin are not different in an individual sense; they are a different *kind*. We Ledom could probably cope with it better than they, but we are still new, young, unpracticed; we are only in our fourth generation ...'

'Really?' said Nasive. 'I thought ... I mean, I *didn't* think. I didn't know.'

'Few of us know; few of us care, because it doesn't matter. We are conditioned to look ahead, not back. But because it bears on our decision of what to do with Quesbu and Soutin, I'll tell you briefly how the Ledom came to be.

'It has to be brief; for we know so little ...

'There was a homo sap., a very great one; whether he was known as such among his kind, I do not know. It seems probable that he was. I think he was a physiologist or a surgeon; he must have been both, and a great deal more. He was sickened by mankind, not so much for the evils it committed, but because of the good in itself it was destroying. It came to him that humankind, having for some thousands of years enslaved itself, was inescapably about to destroy itself, unless a society could be established which would be above all the partisanship which had divided it, and unless this society could be imbued with a loyalty to nothing but humanity.

'He may have worked alone for a long time; I know that at the end, he was joined by a number of like-thinking people. His name, their names, are not known; humanity honors by emulating, and he wished us to copy nothing from homo sap. that could be avoided.

'He and his friends made us, designed our way of life; gave us our religion and the cerebrostyle and the rudiments of the A-field, and helped the first generation to maturity.'

Nasive said suddenly, 'Then some of us must have known them!'

Mielwis shrugged. 'I suppose so. But what did they know? They dressed, acted, spoke like Ledom; one by one they died or disappeared. As an infant, a child, you accept what you see around you. We four are teachers – right? so were they.

'And all they ever asked of us was that we keep humanity alive. Not their art, music, literature, architecture. Them*selves;* in the widest sense, the self of humanity.

'We are not really a species. We are a biological "construct." In a cold-blooded way we might be called a kind of machine with a function. The function is to keep humanity alive while it is murdered, and after it is well dead—

'To give it back!

'And that is the one aspect of Ledom which we never told Charlie Johns, because he would never believe it. No homo sap. would or could. Virtually never in human history has a group in power had the wisdom to abdicate, to relinquish, except under pressure.

'We are to be as we are, stay as we are, keeping the skills of the soil, holding open the two great roads to the inner self – religion, and love – and studying humanity as humanity has never troubled to study before – from the outside in. And from time to time we must meet with homo sap. to see if he is yet ready to live, to love, and to worship without the crutch of implanted bisexuality. When he is – and he will be if it takes us ten thousand, or fifty thousand years, we the Ledom will simply cease. We are not a Utopia. A Utopia is something finished, completed. We are transients; custodians; a bridge, if you like.

'The pure accident of Charlie Johns' arrival here gave us an opportunity to find out how homo sap. would react to the idea of the Ledom. You saw what happened. But the factor of Soutin, now: that presents us with a new opportunity, and our very first to see if homo sap. can be made ready for its own maturity.'

'Mielwis! You mean to set them out to start a new—'

'Not a new homo sap. The old one, with a chance to live without hate. To live, like all young things, with a hand to guide them.'

Grocid and Nasive smiled at one another. 'Our specialty.'

Mielwis smiled back, but shook his head. 'Philos', I think, and Froure's. Let them be together – they've earned it. Let them live at the edge of Ledom – they're used to it. And let the young humans know only them, and remember us; and then let their children and their children's children remember them and make of us a myth …

'And let us always watch them, perhaps help them by accidents and bits of luck; if they don't succeed they will fail and if they fail they will die, as humanity has died before …

'And one day, some other way, we will start humanity again, or perhaps meet humanity again … but somehow, some day (when we know ourselves well) we can be sure, and then Ledom will cease, and humanity will begin at last.'

*

On a starry night Philos and Froure sat outside for a few minutes in the thin cold air. Quesbu and Soutin had left an hour before, after a real family dinner, and had gone back to their snug log-and-sod house out on the wooded mesa.

'Froure …?'

'What is it?'

'The youngsters …'

'I know,' said Froure. 'It's hard to put your finger on it … but there's something wrong.'

'Not a big something … maybe it's just pregnancy.'

'Maybe …'

From the star-silvered dark: 'Philos …?'

'Quesbu! What on earth … did you forget something?'

He came out of the shadows, walking slowly, his head down. 'I wanted to … Philos?'

'Yes, child; I'm here.'

'Philos, Sou is … well, she's unhappy.'

'Whatever's wrong?'

'I …' Suddenly he flung his head up, and in the dim glow of his face, stars stood: tears. 'Sou's so wonderful but … but all the time I love somebody called Laura and I can't help it!' he burst out.

Philos put an arm around his shoulders and laughed; but laughed so softly, with such compassion, that it was a stroking. 'Ah, that's not your Laura, that's Charlie's!' he crooned. 'Charlie's dead now, Ques.'

Froure said, 'Remember the loving, Quesbu; but yes – forget Laura.'

Quesby said, 'But he loved her so much …'

'Froure's right,' said Philos. 'He loved her. Use the love. It's bigger than Charlie – it's still alive. Take it back and give it to Sou.'

Suddenly – Philos thought it was a glory in his face, but it was the sky – suddenly the sky blazed; the stars were gone. Froure cried out. And their familiar mesa was unfamiliar in the silver overcast of a Ledom sky.

'So it comes; at last it comes,' said Philos. He felt very sad. 'I wonder when Seace will be able to take it down again … Ques, run back to Soutin – quick! Tell her it's all right; the silver sky is keeping us safe.'

Quesbu sprinted away. Froure called, 'Tell her you love her!'

Quesbu turned without breaking stride, waved just like Charlie Johns, and was gone through the woods.

Froure sighed, and laughed a little, too.

Philos said, 'I don't think I'll tell him … the love's too good to spoil … poor Charlie. His Laura married someone else, you know.'

'I didn't know!'

'Yes – you know perfectly well you can cut off a cerebrostyle recording at any point. Seace and Mielwis just naturally cut off Charlie's record at a point where he was full of love; he might understand Ledom a bit better. But actually Charlie had a bit more memory than that.'

'He was in that flying thing because he wanted to get away from—'

''Fraid not. He just got tired of her, which is why she married someone else. But that I wouldn't tell Quesbu.'

'Oh, please don't,' said Froure.

'At loving ... amateurs,' chuckled Philos. 'Actually, Charlie was in that plane being flown to a place on the coast not too far from here. They had some bad earthquakes down there that year, and he was a bulldozer operator, you know. *Oh!*' he cried, looking up.

The sky began to shimmer, then to sparkle.

'Oh, pretty!' cried Froure.

'Fallout,' said Philos. 'They're at it again, the idiots.' They began to wait.

POSTSCRIPT

You homo saps are funny people. I just read some figures wherein a large group of my fellow-citizens were asked if they thought all men were equal, and 61% said Yes. The same people were then asked if Negroes were equal to whites and with the very next breath 4% said Yes – and this without the sound of a shifting gear. To illustrate further: I once wrote a fairly vivid story about a man being unfaithful to his wife and no one made any scandalous remarks about me. I then wrote a specific kind of narrative about a woman being unfaithful to her husband and nobody had anything scandalous to say about my wife. *But* I wrote an empathetic sort of tale about some homosexuals and my mailbox filled up with cards drenched with scent and letters written in purple ink with green capitals. As good Philos says herein: *you cannot be objective about sex, especially when it's outside certain parameters.* Hence this disclaimer, friend: keep your troubles to yourself. I wear no silken sporran.

It was my aim in writing *Venus Plus X a)* to write a decent book *b)* about sex. It is impossible to attempt such a thing without touching upon religion, which is impossible to do without touching rather heavily upon some of your toes. If this hurts, I am sorry about the pain. My own toes stand firmly upon two planks in the Bill of Rights, and if you have a book which refutes me, I promise that I shall read it with full attention and that *I will not burn it.*

Finally, I'd like your help in stacking these books spread all over my desk, partly because some of them are heavy and partly because it really might interest you to know whereout some of the *Venus Plus X* material was dredged. (Almost.) Needless to say, I make no claim to having transferred the contents of any of these books *in toto* into my manuscript. But they are, one and all, provocative tomes, and I list them for provocation's sweet sake; and where due and acceptable, to extend my thanks to the authors.

Holy Bible: Oxford Concordance. *The Human Body and How It Works*, by Elbert Tokay, Ph. D., Signet (NAL). *The Transients*, four parts, by Wm. H. Whyte Jr., *Fortune* magazine, 1953. *The Varieties of Religious Experience* by William James, Modern Library (Random). Cunningham's *Manual of Practical Anatomy*, Oxford Medical Pubs., 1937. *Patterns of Culture*, Ruth Benedict, Mentor, 1953. *The Disappearance*, especially Chapter 13, p. 262, by Philip Wylie, Pocket Books edition, 1958. *Psychoanalysis and Religion* by Erich Fromm, Yale University Press, 1950. Various recent magazine articles by Margaret Mead. *Sex in History*, by G. Rattray Taylor, Ballantine, 1960, and *Are Clothes Modern?* by Bernard Rudofsky, Theobald, 1947. (These last two are among the most startling, informative, and thought-provoking books you could pick up.) Most of the Ledom names came from an article by John R. Pierce (J. J. Coupling), 'Science for Art's Sake,' in *Astounding Science Fiction* for November 1950, in listings of 'words' constructed by the use of a table of probabilities and a table of random numbers. 'Ledom' itself comes from a can of my favorite tobacco spelled backwards. All original trade names and advertising slogans herein copyrighted herewith.

NEW YORK
June 1960

If you've enjoyed these books and would like to read more, you'll find literally thousands of classic Science Fiction & Fantasy titles through the **SF Gateway**

*

For the new home of Science Fiction & Fantasy . . .

*

For the most comprehensive collection of classic SF on the internet . . .

*

Visit the SF Gateway

www.sfgateway.com

THEODORE STURGEON (1918–1985)

Theodore Sturgeon was born Edward Hamilton Waldo in New York City in 1918. Sturgeon was not a pseudonym; his name was legally changed after his parents' divorce. After selling his first SF story to *Astounding* in 1939, he travelled for some years, only returning in earnest in 1946. He produced a great body of acclaimed short fiction (SF's premier short story award is named in his honour) as well as a number of novels, including *More Than Human*, which was awarded the 1954 retro-Hugo in 2004. In addition to coining Sturgeon's Law – '90% of everything is crud' – he wrote the screenplays for seminal *Star Trek* episodes 'Shore Leave' and 'Amok Time', inventing the famous Vulcan mating ritual, the *pon farr*.